Dedicated to my soulmate,

my wife Mila

STATE
OF PERMAFROST

Novel by Edward Shane

©2025

Chapter 1

Monday, November 7, 1977. Major Viktor Vitus was floating over the *Taiga*. So low he could touch the tips of the pines and the spruces. It was impossible for him to tell if the surface under the trees was water or ice. Right beneath it, through patches of mist, Viktor could clearly see people's faces. Though he couldn't recognize them, their wide eyes all seemed to ask the same question: *why?*

Vitus forced himself awake. Lately, the same dream would come to him more and more often, always in the early morning. He opened his eyes and glanced at the luminous green digits on his wristwatch. A second later, the alarm clock sounded off on the nightstand. The sound was not loud, but it made him wince in pain. It was six in the morning, and his head was throbbing. The windows were still dark, but a thick frost gave the glass a mysterious glow.

The Major could have used some extra sleep. However, today was a big national holiday, the sixtieth Anniversary of the Great October Revolution, and as a senior detective of the Violent Crimes Department of the Militia, Vitus had no choice but to report for duty. On days like this, all Militia personnel were mobilized to patrol the city, making sure that drunks or other unsavory elements did not stir up any trouble — law and order was the imperative.

"Damn!" Viktor squeezed his temples with both hands, shivered, and cursed himself for forgetting to light the furnace. "I shouldn't have drank so much last night", he thought to himself. "Too late now." Jumping out from under the down comforter, Viktor immediately realized that he was still wearing most of his uniform. His jacket and a heavy, dark blue wool militia overcoat lay on the floor near the bed. Viktor did not remember dropping them there… or much else from the previous night, except that he was on a routine out-of-town assignment. And that he'd gotten very drunk with his local compatriots.

"Those sons of bitches are tough drinkers," he admitted to himself reluctantly. It was a good thing his driver, Sergeant Pyotr Uvalov, who did not drink, had driven him home over 150 km and perhaps even put him to bed. But Viktor wasn't sure exactly when that had happened.

A desperate thought jolted him, and Viktor began to frantically search for his gun. "Where is it, you idiot!?" He'd already searched through half of the apartment before realizing that all the lights were still turned off. "You are still drunk," he thought to himself bitterly. Then he saw the 9mm Makarov on the kitchen counter next to the gas stove.

"Here you are, my true friend!" he sighed. "Pyotr, you bastard, how could you? These kids have no respect for a man's personal weapon."

His mood improved, having solved his first mystery of the day, Viktor jumped in the tub and turned on the cold water full blast. He knew, of course, that if he turned on the hot water, it would still come out at the same near-freezing temperature, so why even pretend? He brushed the taste of liquor from his mouth with tooth powder, shaved quickly, leaving several tiny cuts which he barely noticed, and wiped his face with a cold, wet towel. Breakfast was out of the question—he wasn't sure if there was any food in his refrigerator to begin with, or if he'd be able to keep it down if there was. So, he took two big gulps of pickle brine from a jar that's been sitting for days on his windowsill. And that was breakfast, just like it was the previous morning.

As he was finally ready to face another freezing November day, Viktor heard someone shuffling outside his front door. He looked through the peephole and saw Pyotr's sleepy, freckled face. Viktor opened the door.

"Pyotr! What the hell happened last night? And how did my gun end up in the kitchen? Are you trying to play tricks on me, Sergeant? You're lucky I like you. Never do such a thing again—I always need it next to me. Got it?"

Pyotr nodded his head with urgency. Suddenly, a feeling of anxiety came over Viktor again. "What are you doing here so early?"

Pyotr mustered a kind of regretful smile and announced with a hint of formality:
"They sent me to bring you, Comrade Major. You're needed at headquarters right away; something very important."

"Then what are we waiting for? Let's ride, Sancho!"

"Yes, Comrade Major! Why do you call me that name?"

"Never mind." Viktor assumed Pyotr wasn't familiar with Cervantes, and he ushered the young Sargent out the door with a slight smile on his face.

The two Militiamen climbed into a white and blue UAZ, derogatorily referred to as *kozyol (goat)*; a small off-road vehicle with Militia insignia on the doors. It was a lousy car, notoriously hard to maintain, but it was what they had, so nobody griped too much. The air was too cold for early November. It took time for the heater to crank up, and the frosted windows dissolved the red decorations that covered the buildings along the Muravyov-Amursky Street. Viktor cared little for this garish display of patriotism — all the banners with Party slogans, the portraits of Party leaders, and endless rows of flags. Every holiday was adorned with the same things, three times a year, every year since he could remember: May Day, Victory Day, and today, the Day of the Red October Revolution. A sea of red.

They arrived at the Khabarovsky Krai Internal Affair Administration (UVD) at precisely seven o'clock. The UVD Headquarters was usually not crowded this early in the morning — only a few receptionists and assistants were settling down at their workstations before most of the staff arrived. But today wasn't a regular Monday, and cops of different ranks and positions bustled about, all in full uniform with parade cockades on their caps.

The Major wanted to make a fast stop at his third-floor office to see what had happened in his absence over the last four days, but a low-ranking officer diverted him straight to the boss's office. Vitus let himself into the long and narrow room, dimly lit despite the three tall windows lined up in a row on the wood-paneled walls.

A large, ornate desk filled the far end of the room. High on the wall above it hung a framed picture of Lenin and Dzerzhinsky, the two men looking at each other conspiratorially. Two large flags stood in the corner, near the first window. One flag was simply red with a gold embroidered hammer and sickle and the big letters "CCCP." The other flag had a white, green, and blue background with a black bear clutching to its chest the heraldic symbol of the Khabarovsky Krai.

A long, shiny table sat at ninety degrees to the desk. There were sixteen chairs, eight on each side of the table, perfect for full staff meetings or teleconferences often held here. For this purpose, there was an ugly-looking box speaker attached to the telephone in the middle of the table. On the opposite side of the room, the huge administrative map of the entire region covered the wall, lit by three overhanging spotlights.

Viktor knew this room well, ever since he was a little boy. It was his father's office until two years ago. Back in 1935, twenty-year-old Raymond Alfredovich Vitus arrived in Khabarovsk to maintain the law and order of the new Soviet Russia, presumably at the request of Stalin himself. This small provincial town happened to be the administrative center of a vast territory on the godforsaken, Far-East Siberian outskirt of the Russian empire.

At that time, this no-man's land sprawled from the Sea of Okhotsk in the far north, to the border with China in the far south. It was here that the Red Army captured the territory from "White" Admiral Kolchak and his counter-revolutionary troops. Khabarovsk desperately needed men like Raymond Vitus, the son of a professional revolutionary and a graduate of the Academy of the People's Commissariat of Internal Affairs. And Raymond Vitus devoted himself to his job with an unbridled passion.

The sound of his own name interrupted Viktor's thoughts. Looking away from the map, he saw the silhouette of a plump, middle-aged woman in uniform, standing in the doorway. Her round face was hidden in the shadow of the darkly lit office, but Viktor immediately recognized that soft, humorous voice. Nadezhda Petrovna, his boss's secretary, with her iconic braid of thick blond hair sitting like a crown on top of her head.

"Good morning, Viktor! Why are you standing in the dark?", she asked. "Was it a rough night? I assume you wouldn't mind a strong cup of coffee?"

Such familiarity would have normally angered Viktor, but this was a woman who he'd known his whole life, who once held him on her lap, giving him lollipops and homemade cookies when his father would bring him along to work. She was almost family.

"Of course, I wouldn't mind it! Even if it's instant coffee. Thank you, Nadezhda Petrovna! By the way, where is the boss? He sent for me with such urgency, and now…"

"Oh, he is here. He came in even before I did. The General is in the personnel department but will be back very soon," she reported. "Let me get your coffee."

Vitus returned his attention to the map, and a new wave of memories began to rush in. But not for long; another familiar voice abruptly stopped Viktor's reminiscence.

Closely shaven, with neatly cropped graying - yet plentiful - hair and dressed in his parade uniform, Lieutenant-General Mikhail Grigoriyevich Melekhov looked even more handsome than usual. Tall, broad-shouldered, and slim, he appeared a much younger man than his 57 years. The General's confident, low voice fit his impressive stature. Victor always felt that the man looked like one of those Soviet Realism posters from the post-Revolutionary period.

"Good morning, Comrade Major. I apologize for making you wait." The General flipped the light switch on and quickly made his way behind his desk as he continued. "I had to look at the personnel files of a couple of new academy graduates. It took longer than I realized."

"Of course, Mikhail Grigoriyevich." Viktor casually saluted the General. "I never mind waiting in here, sir. This office always brings back nice memories."

"I understand. Take off your coat and sit down. This is a delicate situation... Oh, here comes your coffee. Dear, can you make one for me too? Thanks." The General waved to Nadezhda Petrovna, then centered a steady gaze on Viktor, now sitting somewhat sheepishly across from this imposing figure.

It was a conversation Vitus did not want to have but knew he could not avoid. And it wasn't the first time the General had broached this subject with him. Yet the atmosphere felt different this time. 'What choice does he have? 'thought Viktor. Melekhov had a duty to reprimand a subordinate for months of inappropriate behavior. Yet, it was not that simple with Viktor, the son of his former boss and his closest friend. Because Melekhov and his wife Alyona did not have any children, they took Viktor and his sister Raisa as their godchildren. They lived in the same building, watched over them, helped rear them as godparents did in those days. To the children, the General was simply "Uncle Misha,".

The sudden and violent death of Raymond Alfredovich Vitus, just three months from retirement, after forty years of service, shook both families to the core. The suicide of a man like General Vitus, who seemed almost indestructible to his friends and colleagues, was not something that anyone could have predicted, or even imagined.

There were no obvious signs of emotional distress or mental illness, no family troubles of any kind. Yet, one sunny afternoon in September of 1975, Raymond Vitus left home for a walk in the nearby park and did not come back. He was found dead, sitting on a bench in a remote area of the park, partly covered with yellow and red leaves, his personalized .22 caliber Browning in his right hand and a matching bullet hole in his right temple. The police found a short-handwritten note in the pocket of his overcoat: *"I beg your forgiveness, but I have to do this. Please, do not blame anyone."*

After an extensive and ultimately fruitless investigation, the case was officially declared a 'suicide 'and closed. It was General Melekhov who put the final stamp on the Vitus file. Sitting across from the man now, Viktor didn't see Uncle Misha anymore. He saw a man who failed him. In spite of his love and respect for Melekhov, in the back of his mind, Viktor developed a resentment that has been eating away at him for the past two years. Along with frustration, anger, and anxiety. The same nagging question stuck in his mind: "Why?" And when the question became unbearable, Viktor started to drink. And, as was his nature, he approached drinking with the same obsessive focus as he approached his investigations.

Yet, in times of sobriety, Viktor understood that his life could not continue down this path. He realized how much hurt he was causing his mother and his sister. His career also started falling apart: no more serious cases were assigned to him, only desk jobs and occasional field inspections. Viktor did not know what to do about it. He was lost.

"Major, you know how highly I think of you." Melekhov started in a low voice but then increased in volume and emotion. "You are like a son I never had and never will. So, let me be blunt. This is your last chance."

From habit, Vitus reached into his pocket for a pack of cigarettes but remembered, unlike his late father, General Melekhov did not smoke and did not allow it in his office. Nadezhda

Petrovna enforced this rule unwaveringly and it drove most of the other officers - all heavy smokers - nearly insane during the long briefings. But it never bothered Vitus… until this moment. Melekhov pretended not to notice and continued in a hushed tone.

"I understand your anguish and your anger... but life goes on. Pull yourself back together. Think about your mother, your sister, your job. Stop punishing yourself. It wasn't your fault."

The General leaned forward, pushing his chest against the desk's edge, and tried to look directly into Viktor's eyes, who turned his head away and attempted to stand up.

"Sit down, Comrade Vitus! I did not dismiss you," Melekhov said forcefully.
Vitus slumped back into the chair.

"Although you are not the most senior member in your unit, people look up to you. And I don't think they do this only out of respect for your late father. You have always been an intelligent officer, an insightful investigator, and a helpful colleague to anyone who needs help. Not so much lately, though." He took another breath. "So, I'm suggesting you get off your drinking binge. Stop being an idiot. Enough of this self-pity! I am fed up with hearing about your escapades. You know what I am talking about! If you drank quietly at home, that's one thing… but on assignment? With colleagues? And that brawl you got into two weeks ago! Embarrassing. To the whole department. Word gets around and I can't shield you anymore, Viktor. "

It seemed like the General was just picking up steam when he suddenly stopped. Viktor looked at him with concern. He did not remember ever seeing the man so emotional, so animated, and yet so bloodlessly pale. Whatever was left of his hangover was gone; his mind was suddenly crystal clear. This wasn't a reprimand. This was the General's last call for action. Viktor lowered his head and stared at the hands laying in his lap. They were trembling.

For the next few moments, the silence in the room thickened as the two officers reflected on the things that had just been said, and those that had not.

Suddenly, the General changed the subject. "How was the inspection trip to Komsomolsk?"

"It went smoothly, sir, except they got me pretty loaded—" Viktor stammered, both grateful for a new avenue of conversation, and frustrated with his own foolish reply.

Melekhov ignored it and continued his questioning calmly. "I heard Freckles drove you there and back home. So, the roads must be in good shape?"

"Yes, the permafrost is rock-solid, compared to a couple of weeks ago. Also, there's no snow on the ground yet. The roads are not messy," Viktor replied without trying to hide the fact that he liked this shift in subject matter. But he sensed something important was still to come. And he was right...

"Viktor, you have to tell me truthfully. Are you tired of this job? Do you want to quit? I will be disappointed, but I'll support your decision and help you start a new career. Perhaps you could be a good jurist, perhaps a prosecutor or a defense attorney. I need to know now before we go any further."

This time Viktor did not look away. He sprung from the chair, stood at attention and spoke in a formal military voice, looking straight into the Generals eyes:

"I have no intention of changing my career, sir. I love my job, and as you, Comrade General admitted yourself... I am good at it. So, I fully intend to stick with what I've committed myself to for the last six years."

Melekhov smiled slightly as Vitus continued.

"I fully understand that my behavior in recent months has fallen short. And - at times - has been completely unacceptable. I beg the General to officially reprimand me in any way you see fit. Perhaps a demotion and a leave without pay may be in order, but I beg the General... "

"Relax, Major!" Melikhov interrupted with a dismissive wave. "Sit back down, please. Your coffee is getting cold."

Vitus did as he was told.

"Listen, Viktor, if you are serious, and I assume you are, I have something important for you. Three days ago, Father Fyodor Rogozhin was brutally murdered in his home at the Izmailovsky hamlet." The General paused for dramatic effect and studied Viktor's reaction. "I've decided that what you need now is a good, juicy case. I think this is the case and I hope you will give it your undivided attention. It should take your mind off... things. And it will keep you away from Khabarovsk for a little while."

Viktor felt relieved, but uneasy. Perhaps the General was right, and a complex case was exactly what he needed now to focus his brain and distract him from... from what? The depression? The doubt? The drink? A drink... Was he even capable of stopping? He honestly didn't know. Was he capable of slowing it down enough to work on a potentially complex case? He didn't know that either. Even without the drink, could he still handle his job at all? Not sure. To the devil with it!

"I'll take the case, any case, anywhere, Comrade General! And I thank you for your confidence in me. I won't let you down this time."

"Yes, of course you won't."

"There's only one request, sir."

Melikhov raised one of his thick eyebrows.

"I ask that no pertinent information be held back from me. Nothing that could blindside me down the line. I will need to know everything."

"That's what you will find in this folder. Review it thoroughly en route." The General smiled again. "Sergeant Uvalov will be your driver to Chegdomyn. It's almost 400 kilometers one way, so it should take three or four days if the weather holds up and the snow stays away. Plenty of time to study all the details we have at this point."

"Yes sir." Vitus silently wondered why the General didn't arrange for a faster train option. Or even a helicopter. But he kept these thoughts to himself.

"Oh, and Lieutenant Nina Toropko will accompany you. She is new but seems very sharp. She will help you with forensics and evidence gathering."

More questions in Viktor's mind: why is he sending a rookie? Or is she there to make sure he stays in line? Or is she KGB?

"Yes, sir! Glad for the additional help."

The General pushed a thick brown folder across the desk toward Vitus. The top right corner was labeled with the name "Fyodor Rogozhin" in faded blue ink. "

"You leave immediately."

* * *

Festivities were in full swing while Pyotr Uvalov navigated the UAZ out of the city, avoiding the streets most crowded with people carrying flags and banners. Viktor sat in the passenger seat, occasionally giving suggestions. Being a good driver and a clever young man, Sergeant Uvalov never argued nor expressed any displeasure with such interference. After spending so much time in this car together over the past three years, he'd learned that the Major's advice was usually sound.

They made a quick stop back at Viktor's apartment, where he packed a small suitcase for the journey. The best part of wearing a uniform is that it makes packing easy. Just the essentials. For a moment, Vitus stared at a flask of vodka on his bedside stand. Then he closed the suitcase and stepped out into the cold.

Junior Lieutenant Nina Toropko was a tall, lanky young woman in her late twenties. She had natural blond hair, cut short in a boyish style that didn't make her look any less feminine. Her wide green eyes had a spark of spontaneity yet projected a certain sadness. Under her heavy black shearling coat, Nina wore dark blue cotton pants. A single star adorned the epaulets on her jacket. She situated herself and all her gear comfortably in the vehicle's back seat, right behind Major Vitus. Viktor couldn't see her unless he turned his entire body at least 90 degrees, but he had no intention to do so.

Uvalov, on the contrary, took every opportunity to glance at Nina in the rear-view mirror, even trying to strike up a conversation. It didn't escape Viktor, who reminded his driver to pay more attention to driving. The Sergeant took the hint and concentrated on the road demonstratively. The change in his boss's demeanor after his meeting with the General that morning was noticeable. He seemed preoccupied and quiet - strictly business. And now with this unexpected journey in the company of the young female Lieutenant whom neither of them had met before... Pyotr decided that it would be wise not to irritate the Major.

By noon, their *kozyol* had left the city behind and hit the open road. The temperature outside was dropping fast, well below the freezing mark, and the car heater struggled. Thick frost covered the insides of the windows, making it challenging to see through. The narrow swatch of the two-lane highway was only visible in two shapeless clearings created by hot air forced from the engine. Moving at a higher speed proved out of the question, so, after exchanging glances with Major Vitus, Sergeant Uvalov eased off the accelerator.

For the next two hours, they slowly pushed their way west. Their first stop was still far away. There were no signs of life on either side of the road—only the sparse growth of short trees and large areas of the permafrost, now hard enough to walk on. A dull sight but an excellent time for the travelers to talk, tell personal stories, or even tell a joke. If Viktor was in the mood to do so, but he wasn't. Several times, he stopped Freckles 'attempts to strike up a conversation. Nina likewise avoided talking to either of them. She didn't want to get off on the wrong foot with her superior officer. An hour in, she began humming a melody, testing if the Major would tolerate it. Viktor didn't mind. Freckles noticed him smiling and joined Nina's improvised musical exercise with gentle whistling.

Viktor lit a cigarette, closed his eyes, and went back to the memories of his late father, imagining how the young Raymond Vitus arrived in Khabarovsk at the start of his career. Those times were harsh: not enough food, or sleep, or warm clothes. Everyday life required enormous efforts and sacrifices. Moscow was far away—over eight thousand kilometers, and Vitus was to bring people to this desolate place—people who knew how to build, how to gather materials, how to create a transportation system, provide social services, run schools, and practice medicine. It took time and patience, but within five years real success was visible. Khabarovsky Krai joined the rest of the country in a collective undertaking of enormous magnitude. The industrialization of the country's economy caused the population to boom. New railroad lines, coal mines, factories for timber processing, gold, and other rare metal prospecting, began popping up in the small towns throughout the region. It was a time of rebirth and excitement.

Raymond Vitus was Latvian by birth, the son of Alfred Vitus, an "old" Bolshevik, one of the original Revolutionary Guard, and a member of the personal security detail for Vladimir Illich Lenin. Raymond was a natural leader who could relate to people of different backgrounds: Russians and Ukrainians, Armenians and Byelorussians, Georgians, and Tatars, Gypsies and Jews. And they were arriving in droves to this remote land to settle down, to work, and to make their lives in this brutal place.

With the success of industrialization, many problems arose. The simple fact was that with more newcomers, more crime was committed; mostly by drifters, petty thieves, con artists looking for easy prey, and armed robbers chasing bigger prizes. And then, a new historical development: the swelling network of forced labor camps. The state security apparatus of NKVD was supplying an abundance of inmates, both criminal and political.

Stalin's purges were as unforgiving as the tundra. Tens of thousands of people from all over the vast country, who only yesterday were regular, educated, or sometimes even famous citizens, considered loyal and productive members of Soviet society, suddenly became "enemies of the people." And they were thrown in the same camps with professional criminals; hard, violent men. It was like two opposite worlds suddenly collided in this land of infinite beauty and extreme climate: one of human aspiration and accomplishment, and another of darkness, betrayal, and misery. It was a volatile mix. The Main Administration of Corrective Labor Camps and Labor Settlements, the GULAG, ran the camps with an iron fist, in the harshest, most difficult-to-reach places on earth. But the diverse prisoner population was ultimately ruled over by the inmates themselves, with their own set of rules and punishments.

Meanwhile, Commissar Vitus, as head of both the regional UVD and the Militia, also had another assignment: recruitment. He somehow managed to gather a group of solid professionals, both local and from around the USSR, to help deal with the problems created by the increase in the prisoner population. He shaped them into a competent and successful police force, and he remained their commander for the next forty years.

A sudden burst of laughter brought Viktor back to the present.

"We are sorry to wake you, Comrade Major." Now Nina and Freckles were both laughing. Pyotr stopped first and apologized. "We didn't mean it. The anecdote Comrade Lieutenant told me was so funny I had to laugh."

"May I hear it?" Viktor inquired with exaggerated indignation in his voice. "Or is it too dirtying for my taste, because…"

Vitus abruptly cut his sentence short as the vehicle came to a sudden, jarring stop. The three officers stared through the windshield with a look of amazement on their faces. Just a few meters in front of their car, a gigantic, large-antlered moose stood in the road directly in front of them. Larger and heavier than a workhorse, the beast stared directly into their eyes. If the car had been moving faster, it would have collided disastrously with the animal.

"What in the hell is this thing doing in the middle of the road?!" Pyotr exclaimed, wiping the sweat from his forehead and pressing on the vehicle's horn. "It could've killed us!"

The moose was most likely crossing the road when their *kozyol* approached rapidly with the frightening, gnashing sound of its brakes. So, instead of running away, the animal froze in its tracks. The sound of the horn scared it even more, totally paralyzing the poor creature. Viktor knew that getting out of the car to chase it away could provoke the moose to attack. Of course, he had no intention of shooting the animal with his 9mm weapon, realizing that it would most likely just make the animal angry. The best thing to do would be to stay calm and wait a few minutes to let the moose come out of its dazed stupor and leave the road on its own.

But Nina, who had never seen such a giant creature in the flesh, screamed at the top of her lungs, more in excitement than fear. The high-pitched sound must have jolted the beast from its trance and sent it into a frenzy. It leaned on its hind legs, lowered its antlers, and produced a battle-like wailing sound. It looked like it was about to charge when Sergeant Uvalov quickly slammed the transmission into reverse and thrust the accelerator to the floor. After a moment's hesitation, the *kozyol* lurched backward, spitting up a cloud of thick dust with its spinning wheels. When the dust settled, the road was clear, and the charging beast had disappeared.

Viktor said nothing but touched his Sancho on the shoulder. Nina whistled two exclamatory high notes, and the trio laughed in relief. From there on, all the way to Birobidjan, they all had a pleasant time exchanging jokes and personal stories. Nina eventually dug out some bologna sandwiches wrapped in oily paper from one of her large bags. She also pulled out a big thermos with hot tea. The food and the tea elevated the mood even further. Good start, Vitus thought to himself. Good start.

It was after four o'clock, and the sky had already turned dark with the big moon shining. The visibility improved so much that Pyotr could increase the vehicle speed to 70 km per hour and by ten o'clock, they reached their first stopover at the Hotel "Sovetskaya" in Birobidjan. Viktor dropped off the instant his head touched the pillow. He slept a deep sleep, and - for the first time in weeks - dreamt of nothing.

*   *   *

The following day began at seven o'clock in the morning and lasted ten hours of non-stop driving. It went on without a hitch, only when they arrived at their second stopover point, the Bira urban settlement, they discovered there was no hotel of any kind. The local Militia chief played the host role by providing a roof over their heads, a hot meal, and provisions for the next day on the road. However, he had only one bed available for the guests. Therefore, Viktor and Pyotr, as gentlemen do, let their female fellow traveler take it, and they both slept on blankets thrown on the cold hard floor. It was difficult to get a good night's rest sleeping like that, but neither complained.

Due to heavy fog in the morning, the third day of the trip started relatively late. Only around noon did the visibility clear up enough to resume driving. Still, the road was treacherous, demanding extra caution. It became obvious they couldn't reach their destination as they had planned that day.

The long trip began taking a toll not only on Pyotr, but also on his passengers. There was not much laughter anymore. Everyone was mostly quiet, conserving energy and keeping their thoughts to themselves.

Vitus took this opportunity to study the contents of the Rogozhin file. The details of the crime itself were minimal and Vitus refrained from putting too much stock in what was on the page. The vast bulk of the material consisted of the victim's personal background, and this was exhaustively detailed. The old priest had lived an eventful quite a life! But Vitus also understood, from his years as an investigator, that such background information could sometimes be a distraction. Most violent crimes, in his experience, had little relation to the victims 'past. Or, at least, not the distant past that was detailed in the file. Most crime, Vitus knew, was a result of opportunism, greed, and desperation. Was this the case here? He lit another cigarette and stared out the window at the windswept tundra, lost - once more - in his memories, accompanied again by Nina's soft humming.

They arrived in Chegdomyn, the administrative center of Verkhneburiyinsky District, in late afternoon the following day. It took them another hour to register at the local hotel, where they were finally able to get a few hours of relatively normal sleep.

Chapter 2

Thursday, November 10. Eight o'clock in the morning. Major Viktor Vitus and Lieutenant Nina Toropko, dressed in their full Militia winter uniforms, stood in the basement of Chegdomyn Hospital. A custodian, at their request, has unlocked the door. A stench of tobacco and death saturated the white tiled walls of the dimly lit room.

There was a human body fully draped with a bloodstained linen sheet laid out on an elevated concrete slab. Viktor was about to pull the shroud off the cadaver when Nina stopped him.

"Let's wait for the coroner. He might not have finished the autopsy yet."

Viktor nodded in agreement. Clutching her Zenith camera, Nina searched the dim room for the light switch. At that moment, a man in a white lab coat swung the door open and stormed in. He reached the switch first. Harsh fluorescent light flooded the room, flickering at first, then going steady.

"I'm Dr. Goldfarb, Anatomy-Pathologist and Verkneburiyinsky District Coroner," he announced. In his mid-forties, the man was tall and burly with a full head of unruly hair sitting on a thick neck. After his official introduction, he added, "You can call me Naum."

He pushed his glasses with a long, smoke-yellowed finger up his impressive nose, bringing them closer to his dark, droopy eyes. He glanced over the visitors and quickly approached the slab.

"And you are?" he asked.

"Major Vitus and Lieutenant Toropko, Khabarovsky UVD, Violent Crime Investigative Unit. You can call me Viktor."

"I would've been done with the autopsy last night if anybody had bothered to alert me of your arrival. I was expecting you tomorrow. I guess it doesn't matter now. There isn't much left to do except putting in some final stitches. I understand you are eager to see the victim." Dr. Goldfarb abruptly pulled the linen sheet off the corpse on the slab. "What a rare human specimen he is!" he exclaimed. "Don't you think?"

Viktor and Nina were stunned by the sight of the man lying in front of them. He was over two meters tall and powerfully built, his long arms and big hands reaching down along his muscular legs. His feet seemed large, even for his impressive frame. Viktor and the doctor exchanged bemused glances when Nina inadvertently stared at the corpse's genitals, also oversized. Everything about this dead man was big: his head with its thick gray hair intermingled with dry blood clumps, fell mane-like down his broad shoulders; his wild beard reached his chest, which was now pried wide open from the neck down to the navel, like a colossal flower petal, exposing his internal organs with their dark, red color.

However, it was not the work of the surgeon that made the body look gruesome. He had washed the blood from a deep, wide crack at the top of the man's head, caused by some sharp object, revealing the rough edges of his broken skull and the wavy brain tissue behind it. Nina centered herself, moved closer to the slab, and began snapping pictures. The strange-looking device attached to the top of her Zenith produced irritating light flashes with every click of the camera's shutter.

"Believe it or not, this nasty blow to the head was not the actual cause of death for this man," Dr. Goldfarb explained, lighting a cigarette. "Fact is, it happened that the man's last breath was taken after a long knife blade went right through his heart after the blow. Do you see these deep stab wounds around his torso? I counted seventeen altogether. I am sure it was not the work of just one assailant. There were at least two of them, armed with axes and knives. The attack was spontaneous, uncontrollably violent, and yet methodical. I bet it wasn't the first time they had killed a man."

"And what are these wounds?" Viktor inquired, turning over one of the man's hands and pointing to his palm.

"The same wound is on the other palm as well," the doctor said as he walked around the slab to show them the other palm.

"These wounds occurred from driving railroad spikes through them. Just like it was done to Jesus, you know?" Goldfarb stopped himself mid-sentence. "What I meant to say is that the old man was nailed to the wall inside the house. The effect was not what his killers had expected, however. The wall wasn't high enough, so his knees were bent, and his feet touched the floor. By the way, this improvised crucifixion took place at least 30 minutes after the old man was already dead. You see, there wasn't sufficient bleeding through these wounds even before I washed the body."

Hearing this curious detail (which was missing from the file), the Major paused writing in his notebook and Nina stopped taking pictures. When Dr. Goldfarb noticed this, he asked loudly and with a hint of surprise, "I must assume that you didn't know about the pictures from the crime scene?"

"Who took these pictures, and where are they? Can we see them?" Viktor asked.

"I have no pictures. I only have a bloody axe found on the floor of the crime scene. I am telling you only what I was told by the New Urgal local Railroad UVD Captain. I can't recall his name now, but before he sent the corpse to Chegdomyn, the Captain informed me that he took a bunch of pictures the very next morning after the murder happened. He received a phone call from his Sergeant in the Listvenny settlement and immediately drove to the small hamlet (*khutor*) Izmailovsky, where the killing took place."

"You mean the Captain was at the site the very next morning?" asked Viktor. "And what exactly was the time of the murder?"

"In my estimation, it must've happened in the late hours of November 3," the Doctor answered without any hesitation.

"So, let's assume the pictures were taken on November 4 and sent for development right away. By any chance, Doctor, is there a photo development service in Chegdomyn?"

"I wouldn't know. I never had a photo camera of any kind, although it would be nice to have one for this job. But it is not in the budget," Dr. Goldfarb said with annoyance. "Where do you expect to develop and print your pictures, Comrade Lieutenant?"

"In Khabarovsk, I know one store on Shevchenko Street where they do that in three to four days tops. Anywhere else, it takes at least a week," said Nina.

"This means the Captain from New Urgal, if he had sent his film by mail, can get the pictures back no earlier than November 13 or even 15. Pity, there aren't any other options," concluded Viktor. "Pictures or no pictures, we'll need to inspect the crime scene as soon as possible. I hope our local Sherlock Holmes didn't destroy all of the evidence during his initial visit and his photo session. By the way, has anybody formally identified the deceased? Was any next of kin notified?"

"I don't know," the doctor replied right away, pointing to a plastic clipboard on a side table. "The paperwork I received with the body had the name Fyodor Feoktistovich Rogozhin: an 81-year-old resident of *khutor* Izmailovsky. I am positive this paperwork had been filled in by the same Captain, who was on the scene first."

Viktor walked to the table, grabbed the clipboard, and studied the top page for a minute or so. "Dr. Goldfarb, thank you for your medical insight. I am sure your official report will follow soon."

"You are welcome, Detective. I promise to finish my autopsy report promptly," the doctor continued in his serious tone. "I hope your investigation will reveal who these killers are and bring them to justice. And I hope you have a safe drive to New Urgal," he concluded with genuine concern. "It is only 28 kilometers from here, but the roads will be hazardous. The permafrost, covered with gravel, can't withstand the constant traffic of those giant trucks. Their drivers are maniacs with total disregard for the other vehicles, and the roads are too narrow."

"Thank you, Doctor," Viktor replied. He turned to Nina. "Lieutenant, please inspect the corpse one more time; try not to miss any details. Don't forget to pack the axe carefully; we might be able to lift some fingerprints. So, wrap it up here quickly, and I will alert Petya to be ready. I want to be in New Urgal to catch this mystery Captain in his office before the end of the day."

Viktor placed his notebook in his sheepskin coat pocket, put his fur hat on, and left the Pathology Room. He took three steps beyond the door into a long corridor and noticed a young woman in a luxurious mink coat sitting on a chair next to the door he had just exited. She sprung from the chair and quickly followed him.

"Are you Major Vitus? I was told you're in charge here, is that correct?" the young woman asked in a surprisingly low voice.

"Yes, I'm in charge of the murder investigation. And you are?"

"My name is Kseniya Krylova." She paused, fixing a black wool shawl that was covering her dark copper hair.

"I recognize you," said Viktor flatly. "You are an actress from the Khabarovsky Theater. I have actually seen you perform. To what do we owe the honor?"

"Kseniya Krylova is my stage name. My real name is Katerina Rogozhina." Her voice trembled slightly. "I am the daughter of the man who was… killed. I am here to see my father."

Women's emotions always made Viktor uncomfortable. He was anxious to progress on the case and this was not a distraction he particularly welcomed. Yet, this woman's frankness and resolve struck a sudden nerve in him.

"I am sorry for your loss, Comrade." He mumbled awkwardly.

Katerina suddenly moved closer and buried her face in Viktor's furry overcoat lapel. The top of her head touched his chin. He could smell, through the shawl, the fragrance of her hair. She sobbed quietly. This made Viktor even more uncomfortable, but he didn't move away. His hands awkwardly patted the young woman's back. They stood like that for several long seconds until Dr. Goldfarb and Nina Toropko came out of the Anatomy-Pathology Room. They were both slightly taken aback by the unexpected scene. The doctor coughed politely and broke the silence, and Viktor sharply has broken the embrace.

"I am sorry, Comrade Major, I forgot to mention that this young woman was trying to get access to the body of the deceased. She claims to be the victim's daughter. I informed her that someone like you, Comrade Major, could resolve this matter. Sorry again if I've caused any inconvenience."

Vitus turned to Kseniya. Or was it Katerina? He was unsure how to refer to her, so he decided to keep it formal.

"Citizen Rogoshina, are you officially requesting to see your father's body?"

"Yes, Major. Is that allowed?"

"I have no objections. Your identification of the victim is actually required. Unfortunately, we cannot do it at this very moment. Am I right, Dr. Goldfarb?"

"I can have the body prepared for you in an hour if you'd like to wait," the doctor said.

"I think so. Thank you, Comrade Vitus. And thank you, Doctor," Katya said with a grateful smile. "I'll wait here if that's all right."

"I think you will be much more comfortable waiting upstairs in the lobby," said the doctor with authority and ushered the group toward the staircase. Viktor hesitated for a second, then addressed Katya again.

"We need to be in New Urgal by tonight. However, I still would like to speak with you, Citizen Rogozhina, and take a detailed statement regarding your father. How long are you planning to stay in Chegdomyn before going back to Khabarovsk?"

"I honestly hadn't thought that far ahead, Major. I took some time off, so I'm in no hurry to get back." Katya said

"If I may make a suggestion, Major," Nina interjected. "Perhaps Citizen Ragozhina should accompany us to New Urgal? It would be more efficient for the investigation and, I believe, it would be much easier for her if she simply travels with us."

Vitus was taken aback by this suggestion, but as Nina looked at him inquisitively, its basic logic couldn't be denied.

"Would that be acceptable to you, Citizen Ragozhina?" He asked.

"I suppose I can go with you, but only after I see my father's body."

Vitus nodded, but his feelings were difficult for Katya to read. Would she be an intrusion into an official investigation? Would it be awkward traveling with strangers? Katya was unsure, but she was certain that she did not want to be alone now. And she appreciated the young Lieutenant's intuition on this point, which clearly factored in her surprising suggestion.

Vitus continued, "I also need to ask you, how familiar are you with your father's house?"

"Quite familiar, Major," she answered without hesitation.

"Very good. Your presence will definitely be of help, then."

"In that case, I will try to finish my job within the hour," The doctor chimed in decisively and marched back into the Pathology Room.

"Should I send my driver to the hotel to bring your luggage?" Viktor asked Katerina as they walked up the stairs to the lobby.

"Yes, please. I left my bag at the clerk's office. I was unsure about staying another night, but there was no storage room for my luggage." Katya explained.

Nina Toropko followed closely behind, trying to keep up so as to not miss anything. In her right hand, she carried an *avoska* (a "just in case" knitted bag) with the bloodied axe carefully packed inside; in her left hand, she clutched her aluminum case.

Viktor prompted Katerina to take the only available armchair in the lobby. He pulled up a regular chair next to it and sat down. Although not teary anymore, Katya's eyes were still puffy. Vitus also observed that her face strongly resembled her late father's. She did not wear much make-up. Her thick hair, naturally arched eyebrows beautifully contrasted her skin and her gray eyes. She was unquestionably beautiful, and, for a moment, Vitus found himself getting lost in those eyes… He had not experienced this kind of instant attraction for a very, very long time.

Viktor's mind drifted back to Yulia, his college love, and the woman he was about to marry. Her sudden death in a traffic accident on the streets of Leningrad, all those years ago, had scarred him deeply and was the main reason for his aversion to serious relationships. There had been quite a few casual dalliances, of course; women found Vitus attractive and charismatic, but his cold demeanor kept most of them at bay, and that's the way he preferred it.

This stunning woman sitting in front of him right now is an important part of this investigation, and he had to remind himself to keep things objective and professional. For a split second, Viktor even entertained a thought that Katerina may turn out to be a suspect, but quickly put this thought on the back burner. He lit a cigarette and gathered himself.

Katya remained seated in her armchair, poised and suddenly emotionless. She seemed drained from the shock of the past two days, and Vitus allowed the silence to hang in the air like the smoke from his cigarette. Lieutenant Toropko stood a few steps behind Viktor's chair with the bundled axe and aluminum case still in her hands, feeling awkward and out of place.

"Lieutenant, please go, put the evidence in the car, and tell Freckles to clear the back seat for the extra passenger. Then, go with him to the hotel and collect Citizen Ragozhina's luggage."

"Yes, Major!" Nina, without delay, hurried out the main entrance door.

Vitus turned to Katerina again.

"I believe you had some questions, Comrade Major?" she asked preemptively and pulled her shawl back on her shoulders, uncovering her hair. This self-conscious move didn't escape Vitus. This is a woman who is well aware of her effect on men, he thought to himself.

"I understand you reside and work in Khabarovsk. What do you know about your father's everyday life as of late?" He began.

"Honestly, not much. I had a habit of visiting my father at least every two to three months. He is - he was - a wonderful human being. Sort of a gentle giant." She slipped into deep thought.

"Does that mean he did not have any enemies that you are aware of?" Viktor interjected.

"I can't say for sure," she continued. "After all, he was incarcerated for almost seven years. Someone put him in a labor camp. He never told me what he was accused of. And you may not believe it, but he once said that he was thankful to God for what happened to him. Otherwise, he would not have had me. That was exactly what he said, and when I asked him about my mother, he would hug me and say in a sorrowful voice: 'Your mother was the best woman I ever knew, but God has taken her and left you instead.'"

Again, Katya's eyes filled with tears. At that moment, Viktor saw Dr. Goldfarb marching confidently up the stairs with a cigarette dangling from the corner of his mouth.

"As I promised, everything is ready for you, Citizen Rogozhina. And you, Major Vitus," the doctor announced. "We can go downstairs."

Viktor grabbed his overcoat and his hat and helped Katerina up. On the way to the Pathology Room, the doctor pulled the Major aside discreetly and reported, "I am glad I finished with her father so quickly because I have another body on ice. The same Captain sent it from Urgal. This time, it's an eighteen-year-old Korean soldier found dead in the woods yesterday near the Listvenny settlement. No other details. At least I can tell you the name of the Captain—Lyubomir Nesterenko." Goldfarb concluded triumphantly.

"Looks like Captain Nesterenko keeps himself very busy these days. By the way, how was the body delivered here?" Viktor inquired.

"A dump trucks." The doctor replied," These monsters run between New Urgal and Chegdomyn through old Urgal, twenty-four hours a day." He noticed that the Major's eyebrows arched up in disbelief. "They just strapped the body bag on top of the huge front bumper. Ingenious, isn't it?"

"Oh, yes. Real Soviet ingenuity." Viktor said and the sarcasm was not lost on Goldfarb. "Well, let's get this over with." He deftly maneuvered himself into the room ahead of Katya, followed by the doctor.

The corpse lay covered by linen from the toes to the body midriff. The chest and the top of the head were neatly stitched, the clumps of blood cleaned from the now-combed hair. The late Fyodor Rogozhin was indeed a large and exceptionally handsome man. Even the violence of his demise did not distort the classic features of his serene, spiritual face.

Katerina remained surprisingly collected upon seeing her father on the morgue slab. She slowly approached the body, leaned to her father's cheek, and kissed it gently. A few of her tears dropped onto the face of the dead man, staying where they fell, suspended as if by some minor miracle. Katya whispered something in his ear and smiled. She straightened up and turned to Viktor.

"It is he. I confirm it." Katya suddenly covered her face with both hands and began sobbing. Viktor stayed immobile this time, though it took some effort. Suddenly, she comported herself and turned to the doctor.

"Where do I need to sign? May I arrange to put him in a decent coffin and ship him to be buried in Khabarovsk? I'll pay for everything." She attempted to sound clear and concise in her questions. Viktor was impressed by her poise, and that thought occurred to him once again. What does she know?

The doctor reacted promptly. "Sign here." He handed her a form and a pen. "And I will escort you to the clerk. She will help you with all your requests and take your payment. However, I am not sure about a cemetery plot in Khabarovsk."

"I could ask someone at UVD Headquarters to make the necessary arrangements with a cemetery," Viktor volunteered, but he did not get any response.

"Thank you, Doctor. You are a good, kind man." Katya gently squeezed Naum's wrist. "I have never seen a dead person, and it had to be my father... I am a mess, aren't I? Please forgive me." She looked at the body one last time, pulled the shawl over her head, and quickly walked straight through the door, followed by Goldfarb. She passed Viktor by like he wasn't even there

* * *

When the Major stepped outside, he saw Pyotr and Nina slapping their thighs and stomping their feet to keep warm. Here in Chegdomyn, it was much colder than in Khabarovsk or even in Birobidjan, and this strange dance was a common way to keep the warm blood pumping.

"You can start the car now," Victor said with slight irritation. "We are losing precious time; it will get dark in a couple of hours."

Nina ran from the vehicle to his side with a cloud of white steam around her head. "Should I go and fetch her?" she said with a smile. Viktor paused.

"No. Let the woman finish the arrangements for her father's burial. It's tough to do when it comes to someone close to you" He sighed, letting out a big cloud of steam.

"I buried my father nine years ago, so I know," Nina replied with sadness in her voice.

"What happened? He must've been relatively young, your dad?" Viktor looked at her with genuine interest.

"Yes, he was only fifty-one. Died in the line of duty. He was ambushed and killed by a thug with a knife." Nina went silent. "It's still hard to talk about it."

"So, he was a cop, and you followed in his footsteps?"

"Yes, Major," replied the Lieutenant in a manner that suggested the end of conversation. Viktor obliged.

"Lieutenant, the Doctor just informed me that another dead body was found in the woods, not far from the same *khutor*," he declared without hesitation. "Only this time, it's a young Korean soldier. That's all I know for now. We will obtain more details after Goldfarb performs an autopsy on him. However, I already have a couple of burning questions about this new development. Why did Captain Nesterenko from New Urgal decide to ship the body here for the autopsy instead of handing him over to the North Korean Military Command? An unusual break in protocol, no?"

"I want to know what the hell North Korean Military personnel were doing on Soviet territory. Was it some training exercise? And how many of them are still here?" Nina fired back.

Viktor went on to explain: "For more than fifteen years now, our government and our North Korean friend Chairman Kim Il-Sen have had a concession agreement to supply North Korea with construction timber. Korean workers do the labor, and half goes to North Korea while the other half stays here. Not a bad deal, eh?"

"But why is it the responsibility of their military?" Nina insisted.

"Very simple: they don't trust their civilians, but their soldiers are more reliable. I read somewhere that 25% of the population in that country is in military uniform anyway. So, they send a military regiment, specializing only in construction. They've set up several tent settlements, about three thousand heads in each camp. The soldiers are unarmed, except for their commanding officers and their security guards." Viktor paused for a breath and continued.

"A couple of years ago, I had a chance to walk through one of their camps on the Amur River. I saw the tarpaulin tents that slept twenty people alongside small food storage chests packed with cans of pork and beans. Oh yeah, and bottles of traditional Korean rice vodka with some kind of a large worm or small snake coiled at the bottom. On the shelves, I saw nothing but canvas shoes with thin rubber soles and cheaply made Chinese quartz watches."

Nina seemed skeptical. She looked over at Pyotr, who interrupted his dance to listen to the Major's story. Vitus continued.

"There were dozens of loudspeakers hung on the trees throughout the camp, playing Korean music non-stop. And though the Koreans were of different ages—some of them looked like teenagers, some in their twenties or thirties, and some in their sixties—they were all dressed the same: canvas shoes, khaki pants, the same green color cap with a long visor in front. And green, cotton-filled, stitched up jackets that reminded me of our Soviet quilted jackets we call "telogreika" (bodywarmer), that construction workers wear."

Viktor was enjoying the undivided attention from his younger colleagues. "To me, the Koreans were almost indistinguishable from one another, but I figured out how they recognized each other's rank: on their jackets, they wore round buttons with a picture of Chairman Kim. These buttons were of various sizes: big, medium, and small. So, the bigger the button, the higher their rank!"

"What I could never understand is how anyone could survive, let alone work, in the woods for eight-plus hours, dressed in only canvas shoes and a quilted jacket, during our winters of minus 50 degrees Celsius?" mused Freckles, to everyone's surprise.

"Maybe this is why I often come across internal reports regarding the bodies of North Korean soldiers found in the *Taiga*, frozen to death. But I think this one may be different." Viktor trailed off, noticing Katerina and Dr. Goldfarb emerging from the hospital entrance.

"Doctor, God forbid, you'll catch pneumonia! Go inside, please!" Katya pleaded with Goldfarb, who was only in his suit and white lab coat. "Thank you again for your help. Goodbye!"

"Don't worry about me! Nothing, a little vodka, and pickled herring won't cure. Take care of yourself, my dear!"

The doctor turned sharply toward Vitus. "Comrade Major, I'll let you know as soon as I've found anything interesting about my next patient. And, please, drive carefully. That permafrost is treacherous." He smiled, waved his hand, and ran back into the dilapidated three-story building called the Chegdomyn Hospital.

* * *

Major Vitus took his usual place in the front passenger's seat. Nina sat directly behind him. This put Katerina in the seat behind Freckles, which gave her a clear sightline at the Major's pensive profile. He's a handsome man in his own way, she thought to herself. But she was wary of starting any conversation and they all proceeded quietly as the *kozyol* cautiously wound its way through the streets of Chegdomyn.

Local children were running home from school alongside bundled-up women toting their meager food supplies in their expandable fishnet *avoska* bags. Men stood in groups of three near a liquor store, many already visibly drunk. The local militia Sergeant patrolled the streets, ready to spring into action if any of these men started any trouble. Just another day in the life of this small Soviet town of about twenty thousand people.

Almost all the men here were either coal miners or railroad workers. The rest of the population consisted of their spouses, children, and extended family. They all lived in furnished apartments with two or three rooms identically arranged, in identical three-story buildings lining identical, treeless streets. Viktor noticed that some of the buildings were leaning to one side or the other. That's what permafrost does, he thought to himself: generates heat under a structure, softening the frozen soil and giving way for the buildings to lean to one side. It was a slightly surreal sight, and Vitus smiled to himself; a smile noticed by Katya, who was more interested in reading the Major's facial expressions than the sad sights of this desolate backwater town; a town she knew all too well.

This particular town began its existence at the end of the 1930s when a rich deposit of black coal was discovered in the Buriya River Valley, near its confluence with the Urgal River. It was the aborigines who called it Chegdomyn. The tiny settlement was built up around several coal mines, but it got its real boost in 1939, when a railroad branch connected it with the Trans-Siberian Mainline. Chegdomyn officially received status as the administrative center of the Verkhneburiyinsky district, and its population doubled within two years. Several thousand experienced coal miners moved from Donbas, Ukraine, to settle down on the newly developed land.

However, the economic boom did not last long. When the Great Patriotic War broke out, the order came to dismantle the railroad and ship the steel tracks for smelting. The Red Army desperately needed tanks and cannons to fight the Germans. Mining resumed only in 1951, when the branch was reinstalled. The town had grown noticeably since: a cinema house, a school, a cultural center, even a recreation park with a statue of a war hero hoisting a flag. In 1974, the Baikal-Amur Mainline came through, 600 km north of the old Trans-Siberian Line on the troublesome border with China. Chegdomyn thus supplied energy for the whole nearby region.

Viktor had actually visited here thirty years ago with his father, then Colonel Raymond Alfredovich Vitus, but his recollection of it was hazy at best. His father had to bring him because of an unexpected hospitalization of his mother Leya, two months after the birth of their second child, Raisa. Colonel Vitus did not have time to arrange for anybody to stay with six-year-old Viktor, so he took the boy with him. It was little Viktor's first time outside his home in Khabarovsk.

Now - as their *kozyol* moved through the streets of Chegdomyn - Viktor understood the real purpose of his father's assignment here three decades earlier. He read the contents of the brown folder, the same folder that Colonel Vitus started right before their trip. The Colonel was to interrogate a resident of *khutor* Izmailovsky, 13 km southeast of Chegdomyn. A man who was arrested three days prior by the local operatives of MGB (The Ministry of State Security). The reason for the arrest was in the brown folder in Colonel Vitus'possession – a poorly phrased, handwritten letter signed by some anonymous hand, stating that Citizen Fyodor Feoktistovich Rogozhin was an anti-Soviet agitator and - potentially - a foreign agent.

But what Viktor could not know was that the fates of his late father and the late Father Rogozhin had crossed even earlier, back in 1939.

Chapter 3

Thursday, November 10, time precisely 13:00. The blue and white *kozyol* left behind the sorry looking streets of Chegdomyn and approached a massive structure on the right side of the two-lane highway. Bulging ripples and wide cracks across the road rattled the vehicle, shooting bolts of pain up the riders' spines.

The driver, Sergeant Uvalov, braced his arms against the steering wheel before each crevice, sparing himself a little of the shock. He occasionally glanced over at the Major with an empathetic smile. Viktor refused to acknowledge Freckle's sympathy and glanced at his watch: there was barely enough time to catch the Captain in New Urgal. They had just passed the 5km mark, with a sign reading: "Urgal 9 km; New Urgal 23 km."

The sprawling structure on the right was the Chegdomyn Electric Power Plant. It burned locally mined black coal, supplying electric power and steam to all nearby facilities. Four towering chimneystacks spewed dark grey clouds into the air. Hundreds of transformer substations surrounded the plant. The broad-shouldered towers looked like marching giants carrying thick braided high-voltage lines in different directions.

From this point on the traffic intensified. Trucks of all sizes were heading to and from the power plant, hauling all types of cargo. Yet Pyotr had no difficulty negotiating the way over the next four kilometers, weaving left and right around monstrous, yellow-colored four-wheelers.

When they reached Urgal, the dilapidated asphalt highway gave way to a gravel-covered, two-lane road. Upon seeing a sign marked "New Urgal 15 km," both Pyotr and Viktor let out sighs of relief. Viktor's watch showed only 14:45. There was enough time to reach their destination, though no one knew what lay ahead.

Very soon, they were squeezed between two huge dump trucks, one behind and one ahead. The trucks' massive, slow grinding wheels spewed gravel and mud all over the tiny *kozyol*. The windshield wipers swung feverishly, trying to provide some visibility. The conditions jeopardized their timely arrival in New Urgal, but it was even more dangerous to jump into the next lane to pass. Czech-built Skoda and Soviet-made KamAZ were barreling down the road in the opposite direction, packed together tightly.

Viktor and Freckles exchanged reassuring glances.

The Major said, almost whispering, "Take it easy. Better safe than sorry."

Pyotr nodded in agreement and leaned back.

"How do you like how huge those wheels are? A truck with tires like that could run over my *Kozyol* and not even notice. I wonder what they are hauling?"

"It seems that all the trucks in the opposite lane are empty, and the trucks in our westbound lane are hauling gravel," answered Viktor, still in a low voice, because he was afraid to wake the women snoozing in the back. "Around here, on the bank of Urgal River, there must be a quarry for good quality gravel," he speculated, turning his head toward the backseat.

Viktor could not see Nina. She was right behind him, slumped in the seat with a fur hat between her head and the frosty car window, sleeping away the exhaustion of the past few days. In his peripheral vision, however, he could see Katerina quite well. She was fully awake, leaning back slightly. Her wide-open eyes caught Viktor's glance. She straightened up and looked with surprise right back at him.

Viktor sensed pain in her look. His heart clenched. He turned almost entirely around to face Katerina and intensely stared at her. Unable to mask his anxiety, Viktor reached out and touched Katya's hand. She did not move an inch; she raised her head with teary eyes, looked straight in his eyes, and smiled. It was a smile of gratitude, with a little bit of hope that the pain would eventually go away. Viktor smiled back but withdrew his hand momentarily. He was afraid to upset Katya once again. However, this time, she did not seem to be upset. She dried her eyes with Viktor's handkerchief, which was still in her possession, and leaned back, pretending to look through the frosted car window.

This tenderly awkward moment did not escape Pyotr's attention. He noticed how pale Viktor's face became and how suddenly the Major turned back around in his seat, pressing his right hand against his chest, trying to calm down his heart palpitation.

The Sergeant got worried and whispered, "Are you all right, Comrade Major?"

"I am fine, my loyal Sancho," answered Viktor." It is getting darker. Turn on the headlights and keep your eyes on the road. Will you?"

"You called me this strange name again, Comrade Major. Who is he?" Pyotr wondered.

"It happened a long time ago in Spain. He was the servant and sidekick of a nobleman named Don Quixote, the Knight of Sadness and the Conqueror of—" Viktor stopped in mid-sentence. "Just read the book."

At this moment, they heard Nina's short but explosive laugh. "Yes, Sergeant, you better listen to your superior officer. Weren't you supposed to read that book in school?" she teased.

"I did finish middle school, you know, but I didn't remember the name of this character. I admit I skipped a lot of books when I was a kid. I wasn't a reader, I guess. I loved physical education—ice hockey, in particular," Pyotr mumbled.

"It is not a big deal," said Viktor with a reassuring voice. "You can always pick it up. That is the great thing about reading. You make yourself start a good book, and pretty soon, you realize you can't put it down. You want to finish it as soon as possible. And then you read another book, and another." Viktor was thinking out loud. "It becomes a routine, a good habit. Trust me."

"Oh, that's what happened to me too," said Nina with a certain hesitation. "In school, I was not an avid reader. I was crazy about science, chemistry and biology, physics, you know. Later, I became obsessed with criminology and forensics, so I had to read a lot. And I did, but not fiction." Nina paused for a moment and then continued.

"At the Militia Academy, my mentor—a very astute man—brought me a book and asked me to read it. It was a book of short stories by Edgar Allen Poe, an American writer. At first, I felt bored a little; the subject matter was very dark and gloomy. You know, human behavior, crime, like in Dostoyevsky's novels, which I had tried to read until the end but failed. However, this time, I got more and more into these books and couldn't stop.

Eventually, I was totally hooked on reading every book of his that I could get my hands on."

Katerina suddenly joined the conversation. "If you like those types of books, I mean, human behavior, psychology, or something of that nature, I recommend reading Charles Dickens. Nobody is better than him when it comes to that stuff."

"I think that is a bit heavy for me," Freckles interjected. "In any case, I will need a motivator, someone to lash the whip, because I'm lazy. Any volunteers? Comrade Lieutenant?"

"Let me think about it." Nina played along, laughing. "N-O. No! Sergeant, there are things in life you have to do by yourself. Becoming a reader is one of those things."

"Maybe I can contribute to your literary education?" Katerina said with a more confident voice. "I would like you to come and see our play for the new season. We are rehearsing it now; it's a very witty Shakespeare comedy: "The Taming of the Shrew." You can be my guests on premier night!" She sounded very excited. "I play Katherine, the Shrew."

"Our own Katerina is portraying the Shakespearian Katherine? Isn't that a marvelous coincidence?" Nina interjected with a hint of humor and a pinch of jealousy in her voice. Everyone paused.

"Please forgive my stupid humor." Nina quickly turned apologetic. "Katya, dear! I didn't mean anything negative, believe me."

"Sorry, I invited you all without even knowing any of you. And, sorry, Comrade Lieutenant, I liked your joke. It was cute, indeed." She turned her head back to the frosted window.

Viktor hurried in to dissipate the awkwardness caused by Nina's seemingly innocent joke. "On the contrary, we all are grateful for you inviting us to your premiere. We will be there to support you, Katya. If, of course, you don't change your mind."

"My invitation stands for all of you." Katerina sighed with relief and smiled. Again, she appreciated Viktor's effort to include her into his friends' circle, as she really needed it at that moment.

"Hey, look!" exclaimed Freckles. "We are almost at our destination, maybe another five or ten minutes. These monster trucks are getting off the road, so we can speed up a little."

It was a correct assessment on Pyotr's part. The dump truck in front of them veered off into a mass of trucks and heavy construction machinery. The cacophony of diesel engines penetrated easily through the thin doors of the Militia UAZ. Each truck in line dumped its gravel load into a shallow ditch then immediately pulled away to allow the next truck to take its spot. An excavator piled the gravel with its long-articulated arm and basket while huge bulldozers shaped it into an elongated trapezoid. This created a bed for laying railroad tracks, which also protected the permafrost underneath from melting during the hot summer months.

Further along, half a kilometer or so from the construction site, a machine with a crane on top and a cargo platform dropped cross ties in perfect parallel spacing on the gravel bed. Those squared, tar-treated wooden blocks were made from Siberian pine logs. A second machine followed closely behind, laying steel rails perpendicular to the ties. Piece by piece they lined them up, accurately gauging each section between the rails and bolting them down with iron spikes. It was slow and tedious work, always subject to the weather. Each crew of about twenty people could lay down no more than three to five kilometers a day. But four hundred working teams like this one stretched across a 4200km construction zone, working day in and day out. Viktor was very familiar with operations like this.

In the early winter of 1974, the *Politburo* of the Communist Party announced the rebuilding of the Baikal-Amur Mainline; they asked the members of the Communist Youth Union to rise to the challenge of this massive undertaking. Of course, the official answer from the Komsomol was "Yes." The young people of the USSR were always at the front lines of every endeavor and every project initiated by Soviet leadership. The problem was, most of these national initiatives were politically motivated, or purely ideological. Too often such industrial projects lacked common sense, cost too much, and were executed poorly with unnecessary loss of human life.

More and more, the post-war generation of Soviet youth recognized each new construction campaign as mere propaganda and simply ignored the calls for labor. So the Moscow Administration began offering significant financial incentives: double pay, completion bonuses, and the like. While not officially advertised, these perks were well promoted by word of mouth. Soon there was no shortage of young professionals and low-qualified laborers volunteering. Some did seek to advance their careers or learn marketable skills. But for everybody, the primary objective was to make as much money as quickly as possible. It seemed unimaginable: the Soviet Socialist system, which prides itself on economic equality and fairness, secretly encouraging Komsomol members to get rich on the auspicious task of building national infrastructure. But in fact, nobody paid much attention to such a glaring paradox.

At the beginning of the 1970s, after Nikita Khrushchev's era, the socialist system's most significant danger was that people finally began paying close attention to the undercurrent of societal developments. The relations in a country of almost a hundred different ethnic groups would not fit into Stalin's traditional concept of one Soviet nation. Moreover, serious cracks in Khrushchev's economic plans indicated the beginning of a severe stagnation.

As a result, people became more disillusioned and skeptical of the Soviet regime. The entire world was at the threshold of the Information Revolution, and the young people of the Soviet Union were yearning for changes. Brezhnev's Politburo members fully realized that to halt the permafrost of the society, a shake-up was needed. But of course, not a meaningless shake-up, but one to excite and to rally them for a while and divert their anxiety from the real troubles.

Moscow leadership strongly believed this might work and began deploying construction teams along the future Mainline with real urgency and a well-organized media blitz. By the end of February 1974, two strategic centers were established: the City of Tynda for the Western section of the BAM; And Urgal—its Eastern counterpart. The Western branch was sponsored by the Komsomol organizations of Moscow and Leningrad, and the Eastern by the Komsomol organizations of Kyiv, Donetsk, and Lviv. The national movement to build the Baikal-Amur Mainline in ten years was on its way to becoming a reality.

* * *

At 16:40, the *kozyol* approached an old wooden building with a large sign that read: "URGAL II." The road branched off just in front of it, crossing the railroad tracks and leading through an arched gateway with letters forming the name: "New Urgal." Pyotr looked at the Major victoriously.

"We are here; I told you we would make it."

"Well done. I didn't have any doubts, Comrade Sergeant. Now we must find Captain Nesterenko office. Let's see if we can find someone."

They pulled in near a strange-looking structure on the right side of the road, sprawled along the track opposite the old Station. This was a huge structure. Two dozen square pillars of steel-reinforced concrete jutted out of the ground, about one-and-a-half meters each, to form a twenty-by-fifty-meter rectangle. At its far end, bright sparks flew into the crisp, cold air. Four workers, wearing orange safety hats, dark goggles, and bulky rubber gloves, were welding a crown of rebar and wire across the skeletal structure. Another group attached wooden box-frames across the steel trestle to be filled by cement slowly pouring from the spinning cone of a mixer. This created an elevated foundation that would keep the heat generated by the sizable structure from affecting the frozen soil during the warm season.

Viktor remembered a recent article in a Khabarovsky newspaper detailing this method for building more permanent architectural structures in permafrost regions. Russian civil engineers first successfully developed the method, which was then exported to all the nearest Arctic European countries, along with the frigid regions of North America. As he tried to illuminate his companions with these finer points, Pyotr abruptly stopped the car next to a foreman surveying the work. The man noticed the dirt-strewn Militia UAZ and faced it. Viktor pushed his side door open and held on to its handle, leaning forward.

"I apologize for interrupting your work, comrade." His voice signaled urgency. "Can you tell us how to find the local Militia precinct?"

"Just keep going down this Donetskaya Street," the man responded in a casual tone. "The road will make a sharp curve, and after you pass the 'Diner', you'll see the Militia office." He waved his hand and returned to what he was doing before.

"Thanks!" Viktor yelled and quickly pulled himself inside the car that was already rolling forward. Minutes later they passed a large log barracks with a 'Diner' sign, and across the street, a cabin with the plaque saying: "The Railroad Militia, New Urgal Precinct." Pyotr nimbly parked his *kozyol* next to a nearly identical vehicle except for a blue domed Mars light on top.

Viktor's wristwatch read 16:50, so in a rush he jumped from his seat and dashed up the cement stairs. Luckily, the door wasn't locked. He passed through a narrow corridor to find himself in a large office with two further doors. Hearing voices behind one of them, he knocked sharply. Without waiting for a response, he pulled the door open only to find two men sitting across from one another at a desk. One man had the uniform of a Militia Captain; his head resembled that of a bald eagle. The man across from him was younger and dressed in plain clothes, giving an air of authority and ostentation. It seems Viktor interrupted their visibly heated discussion and they both stared at the unexpected visitor with expressions of bewilderment.

"I apologize for interrupting. I just arrived in town," Viktor declared. "I'm Major Vitus, the Senior Investigator from Khabarovsky UVD, Violent Crime Investigation Unit."

"Comrade Major.! To be honest, I wasn't expecting you until tomorrow or even Monday. This is great; you are here today. Welcome to New Urgal, I'm the Captain Lyubomir Nesterenko, Commander of the local UVD, Railroad Militia, Forgive me as I wrap up some business here." The Captain said apologetically, sounding Ukrainian and yet a little different from the familiar dialect; Viktor found his melodious speech pattern pleasant.

The tall, handsome young man rose from his seat as well, with no intention to speak but full intention to leave. He was puffing on a Marlboro cigarette, a rarity in the Soviet Union. He made his way to the door, as he gestured to the empty chair.

This man piqued Viktor's curiosity.

" And would you be so kind as to introduce yourself?" Viktor asked.

"Frankly, I don't have to introduce myself to anybody."

Viktor was taken aback by this dramatic response. Viktor also saw the man more clearly as he stood into the light, his olive-skinned face with high cheekbones, narrow lips, and almond-shaped eyes indicating his Kazakh or Tatar blood.

"Forgive me, Major but I am in a hurry. I'm sure we will meet again. And Captain— you should seriously consider what I mentioned to you earlier." The man walked out the door without closing it.

"Who was that? Hold on, let me guess; he is from the KGB?" Viktor could not hide his annoyance.

"Yes, Comrade Major, he is a KGB Captain from the Khabarovsky Regional Office. He curates our section of the BAM. For the last two years, he was stationed in Chegdomyn, but lately he spends most of his time in Old Urgal. And here, of course," the Captain responded in a low voice, in case the man was still in earshot.

"Generally, he is a good guy, but sometimes he irritates the hell out of me, I must admit. I've asked him not to smoke in here because I am allergic to tobacco, but he ignores me."

"I meet people like him at KGB headquarters quite often. I even had a few joint cases with those guys. Some are real pros, but some are all show and no substance."

Viktor decided to switch to another topic.

"I would need to go over the case now, but before we do, allow me to introduce the rest of my team. I am afraid they might be cursing me for leaving them in the car."

Viktor ran outside and waved everyone in. By the time they gathered back in the Captain's office, he had procured chairs enough for all of them. The formal introductions went quickly, except for Katerina. When she told the Captain who she was, he looked at Viktor, a little puzzled. Vitus explained:

"Citizen Rogozhina arrived in Chegdomyn on her own. At my request, she identified the victim as her father and made arrangements for his proper burial."

"I see," replied the Captain. "Please accept my condolences, Citizen Rogozhina. It is good that you were able to say a final goodbye to your father. I knew him; I met him once. He struck me as an exceptional man." Katerina sensed the genuine sincerity in his voice.

"Thank you, Captain, for your kind words." Again, Katerina brought the white handkerchief up to her teary eyes. "I want you to find whoever killed him," she said calmly but with conviction.

For a moment, there was silence in the room. Then, the Captain broke the silence.

"I assure you, we will bring whoever did this to justice."

Katerina looked at Viktor at this moment. Viktor didn't know how to respond, but the Captain interjected again.

"Before we proceed any further, let me make some sleeping arrangements and get something for you to eat. When was the last time you had any food??" Lyubomir pulled the telephone over and dialed an extension number.

"This is Captain Nesterenko. We need to set up a place for a few days: two young women and one young man. Yes, two separate rooms, preferably in the same building. Let me know, as soon as possible. Thanks."

"Six people," Viktor corrected the Captain.

"You, Major, will be staying with my family and I, at my apartment," the Captain replied. "That way, we can discuss the case more thoroughly. Is that okay with you?"

"Is your wife aware you're having guests?"

"She will be. And she'll be delighted. Lyuba loves to feed and entertain guests. They are scarce around here. Since we settled down here almost two years ago, we've only had one other person stay with us. So, please, accept our invitation," the Captain insisted.

"I accept." Viktor agreed while feeling a bit torn about being separated from Katerina.

He immediately dialed another number. This time, the conversation was even shorter. "Good evening, Nastya. Five of us will be over in fifteen minutes. Please, make something hot. See you."

At that moment, the telephone rang. The Captain answered it right away. "Yes? Okay, we are coming."

The telephone rang again as they headed through the door. Lubomir lifted the receiver and listened. He pulled a piece of paper from the desk drawer, grabbed a pen, and began making notes.

"Okay, thanks. I'll bring them after we eat." He put the receiver down and followed everybody outside, closing the door behind him. "We are just going across the street, people. You see the diner, don't you?"

The visitors stepped through a small foyer into a long, well-lit hall with fifty or so square tables for four laid neatly with red and white-checkered cloth. There were salt and peppershakers atop each table. Glass refrigerators displayed appetizers and counters held bread and pastries, but there was no cashier's desk along the wall. A large sign on the opposite wall informed patrons that smoking was prohibited. Everything screamed of cleanliness.

The diner was empty, as dinner started only at seven, but two tables had been pulled together in the middle of the hall, piled with steaming food, which smelled delicious. Anastasiya, the hostess, stood nearby, beckoning to the guests to take their seats.

Dinner had begun, and what a dinner it was: smoked fish appetizers, hot soup with meat, cabbage, potatoes, and beans. Beef Stroganoff on a bed of egg noodles, pickled cucumbers, tomatoes on the side, and finally, freshly brewed hot tea with apple turnovers, honey *kalachkies*, and other local pastries. Everything was delicious.

Nina could not help but ask Anastasiya unceremoniously: "Was it prepared just for us?"

"A meal like this would be impossible to prepare on such short notice, don't you think? You are having the same dishes that are on our evening menu," the hostess explained proudly. "When we started our job at this diner two years ago, we pledged to the hard-working people of BAM that when you come here to eat, you will feel right at home! And so far, this promise has been kept. By the way, the entire personnel of this diner graduated from the same culinary school in Donetsk. Class of 1974."

"You are doing a great job. Thank you from all of us!" Viktor got up and shook the hostess's hand. "It is, indeed, close to home cooking. Please pass on our appreciation to everyone in the kitchen. To whom do we pay for this lovely supper?"

"We do not take money from guests. We are on a collective budget that is created by withholding a reasonable amount from every monthly paycheck of each person who works and lives in New Urgal." The woman could not hide her surprise at the ignorance displayed by the Militia Major.

"I must admit, the number of our customers lately has started to shrink. The workers whose wives and children have joined them here moved from the dormitories to their own apartments with modern kitchens. They prefer eating with their families at home. Recently we opened a produce and grocery store to shop for home cooking. And this is wonderful. But we still have plenty of people to feed," Anastasiya concluded, helping the guests to put their winter coats back on. "Hope to see you all for breakfast!"

As the left the friendly diner, they passed a long line of people just finishing their work shifts. Many were young people, between twenty and thirty-five, but some looked older, maybe in their forties or even fifties. Regardless of age, they had no problems intermingling amicably and respectfully, just like it should be in a tight knit community.

Outside, festively dressed young people strolled in pairs down the walkways lining Donetsk Street. These wooden planks covered the tops of an insulated plumbing network that curved around the terrain, connecting every building in the settlement. The temperature had dropped even lower. The wind was picking up, fluttering flurries in the cold air. Captain Nesterenko led the group through the throng, into a log barracks across the street.

The young woman behind the counter greeted them with a smile. "Welcome to New Urgal Hotel! May I have your passports or some other identification?"

After collecting the documents, she explained: "Women will stay in the left-wing, men in the right. Bathrooms and showers are in between." She pointed to the wall behind her.

"Each room is for two occupants. Sorry, no smoking allowed in the rooms; fire hazard, you know. This isn't a real hotel. Just six months ago, it was a dormitory with bunks. If you are interested, tomorrow I'll show you the real hotel which is being constructed next to these barracks."

Nina smiled. "Can we get a wake-up call?"

Viktor interjected. "The Captain and I will come and pick you up when it is time to drive to Izmailovsky. So, get some good rest. We'll see you tomorrow. Good night."

Before leaving, Viktor glanced at Katerina one more time. She had not looked at him once since they arrived at the Captain's office earlier. But now she gazed directly back, and the faintest shadow of a smile crossed her lips. Viktor could not hold back a wide grin.

In five minutes, he and the Captain were back at the door of the Militia precinct. A young man and woman, both dressed in fashionable shearling coats and fur hats, waited atop the concrete stairs. The woman held a large manila envelope in her hand.

"Polina, Yury, you brought me my photographs, didn't you?" exclaimed Lyubomir with sincere surprise. "I thought they would not be ready until tomorrow. Thanks, and forgive me for making you wait in such cold."

"It's okay, Captain. We have been here for no longer than a few minutes," replied Polina. "We are on our way to a concert, so we're kind of in a hurry. If you need anything else, I'll be glad to help. Bye!"

The Captain put the yellow envelope under his arm and unlocked the door. The very next moment he was behind his desk, opening it gently. "Major, sit down. This will be a great deal of interest to you." He removed a number of black and white photographs and spread them out on the desk surface.

"How did you manage to get them processed so quickly? You did not send film anywhere, did you?" Viktor leaned over and grabbed two or three prints off the top of the pile.

"I didn't have to. There is a photo lab right here in New Urgal," Nesterenko informed him proudly. "Leonid Gordin, our correspondent for the National Railroad Union Newspaper

Gudok, brought it with him. He has embedded himself with the Lviv construction team to record a history of the construction project for the different national publications. Alexandr Borovoy, the Urgal Komsomol Committee Head, also contributed some funds to purchase a photo printing projector, photo paper, and all the necessary chemicals for processing."

"And how is this documentary coming along?" Viktor asked in mock interest.

"I am sure it is coming along well," Lyubomir answered, matching the Major's ironic tone. "You can read a very informative bulletin board, posted in the diner every Saturday, It has pictures and articles written by workers and foremen and project supervisors. I must admit, Polina and Leonid are doing a great job with this bulletin since their arrival here in April of 74." He continued more seriously, "However, Leonid's main job is to write information pieces and articles about the railroad's progress and the people working at the Eastern section of BAM. He has produced hundreds of articles in the last few years. He is actually a close friend. We were neighbors back in Lviv. Leonid was the only person my wife and I knew when we came here in January 1975."

"I would like to meet your friend Leonid," Viktor reacted. "I honestly do like journalists."

"Then, I will introduce him to you soon." The Captain paused for a second and changed the subject to the matter at hand. "You can see these pictures are from the site where the Korean soldier was found. The stab wounds have similarities with the wounds on Rogozhin's body. I'll show you the pictures I took in his house in a moment. I am sure, in both instances, it is the work of rather experienced killers, using the same weapons."

Nesterenko leaned on the other side of the desk and opened the medium size safe. He pulled out a yellow manila envelope and handed it to Viktor. "You can see it yourself."

The Major opened the folder and examined a few pictures with a magnifying glass he picked up from the desk. "I agree, it looks that way. This one shows the ruckus you found at the house. They turned everything upside down, didn't they? What do you think they were looking for?"

"It was impossible to determine if anything was taken away from there," the Captain replied. "But you're right, they did search for something worth killing Rogozhin for."

"I hope his daughter Katerina will be able to shed light on this mystery," Viktor declared with a degree of confidence in his voice. "We may lose some evidence, though, I am afraid. And something else worries me: the killers could come back and search the place again. So, we must go there as soon as possible."

"We must, we must, Comrade Major. But don't worry about losing any evidence. I've had my guy, Sergeant Darsulov, watching the Rogozhin's house since day one!" The Captain smiled.

"Excellent! Good thinking, Captain. Are you sure that your Sergeant can defend the scene from these killers, let alone survive there for so many days? How many people do you have to cover such a large territory under your jurisdiction?" Viktor expressed genuine concern.

"There are five Militia men at my disposal: two in New Urgal, two in Urgal, and one in the Listvenny settlement, where my wife Lyuba happens to manage a dry goods store," said Lyubomir. "Sergeant Darsulov is half Nanai, which is a local tribe. He has no problem surviving in the *Taiga* or protecting himself against any intruders. Nikolai is a very experienced serviceman and an exceptional tracker, hunter, and marksman as well."

"You said half; what's the other half?" asked Viktor.

"His mother is of European descent, new to this land, I guess." Lyubomir answered. "I know from his personnel file that Nikolai was born south of here, in Birobidjan, the Autonomous Jewish region of the Russian Federation."

Viktor quickly changed the subject. "I think we have to alter our plans for tomorrow. It's late. I'll stay here and work more with these photographs. We'll eat and immediately leave for Izmailovsky. Agreed?"

"Agreed," the Captain answered with little hesitation. "But don't fall asleep on the desk; grab your bag and go to the Hotel. There is another bed in your driver's room."

"Of course, that is exactly what I am going to do," Viktor said agreeably. "Remember, I promised to wake everyone up."

"Then I am off." Lubomir got up and slowly walked to the door. "See you in the morning. Get some sleep too, Comrade Major, will you? I am sure Lyuba will be disappointed that I did not bring you home," he waved amicably.

Viktor set himself comfortably in the Captain's chair and scooped up another pile of photographs. He thumbed through them gingerly, sometimes using the magnifying glass. But he could not help thinking about Lyubomir Nesterenko. Viktor liked him, though they had met only three hours ago. However, something in his demeanor made Viktor uneasy. Perhaps he was too friendly, too excessively accommodating. People in this neck of the woods were usually more reserved— they liked to test the water before jumping in.

Viktor's family would be a great example: by nature, his mom Leya was a friendly and hospitable woman, but she was not eager to form close relationships too quickly. Perhaps many years living with her husband, a professional state security man, had taught her that. Viktor and his sister had also grown to be cautious people like their father. So had everybody around them—cousins, and friends. Viktor was not familiar with the cultural habits of newcomers to this land, Ukrainians in particular.

He could only guess that an eagerness for informal relations, even friendship, might be a shared trait.

And when was it that the Captain mentioned he had met the deceased in person? This thought had just popped in Viktor's head. *Must have been when he was still alive, but when? A few days, a few months before Rogozhin's death? I have to ask him tomorrow.*

The Major looked at his watch. It was almost 9 o'clock. He stepped outside for a moment to clear his head from the swirl of thoughts. The night was frigid, dark, and quiet except occasionally for the staccato rattle of rail cars in the distance. Viktor sucked in a few deep breaths of fresh, frosty air and quickly returned to the office. Inside, it was warm and comfortable. He took up the photographs and resumed studying them attentively.

Chapter 4

Friday. Major Vitus, Lieutenant Toropko, and Katerina climbed aboard of the white UAZ, marked "Railroad UVD Novy Urgal." Sergeant Uvalov waved from the precinct stairs. He would stay in contact with the party via a two-way radio for the time being.

All the passengers including the captain were well rested; a warm room and comfortable bed can do miracles for a tired body. The Major on the other hand, looked ragged with dark circles around his eyes, bloodless lips, and pale face. He had slept poorly. So, Viktor immediately closed his eyes as the *kozyol* passed through the arched gate into the woods. Everyone in the car kept a respectful silence.

Thick frost covered the car windows. The headlights pierced the early dawn as the car squeezed between the walls of tall pine trees. Captain Nesterenko drove with the confidence of someone who knew his way around. Twenty minutes passed in silence, until the vehicle climbed over a small hill and abruptly stopped before a small wooden bridge.

Major Vitus opened his eyes in a half daze, "Are we in Izmailovsky?"

"Yes, we are," answered the Captain, still in a low voice. "Only, from this point on, we have to walk."

As they climbed from the car and approached the bridge, a hulking figure bound toward them in what seemed only two or three steps. He wore a long-inverted sheepskin *tulup*, floppy fur hat, and *valenki,* knee-high felt boots. In his left hand he clutched a 22mm rifle that looked small in his huge mitten.

"Sergeant Darsulov at your service!" He addressed Major Vitus, as the senior officer. Then he turned toward Nesterenko and reported, "Everything is in order, Comrade Captain. No one has disturbed the crime scene."

"Thank you, Sergeant. Well done." The Captain replied, sharply touching his head with his stretched hand in formal salute.

"Thank you, Captain. " Darsulov retorted with a smile. His high cheekbones moved even higher, and dark pupils disappeared behind heavy eyelids.

This giant doesn't have any European features, Viktor noted to himself.
"It is obvious that I didn't need to worry about you being here alone," he said aloud, as he slapped Darsulov's large back. "Lead us to the site, please."

"Not yet!" Nina Toropko exclaimed, as she gathered her gear from the vehicle. "Let me go right behind the Sergeant and ahead of you, comrades. I need to see the scene first."

"Of course, Comrade Lieutenant!" said Major Vitus approvingly, waving Katerina and the Captain back. "Let her get the camera ready."

They each took in the sights as they waited. The sun, still close to the horizon, shot its crimson beams through the pine branches to land softly on a small frozen pond, surrounded by short spruces and swamp cranberry bushes. *Khutor* Izmailovsky was a picturesque view of the Siberian Taiga, with four well-kept cedar-log houses with steep, straw roofs, each sitting on top of its own little hill. A narrow, elevated walkway connected each house to another.

Viktor moved his glance from the beautiful scenery and looked at Katerina. Tears filled her eyes as she gently dabbed them with the handkerchief. He got closer and reached for her hand. She did not protest.

The Rogozhin's house was second from the bridge, on the highest hill, visible from every angle. It had a porch alongside the front wall and a long narrow window with small square panes. The six-ended cross of the Old Believer's Faith crowned the entrance, a full meter above the doorframe. Viktor remembered seeing some files on this sect in his father's safe but recalled very little about them.

Perhaps Katerina could help him with this information? Viktor thought.

Lieutenant Toropko finished assembling her gear and marched ahead, just behind Sergeant Darsulov.

A thin crust of ice covered the old cedar planks of the walkway preserving sundry footprints against their weathered grains. Nina quickly passed by the Sergeant and started snapping photos at every second or third step. She squatted down at the junction before the first house on the left, pulled a scalpel from her aluminum case, and scraped something into a small plastic bag.

At that moment, a woman ran from the first house they had passed, wearing only a netted wool shawl wrapped around her upper body. She was screaming, "Where did you take him? Why did you arrest Fyodor? He did nothing wrong. Wasn't it enough that he was in prison for seven years?" She was almost choking on her own words, either from the exertion of running or the frigid morning air.

"Oh, Katya! It is you, isn't it? Tell me, is Fyodor in prison again?"

With both hands, Katerina grabbed the screaming woman by her shoulders and hugged her tightly.

"*Aunt* Anna! Dad wasn't arrested. Please go back inside! It's too cold; you're going to catch cold," she was pleading with her. "After I help these people with some of Dad's stuff, I'll come to see you and tell you everything, I promise."

Viktor helped Katerina guide the distraught old woman back to her house. "Comrade Sergeant, please make sure no one else leaves their homes."

"There's only one more person who is still here, my uncle Saveliy. But he is too old and too ill to leave his house," explained Katya in a calm but sad voice. "My Dad was taking care of his younger sister and older brother for many years. Dear God, who will do it now?" She let out a deep sigh and wiped the tears from her cheeks. "I must inform my cousins about what happened. They should take their parents to live with them," Katerina added.

"What about your Aunt Anna? Why can't she look after her sick brother? She is not that old, is she?" For Viktor, it was clear.

"First, my aunt is not that young; she is 74. And second, for the last few years, she has been afflicted by blindness and some senility," Katerina explained after she gently nudged the old woman inside the house and closed the door behind her. "She can be all right on rare occasions, like now. More often than not she gets confused and can't even recognize some relatives. It would be hard to get any sense out of her."

"Too bad; however, I hope, today, your aunt could share with us some valuable information about what was happening here on the days before your father was killed." said Viktor as they rejoined the rest of the group.

"I have my doubts. We'll see," Katerina replied, almost whispering.

Suddenly they found themselves standing under the cross at the entrance to Fyodor Rogozhin's house. A light green paper stapled to the door offered notice of an official crime scene. Lieutenant Toropko snapped some shots of the porch, and entrance way. She reached for her scalpel again and scraped another sample into an evidence bag.

Sergeant Darsulov removed the padlock from its latch and swung the door wide open. There was a room—more like a tiny entrance hall—with a huge wooden barrel full of water in a corner and a small wooden shelf just over it. A pewter mug hung from the shelf by a long string, next to a kerosene lamp with a smoky glass dome. A pair of high felt boots stood next to the other door.

"I did not touch a thing; everything is as it was when you left, Comrade Captain," reported Sergeant Darsulov. "I stayed in this house to keep it warm. I've got the oven going and slept on it." He sounded a bit apologetic. "Believe me, I know traditional Russian ovens; I've built a couple of them myself, but this one is superb; made by a true master."

"Okay, okay, Sergeant, we believe you. Let's go inside, already." Major Vitus could not hide his impatience. "Do we need some light?"

"I don't think so." The Sergeant waved his right hand, inviting everybody in and stepping aside.

The main room was indeed surprisingly well lit by the two narrow windows with small square panes. Another cross, this time an eight-ended one, hung between the windows; it was even larger than the one outside. Closer to the door, the white-painted brick and clay Russian oven extended all the way to the ceiling like a broad chimney. The oven occupied almost a third of the entire room, and its arched mouth glowed with the smoldering firewood in its deep belly.

There were few furnishings to speak of: a crude wooden table, four crude stools, and a simple two-shelf cabinet. Pewter tableware, ceramic dishes—the meager trappings of an ascetic life were tossed about helter-skelter. A few small icons had been knocked off the wall. The cross was crooked as if someone had tried to tear it from the wall but failed. Dozens of old religious books lay scatted about, their bindings torn with great force. Blood stains splattered the floor, the walls, everywhere. A large, black pool of it had almost dried near the back wall; two bloodied railroad spikes lay next to it. The smell of violent rage and death hung in the air.

The black and white photos Major Vitus studied the night before with the view of the dead body nailed to the wall couldn't prepare him for this livid, gruesome scene. Everyone stood petrified for a moment, even Captain Nesterenko and Sergeant Darsulov who had been here before. Then, a chilling groan pulled everyone's attention to Katerina. She slid down to the floor by the corner of the oven. Sitting with her legs crossed, she swung from side to side and moaned, like the wailing women at an Orthodox funeral.

Nina immediately dropped on the floor next to Katerina. She put her hands around Katya with sincere compassion and looked up, searching for Viktor. Nina's entire demeanor screamed *I told you it was a bad idea to bring Katerina here with us!*

Viktor fully comprehended what the Lieutenant could not say out loud. He sat on the floor facing Katya, attempting to console her as his own frustration mounted. She stopped swinging and moaning, this time staring right through Viktor. She whispered, "When I was little, we gave the oath to protect each other from troubles. He kept his word. I didn't. I know who could've killed him."

"What do you mean, you know who did it?" Viktor asked in disbelief. He tried to look straight into her eyes. "Look at me, Katya; look at me! You know who did this?"

Katerina tried to rise but felt very weak, almost lifeless, like someone had let the air out of her. Nina placed a stool near her.

"Nina, Comrade Captain, please, proceed with what we have to do here. I'll stay with her; we need to talk." Viktor continued to hold and prop Katya up. "Collect any possible artifacts which can become evidence. Photograph and record them. Be careful moving through all this mess. And let me know if anything unusual pops up, okay?"

"Don't worry, Comrade Major. We know what to do," replied Nina with confidence. "We might need the help of Sergeant Darsulov to search the rest of the house, around and underneath it. It is obvious the perpetrators were looking for something extremely important to them."

"And I am pretty sure that they did not find whatever it was," the Captain said. "The Korean Soldier Kim accidentally walked in on them while they were committing this crime. That is why they had to stop their search and go after the unwanted witness. Talk about being at the wrong place at the wrong time!"

"They did come back here the next night, by the way," Sergeant Darsulov interrupted. "Close to midnight, I heard two men snooping around and talking about the Militia order on the locked door. By the time I jumped from the bunker behind the oven and grabbed my rifle, they were gone into the woods. I think they saw me, though."

"Did you notice how they looked, by any chance?" asked Viktor rather anxiously. "You have a keen eye, Sergeant."

"I am sorry, I wasn't able to. When I got on the porch, it was too late even to catch a glimpse of the intruders," said Sergeant apologetically. "I did not have a chance to mention this to you yet. Sorry. But I think if this is so important, they will try to get access to this place again, and then I might be able to catch them red-handed."

"I don't share your optimism, Comrade Sergeant. They know that this place is guarded. They might even be watching us here today from afar. Thus, there is no reason for them to take a risk. Most likely, they will go away, as far as they can, and lay low until everything blows over," the Major concluded with a hint of irritation.

"All right, Comrade Sergeant. Thank you for your valuable input," the Captain interjected, trying to dissipate the tension. "The Major is right; time is running fast. Let's get to work.

The Comrade Lieutenant and I will search here while you Comrade Sergeant will go outside and carefully inspect what is underneath and around the house."

"Permission to precede, Comrade Captain!" The Sergeant saluted and walked out the door stiffly.

Nina and Lyubomir divided the room between them and began sifting through the debris. They carefully sorted each item of interest into a pile to be photographed and recorded in the case ledger.

In the meantime, Katerina and Viktor sat near the oven. The Major hoped to restart the conversation, but Katya continued sobbing. It was, after all, the house where she grew up, where she had lived with her father and now the place where her father had been murdered. Viktor suspected Katya was withholding information as to what had transpired here, as she claimed she knew who had the motive to commit such a terrible act. But the Major could not force her to speak when she was so fragile, so he left her for a while to calm down and gather her composure.

The Major took his heavy shearling coat off and put it on the top of the oven. He noticed a quilted spread thrown over a thin straw-filled mattress there. Viktor had never had the experience of living in a country home where the Russian oven was such a vital necessity, nor did he fully appreciate how central it was to life in such places. People baked bread in this kind of oven; boiled milk and water for bathing; it was also the place to gather and rest after a hard-day work, and to sleep during the long winter nights.

Once, the building of an oven was a high art throughout European and Siberian Russia, and master oven-builders prospered. But all this was in the past. There was no place for traditional Russian ovens in the urban high rise, with their gas ranges and central heating.

"I spent my childhood on top of this oven," Katerina smiled when she noticed how attentively Viktor was studying this piece of history. "The best place in the whole world. Here, I did my schoolwork and my most interesting reading; here, I had my most wonderful dreams. Dad prepared the most delicious meals for me in this oven and always made sure that it stayed warm overnight."

Katya took off her fur coat off and put it on the top of the stove next to Viktor's. Her dark blue pantsuit was very elegant but in need of some cleaning and ironing. She stopped crying and dried her face with Viktor's handkerchief.

"I have to get you a fresh hanky, don't I?" Viktor tried to inject some humor. "Do you feel better?"

"Yes, I do feel better. Thank you," answered Katya in a calm voice. "It was unbearable to see this place in shambles and realize it's where my dad took his last breath. I must apologize for my outburst. I should've prepared myself better before I agreed to accompany you here."

"Never mind, Katya. Everyone understands and respects your feelings." Viktor now sounded serious. "Take your time if you need to. Please relax and calm your nerves. Our talk can wait."

"No, no!" insisted Katerina. "I am here to help, remember?" She made another attempt to smile. "I am fine; I am strong. You can ask me any questions you need to ask."

"Then let's go back to what you said when you were sitting on the floor," Viktor started hesitantly.

"Perhaps it is a little hasty on my part, but I do think I might know a person who might want to take revenge on my father. Dad told me about him once, when I demanded to know what happened to my mother," she said, her voice still trembling. "His name is Myron Zozulya, my dad's fellow-inmate in the labor camp. They shared the same *nary*, what they called a plank bed with no mattress."

"And why do you think he had a motive to hurt your father?"

"He was my mom's husband!" Katerina almost shouted but then continued more calmly. "She went to visit Myron at the camp, where she met the man who would become my father. They fell madly in love, as my dad put it. But my mom could not stay near the camp any longer and had to leave. Once home, she discovered she was pregnant. She confided in her friend, Myron's younger sister Daria, who reminded her that she must think about her first child, Myron's son, four-year-old Roman. Daria recommended an abortion, but she decided to keep the baby. So, here I am, a love child. Sadly, my mom died during my delivery. Aunt Dasha had to care for Roman and me. When I was four, Fyodor Rogozhin showed up at the door of her house. After a short stay, he took me with him back to Khabarovsky Krai. And that is how this house became my home until I was eighteen."

Viktor was captivated by her story, but he had to interject. "Regarding Myron Zozulya, as a potential suspect— Did your dad tell you about him in more detail? Is he still incarcerated?"

"No, he was freed in 1959, five years after my father." Katerina talked hurriedly. "And yet, he wasn't officially re-instated, so he couldn't go home. Instead, he settled in an urban settlement not far from the camp. He even started a new family with a local widow and her two teenage daughters."

"And your father told you all this?" Viktor asked.

"No." She paused to catch her breath. "It was Roman Derenchuk, Myron's son and my half-brother, who told me all this. About a month ago, he visited me at my apartment in Khabarovsk. Of course, I couldn't remember him, so I slammed the door in his face. My dad taught me not to trust anybody. But after he said that he had gotten my address from Fyodor, I let him in."

"And?"

"We had tea and talked past midnight. I asked Roman to stay until the next morning and sleep on the couch. He showed me pictures of his family, his wife and six-year-old daughter." Katerina smiled rather affectionately, "He seems like a good guy, this long lost brother of mine."

"I must ask you, what does all this have to do with your suspicion of Roman's father?" Viktor put it directly. "Did your newly-discovered brother give you any hint that Myron was planning on doing something?"

"He did not give me any indications to support my suspicion, but he told me that his father visited him and stayed with his family for a few days, just before Roman decided to pay me a visit.

"You said it was a month ago. Do you know Roman's whereabouts?" Viktor tried not to show his impatience. "And that's his full name? Roman Derenchuk?"

Overhearing this last question, Captain Nesterenko interrupted before Katerina had a chance to answer.

"I know Roman Derenchuk very well. He is one of the original members of the Lviv detachment," the Captain reported. "He and his family live in New Urgal. Roman is the leader of the electricians crew now."

"Another coincidence?" Viktor was genuinely amused. He turned to Katerina. "So, what else were you talking about with your brother past midnight?"

"Why don't you ask Roman himself? He is just a dozen kilometers away," Katya said with sarcasm.

"No, no. Please go on. Seriously."

"Well, he told me about Aunt Daria, who he called "Mamma Dasha" Katya said reflectively. "He talked about our mom— the way he remembered her and what he learned from his father Myron, his aunt, and my father." Katerina paused for a moment. "While I was listening to his stories, I suddenly recalled an old letter which had arrived two days before my sixteenth birthday. My dad gave me this letter, still sealed, and explained that it came from my Aunt Dasha. I read it immediately. I even read it in front of my dad, although he didn't seem to like that. The letter was very long and very sad. I cried, but dad consoled me. I was only sixteen; I could not fully comprehend it, or the impact it would have on my life."

"Soon I realized my half-brother had no idea his adapted mother Dasha had described the life of my mother Olecya on my sixteen's birthday. During our chat with Roman, I pulled this letter out and we started to read it together. I stopped reading when I noticed Roman fell asleep. In all honesty, it was indeed a long letter full of events and details related to their lives. So, I wasn't upset at all. However, the beginning of it got etched in my memory.

* * *

Myron and Olecya married in May 1945, less than a year after the Red Army liberated the western regions of Ukraine from Nazi occupation. It was the second time the country had been liberated since 1939. In that time, and without warning, a tide of repressions and persecutions swept through the country. This purging campaign ravaged the western regions of Ukraine, Belorussia, and the Baltic Republics. It started with the 1939 liberation and intensified after the Great Patriotic War against Germany and Japan was over.

Like many innocent people before and after him, the purge tragically affected 23-year-old Myron Zazulya, the young father of a toddler boy. One early morning in August 1948, Myron Zozulya was arrested and convicted as the State's enemy under Statute Number 58, Article 1-a of Soviet Penal Code, and sent to life at the state penitentiary system, more specifically the GULAG.

Olecya could not accept such an injustice: her husband Myron was only fourteen when the western regions were reunited with the rest of Soviet Ukraine, and he could not be expected yet to join Red Army. When Germans occupied their land, being already sixteen, Myron did not collaborate with occupiers, did not become a local commando for the SS *politzai*. Dropping out of school, he became a carpenter and worked odd jobs to help to feed his family. So how could this young man be considered as someone who committed treason? Perhaps it happened because Myron was a son of a well-to-do proprietor who owned a horse and a cargo wagon. Who knew?

For the next two years, Olecya spent days and months going from office to office of faceless state officials and judges in Lviv, in the Republic Capital city of Kyiv, and even in Moscow, trying to find the truth about her husband's undeserved conviction—to no avail.

In the early fall of 1950, after endless bureaucratic delays, Olecya finally received permission to visit her husband at the place of his incarceration. It was an unexpected yet significant victory. Her long train journey, from the little town of Obroshino near the city of Lviv, ended in Komsomolsk-on-Amur in Khabarovsky Krai. Then a horse carriage delivered her finally to the small settlement of Zyma, the location of labor camp Lagopunkt №4382. Behind two rows of eight-meter-high barbwire fence, thirty-five thousand inmates of all ages, lived in poorly built and poorly heated wooden barracks. And always under the constant watch of a hundred fifty guards and forty ferocious German shepherds trained to tear apart anyone attempting to escape.

Every morning, after a skimpy meal, the inmates gathered outside their barracks for work distribution. It took at least an hour, standing in the cold and rain, ten months a year, and in extreme heat in the summer. Then they marched to their designated worksites: cutting stone in the limestone queries, laying crossbars or spiking steel rails on the railroads, or more often, cutting and trimming timber in the *Taiga*. It was a grueling eight-hour workday, with only a fifteen-minute lunch break to chew on a piece of stale bread saved from breakfast. Then they walked back to camp for one hour to a plate of fatless cabbage soup, and a night of rest—for those lucky enough to have a plank bed for themselves.

This is how inmates lived day in and day out, month after month, year after year, sometimes for the rest of their lives—if they did not die much sooner from infectious diseases, malnutrition, lack of decent sanitary conditions, or as victims of violence at the hands of the guards or the hardcore criminals, who, in fact, ruled this God-forsaken place.

Olecya settled in the old log house across from the camp sentry building at the iron entry gate. She rented a little room from an old woman, a longtime resident of the settlement. The *babka* Elizaveta was quite sympathetic to the new guest. She told Olecya everything she knew about life behind the barbwire and the commanding officers and guards. She explained to her about the assignments and privileges of the camp's *pridurki*, the inmates chosen by the camp administration to set the norms and distribute the work among the prisoners. Some even worked as *feldshers*, low-level medical personnel, or in the kitchens, bathhouses, and laundries. Also, Olecya learned about the *avtoritety*, the criminal bosses, and their *vor-v-zakone,* the career thieves, abiding by their own code of conduct and presiding over the rest of the *zeks*, especially the *politikals*.

Olecya soon struck up a friendship with Natalia, the wife of the Deputy to the Commandant, and arranged a short meeting with him. This sleazebag wasted no time in starting his sexual innuendo, openly suggesting this was the only way if she wanted to see her husband. Olecya sweetly and innocently informed this predator of the many good things Natalia had said of him: what a good, fair, and kind man he was. The Captain grinned, revealing his crooked, badly nicotine-stained teeth, and awkwardly stroked his thinning yellowish hair. He returned behind his desk and asked a guard to find inmate Zozulya.

When he arrived, it took Olecya several glances to recognize this inmate as her dear Myron. But she remembered the sheer horror in his eyes when he immediately recognized her. Like a sack of potatoes, Myron dropped onto an empty chair and covered his unwashed face with his hands. She could not forget those hands—dirty with bleeding scratches and abrasions, and black lining under cracked nails. Olecya instinctively moved toward him but was thrown back by the strong stench emanating from Myron, perhaps his ragged clothes or his own flesh. It did not escape his attention. He started sobbing and moaning until uncontrollable hiccups began to shake his body. Olecya overcame her disgust and gently hugged him. At first, he did not resist; he even buried his head into her bosom.

In a few moments, his hiccups subsided, and so did his moaning. However, it did not last long. Myron's body became stiff, more strained, like a string ready to be snapped. Olecya felt it and let him go of him. They starred at each other without saying a word. Now, she could observe him better. Myron did not look at all like the young and handsome man she remembered and loved. Her heart ached; a deep sadness overpowered her. It was her turn now. Olecya broke into tears and did not even try to hide it. After calming down, she attempted to start a conversation, showing him a picture of their child Roman. But Myron was absently quiet, like he did not care. His earlier outburst had left him weak. He did not want to be there anymore.

"That's it! Your meeting is over, citizen Zozulya." The Captain got up from his chair, smiling. "Your husband doesn't want to talk to you." The officer called the guard.

"Please don't send him away yet!" Olecya begged, but she did not sound overly convincing. "I did not have a chance to show him his son. He is already four, you know."

"Don't you see, Madam? You are torturing him." This time, the Captain was serious. "He smells awful too. Even my tobacco smoke cannot mask it. Your husband is a strange man. He refuses to attend his scheduled baths. Most inmates would give anything for this privilege, you know."

Myron was escorted from the room. He did not turn back to look at Olecya. She felt sad but at the same time relieved.

More than two months passed since that miserable day. She thought Myron behaved aloof and withdrawn because he really did not want her to see him like that. If the next meeting was longer and with some privacy, she hoped, they would be able to talk. But then, serious doubts rushed into her head. What was the use of all this? Why did she come here? He was not returning home any time soon—probably never—so it was a torment for him.

And something else happened after their first meeting that gave Olecya pause. One day, while perusing the small, scantily stocked village store, she ran into a man. For a split second, they looked at each other, but Olecya did not need any more time to feel like she had known him all her life. This tall, lanky man was handsome, but that was not what stopped her cold—enormous physical and spiritual power emanated from him. No wonder Olecya was taken by this man, and she quickly found herself drawn into his orbit.

The man struck up the conversation first, although it wasn't much of one.

"Who are you? What is your name?" he asked in a deep, soothing voice, looking right into her big, hazel eyes. "What has brought you here and from where, my child?

"I am Olecya, and I am from Lviv." She instinctively answered in the Ukrainian language but switched to Russian right away. "I came here to visit my husband, an inmate."

That was it, no more words. They moved to a corner of the store, out of the main passage, and stood there, silently looking at each other, studying each other's features, taking in each other's image. Soon, they realized that they were creating a spectacle for the store clerk and the few women shopping. The man grasped her hand and whispered, "I am Fyodor, by the way. I am an inmate too, and I must go now. Perhaps I'll see you again, Olecya!"

"Perhaps," she answered with slight embarrassment and rushed out of the store.

It took her only a dozen strides to cross the road and storm into her room. Babka Elyzoveta followed and found her breathing heavily while starring through the window facing the store. Both women observed Fyodor carrying a small package and briskly walking from the store toward the camp's gate. As most people inside the *zona,* he dressed in the standard light green *telogreika*, the same type of pants, *valenki* boots made of felt, and a hat with its earflaps down. His clothes, even his beat up boots, seemed clean and tidy. For sure, this inmate, her new acquaintance, looked nothing like poor Myron.

"Who is he?" asked Olecya. "He talked to me in the store."

"Oh, he is the interesting man!" exclaimed Babka Elizaveta with a certain mysteriousness. "In the Lagopunkt №4382, there are very few like him. I know for sure that he is one of the brigadiers, and yet he is not one of the *pridurki* who usually get the privilege to go outside the zone. I guess inmates and camp bosses equally respect him so that he gets the same privilege. He goes by the name 'Father Feodor', but his secular name is Fyodor."

"That was the name he revealed to me. So, is he some kind of priest?" asked Olecya. "He did not strike me as a holy man."

"Someone told me he was the local leader of the Old Believers sect." Babka Elizaveta tried to explain. "Maybe that's why he is here."

"Old Believers. What kind of religion is that?" Olecya sounded a little worried. "Are they Christians? So, they are like Pentecostals, Jehovah's Witnesses, or Baptists?"

"Honestly, I don't know," she replied. "But why are you so interested in that?
Oh, I got it— you like Fyodor, don't you, you silly girl?"

"I am not sure… " Olecya dropped on the bed and buried her head under the pillow. She was certain Elizaveta could hear her heartbeat.

A few days later, they met again. This time, despite the excitement, they were better prepared to not reveal their feelings with the same intensity of their first meeting. Although the electricity between them still flowed strongly, they exchanged less than a few words. Olecya told Fyodor where she stayed and who her husband was.

Fyodor said, "I'll try to find him and help him."

Now, she was consumed by the magnetism of this man. His large grey eyes scanned Olecya with uncanny interest and genuine adoration. They desperately wanted to touch each other but couldn't. When Fyodor noticed the attention they attracted from store visitors, he stepped aside and said, "Excuse me, Olecya," he whispered, "I'll come to see you. Will you be here?"

"Yes," Olecya whispered back and rushed to the exit.

* * *

Katerina took a pause from relaying the story to Viktor, when suddenly the door swung open and Sergeant Darsulov appeared.

"Look what I found!" he shouted excitedly as he placed a dark, shapeless lump before the Captain at the table.

The Captain glanced at it quizzically before enquiring, "Where did you find it? Was it the only one?"

"I found it under this house, behind one of the support beams," the Sergeant reported. "I did not go far from the house, though."

The Captain picked up the folded piece of fabric; it looked like burlap or the shreds of a dark brown potato sack. The Lieutenant and Major rushed to the table. Using the tweezers, Nina pulled the thing from the Captain's hand and began studying it with a magnifying glass.

"Huh, interesting," she mumbled to herself but then concluded loudly. "There's some kind of dust on this. I am not sure yet what, but it's shiny," she said. "I'll tell you exactly what it is after a spectrum analysis."

"If we have to wait, we have to wait," Viktor said. "What else have you found?"

"We found only a few things, which, in my opinion, did not belong in this house," Nina explained. "Maybe Katya can help us to sort some things out."

Katerina approached the table. "What do you want me to look at?" she asked.

"First, this benzene lighter. Do you think it belonged to your father?" Nina pushed forward a lighter constructed from a bullet cartridge.

Katerina looked at the lighter. "I don't think so. My dad never smoked. I have never seen it in the house."

"Next, these two books." Nina slid them closer to Katerina. "Have you seen them before?"

Katerina picked up one book— Dostoyevsky's *Brothers Karamazov*. She fanned through its pages, and then did the same with the other, L. Tolstoy's *War and Peace*. "Both books are from New Urgal Library; here is the stamp," she offered. "I did not know my dad read Tolstoy. I only remember him reading the Bible."

"Do you think some of his visitors could've left them here?" asked Nina. "Strangely enough, I found them in the quilt on the top of the oven."

"Perhaps Comrade Sergeant had these books with him to read," suggested Katerina, but the Sergeant shook his head with confusion.

Captain Nesterenko pulled the books closer and, after making some notes in the ledger, placed them in the bag, saying, "I'll check with the library and find out who signed for those books."

The Lieutenant placed a few photographs in front of Katya: two 4x5cm pictures, and a smaller portrait. This last was very old, more yellow than grey, with a deep crease above the image of a young man's head. "Katya, what about these photographs? Did you ever see these photographs in your father's possession?"

"Yes, I did." Katerina picked up the larger photographs and looked them over with fondness. "Here I am with Dad, Aunt Anna, and Uncle Saveliy in Chegdomyn. I was eight or nine then. And, in this one, I was with Dad right here on the porch. It was taken by my cousin Matvey, Saveliy's youngest son, before he took me to Khabarovsk."

"What about this little one?" asked Nina.

"I think I've seen this photo before." Katerina paused for a second. "I found it accidentally between the pages of one of Dad's religious books. I asked him about the young man in the photo. Dad got irritated and explained, that this was my half-brother, Ivan. He was killed in the war. When I wanted to know more, Dad became really upset and blew it off. I never asked him about Ivan again."

"And that's it? You know nothing about your half-brother?" Nina pressed.

"I tried to find out about him from Aunt Anna, but she only gave me the barest details," Katerina answered evasively. "She told me that Ivan and her son Dmitry were sort of troublemakers in their teenage years, and there was bad blood between Fyodor and Ivan very early on. Their feud had intensified after Ivan and Dmitry were arrested and sent to a juvenile correction camp for two years."

"What happened after that?" Viktor asked.

"In the fall of 1941, the cousins volunteered to join the Red Army and went to war. They were both eighteen. Dad and my aunt never saw them again. In the spring of 1943, the Military Commissariat sent Dad an official notification that Ivan went missing in action and was presumed dead. A few months later, Aunt Anna and her husband received a similar note regarding Dmitry. That's all I know," Katerina finished with a long sigh.

"This old and murky picture, was most likely taken for his passport when Ivan was sixteen." Katya added.

"Your brother was handsome, wasn't he?" Viktor tried to cheer Katya up. "Just like your father." He looked at the photographs once again and put them back on the table.

Katerina remained silent for a while. Then, before retreating to her chair near the oven, she asked, "Will I be allowed to take these photographs with me? Of course, after you have processed them."

"No problem, Katya; you can have them and anything else from this house as soon as Nina and the Captain have finished their job here. What about those icons? They look very old and are certainly very valuable." Viktor motioned to two small Byzantine-style icons, one of the Virgin Mary with little Jesus on her lap and another of Jesus holding two slightly folded fingers for a cross sign.

"Yes, Dad felt proud of those— they are both over four hundred years old, at least," Katerina informed. "Dad mentioned the fact that those icons were handed down from generation to generation of Rogozhins."

"By law, now they are yours, Katya," Viktor said. "But you have to promise to tell me more about the religion of the Old Believers and about the traditions of its followers."

"You want me to tell you about this now?" Katerina sounded a little tired. "I do not know much about it. I remember my father conducting the liturgy in this house for hours. I always loved watching him preach here in front of a couple dozen people. But my father, although very pious, never pushed me to follow him and his flock. He just taught me how to be a good person so God can watch over me."

Viktor noticed her discomfort in talking about this and changed the subject. "We don't have to talk about it now, Katya. I hope we will come back to this later after we are done here."

"I am sure Aunt Anna would be a better source of information on religious matters. She always was in our house during services." Katerina thought for a moment, then added, "Let's just hope she is in a condition to talk."

"By the way, you did not finish telling me about your mother and her visit to the labor camp," Viktor said in a low voice. "This can wait until later too. Perhaps, I can see the letter you mentioned when we are back in Khabarovsk."

"Of course, Comrade Major," Katya assured him.

"We are almost done here," Lieutenant Toropko reported. "One more item left to process. You should see it, Comrade Major."

The Lieutenant handed Viktor a small plastic bag, sealed at the top. Inside was a plastic button, still attached to a piece of quilted fabric, torn from a green *telogreika*.

"I found it on the floor right by the wall next to the icons," Nina explained. "This button got ripped off, together with a piece of fabric. Possibly in a struggle."

Lieutenant Toropko placed several plastic bags in her aluminum case and the rest of the evidence in a big brown paper sack. She put her winter sheepskin coat on. The rest of the group took this as a signal that the job was finished and did the same.

Viktor looked at his watch: it was 12:35. They less than three hours before dusk. He hoped it would give them enough time to speak with Aunt Anna.

"Comrade Sergeant," Viktor addressed Darsulov. "We are done here for now. You must stay here another two days. Keep in touch with the Comrade Captain by radio. I hope it's working." The Major paused, and then explained, "We might be back again. Please secure the perimeter and keep your eyes open. They might return."

"Yes, Comrade Major!" the Sergeant said distinctly. "I have checked the radio; You want me to leave everything as is?" He paused and looked at the Major.

Viktor looked in the direction of Lieutenant Toropko. She nodded.

"You can put the furniture in its place and clean up the blood, please." Viktor spoke slowly, with some hesitation. "Try not to disturb anything else."

Chapter 5

A unt Anna was sitting in a rocking chair by the window, near an oven similar to the one in her brother's cabin. The stove inside was barely warm. The old woman still had the wool knitted shawl wrapped around her upper body, its two corners knotted across her chest. She was slumbering the way only old people do—her head was thrown far back, eyes closed and mouth wide-gaped, producing a rather loud snore. She jolted upright as the door creaked open, straining to focus on the visitors.

"Dyma, is that you?" she shrieked. "Come closer. I am here, my Son."

Katerina waved to Viktor and his colleagues to stay back and rushed to Anna alone.

"It's me, Katya." She kneeled in front of the old woman and tried to calm her down.

The old woman's half-smile indicated that she could see better. "Oh, Katya, dear!" A genuine surprise sounded in her voice. "What has brought you here?"

"You saw me this morning already. Remember, dear Auntie?" Katerina asked in a calm, soothing voice. "I promised to visit with you, remember?"

"And who are those people?" The old woman's head turned toward the door.

"You saw them this morning too, outside," continued Katya even more calmly. "They are from the Militia. They are friends. Do not be alarmed, Auntie. They are here because of your brother, my dad. Comrade Major Vitus would like to speak with you."

"Who? Vitus?" Katerina felt a shudder pass through Anna's body. "I already talked to the Comrade Nachalnik. I've told him everything I know. I don't want to talk to anyone else."

Noticing the old woman's agitation, Viktor started to advance toward her.

"Don't you see she is frightened?" Katya almost whispered. "Go back. I'll try to calm her down."

"What is she talking about?" Viktor whispered back while retreating. "I hope you know I have never seen her before today."

"I do, I do. Aunty might be confusing you with someone from the past; she often mixes things up in her head lately. This is exactly what I was afraid of." Katya sounded upset. "We will not get anything out of her if we startle her further."

"Of course, I understand; we have to be patient." Viktor nodded.

"Let me handle this." Katya paused for a moment. "You and the Captain, bring firewood from outside—the more, the better. It is cold in here; we have to fire up the oven." Now she sounded confident, like a woman of action. "Nina, please, look for anything that could be cooked. You can most likely find supplies in the pantry behind the oven. We must feed Aunt Anna. Who knows when she last ate? And now, I shall try to put her at ease and engage her in some conversation. That helps her to focus better."

"Okay, then. Let's do that." Viktor swiveled back out the door, gently pushing Captain Nesterenko before him. Nina left her coat at the door and looked for something to cook. Katya took off her fur coat and, dragging a kitchen stool behind her, returned to Anna. She sat down close to her and took the old woman's hand.

"Are you hungry? Are you cold, Auntie?" Katya kept asking. She touched the woman's grey hair gently. "When was the last time you had anything hot to eat?"

"I am a little hungry, but it's no big deal." She wasn't agitated anymore. "Fyodor will be back from hunting soon; he will fix some food."

"We don't have to wait for him to come back." Katya navigated the subject of Fyodor Rogozhin's death carefully. "Auntie, we'll prepare dinner for you. You just relax and tell me about what's been going on lately. Okay?"

At that moment, Viktor and Lyubomir came back with firewood and coal. The Captain pulled the half-moon cover from the oven and set it on the floor. Only two or three pieces of charcoal still glowed in the ashes. Lyubomir grabbed an iron poker and piled up the charcoal in the middle of the oven's belly, stirring up the sparks and re-igniting the flame. It seemed he knew what he was doing.

"I grew up in a house with an oven like this," he explained modestly. "All right, Comrade Major, you can hand me the wood now, one log at a time. We don't want to overwhelm the flame."

Very soon the new logs started to crackle, catching ablaze. A small patch of smoke wafted from the oven's mouth and crept up toward a narrow slot in the ceiling. The Captain pulled a lever in the grate of the oven's mouth, letting the smoke dissipate and leaving behind just a little soot. He threw a few more logs and coal into the fire, then set the metal cover back in its place, dampening the sound of the now roaring blaze. He beamed with pride.

In the meantime, the Major and Nina were peeling potatoes at full speed, tossing them into a big fireclay pot filled with water. Everything Nina could find in the pantry was now on the table: tin cans of pork, onions, beets, and bunches of spinach.

Occasionally, Viktor glanced over at the old woman and her niece. They were still sitting by the window, murmuring together. Finally, Katerina signaled that he could come over and join them. Viktor dropped a knife on the table and approached the women. He pulled up another three-legged stool and sat facing them. This time, Anna looked at him with clear eyes rather inquisitively.

"Thank you, Comrade Nachalnik, for keeping your word. Fyodor had a very high opinion of you," she proclaimed. "Why are you here? Is it Fyodor again? And what is it with your uniform; where is your mustache?"

Viktor felt like he was missing something, so he looked at Katya for help.

"Auntie, Major Vitus never met my dad. He is here for the first time. You saw him outside your house this morning. He arrived here from Khabarovsk." Katerina paused, searching for the right words or questions to bring her aunt back to reality. "What is it about his uniform and mustache?"

"I know he is from Khabarovsk; he told us!" Anna snapped back at Katya with irritation, totally ignoring what the young woman had just said. "I still don't understand why he came back. What do they want from Fyodor? He promised to leave him and all of us alone." She pulled the end of her shawl and touched her teary eyes with it.

Katerina and Viktor exchanged glances. This conversation brought more confusion than clarity, so Viktor took up the questioning.

"Please don't cry. We came here meaning no harm to you," Viktor attempted to put the old woman at ease. "How was I dressed last time you saw me?"

"You had a long leather coat, high shiny leather boots, and leather hat with the red star. I remember. You are a handsome man in a new uniform too, but in the old one, you looked better," Anna said.

Katerina and Viktor exchanged glances again. This time, the young woman could not hide her confusion, while Viktor could not contain his smile. Could it be that this woman was confusing Viktor for his father? In 1947, when Fyodor Rogozhin was first arrested and interrogated, Colonel Raymond Vitus would have worn the standard MGB Militia uniform. The uniform Anna described was older. *That means Anna must remember an earlier encounter with my father*, Viktor realized with sudden surprise.

Viktor suddenly recalled the oldest file in his father's papers regarding Fyodor Rogozhin. It was dated August of 1938, and the folder was thin, just two documents: a handwritten letter with clumsy accusations, and a typed report on the formal interrogation of Citizen Fyodor Rogozhin and the testimonies of his family members. At the end of this document, there was a handwritten note signed by Raymond Vitus: "Not enough evidence to support the claim. Case closed."

Viktor was astonished by this sudden discovery. It happened almost forty years ago; how did this half-senile old woman remember Commissar Vitus and his visit to this godforsaken place? He had to explain this improbable revelation to her grief-stricken niece. Otherwise, how could Viktor proceed with further questioning? He noticed that Anna, feeling the warmth from the oven, leaned back in her chair and dozed off. Viktor whispered his discovery into Katya's ear. Her big eyes grew wide with excitement, and her breath became heavy and rapid.

"Are you sure?" she exclaimed, loudly enough to wake Anna up, then reverted to a whisper. "The fact that she might remember something like that doesn't surprise me a bit. Quite often, Auntie will pull from her memory a story or two so ancient that even my dad and Uncle Saveliy would be in total disbelief. And then she cannot recall what happened to her yesterday."

"I guess the human memory can indeed play all kinds of tricks on us," Viktor concluded. "So, is it possible that she remembers what happened back in 1938?"

"Yes. But how does that relate to what is happening now?" Katya sounded perplexed.

"Perhaps it doesn't." Viktor replied and paused for a moment. "It just gives me hope that Aunt Anna can provide us with valuable information after all. Of course, you, Katya, shall help me to navigate her hazy memory. She trusts you."
"I'll try my best." Katya responded.

*   *   *

"Food is ready!" Lieutenant Toropko announced loudly. "Katya, you can walk your aunt to the table. Okay, Comrade Captain, you may do your job."

The Captain opened the cover and, using a special paddle on a long wood shank, retrieved the pot from deep inside the oven's belly and placed it on the oven's edge. The steam pushed the lid upward, filling the room with an irresistible aroma.

"Katya, let's resume our conversation after she eats." Viktor got up and stood beside Anna. "I'll help walk her to the table." The sumptuous smell had fully awakened her.

"I don't need your help, Comrade Nachalnik." Anna rose from the chair unassisted and quickly crossed the room to the kitchen table.

"Comrades, thank you for preparing food for my aunt. Maybe somebody should call the Sergeant?"

At first, the Major tried to explain that it would be inappropriate for civil servants working in an official capacity to dine in a private home, but Katerina would hear none of it. Lyubomir ran outside and quickly returned with Sergeant Darsulov. Nina placed aluminum plates and all the spoons she could find on the table and then pulled all four stools around it.

"I am afraid two of us have to find seats away from the table," she apologized.

Everyone reached for the bread which was sliced into thin pieces in a shallow wicker basket in the middle of the table. The dinner proceeded in total silence and was finished hurriedly. Afterward, Sergeant Darsulov started clearing the table without any orders, while the Captain pulled another pot, this time with hot water, out of the oven. Nina began washing plates and utensils in the small painted white iron sink attached to the sidewall. Lyubomir, after helping her with the hot water, dried the dishes, using a little linen towel.

"I'll run to Uncle Saveliy. I am sure he is hungry too," said Katya, but the Captain stopped her.

"Sergeant Darsulov, please divide whatever is left there in another pot and take it to the old man," ordered the Captain. "Put some more firewood into his oven too, will you? Make sure he is comfortable. Then return to your post."

"Yes, Comrade Captain." The Sergeant acknowledged the Captain's order with a hand salute and soon left the house, holding the pot of stew with his earflap hat to keep it warm.

Katya and Viktor helped Aunt Anna back to her rocking chair. The old woman's demeanor was calm, even serene. It seemed she was ready to slumber, but instead, she looked at Viktor and said, "Thanks for feeding me and stoking my oven. It's nice of you, Comrade Nachalnik." Her sturdy voice was confident. "You still haven't told me the truth, though. Why are you here, and what have you done to Fyodor?"

"Fyodor has passed away," Katya blurted out, not wanting Viktor to answer the question. "My dad, your brother, is not among us anymore, dear Auntie." She buried her face in the woman's lap and began sobbing, her shoulders shuddering uncontrollably.

Viktor had not expected Katya would say this to her aunt without preparing the old woman for the truth. He looked at Anna, waiting for a storm of emotions. He saw none: Anna sat perfectly straight, stroking her niece's hair with her right hand; her eyes were directed upward, and a grim half-smile touched her bloodless lips. The old woman was mumbling some words, which Viktor could not understand.

Neither could Katya. She stopped sobbing and trembling, lifted her head, and looked at Anna's face.

"At last, at last. God has taken him to be reunited with the people he loved," Anna proclaimed strongly and clearly. "He is now where he belongs, with his Lord, the Savior."

She began chanting in a high pitch voice, crossing herself feverishly. With the index and middle fingers pressed together tightly, her right hand flew from her forehead to her midriff, then from the left shoulder to the right, again and again.

Katya calmly stepped aside. She then dropped to her knees, facing the wall with the eight-ended cross and a little icon of Jesus. Then she stretched her hands forward until her forehead briefly touched the floor. She started praying again, bowing her upper body up and down repeatedly. This lasted for at least fifteen minutes. She rose up and turned to Viktor.

"We still have to tell her the real truth, Katya," said Viktor. "I suspect her attitude might change. What do you think?"

"I am sure it will not be easy," Katerina agreed. "We cannot keep the entire truth from her, but let's tread lightly."

"Do you want me to start?" Viktor asked.

"It's better if you do. I will break into tears again, you know." She was on the verge of sobbing already.

"Please try not to cry, Katya," begged Viktor. "You have to be calm if we want to get any information out of your aunt."

"I'll do my best." Her voice betrayed her uncertainty.

By now, Anna had stopped her chanting and lay flat on the floor. Katya and Viktor rushed to help her but were waved off. The old woman remained motionless for a little longer. Then she returned to her knees and slowly got up, grabbing the armchair with both hands.

"Dear Auntie, please sit down." Katya took her hand and led her back to the armchair. "Comrade Major must tell you something else, something vitally important."

"What Major? You mean Comrade Nachalnik Vitus?" Anna sounded exhausted and was breathing heavily. "What else in God's name can he tell me that I don't know already?"

Viktor pulled over a three-legged stool and sat next to the old woman. He even offered his hand, but she refused it, quickly pulling both hands to her chest. Katya noticed a change in Anna's demeanor; she moved behind the old woman and gently touched her shoulders.

"Anna, I am not Comrade Nachalnik Vitus. I am his son. You have an amazing memory. Is there a resemblance?"

"You do look like Comrade Nachalnik, only without the mustache. Your father— what happened to him?" She sounded puzzled.

"My dad passed away two years ago," said Viktor as he looked straight into Anna's eyes

"Fyodor told me many times that Nachalnik Vitus was a decent and reasonable man," Anna said with genuine sadness in her voice. "He did not change his opinion even after coming back from prison."

"I believe your brother was a decent and reasonable man too. But I need more information. Can you tell me about Fyodor and your family?"

"Young man, you want to hear my family story? Why?" Anna asked with genuine surprise and looked at Katerina.

Katya responded with a nod. "Dear Auntie, please. We need to know everything." Katya said. "Don't you think I also deserve to hear it? My dad never liked talking about himself or the family's past."

Nina Toropko and Captain Nesterenko approached closer to hear the old woman better.

"I might not remember much," Anna hesitated.

"Don't worry," Viktor reassured her. "Whatever you can remember."

So, Aunt Anna began to tell the story of the Rogozhin family.

* * *

For at least two hundred fifty years, since the Russian Orthodox Church's second schism, the Rogozhin family lived in the Korovino Village of the Nizhny-Novgorod Region, about 350km northeast of Moscow. This village was situated 20km south of the Guberniya capitol Nizhny Novgorod, on the banks of the Sava River, which fell into the Volga River, right at the edge of the Vetchnakovsky Less (the forest).

Nobody in the family knew from where their ancestor Mitrophan Rogozhin and his six sons hailed originally. They belonged to the Old Believers, and from time to time they had serious run-ins with the Czarist authorities and the official Russian Church. The men of the Old Believers were not trusted to serve in the army, nor in any public service. They were practically banned from traditional education. On top of an already high tax burden, the Old Believers were punished with extra taxes on the wearing of their beards.

Nevertheless, the large Rogozhin family survived and prospered through their perseverance. They always used the help of numerous seasonal workers. They held significant livestock, horses, bulls, cows, goats, pigs, and domestic fowl. The rich, fertile land of the upper Volga River basin was a blessing for the four generations of Rogozhins who labored upon it.

Fyodor Rogozhin was born in the fall of 1896. His father Feoktist was the oldest among four brothers, and three sisters resided in the same village. Like his father, Feoktist became the leader of the entire regional Old Believers community, its priest-less Bezpopovtsy denomination. Every weekend, a few dozen worshipers, many of them his close and distant kin, arrived from all corners of the Nizhny-Novgorod Guberniya to pray together and to hear his weekly sermon.

The religious services were held in his house in Korovino. In the same house, he reared four sons, Saveliy, Fyodor, Ivan, Pavel, and the youngest child, his daughter Anna. On the weekdays, all the children participated in the keeping of the household. They worked in the fields, harvesting wheat and digging out potatoes. They tended to the cows in the barn, and they produced cheese in the creamery. They sold the fruits of their hard labor for good profit in the markets of Novgorod, even in Moscow. On Sundays the children assisted their father in his religious duties.

Fyodor happened to be the strongest and the smartest in the family. He taught himself to read and write when he was six. By his eleventh birthday, Fyodor knew the Old Bible by heart and helped his father prepare the weekly sermon. When he was eighteen, he could lift a two-year-old *goby* and carry the 150-kilogram calf a dozen steps. For miles around no one dared to challenge this handsome young man to a fight.

When Fyodor reached twenty, he was introduced to the quiet girl Varvara, the lovely daughter of a wealthy farmer from a neighboring village. They married one year later in a boisterous ceremony in the Old Believer's tradition, filled with singing and dancing. The young couple settled down in a house built by the Rogozhin brothers, just as his oldest brother Saveliy and his bride had done three years prior. In the next four years, the village of Korovino was expanded with three more houses, where his two younger brothers and Fyodor's sister also got married. The Rogozhin family was growing, and so was the family's fortune.

They always praised God for their prosperity and never complained about difficulties. There were setbacks through the years of course: diminished harvests from floods and the death of livestock from diseases. The Rogozhins also had their share of unforeseen tragedies. Ivan's twin sons succumbed to the 1919 typhus epidemic that swept through the entire Volga River basin. The next year, a timber cutting accident crippled Pavel permanently. And in 1921, after their first child Mariya reached the age of four, Fyodor's wife Varvara began coughing blood.

The local country doctor diagnosed her with tuberculosis. In the healing of human sickness, the Old Believer's trusted their own traditional ways and their spirituality over modern medicine. The *babka* shaman fed Varvara with all manner of extracts distilled from plants gathered in the fields and forests nearby. And miraculously, this terrible disease retreated for a couple of years, or so it seemed. Varvara even became pregnant again and, in October of 1923, she gave birth to a second child, their son Ivan. But her illness returned with a vengeance soon after the birth. Over Fyodor's strong objection, the doctor examined Varvara again and determined that her tuberculosis had reached the final stage. Her end was imminent.

Fyodor, who had assumed the leadership of their community, faced an agonizing dilemma— to leave the care of his wife in God's hands, or to break with the Old Believer's doctrine and fight to prolong Varvara's life with every way known modern medicine. He chose to fight. The doctor helped Fyodor obtain the most potent drugs and potions from Moscow. He visited Varvara every day, supervising her medication regimen. But it was too late: in December of 1924, Varvara passed.

Fyodor's travails did not end there. Three months later, a smallpox epidemic, raging for the last two years throughout the neighboring Guberniyas, claimed the life of his seven-year-old daughter, Mariya. She was still too young to work in the barn with the cows or horses, and so she had not yet developed any immunity to this horrible disease.

In this time, Anna nursed his infant son Ivan together with her own son Dmitry. The cousins were born only days apart.

And it was not only his personal tragedies that devastated Fyodor. Since the Bolshevik Revolution of 1917, the entire country was going through turbulent times and drastic changes, troubles that did not pass by Korovino.

Although the village was too remote and too insignificant to have any permanent state officials, the commissars in Nizhny Novgorod never forgot its existence when they needed food to feed the starving revolutionary proletariat. Often, the entire Rogozhin family was robbed of almost all its wealth during the civil war. One week, soldiers of the Red Army, with their leather-clad Bolshevik commissars, would come take everything by force. The next week, White Army soldiers, led by their officers with Czarist cockades, would storm into the homes. They would cross themselves, bow toward an iconostasis, and then clean every pantry or nook of meat, flour, and potatoes—anything that was not hidden.

And that was how it was, until one day when a commissar with a huge Mauser pistol on his hip came to Korovino. He assured the villagers that they didn't have to worry about anything anymore: the Bolsheviks had prevailed. For the inhabitants of Korovino, as much as for the millions of Russian peasants, it was a reprieve, a real opportunity to rebuild their homes and farms, destroyed by two wars and two Revolutions in only ten years. And so through the 1920s the Rogozhin's regained their footing in the prosperity of the New Economic Policy. But it was not to last.

One cold morning in March 1930, the OGPU *nachalnik* led a train of four horse-drawn carts into Korovino, and demanded the villagers surrender the bulk of their provisions: the livestock, the produce, even the grain seed reserve. Fyodor tried to negotiate with this little man in an oversized uniform and thick wireframe glasses, but he failed. Moreover, he was threatened with arrest. Fyodor understood that resistance would endanger every member of his family. But over his objections, his brothers Ivan and Pavel, armed and flanked by their sons, confronted the commander and refused to surrender their goods. The unwelcome visitors turned around and left.

A week later the same *nachalnik* returned, accompanied by thirty heavily armed NKVD soldiers and a machine gun perched on the top of a carriage. Fyodor was right; any resistance would be lethal. The soldiers gathered all the inhabitants of Korovino in the center of the village, near the water well. They were divided into two groups: members of the Rogozhin family and the seasonal workers. Recognizing him as the leader of the community, the *nachalnik* approached Fyodor with an unfolded paper in his outstretched hand.

It was some kind of official decree. He read it loudly and resolutely, with no pauses between paragraphs. According to this document, the adult members of the Rogozhin family had proven themselves as *kulaks*, the remnants of the bourgeois class and therefore the enemy of the working people of the Russian Socialist Federation Republic. By Decree of the Novgorod Regional special investigative commission for uncovering sabotage or any other anti-Soviet activities, the Rogozhins were subject to deportation with confiscation of all possessions.

"This decree is to be executed immediately," concluded the little man with thick glasses. A silence of disbelief lasted only a few moments, replaced by the wailing of women and the crying of children. The *nachalnik* turned sharply on the heel of his shiny boots and barked commands to his subordinates.

Soldiers went from house to house collecting any weapons. When all rifles and shotguns were secured on one of the carts under two guards, the Rogozhins were ordered to grab only their personal belongings and take seats in another cart. In the meantime, the soldiers emptied the houses of everything of value. After this was done, they turned to the silos, the underground storage, the barns, and the home pantries to collect every jar of milk, every ounce of animal feed, every handful of grain down to the last crust of bread. Under the soldiers' supervision, the seasonal workers rounded up all domestic animals, every chicken and duck, every cow and goat, and tethered them one by one to the last wagon in the train.

It was almost dusk when the *nachalnik* quickly inspected every house again and gave the order to move out. Every member of the Rogozhin family wept as they turned their heads to look at their abandoned homes one last time.

By midnight, when the horses finally stopped, Fyodor recognized the Nizhny Novgorod Railroad station. Only two carts remained in the train: one with the Rogozhins and one with the *nachalnik*, his three soldiers, and the machine gun. The rest had disappeared somewhere along the way.

Another OGPU officer spoke quietly with the *nachalnik*, who nodded and pointed in the direction of Ivan. Five minutes later, their brother, his wife Marfa, and his two teenage sons were ordered to get off the cart and were taken away. Fyodor did not have a chance to protest, and it was lucky for him: without a doubt he would have shared the same fate as Ivan. But the Rogozhin's never found out what that fate was, or where their brother's family landed; most likely they perished.

Anna paused telling her story and sighed. "It happened so many years ago when I was still young. I expected this horror was out of my memory for good. I guess not." Two big tears rolled down her cheeks. She closed her eyes and went silent. So did everyone else in the room.

A few moments later, Major Vitus inconspicuously glanced at his wristwatch: it was almost 15:30. *In less than two hours, it will be dark,* he thought. *And yet, we can't hurry the old woman up. She might clam up, and there will be no more stories.*

Katerina noticed Viktor's glance at his watch and understood his concern. She sat on the floor next to Anna and gently squeezed her hands.

"Take your time, Auntie, take your time," Katya said calmly. "Dad was never a talker; I wished you had told me this story before."

Anna opened her eyes, made a deep sigh again, and went on with the story.

* * *

Soon, the Rogozhins merged with a larger group of people looking just as confused and frightened. The soldiers led them to a string of cattle cars and ordered them to climb aboard the nearest car. A thin layer of wet hay covered the floor. There was an empty bucket in the corner. The soldier explained: "Use this bucket to relieve yourself. When the train stops, you will be allowed to get rid of your shit. Understood?" And he slid the door shut.

It was a torturous, two-month long journey, across thousands of kilometers in the cold, stinking cattle car with only a piece of bread and a mug of water each day. Soon the women did not have enough milk to nurse infants; children and the elderly alike sickened from the hunger. Some died. Despair filled the air inside those cars. Every morning and every night, Fyodor led the family in prayer, asking Almighty God for forgiveness and help. And God must have listened, as the Rogozhins survived their terrible journey.

The condemned deportees arrived at their destination in the middle of May. It was the Urgal Railroad Station in the Western part of the Khabarovsky Krai, in the middle of the *Taiga*. Here, by order of a local OGPU *nachalnik*, they were divided into their families—men, their wives, and children—and dispatched on the horse-driven carts to the nearby small settlements and village. The entire Rogozhin family ended up at the *khutor* Izmailovsky.

Their new life began with two funerals. Izmailovsky consisted of four dilapidated log houses, abandoned for the last twenty years. The Rogozhins had no choice but to move into those ruins. In two of them, they found human skeletons. One lay on top of the oven, covered with a rotten quilt; the other sat in a broken old rocking chair. There was no way to determine to whom these skeletons once belonged, but from their arched spines they must have been in the declining years of their lives. Who knows who they were or what happened to them? Perhaps they were too old to move with the rest and were left behind to die, or simply refused to leave their birthplace. Anyway, they had to be buried according to Christian traditions.

When this was done, the Rogozhins, all able men, women, and adolescent children, began fixing their new habitat. Thanks to the *nachalnik* who had brought them here, there were a few tools at their disposal—long reciprocal saws, hammers, axes, etc. They also found some rusty but usable carpenter's tools, nails, and spikes in the sheds behind the houses. There was no shortage of wood around either. Everyone joined the effort to make this dead place livable again.

It soon became clear those houses were beyond repair, their battered ovens and rotten walls no longer able to withstand the harsh Siberian climate. The Rogozhins realized new homes needed to be built soon, but for now they had improvised stoves to keep the young children warm during the cold May nights in May. Help came from the local *soviet*, which delivered half a dozen metal tubes, screens, and old steel barrels. Under Fyodor's leadership and his brother Pavel's supervision, they converted these into ovens in five or six hours. Pavel, since his childhood, was known as a very handy fellow.

The life of the Rogozhin family in this inhospitable place improved rather quickly. Old and young alike learned how to trap small animals in the *Taiga*, to forage edible tree nuts and berries, and to grow their own essential crops. They acquired a few chicks from the distant neighbors, which grew into roosters and hens, and they caught and domesticated a few ducks and geese to start their own flock of waterfowl. By the end of September, all four dilapidated abodes had been demolished and replaced with spacious cedar log houses, elevated over the permafrost by wooden beams. They built barns as well, although it took another three years before cows, pigs, and horses occupied them.

It was in the blood of the Rogozhins to work hard and keep their faith, and Fyodor led his family back into prosperity. But the sky over their heads was not always blue and calm, as the storms of progress rained down new troubles upon them. In 1933, commissars from Chegdomyn and even from Khabarovsk began visiting Izmailovsky more often, pressuring families to join their lands together into *kolkhoz* collective farms. It was obvious such enterprises were doomed to fail, given the local conditions and distances between farms. But inspired by Stalin, the party members insisted on joining this national campaign, even threatening to prosecute those who refused as the *kulaks*—well to do agricultural proprietors and therefor the enemies of the Soviet State.

Fyodor understood the threat. After several consultations among the families living in neighboring villages, he devised a proposal to create a collective farm as a state enterprise. The government would contribute half of the assets, in the form of the communal land and equipment, while each participating family would contribute the other half. The farm would specialize in growing vegetables, mainly potatoes, and producing dairy for the miners and rail workers in the urban settlements nearby. Eighty percent of the farm's production output would be distributed exclusively through governmental channels, and twenty percent would belong to the members of the collective Soviet state enterprise called the Sovkhoz New Dawn.

The local Party officials rejected Fyodor's proposal: "Not in line with the Socialist economic norms." A strict order followed, to create the *kolkhoz* with the members' private assets only. The government would sell them two tractors on credit, with all necessary implements, and allocate the communal land, which needed to be cleared of timber by the *kolkhoz* members themselves. All future production would go to the state at nominal prices, while members would be allowed to retain their small private parcels of land and a limited number of domestic animals for their own sustenance. In addition to the potential monetary compensation or barter consideration, members' earnings would depend on the results of the farms' annual agricultural activities, primarily the compliance with governmental production quotas. In simple terms, if the *kolkhoz* failed to meet these quotas, its members would get no money for their hard work—nor potatoes, cabbage, and meat. They would have to rely solely on their own miniscule private capacities and labor to feed their families until the next year's harvest.

There was no choice, so in the spring of 1933, the *kolkhoz* New Dawn was established. For the next twenty-five years, this ill-conceived enterprise struggled to stay afloat, rarely meeting its production quotas and causing its often-changing managers serious problems with Soviet authorities. Kolkhoz New Dawn remained on the books until the end of the fifties. Its existence finally ceased in 1962, after many of the original members had died or become too frail to work and the younger generation had abandoned the *Taiga* for urban life.

From the start Fyodor knew this Socialist economic experiment would not work. He went along with the Bolsheviks to save the freedom and, in some cases, the lives of his brothers and sisters. But his frustration with their everyday economic struggles never dissipated. What disappointed and disturbed him most was the state law on compulsory public-school education. Throughout their history, the Old Believers homeschooled their children, instilling in each new generation their canon and their moral values and work ethic. He doubted very much that Soviet public education, enforced by communist ideology that rejects God, human individualism, and the entrepreneurial spirit, would foster those values so revered and cherished by people of faith.

However, the law could not be ignored without serious consequences. So, all the Rogozhin children were sent for the whole day to school at settlements in Listvenny and Urgal. And soon the children no longer followed in their god-fearing parents' footsteps; in two to three years, Fyodor no longer saw their familiar young faces in his Sunday services.

The children adapted to the new system in their own ways, and the Rogozhin family was no exception: some were more obedient than others, some more rebellious or plain unruly. By the age of ten, Ivan and Dmitry manifested disobedient tendencies and a propensity for violence. They bullied their fellow students and terrorized schoolgirls. Their teachers complained of such unacceptable behavior to their parents many times. But Fyodor and Anna's reprimands never had any lasting effect.

The signs of real trouble became obvious as the boys reached puberty. Often Ivan instigated these violent acts, and he began to strangely demonstrate an aptitude for leadership. The school authorities often detained the cousins. Anna's husband Nikolai would give his unruly son a good beating, but Dmitry grew even more stubborn and spiteful toward his frustrated father.

Although Ivan, despite his young age, had grown, just like his dad, into a large and strong young man, Fyodor was still able to physically overpower his adolescent son in an attempt to discipline him. However, he understood that corporal punishment would not rectify a bad behavioral problem. So, being the priest of the Old Believers and spiritual leader for the community, he tried to deal with the boy's rowdiness differently: reasoning with him, calmly talking to the boy, reading him passages from the Bible, and shaming him for his actions. But Ivan would laugh in his father's face, lashing back with profanities. In those moments, fear would overcome Fyodor; he saw in the eyes of his only son the boy's tormented soul possessed by the devil. The sight terrified Fyodor, but he knew that there was no other way to drive the evil spirit out but through love and prayer.

Sadly, no divine help came. At the beginning of the summer of 1938, a terrifying event happened: a thirteen-year-old girl, a daughter of the Urgal Railroad Station supervisor and a student at the local school, was gang raped, brutally beaten, and left to die in an abandoned barn on the settlement outskirts. However, she did not die and was brought unconscious to a hospital in Chegdomyn.

The event shook the entire community of the Verkhneburiyinsky District. A week after the tragic incident, its victim remained in shock and could hardly speak. Nevertheless, to identify her attackers, the militia investigator compiled a list of the local hooligans who might have perpetrated the crime. Suspicion fell on the Rogozhin cousins, who by the age of fifteen had already earned an unshakable reputation as vicious bullies. Of course, they flatly denied any involvement, and many adults in the community insisted that teenagers could not possibly have committed a crime like this. But many in the family, and Fyodor most of all, felt certain the two were connected to the rape or knew who was. No matter how hard the militia investigator pressed, he could not pull a word out of them.

After two weeks of clinging to life by a thread, the poor girl finally succumbed to death. Driven to the point of desperation, the local Soviet and Communist party authorities pressured the Chegdomyn Militia to restore justice. The Khabarovsky NKVD headquarters sent their most experienced investigators to crack the case. They detained all the suspects, twelve young men in total, and subjected them to intense interrogation, and borderline torture for several days. Afterward, some continued to be detained while others were released, but there was no breakthrough.

Ivan and Dmitry returned home covered in bruises. They looked somber and weary but somewhat victorious; they had not cracked. It was driving Fyodor mad. He decided he must confront this evil directly and with force. Disregarding Anna's and Nikolai's protests, he locked his son Ivan and his nephew Dmitry in his own house for two days.

No one would ever know what went on in there during those two days. Eventually all three left the house, climbed into a wagon, and left *khutor* Izmailovsky. Late that evening, Fyodor returned home alone, locked himself away, and prayed for the next twenty-four hours non-stop.

A few days later, news arrived from Chegdomyn: "The case of the rape and killing of a local teenage schoolgirl has been solved; seven perpetrators have confessed to the crime.

The panel of three appointed judges, after reviewing all evidence and hearing out all the witnesses, will determine the extent of their participation and the appropriate punishment for each of the accused."

Later that summer, the Rogozhins learned that five of the men were sentenced to life in prison for the crime. Because of their age, Ivan and Dmitry were deemed as willing bystanders and found guilty of conspiring to cover up the crime. They were incarcerated for a minimum of two years in a youth labor correctional facility.

This resolution filled Fyodor with a deep sadness, but also a sliver of hope that his son and nephew would overcome the evil spirit that gripped them, and to find their way to a life of serving God and people of faith. But this hope died with the arrival of a letter from Ivan, filled with venomous hatred and threats. From then on, he avoided even speaking about his son at all.

Then in late October came Fyodor's arrest and his subsequent interrogations by the Nachalnik from Khabarovsk, Commissar Raymond Vitus. After visiting Izmailovsky and questioning Fyodor's brother Pavel and sister Anna, Vitus informed them of his decision to release Fyodor without pressing any charges. More than once in the investigation, the Commissar and the priest spoke extensively on matters of religion, civil obedience, law and order, public education, and the rearing of children. It was obvious that these two men had developed a good deal of respect for each other.

Commissar Vitus had shown Fyodor the letter of his accuser, and he knew that its author was his own son. Perhaps he guessed that only Ivan had a reason for revenge on him. Either way, Fyodor continued to pray for his son's soul, but he made no attempt to see him, even when Ivan and Dmitri were released. In July 1941, the cousins volunteered to fight the Germans and eventually perished in that devastating war.

*   *   *

During this rather long story, Anna stopped several times to catch her breath, overcome with emotion. The interruptions lasted a few minutes, sometimes longer. Major Vitus and Katerina had enough patience not to rush the old woman.

Finally, Anna closed her eyes and paused again, just for a little while. Then she smiled and said, "All these years, I thought I had lost my boy forever. But Dmitry has survived and come back home."

"What do you mean, Dmitry came back home, Auntie? Are you sure it was him?" Katerina asked, looking at Anna very closely. "Many years have passed since you saw him before he went to war. People might change a lot."

"Katya, do you think I would not recognize my own blood?" Anna snapped back. "Girl, you've never had a child, have you?"

"It's okay; we believe you, Aunt Anna," Viktor intervened. "But tell us, when did he come back here, and was he alone?"

"I am not sure. I guess two weeks ago," Anna began hesitantly, trying to recall. "I got so excited, you know, when I opened my door. It was dusk, but I recognized him right away. I almost screamed, but he put his hand over my mouth and pushed me inside, you know, gently." She paused for a moment and then continued with more confidence. "There was another man with him. He had a large scar across his upper lip and left cheek, which pulled the corner of his eyelid down so that he could not blink. Even a thick, bushy beard could not hide this ugly scar. The man gave me the creeps."

"And did you notice anything unusual about Dmitry?" Katerina asked.

"I told you; they came at dusk. I could not see clearly, but it was Dmitry—no doubt." Now Anna had a slight hesitation in her voice. "I was beside myself, really: my son returned from the dead, you know. But, later, inside, I did notice some strange things. First, I noticed he was limping because of his stiff left leg. Second, not even once did he address me as 'Mom.' No hug, no kiss, no nothing. He was just nervously pacing the room, back and forth, non-stop."

"How did they explain their visit?" Viktor asked.

"They didn't. Dmitry asked for food; I gave them food. While they were eating, I thought I would quickly run to Fyodor with this wonderful news, but Dmitry stopped me, saying that they would pay him a visit later." Anna continued angrily. "That was exactly how he put it. To be honest, I was disappointed, but he insisted. Another disturbing thing, while I was placing dishes and spoons on the table, the ugly man pulled a bottle of vodka from his *telogreika* and demanded glasses. I tried to explain that there shouldn't be any drinking in an Old Believers' house, but this awful godless soul started laughing. What hurt me the most, Dmitry was laughing too. He should've known better."

"So, what did they say when dinner was over?" Viktor sounded impatient. Katerina shot him a stern glance.

"Nothing to me. The two men were mumbling among themselves and giggling, like two silly boys conspiring to no good," she answered. "Soon, they got so drunk that they couldn't speak at all. They did not bother to take off their clothes. They climbed on top of the warm stove and snored away. At dawn, they left."

"Just like that? Your visitors did not say a word, did not tell you if they were coming back?" Viktor felt that what Anna was saying didn't make sense. Perhaps that was how the old woman's dementia manifested itself. Again, Katerina seemed annoyed at Viktor's impatience.

"It was too early in the morning. Dmitry and his friend asked for some pickle brine to quench their hangover," Anna said. "I don't believe you've ever needed that, Nachalnik? Did you?"

"Yes, maybe a few times," Viktor replied. "But what happened after that?"

"Before they left, Dmitry handed me a small but rather heavy bundle wrapped in a brown burlap sack tightened with a shoelace. He ordered me to hide it well until they came back," Anna answered. "Make sure nobody knows about it," the man with the scar said, and he moved his hand against his throat, like he was cutting it. It wasn't a joke."

The Major, Captain, and Lieutenant exchanged glances in stunned silence.

"Do you still have this package?" Viktor did not know what answer he expected to hear.

"I was afraid I'd forget where I had hidden it, so I immediately took the package to Fyodor," Anna explained simply. "He could not believe what I told him. He took the package and promised to take care of it. "Tell them to come and see me," he said. And that was exactly what I did."

"Do you remember when the second visit took place?"

"They came back about a week ago, I would say," Anna replied without any hesitation. "Those two went berserk. The ugly man grabbed me by my throat. I got so scared; I couldn't even scream. He would have choked me if Dmitry hadn't stopped him. They did not say a word; they just looked at each other and stormed out the door. I don't know how long I was lying on the floor, crying."

Everyone in the room had their eyes fixed on the old woman.

" The next morning, Dmitry came back here, only this time alone." Anna was just about to start sobbing. "He was disheveled and dirty; he took off his *telogreika* and dumped it on the table. He asked me if I had another warm jacket he could use. I suggested looking through his late father's clothes." She paused to collect herself. "I thought he would know where they were. He screamed at me, demanding that I should get it for him. I went to the room behind the oven, and he began washing his face and hands over the barrel with drinking water. I was upset but did not say a word. He dried himself with a towel and put his father's warm jacket on. What a handsome man he was, even with that untrimmed beard. I tried to hug him, but he would not let me. "Stay home," he said, "and do not go anywhere until I come back. Understood?" I promised to stay put. When Dmitry left, I fell asleep. And then you came."

Anna closed her eyes. She seemed exhausted. At that moment, Lieutenant Toropko emerged from behind the oven with a dirty, bloodstained green *telogreika* in her hands. She approached Viktor and whispered, "Sorry I snooped around, but after I heard what happened, I knew that this important evidence must've been here. And here it is. You see a torn spot. The poor woman forgot to clean and fix this jacket."

"I hope you know that we need a search warrant in a case like this, don't you, Comrade Lieutenant?" The Major did not sound like he was joking. "Thank you anyway, but please be more careful next time."

"I will, Comrade Major. You have my word," Nina replied and packed the *telogreika* into a large evidence bag.

Viktor pointed to his wristwatch and ordered everyone out quietly to not disturb Anna. Katerina covered her aunt with a blanket, closed the door behind her, and followed Viktor to the car. Before getting into the vehicle, Katya looked around, realizing that she would never see Izmailovsky again.

Chapter 6

Friday, November 11, 19:45. Settlement Listvenny. Lyubomir parked his *Kozyol* as close as possible to the three-story apartment building entrance door. He turned the engine off and looked at Major Vitus, who just a second ago had opened his eyes and wondered, "Where are we?"

"We are in Listvenny, Comrade Major. We are going to have supper at my home; my wife has prepared food and expected us an hour ago." Lyubomir Nesterenko said it rather formally, perhaps anticipating some objections. "I also invited Sergeant Lutsenko from my squad, so you can ask him some questions about his initial encounter with Soldier Kim."

"Oh, that's a good idea, Comrade Captain," Viktor replied, smiling. "Are you sure this won't be inconveniencing your wife?"

"Please believe me, it was no inconvenience at all. My Lyuba loves to feed and entertain guests; I told you." The Captain sounded very convincing. "Besides, we all need to get away from reality once in a while, don't we? Double homicides like this don't happen often around here; many people are scared or stressed out. And again, it would save you an extra trip to Listvenny to get the necessary information. Don't you agree, Comrade Major?"

"Yes, it makes perfect sense," Viktor replied with a hint of hesitation. "I just hate to have you drive us to New Urgal and go back home so late, Captain."

"Honestly, I did not plan to drive you to New Urgal. You all should spend the night here: the women can sleep in my daughter's room, and you, Comrade Major, can stay with Sergeant Lutsenko. He lives alone in an apartment on the first floor of this building." Lyubomir uttered the entire sentence in a single breath.

"It seemed you thought the entire plan out, Comrade Captain." Viktor turned to Nina and Katya. "I hope you won't object?"

They both nodded enthusiastically.

"Then let's not waste any time before our hostess changes her mind," Viktor replied casually, then changed his tone: "If we stay here, Captain, can we pay a visit to the Korean commander tomorrow? We will need to talk to him about his soldier sooner or later anyway."

"Yes, Comrade Major, we'll pay him a visit tomorrow," replied Captain Nesterenko. He got out of the vehicle, led everyone to his apartment on the second floor, and rang the bell instead of using his key.

"I have to give Lyuba a little heads up," the Captain explained.

The next second, a good-looking young man in a Militia uniform opened the door.

"Good evening, Comrade Captain!" He addressed Nesterenko first but noticing Major Vitus he tried to correct his mistake. "Greetings, Comrade Major! Sorry for breaking the rules."

"Never mind, Sergeant, we are here for a mostly unofficial event." Viktor helped Katerina with her coat, took off his, and handed both to the Sergeant. "Your name is?"

"I am Sergeant Lutsenko, Comrade Major," reported the young Militiaman. "Nikolai Lutsenko."

Lyubomir took the coat from Lieutenant Toropko and invited the guests to the living room. Here, the Captain's wife Lyuba, a tall, rather plump and big-bosomed woman, greeted them. Her deep blue eyes and olive skin beautifully contrasted her tar black hair, braided into a thick plait around her head. She looked like Scheherazade from the *Arabian Nights* tales.

Lyuba bustled around the table, setting out plates of thin pancakes, red caviar, luncheon meats, pickled tomatoes and cucumbers, smoked fish, rye bread, and butter— a distinctly Russian assortment of appetizers.

In the middle of this bountiful culinary cornucopia, there was a frosty bottle of pure grain Russian vodka, the kind that ordinary people couldn't buy in a standard grocery store. The hostess's eyes were beaming with pride and delight.

"Lyubochka, darling, you have outdone yourself." Lyubomir approached his wife and kissed her on the cheek. "Let me introduce you to our guests: Major Viktor Vitus and Lieutenant Nina Toropko from Khabarovsky UVD. Katerina Rogozhin, or by stage name Kseniya Krylova, is an actress of Khabarovsky Drama Theater. She is our guest by unfortunate circumstances…"

"Yes, the entire settlement heard about the tragedy. My heart goes out to you, honey." Lyuba rather unceremoniously but sincerely hugged Katya, as only a mother can. "I know how you feel, dear. If you ever need a shoulder, mine is always here for you. Come sit here. This is the best seat in this house."

Everybody joined Katerina and took their places around the table. The small meal in Aunt Anna's house at noon had not tided them over. Still, only Lyubomir and Sergeant Lutsenko, not entirely strangers in this home, began loading their plates without further ado; Viktor, Nina, and Katya still held back.

The hostess seemed upset. "Please don't be shy. Everything here I have prepared for you, my dear friends." Lyuba picked up a fork and started putting different delicacies on the guest's plates. "Please try everything. Lyubomir be a good host; go ahead and pour the vodka."

"Oh yes, how could I overlook my responsibilities?" Lyubomir grabbed the frosty bottle and twisted off the cork. "Katya, I propose a drink to your father Fyodor Rogozhin. Only once did I have the privilege to speak with him briefly, two weeks ago. He came to seek my advice, but we were unexpectedly interrupted, and I had to leave him alone for a while. When I returned, he was gone. And I never got the chance to find out what actually brought him to my office that day." The captain paused for a few seconds, holding in his hand a crystal glass filled up to its rim with vodka. "Ever since, I cannot help thinking, what if I had learned the reason for Fyodor's visit?" He became silent from the lump in his throat and drank his vodka in one big gulp.

Katerina began to hold back her tears. Sitting next to her, Lyuba put her hands around her shoulder and whispered to Katya, "Have your drink, girl; it will calm your pain. I promise."

Katya straightened her body and raised the crystal glass. She sipped the vodka, stopped for a second to wipe away her tears, and then slowly emptied the glass. She wasn't a drinker at all, having grown up in a family of Old Believers. Everybody followed suit and emptied their glasses, then reached for some food to chase the strong drink down. Katya looked around the table and smiled. The host and hostess felt relieved and encouraged their guests to eat even more enthusiastically. Lyuba's eyes beamed with delight as she observed her guests going at the pancakes topped with caviar, salami, and smoked sturgeon smothered with horseradish.

"Lyubomir, please, pour more vodka into the glasses. It is my turn for a toast." The hostess got up. "I love men in Militia uniform. I am happily married to one of those men. I am proud of the job you do every day, protecting us from harm. I drink to you, people!" Lyuba emptied the glass, kissed her husband, and set the glass back down. Then she added, "As much as I'm glad to see you all enjoying the food, I have to warn you not to stuff yourself with appetizers because the main course is yet to come."

Everyone froze reaching for another helping of pancakes and caviar. Then Nina burst into laughter. Everyone joined her.

Viktor sipped a little vodka from his glass and rose. "Dear Hostess, everything on this table is prepared with such love and care. Thank you for your kind words and thank you for your hospitality. I'll speak for my colleagues in saying that we really feel at home here."

Lyuba, visibly overwhelmed with emotion, graciously nodded, and quickly retreated to the kitchen.

"Please take it one notch down, Comrade Vitus. You'll spoil my wife," said Lyubomir jovially. "She is an Eastern Ukrainian woman, you know; hospitality runs in their veins."

"My mom is the same way," said Nina joyfully. "You bet we are like that."

"My mom is originally from Odessa." Viktor added in agreement. "She also loves to entertain her relatives and close friends any time of the day or night, even when she is not well."

"So, let's drink to all the women around this table and around the world!"

"Excellent toast, Comrade Nesterenko," Nina raised her glass. "I don't remember who said it, but surely someone very clever: behind every great man, there is a great woman. Isn't it true?"

"Hey, now I understand why there are so many great men among us," Viktor said with genuine sincerity, although everyone took it as a joke and laughed.

"I wasn't kidding." He tried to clarify what he had said. "I am really convinced that it is true when I think of my parents, you and your wife, Lyubomir, your mom and your dad, Nina."

"And my mom and dad." Katerina whispered.

"Yes, Katya, the same goes for your parents too!" Viktor exclaimed and looked at her long and affectionately.

Katya responded with a similar affection. At that moment, she could not explain her feelings, but it had become more and more obvious that these people, and especially this handsome Militia Major, genuinely cared about her.

Viktor and Katya's exchange of glances did not escape Lyuba, who had just emerged from the kitchen with a steaming pot in her hands. Lyubomir cleared the table corner, placed an empty plate there, and helped his wife settle the large pot.

"Did I miss anything important?" Lyuba asked in a humorously inquisitive tone. She looked at Katya conspiratorially.

Ignoring the suggestive look, Katerina answered simply, "I didn't think you missed anything important except Comrade Captain's lovely toast to the women."

"What women did my husband toast—any particular woman? He was always the master of wooing young ladies." Lyuba pulled off her kitchen mittens and gently pinched Lyubomir's ear. "Did you know I was only eighteen when I surrendered to his spell? Tell them, Lyubko."

She blended Russian and Ukrainian words in a clumsy but pleasant-sounding way. Although embarrassed, Lyubomir got a real kick out of her teasing.

"It is true. But it wasn't easy; this woman had a lot of suitors." He blushed and tried to change the subject. "Better tell us what you cooked for us today."

"Borsch!" Lyuba lifted the lid and let a toothsome steam cascade from the pot.

"I have cooked it the way my mother always did. It is a pity; she left for Lviv with our daughter just two weeks ago. Her borsch would be even better, but I hope you will like mine too."

"Don't you worry, honey. I am sure we will." Lyubomir kissed her on the cheek. "Please start pouring it, dear. And I'll pour more vodka."

The borsch was fabulous — hearty yet light, and very tasty. Well-chopped carrots, potatoes, and cabbage together with beans and pieces of meat swam in the dark red broth of the beets. The hostess went from one guest to another, ensuring that everyone had enough sour cream with the borsch. For Viktor and Katerina, this type of soup was a rare delicacy, and they enjoyed it immensely, sighing with delight after every sip. The others, for whom the borsch was a familiar thing, could not hide their satisfaction either; they dipped their bread in it and slurped away whatever was left on the bottom of the deep plate. No one talked: the only sound in the room was the clanking of the spoons against thick ceramic dinnerware.

Lyubomir attempted to break the silence with another toast, but no one followed his initiative. Viktor felt some relief at this: at the start of the evening, the sight of the bottle had filled him with trepidation — that he might not be able to stop. This thought terrified him, especially now that he had given his word to the general; especially in front of this woman he found so undeniably attractive. And yet, because he felt in the company of real friends, Viktor could not say "no" to a couple of drinks. He was glad he didn't. Tonight, Viktor felt fully relaxed but totally in control; he liked this state of mind, but he realized no more drinks from this moment on.

He covered his glass with his left palm as Captain Nesterenko brought the bottle around the table once again. Recognizing the signal, the Captain discretely passed him by and filled the rest of glasses. At first, girls protested but then giggled, saying: "Go ahead, pour it. We can handle it."

"Now I have a toast." Nina stood up, holding her glass high. She seemed a little tipsy. "I want to drink to the men in our lives. They don't always know how to be good to us, women. And this is unfortunate. But we need them and often love them as they are."

She dropped back on her chair and proceeded with her drink. Everyone around the table understood that there was much more behind what Nina had just said but kept their silence as they drained their glasses. Feeling the awkwardness that she had created with her toast, Nina exclaimed, "Come on, people; I mean, I love you! That's all."

"We've got it, Comrade Lieutenant." Now Sergeant Lutsenko surprised everybody. "We cannot live without you girls, either."

Embarrassed, Nikolai lowered his head and returned to his unfinished borsch. Lyuba sprung from her chair and almost shouted, "Oh, dear God. I've totally forgotten about my pirogues."

She stormed into the kitchen.

Lyubomir followed her with an empty soup pot. "Let me help you, honey. What kind of pirogues have you prepared this time?"

"With cabbage and mushrooms," she answered so that everyone could hear.

Everyone heard her, and they exchanged glances in horror.

"Dear hostess, we may die from another bite of food," Katya said. "We are full."

"You will not regret it, I assure you," Nikolai replied with confidence. "Lyuba makes amazing pirogues, especially with white mushrooms. I helped to gather them myself four weeks ago."

"This is true." Lyubomir had emerged from the kitchen with a large ceramic plate full of steaming dumplings. Lyuba was right behind him, carrying two more saucers of sour cream. "Nikolai proved himself a master mushroom hunter. You know, this is not easy to do in the *Taiga*."

As soon as the plate landed at the center of the table, Lyubomir began scooping pirogues onto the guests' plates with a huge, lacquered spoon. Lyuba spread the sour cream over them, solemnly declaring: "I have poured my heart into this dish. It is not going to hurt you; it will be good for you. I promise you, my dear friends. Luybko, make sure everyone has vodka. Let's drink to that."

The main course sat easily in their full stomachs, just as the hostess had promised. She offered hot tea to wash everything down, with cookies and cupcakes. The lovely evening was coming to an end. The guests were tired and sleepy. Lyuba led Nina and Katya to her daughter's room, where two narrow beds were already made.

Sergeant Lutsenko stood by the door, waiting for the Major to exchange some words of appreciation with Captain Nesterenko and his lovely wife Lyuba.

"We can go, Sergeant." Viktor wished good night to the host and hostess and grabbed his coat and hat. "I guess we will talk some business in your apartment."

"Yes, Comrade Major, I am ready," the Sergeant replied, leading Viktor down the stairs to the first floor.

Lutsenko's one-room apartment looked modest; the narrow metal frame bed, a couch, an armoire, a three-drawer dresser, and a tall floor lamp. A table stood against the wall across from an electric stove, and a couple of three-legged stools were in the small kitchen. A double door cabinet hung above a kitchen table. It was the typical dwelling of a bachelor.

"Welcome to my humble abode, Comrade Major!" Nikolai proclaimed with a theatrical flair. The rich, delicious food, rare in his everyday life, and the few drinks had mellowed the Sergeant. "I put clean sheets on the bed for you. I'll sleep on the couch."

"Thank you, Sergeant, for your hospitality," Viktor replied with sincere gratitude. "When you happen to visit Khabarovsk, I will be happy to have you as a guest in my home. It is not large either, but cozy. Where do you want us to sit and talk?"

"I guess the table will be more comfortable; you can write something down if you need to." Nikolai waved his hand toward the kitchen.

"Okay, that will work." Viktor pulled his small notebook and a pencil from his pocket and sat at the table, ready to hear the Sergeant's statement.

*   *   *

At 6:45 that morning — Friday, November 4 — Sergeant Lutsenko walked from his apartment building to the local Militia precinct along the settlement's unlit main street. It was dark and bitterly cold. Barely awake, Lutsenko concentrated on the rough frozen pavement underneath his feet; it was easy to stumble and fall. Still, he caught the red glow of a cigarette in his trained peripheral vision: someone was smoking, standing in the shadow of the cedar tree next to the retail store. He did not turn his head, but it was clear that there was another silhouette next to the smoker. Noticing the Sergeant, they retreated behind the tree's wide trunk.

Soldiers from the construction battalion. Too early, though, Nikolai thought as he kept walking.

Arriving at the precinct, he turned on the lights, sat behind the desk next to the still warm iron stove, and checked to see if the phone worked. It did. At that moment, the door slid open slightly; a dark shape squeezed into the room and closed the door tightly. The Sergeant put the telephone receiver down and looked at the unexpected intruder. It was a small person, more like a kid, dressed in a quilted jacket, oversized trousers, and earflap hat, all covered in thick frost. His face and hands were dangerously puffy and red, his brows and eyelashes were snow-white, and his lips blue. Whoever this person was, he'd been exposed to the cold for several hours.

Nikolai rushed out from behind his desk and pulled the visitor to the stove. The stranger's entire body shook uncontrollably. In the light the Sergeant recognized him as a Korean soldier named Kim. He had seen Kim around the retail store on several occasions trying to sell Japanese watches or bottles of the Korean vodka. He typically avoided the Militia persons retreating into the woods when he spotted them.

Nikolai could hear the sound of Kim's upper teeth knocking against his lower jaw, as the poor fellow settle down. His body was shaking. The Sergeant immediately phoned the

Korean camp to consult with their commander. Seeing this, Kim raised his hands in protest, trying but still unable to speak. Nikolai placed the receiver back on the cradle. He understood that the Korean didn't want his commander to know where he was now; clearly something important had kept him hiding in the woods in the brutal cold.

Another thirty minutes passed in silence before Kim stopped shuddering. He was fully thawed—his lips were no longer blue, although his face and hands were still red and swollen. The frost had melted from his clothes, steaming in the heat from the stove. The Sergeant tried to help his visitor stand up on his feet, but the man's legs, most likely frostbitten, would not support him. Sergeant Lutsenko did not wait; he grabbed Kim across his body, lifted him like a child, and put him in the chair. Nikolai was anxious to listen, and Kim was finally ready to talk.

Despite his heavy accent, Kim's Russian was good. He spoke slowly and sporadically in his nervous, exhausted state: he witnessed the brutal murder of a man he knew personally, Fyodor Rogozhin, the local Orthodox priest; this murder took place in the man's home in *khutor* Izmailovsky last night, around 22:30.

Kim also explained how he happened to be there. It was extremely cold the night of November 3. He was passing by Izmailovsky on the way to his camp and decided to pay a visit to his friend who never refused him the warm comfort of his Russian oven and a plate of hot cabbage soup. When he arrived on the porch of Fyodor's house, he heard a struggle inside. Through the window he saw two men, one tall and the other short and stocky, stabbing Fyodor repeatedly with knives. Then they hoisted his dead body high on the wall, driving metal spikes through his palms.

This terrifying scene caused Kim to panic; he drew the attention of the killers when he turned to run. They stormed outside and chased after him. But they had difficulty tracking him in the darkness, and they seemed unfamiliar with the terrain. He managed to lose them near Listvenny. Instead of running all the way to his camp, he remained there to report what he saw, even though he would be severely punished by his commander for returning after curfew.

The soldier's story shocked Nikolai: he had never experienced anything remotely like this during his entire career as a Militia serviceman. He asked the soldier to sit tight while he reported in. Nikolai urgently dialed the phone and found the Captain in his New Urgal office. Captain Nesterenko told Nikolai that he and Sergeant Darsulov would be in Listvenny as soon as possible. He also instructed Sergeant Lutsenko to retain Kim for the time being and to call the Korean camp commander to alert him.

Lutsenko waved to Kim to stay put and proceeded to phone the Korean camp. When he got the connection and asked to speak with the camp commander, Kim sprang from his chair and dashed out the door, groaning as he overcame the pain in his feet. The Sergeant dropped the telephone receiver and ran after him, but somehow Kim had already disappeared into the fog of late dawn. Sergeant Lutsenko frantically checked building to building, hoping to find Kim, but the runaway was nowhere in sight. Kim was gone.

The Sergeant ran back to the precinct and grabbed the radio, calling Captain Nesterenko in his vehicle. For a while, the radio speaker crackled noisily; then the Captain's voice came through.

"We are on our way. What is going on?" the Captain asked.

Lutsenko reported what had just happened and asked for instructions. Nesterenko could not hide his disappointment but did not express any reprimand. He paused and calmly informed Nikolai that he and Sergeant Darsulov would not stop in Listvenny but would rather go directly to Izmailovsky to secure and inspect the crime scene. He ordered Lutsenko to remain at his post on heightened alert.

The next morning, two soldiers from the construction battalion stumbled upon Kim's dead body in the woods. He was covered in blood, with his throat cut and multiple stab wounds. They reported their finding immediately to the Listvenny Militia precinct. Captain Nesterenko retrieved the body, inspected and photographed it, then sent it to Chegdomyn for an autopsy by Doctor Goldfarb.

*   *   *

So far Sergeant Lutsenko had the most complete account of what had happened at the Listvenny settlement, thought Viktor.

"Did the Korean soldier have anything with him, like a bag or sack?" Viktor asked rather casually.

"I didn't see any such things." Nikolai sounded certain. "I did notice, though, a few times he reached under his jacket like something was bothering him there. But I thought he just felt pain or discomfort. That's all."

"So, you never made that call to the Korean camp commander, did you?" asked Viktor after a short pause.

"No, I did not," Lutsenko replied. "It was my fault what happened to Kim. I should've made sure he stayed put; he could be alive today." The Sergeant became visibly upset.

The Major tried to assure him. "Don't beat yourself up, Sergeant. You could not anticipate that he would take off like that. He must've had a very good reason to not want to be found in your custody. I hope that the Captain and I will find out about it tomorrow. Let's get some rest."

Chapter 7

Saturday, November 12. 7:00 in the morning. Viktor was finishing his tea at the kitchen table when he heard a knock on the door. It was dark outside, and Sergeant Lutsenko had left fifteen minutes earlier to start his shift at the precinct. He took the last sip and opened the door. Captain Nesterenko, with a serious face and in full uniform, stood at the threshold.

"Why so formal, Comrade Captain?" asked Viktor as he let Lyubomir in. "Isn't it your day-off?"

"Yes, I don't have to be dressed like this, but we are going to visit a representative of a foreign country, aren't we?" the Captain replied with hesitation.

"I guess you are right, Captain," the Major agreed reluctantly, and donned his winter uniform jacket. "I suppose it should be a formal visit. How far do we need to drive?"

"Not far; less than 5km by a narrow road. The problem is that the weather is just about to get nasty." He sounded concerned. "This year's first snowfall is coming, and it could be heavy."

"Then let's get going." The Major rushed down the stairs and hopped into the *Kozyol*. The Captain followed, slamming the door behind him.

The car engine started after only three or four cranks. Nesterenko revved the engine while they waited for the heater to cut through the frost on the windshield. They sat quietly, each occupied by their own thoughts.

The Major broke the silence first. "How is everybody? Did the women sleep well?" Viktor fished without much subtlety.

"The women are fine. It looks like they slept well, and Lyuba is feeding them a royal breakfast. If you must know, Comrade Major, Citizen Rogozhina, I meant Katya, seemed to be much less upset than she was yesterday," the Captain added thoughtfully. "So, what do you think about the Soldier Kim's involvement?"

"I would not jump to any conclusions just yet: I don't think we have the full picture yet," the Major replied evasively, trying to gather his thoughts. "His timing at Rogozhin's place looks too coincidental to me, although he claimed they had known each."

"It did cross my mind as well. How did this poor fellow end up being a witness to such a heinous crime? But it provides a clear motive for his murder: he could have identified the killers.

"And we presumably know who Sergeant Lutsenko noticed hiding in the shadows that morning," the Major continued the thought. "The killers tracked Kim to the precinct here and waited to strike. But let's hurry—your prediction looks correct," noted Viktor. "The snow's already begun."

Lyubomir turned the headlights on, put the gear in reverse, and quickly negotiated his way onto the main street. In just a few minutes his Militia *Kozyol* entered a narrow forest clearing, tightly paved across with short cedar logs. The ride was very smooth, even pleasant across the frozen topsoil. Big, fluffy flakes were coming down fast, blanketing the surrounding forest in white. Viktor had watched the first snowfall in the *Taiga* many times before, and still its enchanting beauty always amazed him.

They weaved through the forest and up a hill on the Buriya River's western bank, not far from its confluence with the Urgal River. The Captain stopped the car and waved his hand toward a wooden gate marked in Korean signage.

"We are here, Comrade Major. Get ready to show your documents," Lyubomir said. "I was here last winter with a body of one of their soldiers who froze to death. They weren't very friendly."

"Let's see if they will do better this time," Major replied. "I guess you can shut off the engine and lights."

They walked to the gate and waited a full two minutes before a soldier emerged from the tiny log hut. He stared at them from behind a red and white striped gate without saying a word.

"We are here to speak with your Commander. I am Major Vitas from Khabarovsky UVD, and this is Captain Nesterenko, the New Urgal Militia Commander. Here are our IDs." Viktor tried to hand their documents to the soldier, who remained motionless. Instead, another soldier appeared under the spotlight, said something to the guard, and took the visitors' documents before disappearing into the snowstorm.

Three more minutes passed in total silence until the officer returned. Now he smiled stiffly, making little effort of disguising his pretense. He motioned the gate open and waved them into the camp. He led them into a long cedar log house with doors on either side.

Evidently, the small and well-heated room served as both an office and sleeping quarters. There was a desk with a portrait of Chairman Kim Il-Chung above it, a relatively bare wood bookcase, and in the corner a narrow metal frame bed covered with a green blanket. The strong smell of tobacco permeated the air.

"Please forgive Comrade Commander Riyn Chul-Moo. Our Commander has an important matter to attend to, but he will greet you very shortly," the officer said in Russian with a heavy accent. He smiled again, putting the visitors' IDs on the desk. Then he left the room.

There was only one chair, so they had to stand as they waited for Commander Riyn to return. The Major looked around. History books in Korean and Russian lined the shelf, along with small portraits of Lenin and Marx. On the desk, there was a photo of a woman and two children—the Commander's family, Viktor guessed.

Color magazines lay scattered on the floor around the desk. Viktor lifted a Russian language copy of "People's Korea" with a cover photo of Chairman Kim accepting presents from the teeming masses. Inside, they found lyrics printed in Russian of an opera, glorifying Kim as the sun that shines from above.

"Without you— our sun, Chairman Kim— there will never be a Korean nation!" Viktor read aloud, amused by the poetic lunacy. They were both old enough to remember similar 'artistic' odes for the father of the Soviet people, Comrade Stalin. Even in recent years one would find some new attempt to erect the cult of personality, now for Comrade Brezhnev. But the words here were so blunt and silly they could not stifle their laughter.

Commander Riyn Chul-Moo entered the room silently, discretely ignoring the visitor's inopportune levity. He offered the same false smile, shook Viktor and Lyubomir's hands, and sat in the chair behind the desk.

"Major Vitus, you came here from Khabarovsk?" he enquired in Russian almost devoid of any accent.

"Yes," Major Vitus answered. "One would think you were from our side as well, Commander, with how well you speak Russian."

"I completed my studies at Moscow Patrice Lumumba Institute of Nations Friendship in 1966."

"I must admit, it is remarkable, Comrade Riyn Chul-Moo. What else, besides Russian, did you study?" Viktor was sincerely amazed.

"History and International Politics," Riyn Chul-Moo replied. "But history is my passion."

"I see this from the books on your shelves." Viktor paused and then asked, "And how did you end up here?"

Riyn Chul-Moo did not expect such a direct question. He ceased smiling and stared out the window. "It is a long story; I don't want to bore you with it. By the way, did you know that our Worker's Party Secretary Kim Jong-Il, the son of Chairman Kim, was born not far from Khabarovsk?" Riyn changed the subject abruptly. "Of course, that is not the official party line, but I think it is true. I've read it in the Soviet sources."

"I did not know that." Sensing the Commander's discomfort, Viktor cut directly to the business at hand. "I am afraid we have bad news for you, Comrade Commander. It is about one of your soldiers. I believe his last name is Kim. He is a well-known fellow around Listvenny— New Urgal— Even in Urgal."

"Is he dead? Another one frozen to death?" The Commander's voice did not express any surprise or sympathy.

"Soldier Kim was murdered." Viktor exclaimed.

Viktor paused as he noticed the Commander's facial expression had turned puzzled.

"When did this happen?" Asked the Commander.

"November 4... he was discovered the next morning near Listvenny," replied Viktor.

"If this is the case, why isn't his body here yet?" Riyn Chul-Moo asked, getting up from his chair.

" You see, this is where it gets a little complicated. We believe he was a witness to a murder himself. Perhaps even a culprit. We don't know yet. This is why his body is still in Chegdomyn, being inspected by the district coroner. We hoped you could identify Kim."

The Major retrieved the photos from his leather satchel and placed them on the desk. Riyn Chul-Moo immediately scooped them up and brought them close to his eyes. Apparently, he was severely near sighted; it took him two minutes to look through them one by one.

"Yes. He was my soldier. His full name is Kim Su-Young." The Commander could not hide the distress in his voice. He lowered his shoulders and dropped his head to his chest for just a moment but quickly recovered. "Can you tell me, Comrade Major, how did this happen?"

"We're still gathering details," the Major was purposefully vague. "Possibly he was in the wrong place at the wrong time. By the way, how old was he?"

"I'm not sure—seventeen, no older than eighteen. Kim was born here a few years before I took command of this camp." Riyn Chul-Moo still sounded distressed. "It is unfortunate that occasionally soldiers freeze in the wintertime. I admit their clothes are not adequate, but it's not up to me to do anything about it. However, this is a different case, isn't it?"

"Yes, it is. But tell me, why was this soldier able to wander out of the camp so far and so often? Did he have your permission for such a privilege?"

"Of course not!" the Commander replied defiantly. "What are you implying, Comrade Major?"

"I am implying nothing, Comrade Commander." Viktor tried to be polite, realizing that he was not interrogating a suspect. "I am just stating the fact: Soldier Kim was stopped by Militia servicemen a number of times for loitering around nearby settlements and selling contraband merchandise to our citizens. So, please, give me your honest answer. Were you aware of his activities?"

"Alright, alright, Major. I might be able to answer your question." Riyn Chul-Moo sounded more agreeable. "But first, I have my own question: did you find anything on him—let's say, a sack?" He pulled a green tarpaulin sack from a drawer. "It would look like this?"

Captain Nesterenko interjected before the Major could answer. "We found this button. The rest of his clothes are still in the hands of forensics." The Captain placed a little button with Kim Il-Sung's likeness on the desk. "But there was no sack. There was a strap like the one on your sack, cut off by a sharp object. The soldiers who found the body found nothing else, and I made sure they did not touch a thing."

"Was there something of importance in his sack, Comrade Commander?" asked Viktor.

"How should I know?" exclaimed Riyn Chul-Moo irritably.

The Major did not acknowledge this inconsistency, but returned to his previous question: "Did you or didn't you know about Kim's activity outside your camp, Comrade Commander?"

"Not to the full extent, Major." The Commander's smile returned. "Look, Kim was the youngest soldier among thousands in this camp. He was still a boy, and everyone treated him as such. Kim could not work anyway, so his superiors turned a blind eye when it would come to his daily whereabouts. His Russian was good, and he was a very likable young man with the ability to sell stuff for himself and his fellow soldiers. Can you blame him for wanting a little bit more than what he was getting here? I admit I had a soft spot for this kid."

Riyn Chul-Moo picked the visitors' IDs from the desk and handed them back to Viktor and Lyubomir, indicating that the conversation was over.

"We thank you, Comrade Commander, for your help. You shall receive the soldier's body in the next couple of days. The Captain will see to it. Please pass our condolences to Kim's parents."

"Don't be concerned with this, Comrade Major. Soldier Kim Sul-Young was an orphan. His mother, our diner worker, died at his delivery." Riyn Chul-Moo concluded with a pinch of vitriol. "By the way, I couldn't help noticing you laughing while reading our national magazine. You can have a copy or two for your pleasure. Do you know the difference between us, Major?"

"I do not," the Major replied. "But I have a feeling you will enlighten us, Commander."

"We don't abandon our historic idols; we revere our national leaders like Korean Eternal President Kim or Chinese Chairman Mao or Vietnam's hero President Ho Chi Minh. And what happened to the beloved father of your nation, Josef Stalin? How often do you hear the name of the great Vladimir Lenin lately? Not often—except on holidays, you must agree? The problem is that you erect your heroes just as quickly as you destroy them."

He rose from his chair and called another officer to show the visitors to the gate.

Outside, the morning light had fully dispelled the darkness of dawn. The snow continued to fall, only a little slower.

They strode back to their vehicle, and drove down the hill, leaving the camp behind. Covered with a thick layer of pristine snow, its tents looked like surreal cottages from some fairy tale; they observed with delight the metamorphosis of the forest surrounding this magical world.

* * *

They rode back to Listvenny in silence, arriving at Lyubomir's apartment at 10:45. They found the women having tea with pastries at the table in the main room. They all looked well rested and relaxed.

"I am sorry to spoil your Saturday morning, but we must move on," Viktor said with authority. "We still have a job to do in New Urgal." Then he looked at Katerina and added,

"If you are thinking of going back to Khabarovsk soon, we have to catch the train later tonight."

"Yes, I would like to get back to Khabarovsk… if you don't need my help anymore," Katya replied.

"You don't have to leave tonight, Citizen Rogozhina. We could use your advice in analyzing the facts we have gathered so far. If you stay, we can drive back to Khabarovsk together in our car."

"I don't know what kind of expertise I can offer. But if you insist, I will stay with you a few days longer," Katya said, blushing. "Please forgive me; I'll be right back."

She rushed to the bathroom. Nina and Lyuba, standing at the door, exchanged smiles at the awkward expression on Viktor's face.

Soon after, everyone was ready to leave, and they made their way to the car. Soon, the *kozyol* headed down Donetskaya Street and parked at the New Urgal Hotel entrance, where the women disembarked. The Major and the Captain continued on to the precinct, where they found Pyotr sitting behind the desk, scanning the radio. The moment he saw the Major and Captain, he sprung from his chair and saluted.

"Do you have anything to report, Sergeant Uvalov?" Viktor was glad to see Freckles but tried not to show it.

"Comrade Major, I have very little to report except for one thing—a phone call from Doctor Goldfarb." The Sergeant handed Viktor a piece of paper. "Here is the number you can reach him today."

" Anything else?"

"Yes, for Comrade Captain. Someone by the name of Valery stopped by yesterday looking for you."

Lyubomir and Viktor exchanged a glance as they entered the Captain's office and closed the door behind them.

"Let me call Doctor Goldfarb first." Viktor dialed the number he had gotten from Pyotr. "It's ringing, but he is not picking it up." He was about to put the phone down when he said, "Oh, Doctor, is it you? Sorry to bother you at home on your day-off." Viktor sighed with relief. "Oh, this is the hospital number. Understood. I see. I am listening."

The Major pulled a piece of paper and a pencil close to him and listened attentively, occasionally nodding his head and making notes. Doctor Goldfarb spoke so loudly through the receiver that Lyubomir could hear him from across the room, but he couldn't make sense of what he was saying.

When Viktor put the receiver down, Lyubomir could not hide his curiosity. "What was so urgent that he did not want to wait until Monday?"

"Can you believe Doctor Goldfarb doesn't have a telephone at home? He has been on a waiting list since he arrived in Chegdomyn five years ago. The local Party Secretary has a phone at home, but the surgeon and district coroner does not. Strange, isn't it?"

"Nothing strange around here," Lyubomir replied. "But what did he say?"

"It was about the autopsy on the Korean soldier." Viktor pushed his notes toward the Captain. "Similar cuts and stabs by the same knives. They butchered the poor kid. The doctor found something else that was unusual: two imprints on the victim's back that look like horse hooves. We should get his written report with sketches tomorrow."

"They chased him on horseback?" The Captain sounded confounded. He paused to think. "When we searched the the Rogozhins' barn, the buggy was there, but no horse. Maybe they took the horse?"

"It looks that way," Viktor agreed. "Sergeant Lutsenko did not see any horses that morning. Although those two strangers he did see could've been hiding it behind a tree."

"Nevertheless, I am sure it might help to catch them." Lyubomir sat at the desk and began writing the report. "I believe I saw this horse when Fyodor came to speak to me a couple of weeks ago. I can definitely describe it: a large, dark brown mare, with a long thick mane and tail. And, what else? Oh yes, and a white streak between her ears going all the way down to her nostrils. "

"Rogozhin came to you to discuss something very important that day. I would like to find out more about it."

"I am sure someone whom he trusted suggested that he seeks my advice." The Captain was nervously stroking his balding head. "I know who this someone could be! I thought of him all along. And when I saw those two library books in Rogozhin's home his name crossed my mind right away."

"Whose name is it?" the Major asked impatiently.

"Yury Orlovsky. He is the crew master of the Drilling unit; he came with the Donetsk Construction crew. You met him and his fiancé Polina on the day you arrived," explained Lyubomir.

"Polina is the one who developed and printed the pictures from the crime scenes, wasn't she?" the Major continued. "So, I assume Yury could have seen those pictures and knew very well what happened. But how does it connect him personally to this homicide?"

"During the last year and a half, Yury developed a close relationship with Fyodor Rogozhin. He was visiting him at Izmailovsky regularly. Very often, he took Polina with him on these visits." The Captain paused. "I know about this from Polina. When you arrived, you witnessed my argument with Valery. Remember? He tried to persuade me to turn Polina into my informant. I refused, and it made Valery mad."

"Hold on, Captain. Let me get this straight: he needed Polina to inform on Yury. Why?" Viktor got up from the chair and moved closer to Lyubomir. "Does Valery have a special interest in Yury Orlovsky?" Asked Viktor in a lowered voice.

"I truly believe this guy has a secret file on everyone, but some of us draw his attention more than others. Yes, he does have a special interest in Orlovsky. Valery never shared this information with me, but from talking to Polina, I guessed it has something to do with his late father or his relatives. Polina knew Yury from her childhood." The Captain was almost whispering now.

"This means that Valery is also aware of the friendship between Rogozhin and Orlovsky, and doesn't want this fact exposed by our investigation." The Major became visibly satisfied with his logical conclusion. He smiled. "We have to talk to Yury immediately before he is fire-walled by KGB shenanigans. But for now, let's keep our cards close to the vest, as they say."

At this very moment, the door opened, and Freckles face appeared. "You have a visitor. It is Valery. May I send him in?"

Major did not have time to answer; Valery unceremoniously pushed Pyotr out of his way and pulled the door open.

"Good morning, comrades. I hope it was a good morning for you." Valery sat on the chair without waiting for the invitation. "I need to speak with you, Captain."

"I don't recall your name, Captain; I believe it is Captain?" Viktor affected a calm, formal demeanor. "You disregard the fact that in this room, I am the superior ranking officer. You forgot to ask my permission to enter here and to speak to Captain Nesterenko. You don't want me to report such insubordination to your commanding officer, do you?"

His face turning red, Valery slowly rose from the chair and saluted with his right hand. "I apologize, Comrade Major. I meant no disrespect. I am asking your permission to speak to Captain Nesterenko."

"Permission granted, Captain…?" Viktor insisted on getting Valery's last name.

"Captain Kirsanov, Comrade Major."

"Now, you can speak to us, Captain Kirsanov." Viktor waved him to take his seat again. "What is so urgent that you have to discuss?"

Valery hesitated, hoping to mask his frustration with the Major's humiliating admonishment in front of Captain Nesterenko.

Both Viktor and Lyubomir stared at him with exaggerated attention, making the officer even more uncomfortable. He stood up and said rather casually, "I was concerned about the situation with the murder of the Korean soldier, but I also heard that this morning you visited Commander Riyn Chul-Moo, so any possible complications were avoided. Is my assumption correct?"

"Yes, Comrade Captain, your assumption is correct." Major Vitus sounded formal. "The district coroner just let me know that he has completed Kim's autopsy. Tomorrow, Captain Nesterenko will see that the soldier's body is delivered to the Korean camp. Anything else, Comrade Kirsanov?"

Again, Valery took his time in answering, looking in turn at Viktor and then at Lyubomir. It was obvious that he did have something else on his mind. Nonetheless, he decided to leave.

"Good evening, Comrades," Valery said politely. "Thanks for your cooperation."

"You are welcome, Captain," Viktor replied in a friendly manner. "If not here, I might see you later in Khabarovsk."

"I would be honored, Major Vitus." Kirsanov turned around sharply, put his fur hat on, and left the room.

"Ooh, you were magnificent in your fury, Comrade Major. It did throw him off and put him in his proper place. Who does he think he is, after all?" Lyubomir was still speaking in a low voice but with a smile. "It doesn't matter how much he knows. It is important that we did not have to inform him about our investigation."

"I think you are right, Captain," Viktor agreed. "However, we have to hurry to get a statement from Yury Orlovsky. Can you help find him and bring him in ASAP?"

Nesterenko grabbed his coat and hat, ready to run. "His barracks are not far from here. We'll be back soon."

But he stopped abruptly in the receiving room right in front of Polina, who had at that moment entered the door of the precinct.

"Hi Polina. I was just going to run to bring Yury here," Lyubomir explained. "Has he come with you? Call him in."

"No, he is not with me, Comrade Captain." Polina swiped the tears from her cheeks with her mitten. "I cannot do anything with him; he is drunk and crazy. You've got to help him."

"I was just on my way to see him." The Captain took Polina by the hand and led her into his office. "I believe you have already met Major Vitus the other day. Stay here and talk to him. I'll run to the dormitory and try to calm Yury down."

"Wait, Captain. I have the quickest way to sober him up." Viktor reacted. "Stop by the diner, ask for a jar of tomato juice, two fresh eggs, and a glass of pickle brine. Mix them up in a glass and make Yury drink it at once. Then bring him here."

"I'll try to remember that," Lyubomir shouted as he hurried out the door.

Viktor sat Polina in the chair and went to the opposite side of the desk to look for coffee.

"Comrade Sergeant!" called the Major. "Please find all the available cups and bring them here."

The young woman pulled an envelope from her pocket. "Here are the pictures I processed yesterday. Comrade Lieutenant asked me for them." Polina leaned forward and put the envelope on the desk in front of Viktor. "Those pictures were taken at Izmailovsky."

"You're right. I've heard you are well acquainted with this place, aren't you?" The Major tried to sound merely curious rather than formal. "You visited Fyodor Rogozhin there?"

"The last weekend before the Red October Day celebration. Yury took me. I don't know why." Polina spoke slowly as if she was searching for the right words. "Fyodor promised to teach Yury how to trap a sable or fox. He got this idea to make a fur coat for me. Don't you find it silly? Fyodor did not. I think he gave Yury this idea after telling him how he made a mink coat for his daughter Katerina. She is very pretty; we saw her picture. She is an actress and lives in Khabarovsk."

Viktor pulled his chair closer to Polina. "So, you and Yury were in Rogozhin's house Saturday and Sunday of October 29 and 30, staying overnight?"

"Actually, we slept in his house two nights because we went there Friday late afternoon," Polina told the Major. "Yury was working that day until five."

"So, tell me more about your last visit." asked Viktor.

"Fyodor was very happy to see us. He fed us with his tasty meat and cabbage soup and let us sleep on the oven top. He really liked Yury, and Yury loved the old man. They could talk for hours about all kinds of stuff." Polina slowed down again, trying to gather her memories. "And yet, that time, Fyodor looked preoccupied with something, worried about something. When they were leaving for the *Taiga* early the next morning, Fyodor told me to always keep the door locked with both steel bolts -I did not recall him locking his doors ever before, but I hadn't given it too much thought until…"

"Until?" Viktor became impatient. "Something happened while Fyodor and Yury were away?"

"Thank God, nothing happened to me, but…" She paused for a second or two and re-started her story. "Around dusk, I was just about to climb back to my warm nest on the top of the oven and read one of the books which Yury had brought for Fyodor when I heard heavy steps on the porch. Then there was a nudge on the door. I knew that Fyodor and Yury could not have returned so soon, and I remembered not to open the door for anyone else. I decided to stay quiet. I could hear them talking, and rather loudly, so it was possible to understand…"

"Could you see them? Were there two of them?" Viktor interrupted.

"I could not see them; I was afraid to look through the window facing the porch because they might have noticed me," Polina explained. "But I heard two distinctive voices in their conversation. One was clear, a little bit high-pitched, and the other husky, guttural."

Viktor encouraged the young woman to continue. "Please go on. What were they talking about?"

"The high-pitched voice said he could not believe how stubborn and obnoxious this old man had been during their first meeting and how it was disgusting when the old man threw a picture of his pretty young daughter in his face. He said he had a strong urge to hurt the old man right at that moment but, somehow, he restrained himself because their dealings were not over. The man with the husky voice praised his friend for being wise and asked about the old man's whereabouts. The reply was that if the horse and buggy were in the barn, the old man could've gone by train to Khabarovsk to alert his "prima-donna daughter.""

Viktor made a sudden gesture to halt Polina's story and exclaimed, "Alert her of what?" He could not hide his agitation.

"I'm not sure." Polina was taken aback. "First of all, they were pacing the porch while speaking, and secondly, I couldn't always understand the words they were using—some weird words, like they spoke in tongues. Nevertheless, it was obvious that they wouldn't mind getting hold of the old man's daughter to hurt her too."

Polina went silent. So did Viktor for a minute, trying to digest what he had just learned.

"Of course, you shared all this with Fyodor and Yury when they came back."

"Yes, I did. Fyodor assured us that it was nothing to worry about, that he knew how to deal with those strangers," the young woman replied.

"But you didn't say a word about it to Captain Nesterenko? Why, may I ask?" Viktor sounded a bit irritated.

"Yury told me not to discuss their visit to Izmailovsky with anyone. That morning in the *Taiga*, he told me Fyodor asked him about Captain Nesterenko. After Yury told him how well-respected the Captain was and how much he personally liked him, Fyodor acknowledged his intention to visit the Captain in the next couple of days to discuss some very important private matters. This is why I was quiet until now." Tears began to run down Polina's cheeks. "Yury took Fyodor's death very hard. In the last few days, I've watched him completely fall apart and I cannot help him. And when Yury is broken, it takes a long time to fix him."

"Don't be so pessimistic." Viktor felt sympathetic and stroked Polina's head. "The Captain and I will do everything to help him with his grieving. And do you know the best way to do this? To concentrate on catching those bastards who killed Fyodor and threatened his daughter Katerina. By the way, she is here, in New Urgal, and will be happy to meet you and Yury, friends of her late father."

"Seriously?" The young woman raised her head and looked at Major with hope. "I am sure that will cheer Yury up. But first, he has to get out of this drunken stupor."

"I completely agree with you." Viktor returned to the chair behind the desk. "So, how about a cup of coffee?"

"I would love it."

Viktor unwound the electric cord and looked for a wall outlet when he heard a noise in the reception room. It was Captain Nesterenko, who had just rushed into the office, visibly overwrought.

"You are alone!" Viktor exclaimed. "Where is Citizen Orlovsky? I presume my remedy did not work."

"I would say it did work." Lyubomir sounded a bit rattled. "It took some time, though, to make him drink your recipe cocktail. I must admit, the guy drank a load—at least two bottles of pure alcohol. I wonder how he obtained the stuff when we have a strict prohibition policy in New Urgal since BAM started. Can anyone explain it for me?" He glanced at Polina.

"The truck drivers bring this stuff from Chegdomyn if you pay a few extra Rubles," Polina reluctantly informed them without going into details.

"I see. Thanks. Now I'll know this trick too." It was hard to say whether Captain Nesterenko was joking or not. "Where was I? Oh yes, Yury was mumbling something about his late father and mother, his uncle, and about the people of the city of Zaporizhe in general who died of some calamity. It was hard to make any sense of what he was saying. When Yury recognized me, his mumbling transformed into an expression of his utmost respect toward me. Then he demanded to know whether I had respect for him. He blurted out the question a dozen times. After I assured him of our mutual respect, he agreed to drink your remedy, Comrade Major."

"And then what happened?" both Viktor and Polina asked almost simultaneously.

"Yury grabbed his guitar and started singing from the repertoire of Vladimir Vysotsky. Then he began sobbing profusely, returning to the subjects of his dead parents, his sorrow for Fyodor, his love for you, Polina, and, again, about his respect for me. He even hugged me." Lyubomir paused and smiled. "Eventually, I noticed that the remedy had achieved its sobering effect; he stopped sobbing and mumbling, his eyes were no longer watery, his speech became more coherent. So, I suggested that he take a quick warm shower and come with me to the precinct, where Polina was waiting. He reluctantly agreed and even looked around for soap and towel."

"So, why are you here, and he is not?" Viktor asked.

"Because he suddenly felt dizzy and weak, almost falling. I helped him to his bed. He lay down and closed his eyes. In a minute, he was asleep." Lyubomir concluded, "I don't think we are going to hear from him until tomorrow or the next day."

"He must go to work on Monday," Polina added. "An entire drilling unit depends on him."

"I'm sure he will." Viktor felt disappointed. "I was hoping to get his statement today and be able to leave for Khabarovsk as soon as possible. We have a lot of evidence to process in the forensic lab and a lot of gathered facts to check."

"Are there any other people you would like to talk to?" Captain Nesterenko tried to alleviate the Major's concerns. "So, the rest of today will not be wasted?"

Viktor perused the notes in his black pocketbook, turning pages back and forth. "How about Roman Derenchuk, Myron's son?" he asked after staring at one of the pages. "You mentioned that he was also a person of interest for our friend Valery. Am I correct?"

"You are correct, Comrade Major. Of course, I can send for him right away," Lyubomir responded and walked out of the office.

Viktor turned to the young woman still sitting in the chair on the opposite side of the desk.

"Polina, dear, I am afraid we have to postpone our coffee. It would be best if you now attend to Yury and nurse him back to a sober state, so he can work on Monday. Make sure to bring him here tomorrow, the latest after the end of his shift on Monday. I will introduce you to Katerina. Our trip back home can be delayed for another day or two, I think."

"Okay, then. I'll go." Polina got up and put her fur hat on. "Most likely, he'll see you Monday around five."

"Thanks."

Now Viktor was alone and could put his thoughts in order. He considered what he would ask Roman; he and his father had a lot to contribute to the story of Fyodor Rogozhin. Maybe there was a link between Fyodor's life in the GULAG and his demise. Or, perhaps, his tragic end was the result of an unsettled family feud. Who knew? Viktor wouldn't even discount some religious motive for the man's murder. Thoughts like these buzzed about his head like bees. One thing was clear—he needed more background and more personal information to fully understand the world of Fyodor Rogozhin, his connection to God, his relationship with his children, and his feelings about the country that had been so unkind to him and his people, the Old Believers.

And then there was Katerina Rogozhina. Thinking of her more and more often, Viktor felt emotionally torn: his attraction and longing for her affection mingled with doubt— an almost visceral fear of rejection that seemed to threaten his very existence. These feelings had tormented Viktor since he laid eyes upon this remarkable woman, yet she was a source of joy and hope for future happiness.

Suddenly, it dawned on him: now Katerina could be in danger too. Wasn't it a real threat that Polina heard from the men who tried to get a hold of Fyodor the days before killing him? He must protect her. But how? It would be almost impossible to guard her around the clock. Besides, who would authorize him to assign twenty-four-hour security details for a common citizen? It was unheard of in the history of Khabarovsky UVD.

For Viktor, it had become obvious. The only sure way to remove the danger was to catch those killers before they could make good on their threat—easier said than done. There were still so many unanswered questions regarding who and why. He had to find these answers quickly.

At this point, Viktor began doubting his decision to delay their return to Khabarovsk. What additional information would he gain by spending an extra day here in New Urgal? But his detective's intuition wanted him to talk to Roman Derenchuk and Yury Orlovsky. Viktor was sure these two men could give him a glimpse into the last couple of weeks of Fyodor's life, and at least a hint of the real motive behind the murder. Yes, he had made the right decision. There was another benefit: the longer Katya stayed in his company, the safer she was.

Chapter 8

When he heard the entrance door open and close a second later, Viktor glanced at his watch. It was five after six. Captain Nesterenko came back empty-handed again, but he did not look upset.

"I found Roman," Lyubomir reported. "He is at home. He must finish important family stuff, and he will be here in thirty to forty minutes. I suggest we go to the diner and grab something to eat."

"That is a good idea," Viktor agreed. "What about Katya and Nina? They probably wouldn't mind joining us."

"Let me call the hotel and find it out." Lyubomir grabbed the telephone. "I think we also have to ask Pyotr if he is hungry. By the way, his day shift is over."

Shortly, everyone gathered at the diner for supper. The women looked well rested. Once seated, the ladies seemed to pick up a rather pleasant and humorous conversation which was constantly interrupted by their laughter.

"Did you have a good day, ladies?" Viktor interjected in a jokingly gallant manner.

"Oh yes, we did, indeed." Nina was reluctant to break away from something she was saying at that moment and replied with delay. "We spent some time getting acquainted with the lovely new settlement, with some help from the local Komsomol Secretary Alexandre Golovin. After his tour, we returned to the hotel, where another visitor was waiting to speak to us, the reporter from the newspaper *Gudok*, Leonid Gordin."

"What did he want to speak about?" Viktor asked rather alarmingly. "I hope you did not tell him anything related to the investigation."

"I don't believe Leonid would ask questions like that." Captain Nesterenko jumped right in. "He was away for a few days, visiting his colleagues at Birobidjan regional newspaper, and I doubt he knew about the murder at all to begin with."

"Believe it or not, he did hear about what happened in Izmailovsky," Nina replied. "After Katya told him who she was, he acknowledged that he knew Fyodor Rogozhin and had even met him once."

"Did Leonid say where he met Fyodor?" Lyubomir asked.

Katerina joined the conversation. "No, he did not elaborate, but I understood their meeting hadn't taken place at Izmailovsky. He alluded to the fact that he had never visited this picturesque hamlet, although he had been invited to do so a few weeks back."

"I think I have an idea who told him about Izmailovsky and about Rogozhin," the Captain said and paused for a while, falling into deep thought. "Only Polina or Yury. Most likely Polina— she and Leonid are friends."

"And that was the extent of your conversation with Gordin related to the case? Nothing more?" Viktor asked. Seeing both women nodding in agreement, he continued. "Did you have a good time after that?"

"Yes. We spent the rest of the day in our comfy room, relaxing and bonding. Didn't we, Ninochka?" Katerina replied, smiling. "But now, we are starved. Shall we eat?"

"Great suggestion." Viktor looked at Katya and smiled too. "We must be back at the precinct very soon, to not miss our next visitor."

"Who would that be?" Katerina asked. "Anybody I know?"

"Yes, indeed." Viktor was taken by surprise and replied reluctantly. "It is your half-brother Roman Derenchuk."

"Seriously?"

"Yes, Citizen Rogozhina. As a matter of fact, you may join us for this meeting," Viktor said.

The rest of the time went by rather quickly and in relative silence, Pyotr helped Nina with her coat, and they left for the hotel. Katerina, following the Major and Captain, crossed the street to the precinct. They did not find any visitors in the reception room and proceeded into Nesterenko's office.

Lyubomir sat Katerina in one of the chairs in the room corner near the lamp and gave her a magazine he had accidentally taken with him that morning at the Korean camp. "Please read it. I highly recommend it. It is so funny. I could not leave it behind."

Katerina politely followed his advice and began reading the Russian version of "People's Korea."

When the Captain saw her smile, he turned to Viktor and waved him to the reception room. There, after closing the door behind them, he said in a low voice, "Did you remember, during our conversation at supper, I mentioned that I had an idea who told Gordin about Fyodor?

"Yes, I did take notice of it. And?" Viktor replied, whispering as well.

"It hit me then, but I did not want to say it in Katya's presence and upset her." Lyubomir could not hide his agitation. "It dawned on me why Fyodor couldn't wait for my return at the office. In my absence, Leonid Gordin walked in and tried to strike a conversation with the man who would impress anyone."

"How would it force Fyodor to leave so abruptly and not to let you know?" Viktor continued, still whispering.

"I am not sure. Perhaps something that Leonid said prompted him to leave and postpone talking to me." Lyubomir paused. "Tomorrow, I will find out from Gordin what happened then."

"You do that. I am more concerned with Derenchuk avoiding us, Captain," Viktor said in a higher tone of voice. "Perhaps our friend Valery had something to do with it?"

"I cannot say, I don't know. However, I have a better question." Lyubomir said forcefully yet in a lower voice. "Do you really need to have Katerina here during our questioning of Derenchuk?"

"I do have my reasons, Comrade Captain," the Major replied, trying to sound more official. "Considering that our man of interest was handled previously by a KGB officer and wasn't very forthcoming, I want him to be a little distracted, slightly off balance. That's why I asked her to come."

At this very moment, the front door swung wide open, and a rather tall, athletically built man in his early thirties entered the reception room. There was an apologetic smile on his large round face. He took his fur hat off and fixed his unruly blond hair.

"I am sorry for making you wait. Some never-ending parenting business: my daughter has a math test at school. She is only seven."

"Don't worry, Citizen Derenchuk. Thank you for coming." The Major stepped toward the long-awaited visitor and shook his hand. "Let's go into the Captain's office and talk. Shall we?"

Everyone took their places: Captain Nesterenko behind his desk, Major Vitus perched at the edge of the desk, and Roman Derenchuk across from them. When he lowered his body into the chair, he noticed Katerina, who had stopped reading and stared at him steadfastly. He was surprised but tried not to show that to the officers. He sprung up, approached Katya, and tried to kiss her on the cheek. It looked rather awkward and inappropriate. They both felt embarrassed, and Roman hastily returned to his seat.

"It's getting late, so let's not waste any time," the Major began. "Do you know what happened at Izmailovsky a few days ago?"

"Yes, I do. The entire settlement is in shock." Roman turned in the direction of Katerina with a sympathetic expression on his face. She did not show any reaction; she just lowered her head.

The Major noticed it and continued, "Do you have any idea who had a motive to hurt Fyodor Rogozhin?"

"What makes you think I do, Comrade Major?" Derenchuk replied, looking directly at Viktor.

"For starters, you visited Rogozhin at Izmailovsky not long ago. Didn't you? Can you elaborate on this?"

"Actually, it was more than a month ago. I never knew Fyodor before." Roman answered. "In her last letter, Mama Dasha informed me that my half-sister lived with her father Fyodor Rogozhin in *khutor* Izmailovsky, somewhere in the western part of Khabarovsky Krai. When I learned that this hamlet was only 13km from New Urgal, I decided to pay them a visit. That's all."

The Major pressed on. "Who else did you find in Khabarovsky Krai?"

"He found me."

"Who found you?"

"My father did, Myron Zozulya." Roman was almost mumbling.

"How did this happen? Please speak more clearly," Viktor insisted.

"I think Mama Dasha had been in touch with him for some time after he was released from the camp. She gave him my address in New Urgal, so he could write to me."

"Have you visited him lately?"

"He wrote me a letter, asking to visit with us in New Urgal. I couldn't say no, so he came at the end of September and stayed with us for almost three weeks."

"Did you tell Captain Kirsanov about your guest?"

This question found Roman unprepared. He hesitated to answer for a while. Katerina also looked at Viktor with some confusion but remained silent.

"Yes, we had talked about my father's visit," Roman replied reluctantly. "I guessed Kirsanov didn't care…"

"So, did you visit Rogozhin alone or together with your father?" Viktor cut him off.

"The first time, I was alone. I did not know how Fyodor would react to my visit to begin with." Roman explained. "He wasn't thrilled, but he was friendly. He asked me if I remembered my late mother. I did not know what to tell him; I was too little when she died. The only mother I knew was Mama Dasha." Roman became emotional and stopped talking.

Viktor gave him only a minute to get hold of himself and then asked, "So, did you tell Fyodor that your father Myron Zozulya had come to visit and was staying with you at New Urgal?"

"I did. I did tell him about that. He got excited and asked if we could all meet next time, either at his home or mine." Now Roman's voice sounded more confident. "I invited him to my home, although I wasn't sure how my wife Valentina would take it. She didn't feel comfortable with my father, a former *zek*, sleeping in the next room with our daughter, you know."

Viktor considered this for only a moment, then resumed his questioning. He wanted to keep up the pace, to not afford Derenchuk time to weigh his answers. "And, when did this next meeting take place?"

"It happened three days later, on Saturday," Roman replied. "Fyodor arrived in his buggy around noon. Before that, Valentina prepared a nice dinner, left it on the stove, then took our daughter to a musical rehearsal at school. My father had been very jittery the previous night. I do not think he slept at all. Nevertheless, when they met, there were some hugs and some scant tears. Later, we had dinner together; some drinks too, quite a few of them— between my father and me, of course. Then Fyodor and Myron reminisced about their miserable life in the camp. It seemed they forgot I was even there. I just sat and listened."

* * *

Myron Zozulya had been in the GULAG Lagopunkt № 4382 for two months already when Fyodor Rogozhin arrived there at the end of 1947. It was unlikely that they would ever meet in a camp of almost two thousand prisoners. They differed in their age; they had their own distinctive personalities and life experiences; they came from places that were a world apart. Nevertheless, at the end of 1949, the paths of these men did cross.

For any newcomer, life in the first few months was extremely tough. The guards sought to break their spirits from the start, to take away the will to do anything but work, sleep, and eat. They managed this through constant emotional and physical humiliation: assigning them to the dirtiest duties. Some guards enjoyed all this, while others were so lazy they would delegate the task to the criminal *zeks*. All complaints were ignored or even punished with more beating and humiliation.

Good looking and somewhat spoiled by his relatively comfortable life, Myron became one of the "lucky" ones. He fell under the wings of a career criminal, nicknamed Goose. Perhaps it was his beak of a nose or abnormally large Adam's apple that earned him such a respectable name. No one cared. Despite his small stature, the man was extremely violent, as Myron learned on his first visit to clean himself in the bathhouse. With two huge bodyguards at his wings, Goose approached the naked Myron and informed him that he would now be Goose's *suka (a bitch)*.

The naïve prisoner did not understand what this meant, did not know the language of the *zona*, that strange dialect called *phenya* invented by the criminals of the Czarist prisons a hundred years earlier and still in use today.

Myron eventually took the meaning when Goose proceeded with his intentions. Myron pushed back; he was taller and stronger and could have snapped Goose's neck like a twig. But the other men jumped Myron, grabbed him across the body, clamped his head, and forced him to kneel. He could not resist anymore. He screamed, but no one came to help. He cried, but it did not stop Goose and his *pakhans* from violating his human dignity and manhood.

These incidents soon became routine, part of every scheduled visit to the bathhouse. Soon Myron refused to wash. After his work detail, he would crawl under his *nary* with his daily bowl of meatless cabbage soup and hide from the goons until bedtime. Still, they would drag him from underneath, confiscate his food ration, and give him another beating. The message was clear: Myron must accept his fate. There was no escape from this living hell, except for Myron to shut down all his mental faculties. He became a broken man, a zombie without willpower, desire, or ambition. He only worked, ate, slept, and above all, obeyed.

One cold morning, Myron was called into Captain Vasyuta's office, where he found his wife, Olecya. Myron could not believe his eyes; he thought it must be a fantasy of his own making. But he knew it wasn't a dream by the look on Olecya's face, the love of his life and the mother of his child. He saw in her eyes the reflection of a monster. No wonder she did not recognize him at first, and when she did, it frightened her so much she couldn't stop crying.

Myron's reaction was typical for a person in his mental state. He felt less of a man, less of a human being. He felt pity from Olecya, who wiped her tears and moved towards him, trying to grab his hands. His hands were so dirty, the stench from his body so repulsive, that she instinctively sprang back and covered her face. By the pity in her eyes, he felt himself not a human. Myron wanted to run and crawl under his *nary*. Even in his feeble mind, he knew that Olecya must be spared from such misery. Myron shut down his mind again, falling into a deep stupor. He refused to remain in the room with his wife.

"I remember reading about this meeting in Darya's letter," Katerina said in a quiet voice, as if talking to herself. "They had one more encounter later. Didn't they?"

"Oh, yes, they did," Roman replied eagerly. "Their next and last meeting was long, and just as miserable."

"How did your father cross paths with Fyodor?" Viktor interjected. He did not want Roman to upset Katya by continuing this subject.

"My understanding is that it happened after Fyodor met my mother," Roman resumed. "She recognized the fact that Fyodor was more fortunate and asked him to help Myron, who was in a dire situation."

* * *

Indeed, Fyodor's fate in the GULAG Lagopunkt № 4382 was dramatically different from Myron's. The guards and their deputy *zeks* tried to break him the same as any new political prisoner, but he prevailed over his would-be tormentors. How? Yes, he cracked a few skulls his first week in camp, for which he was punished with twenty-four hours of solitary confinement. But more than his extraordinary physical strength, it was his indomitable spirit drawn from his deep religious conviction. The man exuded a power of will so fierce that the other prisoners had almost no choice but granting him their respect and trust.

He was always calm and collected. He spoke in a low tone, never raising his voice. His clear blue eyes expressed nothing but compassion. Although his head and beard were shaved, Fyodor still had the look of a biblical figure. It was easy to recognize the preacher in him. Prisoners, both political and criminal, even the guards began seeking his advice, or just some solace in their everyday struggle.

This didn't go unnoticed by the Lagopunkt № 4382 administration. Several times, Major Krotov, the camp commandant, offered Fyodor the position of brigadier. He would report any suspicious activity in exchange for certain perks and privileges. He accepted, though he refused outright to snitch; he was no *pridurok*.

So Fyodor took under his command misfits and problem prisoners, treating them fairly and protecting them from unnecessary injury or abuse. His brigade was deliberately given the hardest job assignments with the highest output norms, and he met all challenges; his men always performed the best work possible, even in adverse weather conditions.

And the perks for his brigade soon followed: lightened workloads, larger rations, extra cigarettes and the like. As the brigadier, Fyodor received his own privileges: his own bed, days off, and visits to the dry goods store outside the *zona*. There he could buy fresh carrots and radishes, stationary, and most importantly candles, which were forbidden inside the wire fence.

Fyodor needed the candles for the prayer services he conducted in secrecy. The risk was great and the punishment severe, but he knew the importance of faith in God for the lives of the prisoners. Every Sunday morning nearly a hundred prisoners and even some guards gathered in Fyodor's barracks to hear his sermon and join him in prayer. Only once, some *pridurok* from a rival brigade informed on them, but some loyal guards smoothed it over with Commandant Krotov.

In late December 1950, Fyodor met Olecya while visiting the village store. Their affinity was instant, transforming into irresistible attraction in their next few meetings. It was an unexpected and long-forgotten feeling for Fyodor, and he embraced it with all his heart. Olecya, on the contrary, found the prospect of falling in love with a prisoner—a much older and religious man no less—confusing and frightening. She came to this forsaken land to find her wrongly accused husband, expecting to give him support and hope. Instead, she found a man broken beyond hope, who could not even stand the sight of her. Olecya was devastated, and perhaps this vulnerability was the force that pulled her closer and closer to Fyodor. She felt loved and secure when she was next to him.

Perhaps it was his love for Olecya that moved Fyodor to take her husband under his wing? He convinced Goose to forsake his favorite victim, whether through the power of his will or the strength of his hands. Fyodor moved Myron to his barracks and assigned him a place on a plank close to his own. Everyone understood that this unfortunate young man had come under Fyodor's personal protection. Little by little, Myron regained his old personality, his confidence, and a sense of security in his new life. The two men became friends.

*   *   *

Viktor interrupted Roman. "How did Myron react when he found out about your mother and Fyodor?"

"It ended their friendship," Roman replied. "However, that didn't happen until the fall of 1951, when Myron received the news."

The letter Myron received from Dasha was like a bomb exploding in his face. She informed him of Olesya's untimely death while delivering a baby girl. Darya learned the truth from Olecya about Fyodor and their relationship.

Myron read and reread the letter, trying to comprehend it. He thought himself healed from the nightmare of that winter when Olecya had come to visit. Now, his Olecya had died; she left behind a child, but the child was not his. It was his dear friend's, who secretly had an affair with his wife. Myron's head spun. He shrieked like a wounded animal and threw his body on the floor, crying.

His fellow-prisoners gathered around him, consoling him, trying to find out what was wrong with him. Myron sat straight but continued wailing until he noticed his friend, who was rushing toward him with a worried expression on the face. He sprang to his feet, grabbing Fyodor by his neck and squeezing with all the strength he could muster. Fyodor stumbled at first, but he quickly regained his footing and shook Myron off. He then pinned

Myron on the floor and held him down tightly yet gently. He did not want to hurt him, just to calm him. Fyodor waved to the people surrounding them to disperse. Everybody obeyed, leaving them alone in the middle of the barracks.

Myron lay on the floor, now in a fetal position, sobbing. Fyodor was hovering over him, stroking his closely cropped head with his left hand, trying to comfort him, when he noticed the letter that Myron clutched in his fist. Fyodor reached for it, but Myron buried his hand underneath his body and looked up at Fyodor with anger.

At that moment, Fyodor understood the letter concerned Olecya, and the reason for his young friend's anger. Who wouldn't be? What apology could he offer Myron that would ease his pain? There was none, especially now when the wound was so fresh and raw. Better to leave him alone, let him cool off, and digest what he had just learned. Fyodor walked away from Myron; sure he would have his chance to apologize later. He did not know then that he had lost the love of his life in exchange for a daughter whom Fyodor would adore and cherish for the rest of his days.

The friends did not speak to each other for the next two weeks. Fyodor felt sorry for Myron, but what happened had happened for a reason known only to God. For his part, Myron could not reconcile his love and admiration for his friend and protector with his betrayal, the deep-burning anger and desire for vengeance it wrought. But the more he contemplated the matter, the more he concluded that revenge would not bring Olecya back and would not bring him solace.

* * *

"And what did you observe during their reunion? Did you feel any animosity Myron might have harbored toward Fyodor after all these years?" Viktor again interrupted Roman.

"No animosity, not at all," protested Roman. "They were laughing, clapping each other on the shoulders, crying a little when speaking about my mother. They hugged when they said goodbye. I observed plenty of that. But animosity? No, there was not even a hint of ill will between them."

"Thank you for the invaluable information you have provided, Citizen Derenchuk." Viktor shook Roman's hand, letting him know he could leave, before asking, "Do you remember exactly when your father left New Urgal, and did you ever hear from him afterwards?"

"I put him on the train to Komsomolsk with a stopover in Khabarovsk at 21:05 on October 27," Roman replied without any hesitation. "I am not sure what day it was, though. I received a letter from him a couple of days ago, informing me that he had arrived home at Zyma safely, without any problem, on October 29, and found his young, adopted daughters in good health."

He stood up and pulled the folded envelope from his trouser pocket, ready to hand it to the Major. Viktor ignored it but walked with him to the door, waiting for it to close before turning to the others.

"So, what are your feelings about his father's story?" Viktor addressed both the Captain and Katya. "Sounded fairly credible, didn't it?"

"Yes, it did. Roman's observations were very keen too," Lyubomir replied and turned to Katya. "Don't you think, Citizen Rogozhina?

She nodded. "I believe Roman."

"I wouldn't mind talking to somebody else from the camp though," Viktor said slowly and glanced at his watch. "Hey, it's quarter to nine. Let's call it a day. We accomplished a lot, didn't we? We are all exhausted. Go home to your lovely wife, Captain. Get some good rest. I don't want to see you here until Monday. Understood?"

"Yes, Comrade Major. See you then at 14:00." Lyubomir saluted Katerina and Viktor, grabbed his winter coat, and rushed outside to his car.

Viktor desperately wanted to stay here with Katya for a little longer. He hoped they would have a conversation or just sit in silence, looking at each other. He would be happy either way. However, it seemed Katerina did not share Viktor's feelings in this moment. She got up from the chair, pulled her shawl over her head, and beckoned him to the exit.

"Don't forget to turn the lights off and close the door tight, Comrade Major. It is going to be a very cold night. We will need this room warm," Katya said with a hint of uneasiness.

Since early afternoon, the weather had changed dramatically. The heavy snowfall had ended. The thick clouds had moved west, replaced by extremely cold arctic air from the north. The sky was strewn with thousands of small twinkling dots and one big full moon rising over the tall pines on the edge of the *Taiga*. The virgin snow covering the little settlement glowed in its bright light.

On the way to the hotel, Katerina and Viktor remained silent— only their steps in the crisp snow could be heard. He followed her at a distance, but close enough to catch her in case she slipped. Arriving at the hotel, they muttered 'good night' and went in opposite directions.

Chapter 9

Monday, November 14, 6:00 o'clock. Khutor Izmailovski.
Sargent Darsulov sat quietly in a chair next to the cabin door, the rifle across his lap. It was the darkest spot on the porch. The moon was full and the air bitterly cold. The deep frost didn't bother Darsulov. Since he was very young, his father would order him to bathe in cold winter streams. It was never pleasant, the anticipation of being engulfed in freezing water never eased and neither did its initial shock. As a boy, he hated his father for forcing him to endure it. But the old man's motives made sense to him now; he had grown impervious to extreme cold. And this ability had served him well his entire adult life, just as it was serving him now.

Staying awake was another matter. Like many Soviet men his age, Darsulov fought in the War. He joined in '44, when he was only 16. He was with the Red Army when they took Berlin. The army taught him how to keep watch; fight off the sleep while remaining focused. Still, after sitting here for hours, the Sargent found himself struggling to stay vigilant. He shook his head and decided to go inside to make more coffee.

It was then that he heard a crunch of frosted snow and a low rumble of male voices. The sounds were coming from a cluster of trees to the left of the cabin. He lifted the rifle to his shoulder on zeroed on the tree line. within seconds two silhouettes slowly walked into the moonlit clear. One was much larger than the other.

"Halt where you are!" Darsulov said in calm tone that surprised the two intruders. The shorter man crouched and dove behind the cabin. The larger man sprinted back towards the tree line. Darsulov fired one round, but missed, cursing himself for his poor aim and for revealing his position. He leapt over the porch railing and took cover behind a pile of chopped wood in front of the house. His senses razor sharp again, like in the war. He remembered how much he enjoyed this, fear and all. He heard the crunch of feet on frosty snow moving around the cabin, trying to outflank him. These men were veterans too, he thought to himself as he braced his back against the wood pile and aimed his rifle.

He saw the smaller man now, large knife in hand, rolling out from behind the cover of the cabin wall. The man made himself the smallest target he could and moved quickly toward Darsulov. The Sargent exhaled and fired. One shot. It hit something heavy and the small man went limp without a sound. Darsulov moved again rapidly, rolling to his left between the woodpile and the cabin, landing in a crouch with rifle at the shoulder, facing the direction of the trees. He watched the big man run at him, full gallop, axe in hand, savage scream on his lips. He aimed again, exhaled again, and fired his third shot. The big man spun around and went down, his war cry silenced.

Darsulov's ears still rang from the gunfire, but he perceived the sound of movement. The little man was right behind him, staggering but still fast, knife glistening in the moonlight. No time to fire, Darsulov spun around, driving the stock of his rifle into the attacker's wrist. The knife slid away on the snow. But the little man was tough and agile. He kicked at Darsulov's knee, and the sergeant lost his balance for just a second. That second was enough to make a difference. The little man lunged toward him with his knife. In another second, the heavy blade was in his hand again; he attacked using an underhand stroke. Darsulov regained his balance and blocked the attack with the rifle, the blade just missing his ribs. He followed up quickly, using the rifle stock to put the little man down for good. He was sure the big man would be right behind him as he spun around into a crouch. Emptiness. The big man wasn't there. He had disappeared back into the trees. Darsulov ran towards where the big man went down. No blood. How?! He was sure he hit the target. He followed the tracks into the woods, where the moonlight was barely helpful. He continued tracking the big man for a good kilometer until he reached a flowing creek, where the tracks disappeared. It was useless now. The man had vanished into the fog of the early dawn.

* * *

7:00 that same morning. **New Urgal**. Katerina heard heavy footsteps outside the door and opened her eyes. Just one look at the vaulted ceiling of this former barracks returned her from her dream to reality. Like every dream in times of tragedy, this one was very illusive, full of chimeras and deceptive visions.

The last four days had been extremely emotional, but not just in a negative way. Katerina considered herself a confident yet reserved person, who can handle any stressful situation calmly. No doubt that was something she had inherited from her father. And now, Katya learned that it was okay to reveal her grief to strangers, to share some of her pain with them. And these strangers responded with support and compassion.

Major Vitus was another story. Katerina could not deny her attraction to him, though he was far more reserved than the men she was normally surrounded by in the creative world.

He was handsome, for sure, well-read and cultured, with a wide range of interests. Yet there was a darkness in him - perhaps an inevitable byproduct of his job - that Katerina feared was impenetrable. In spite of this, Viktor immediately felt like someone she could trust completely. At the same time, he also made her realize how vulnerable she suddenly was. There was the unexpected departure of her only friend, mentor, and lover, the Theater Director Alexandre Garanin. She had her first starring role in an upcoming production of Shakespeare (the cursed play! she mused to herself bitterly), and now the tragic death of her father, whom Katerina knew she would miss immensely, though lately they had not been on good terms. No matter how much he adored his daughter, Fyodor had expressed his disapproval of Katya's relationship with Garanin, a married man. She knew his disapproval was not so much a religious one, but more a genuine concern of a protective father. Katerina, in turn, had argued that of all people, Fyodor should be the last person who had the right to blame her for such indiscretion, especially given her lover's circumstances.

Alexandre and his wife Olga Shatalova, the Drama Theater's veteran actress, were already separated a few years pending a scandalous divorce. Katerina did not bear any responsibility for that. The family was on the brink of falling apart long before Katerina transferred to the Drama Theater from the Children's Theater. She did not initiate her relationship with Garanin either. Alexandre had approached Katya and proclaimed his love, which he professed to carrying for quite a while. She couldn't deny that she liked this elegant man, a true Moscow-bred intellectual and talented drama director.

At first, Katerina doubted his intentions, but she eventually accepted Alexandre's advances. Perhaps she wanted to believe that his feelings were genuine. She needed a man who would wake up the woman in her, satisfy her intellectual curiosity, guide her in her acting career and provide support in her everyday life. For the last two years, Katerina honestly believed that Alexandre was that man and hoped that their relationship would become permanent.

And yet, Fyodor, who supported her daughter's aspirations ever since she applied to the Khabarovsky School of Dramatic Arts, did not trust Garanin and did not approve of their liaison. Perhaps, being her wise father, he knew better.

Today, Katerina began seeing things in a different light. Alexandre had never discussed with her the prospect of getting married nor having children. He hadn't consulted her before accepting an invitation by one of the Moscow theaters to direct a play. He hadn't even mentioned that he would call her to come to Moscow as soon as he settled down over there. He just jumped on a plane and left. She needs to see her father; to hear his voice. But now, she would hear it only in her dreams.

Katerina closed her eyes and began falling back asleep when she heard it again. It was a sort of mumbling that had come from Nina Toropko each morning these last two days. It seemed the woman was talking in her sleep. Judging by her smile, this dream appeared to be a pleasant one. In general, Nina was a good-natured person and had a lovely face with strong child-like features, which made her look much younger than she was. Still, occasionally, she could be so direct and unceremonious that she rubbed people the wrong way.

Katya wasn't sure whether she should wake Nina up. But Nina opened her eyes and looked around. When she saw Katya, she smiled.

"Good morning, Katya!" Nina exclaimed. "I hope you have rested like I have."

Katya couldn't help but smile back at her.

"Yes, Ninochka, I have." She lied.

"Then let's get dressed and go for breakfast," Nina said, jumping out of bed. "I am hungry!"

* * *

On the opposite side of this makeshift hotel, in the room identical to all the others, an old round alarm clock showed 7:00. Major Vitus had already been awake for two hours. After sleeping for six hours straight, he felt well rested, even invigorated. Saturday had been an intense day. Lying in bed, Viktor analyzed the events and sorted the facts they managed to gather so far. Some of those facts were directly related to the murder case. The others were circumstantial at best, but still useful. For instance, the story told by Aunt Anna painted a vivid picture of Rogozhin's family life.

Viktor was particularly fascinated by a document that was given to him by General Melekhov in Khabarovsk. It was an in-depth report about the history of the Old Believers branch of the Russian Orthodox Church. Most likely, Colonel Raymond Vitus had requested this document as evidence back in 1947, when he investigated Fyodor Rogozhin.

The year was 1652. Czar Alexei Mikhayilovich ruled over Russia, the second monarch from the Romanov Lineage. The Moscow Metropolit, Patriarch Nikon, presided over the Russian Orthodox Church. As a result of successful wars against Poland, Lithuania, and the Ottoman Empire, Russia took possession of its southwestern provinces and Ukraine. After a first schism (Raskol) one hundred years prior, Czar Mikhayil Fyodorovich— Alexei's father and the first Romanov—divided the authority of the Patriarch Filaret of the Eastern Orthodox Church between the traditional Russian Orthodox Moscow Patriarchy and the Southwestern Metropolitan. The latter gradually fell under the influence of Latinism, eventually becoming the Greco-Catholic Church in service to the kings of Poland and Lithuania. Czar Alexei needed strong ecclesiastical support to effectively rule these newly acquired territories. At the same time, Patriarch Nikon sought to establish concordance in the practices of rites and services—which varied from parish to parish— with the Greek liturgical rules derived from Holy Scripture. These, in turn, contained numerous errors, contradictions, and deviations from the originals, having been hand copied over the centuries by many different monks into antiquated Russian.

Thus, Nikon undertook the re-writing of the holy books. He employed a Greek by the name of Arseniy to supervise the enormous task. This person was an opportunistic con artist with a very questionable education. He claimed to be a student of the Jesuits; later, he converted to Islam and was circumcised, before being rechristened into Eastern Orthodoxy. Before his employment with Nikon, he settled in Moscow earned a very modest living through an illegal racket. Much later, he was convicted and sent to the remote Solovetsky Monastery in the Solovki Islands in the north of Russia, the precursor of the GULAG labor camps.

The revision of the old scriptures took almost fourteen years under the guidance of Nikon and his so-called expert Arseniy. The process led to many new textual errors and even canonical distortions. Many of these changes were insignificant: a change in the number of times "Halleluiah" was to be repeated during the praising of God's Word; the pronunciation of Jesus' name in Russian, from a single initial vowel to double; or the direction of the liturgical procession from clockwise to counterclockwise. Other changes amounted to "cosmetic innovations": the change of the cross from its traditional six or eight-ended design to a four-ended design; a switch from conventional monotonic singing, derived from the Old Testament Heruviem Hymn to a more sophisticated polyphonic sound influenced by Western Liturgy; easing of the rules for bowing and prostration during prayer and chant.

But the most profound change happened in the ecumenical arena. The reform forced believers to discard the widely accepted Russian Orthodoxy dogma of the duality of Jesus' role—as Son of God and God himself—to the concept of the Holy Trinity, of God the Father, the Son, and the Holy Spirit. This shift abolished the two-fingered sign of the cross (with index and middle finger slightly bent), representing duality, in favor of the three-fingered sign (with the thumb holding the tips of the middle and index finger) as a symbol of the Trinity. Thus, the Russian Orthodoxy merged closer with the Greco-Constantinople Eastern Orthodox Church.

The people responded with massive revolt. The new schism (Raskol) affected society from top to bottom, from the clergy to the nobility— boyars of the Czarist courts, to the urban commoners and rural peasants across the Empire. Many thousands that rebelled were simply anathematized, but many more were persecuted. Patriarch Avvacum was killed for his ardent opposition to the reforms. Boyarynya Morozova faced exile for blasphemy and treason for rejecting the new rules, later depicted in a painting by the famous Vasily Surikov, being whisked away in a sled while holding her right hand high in the two-fingered sign of the cross. Entire village communities on the Lower Volga or Vyatka rivers refused to alter their faith and were mercilessly uprooted and relocated to Siberia.

*Nikon's reform widely succeeded, although the persecution and terror did not stop the now heretical groups, whom Church and State authorities called **raskolniki** (schismatics) but who called themselves **Old Believers**. Ironically, Nikon himself did not live long enough to see the fruits of his labor. Fearing the Patriarch Nikon held too much power, Czar Alexei Mikhayilovich sent him to the Solovetsky Monastery, followed by his protégé Arseniy. They both died there soon after.*

The Old Believer's opposition survived but weakened considerably through the years. They broke into two major denominations: the Popovtsy (with priesthood), who retained those few courageous bishops and grew a new generation of clergy, and the Bezpopovsty (priest-less), who held that clergy of the Old Rite would soon be extinct. Much later, the Edinovertsy (People of the Common Faith) denomination emerged from the Old Believers, joining the Russian Orthodox Church while retaining the Old Rites.

Persecutions intensified after 1672, often including torture and summary executions. Many Old Believers fled Russia for good. However, they established a dominant presence in some other regions, including Pomorie in far north, Siberia, and the Urals. Strong communities also existed in Ukraine and Estonia. The oppression eased somewhat during the reign of Peter the Great (1682-1725), taking on a more economic tone: Old Believer households were subject to double taxation, with a separate tax for men with beards.

However, no matter what Czar reigned, the Russian Church and State always considered the Old Believers a threat to the Empire. This same attitude carried into the Soviet era. State Security services closely scrutinized them, first the VeCheKa, and later the OGPU, NKVD, MGB and finally the KGB. And yet in the last Imperial Russian Census, just before 1917, approximately ten percent of the Empire's population indicated they still practiced the faith of Old Believers.

In 1905, Czar Nicholas II signed the Religious Freedom Act, which ended the persecution of religious minorities in Russia. The Old Believers gained the right to build churches, ring church bells, hold processions, and organize themselves. People often refer to the period between 1905 and 1917 as "the Golden Age of the Old Faith."

* * *

Viktor recalled that in 1975, the Moscow Synod of the Russian Orthodox Church had finally lifted the Anathema on the Old Believers, which had been in effect for the last three hundred years. As interesting an intellectual exercise as this was for Viktor, he was still curious how this history connected for his father's investigation thirty years ago? And if it has any relevancy on this case, now?

The sound of a loud yawn interrupted Viktor's thoughts. It was Pyotr, who had just awakened and sat straight up in the bed, scratching his head.

"You are not asleep, Comrade Major?" asked Pyotr apologetically. "I hope I didn't wake you up."

"No, you did not. I was just about to get up." Viktor pulled off the blanket and sat up, his bare feet touching the plank floor. "It's cold! A real winter day, isn't it?"

"Oh, yes. At least thirty below zero." Pyotr shivered as he pulled his blue uniform trousers and a grey wool sweater over his long white linen underwear.

Viktor did the same in a hurry. Soon, both men stood before the washroom mirror, brushing their teeth and shaving. They met Katerina and Nina, already dressed to face the bitter cold, at 8:30 by the reception desk. The women weren't sure whether they had to check out and who would be paying the hotel bill. Viktor explained that they might be staying in New Urgal one more day, so squaring the account would wait until the following morning. For now, the group needed to run to the diner for a good hearty breakfast.

The streets of New Urgal were empty: the adult population was already at work, and the children were at school. They did not find any visitors in the diner either. From their corner table near the kitchen, they could see several young cooks, mostly girls, bustling about preparing the midday meal. It wasn't clear who had prepared their breakfast, but the food arrived very quickly. The classic: oat porridge, a couple of scrambled eggs with a slice of buttered bread, and hot tea.

Everyone devoured the food in total silence. Nina initiated the conversation only with the first sip of tea.

"I thought we were going to leave for Khabarovsk today. What changed if you don't mind me asking?" Lieutenant Toropko asked, turning to the Major.

"We need to interview one more witness," Viktor replied in the same manner. "We hoped to talk to him yesterday, but it didn't happen."

"So, this is what we are doing after finishing our breakfast?" asked Nina rather pertinaciously.

"We are not." The Major could not mask his slight irritation. "The witness must work all day, so we have to wait until after five."

Katerina put her teacup down on the table and glanced at Viktor with curiosity. She lowered her head and smiled imperceptibly. Her earlier guess about Viktor's state of mind was confirmed: he obviously seemed disappointed about last night and therefore avoided looking directly in Katya's direction. Suddenly, Katya raised her head and found Viktor staring directly at her. His wide, dark eyes expressed his unabashed amazement and adoration. These eyes hypnotized her so much, that she couldn't move for a moment, She broke free of the stare and noticed Nina and Pyotr staring at her as well.

"Why are you all looking at me? Is there something wrong?"

"No, quite on the contrary. The light is casting a rainbow on your face," Nina explained.

Indeed, the thick frost on the window refracted the sun's intense rays like through a crystal. The rainbow of colors showered Katerina in a magnificent spectacle. It lasted only a moment, but Viktor's gaze became locked at this moment, as was everyone else's. Katerina felt relieved and took it as a sign of hope. They all laughed.

* * *

When Major Vitus and company entered the precinct, the Militia serviceman on duty greeted them.

"Private Kapustin is at your service, Comrade Major," he reported. "Captain Nesterenko just called and asked you to contact him ASAP. He is in Listvenny. Would you like to be connected immediately?"

"Yes, please, Private Kapustin."

Shortly afterwards, Major Vitus sat behind the Captain's desk, holding the telephone receiver. At first, he did not speak but only listened to Nesterenko. The expression on his face turned worrisome.

"It looks like he was caught a bit off guard. Was he hurt?" Viktor asked. "

After he heard the reply on the other end of the line, Viktor sighed with relief. "Thank God he wasn't. You said he injured one and possibly wounded another? One was captured but the other escaped. What a hero, this Sergeant of yours. I must admit, Captain, I did underestimate Darsulov's abilities. Please thank him and tell him I am impressed."

He continued listening without interrupting for a few minutes but then erupted: "I understand what your concern is, Captain. I realize you don't have enough manpower, but you cannot rely on Darsulov alone to watch the arrested perpetrator and secure an entire khutor Izmailovsky. Perhaps the remaining killer is hiding in the empty house at the edge of the village? There must be something very important in that house. We just don't know what it is yet." He paused and listened to the Captain for a while.

"It makes sense— we should initiate a manhunt, but, as you just said, we don't have the people to do this. So, for now, let's do what we can: immediately place two more servicemen at your disposal in Aunt Anna's house and in the empty one, provide your people with adequate firepower and tell them to lock the village down. Hopefully, this will flush him out somewhere else, where it will be easier to identify and catch him. Since both had injuries caused by Sergeant Darsulov, alert all nearby medical facilities, no matter how small they may be. Oh yes, one more thing: inform the BAM administration in Tynda about the situation and request some additional personnel immediately."

The Major hung up the telephone as he began to think. He pulled out the photographs from his leather sash and began to study them slowly, one by one, occasionally using the magnifying glass. He looked at his wristwatch and called Lieutenant Toropko, who all this time remained in the reception room together with Katerina and Pyotr, talking to Private Kapustin. Viktor asked her to take a seat across the desk.

"I went through all your pictures at the crime scene and Captain Nesterenko's pictures. It is quite a complete representation of the collected evidence and the interior of the room where the killing took place," Viktor said. "And yet, we are still missing something very important, some piece of evidence without which it will be difficult to solve this case."

"I haven't processed all the evidence yet," Nina objected. "It can be done only in our Khabarovsky Lab. I am sure the results will point to the best direction for this investigation."

"I agree with you, we need more details for a complete picture," Viktor interrupted her hastily. "What I meant is that we haven't determined the real motive for this homicide yet. The more I think about it, the more it becomes obvious that the package given to Anna and then passed to Fyodor has a direct connection with the motive."

"That fabric found outside Fyodor's house could help us identify what was in the package," the Lieutenant came back pertly. "I could see some kind of residue, but only a chemical analysis will tell me precisely what it was."

"My question is, will such a small sample be enough to do that?" Viktor asked, gazing at one of the pictures. "And how do we know that this residue was not just circumstantial contamination with no connection to the evidence we're looking for?"

"Circumstantial contamination?" Nina sounded a bit baffled.

"I mean that this burlap fabric could've been used for wrapping something else before," explained Viktor. "In other words, this torn piece, carrying this residue, could've been a part of a much bigger sheet of fabric, which was used to wrap many different things in the past."

"And it would not have the same residue," Nina continued Viktor's thought. "In this case, we would be better off not to rely on this evidence too much."

"Yes and no," Viktor interrupted heartily. "Let's not jump to any conclusions before we analyze all of it. However, I would prefer to have more substantial support for this theory."

"I would too," Nina agreed. "We should have expanded our search outside Fyodor's house. Should we go back and give it another crack?"

"I'm not sure," Viktor replied in a worrisome tone. "Captain Nesterenko just informed me that the suspects returned to the house early this morning and had a run in with Sergeant Darsulov. "

"Is he unharmed?"

"Fortunately, he is. As for the suspects, not so much: one escaped with a possible bullet wound in his abdomen and the other was captured, with a hole in his behind and a bashed head." Viktor sounded concerned. "There is something in that house, or at least they think there is, that they desperately need. My guess is that it is the package that we are discussing."

"Maybe that is all the more reason for us to go back to Izmailovsky?" Nina suggested. "It will give us another chance to look around and to reinforce security."

"The Captain will do that with two more of his men," Viktor began hesitantly. "Frankly, I am inclined to agree with you. Would you be willing to drive with Pyotr to Izmailovsky now? Hopefully, you can collect some additional evidence and make sure that Anna and her older brother are safe. I am sure you can be back here before dusk, so we are still set to leave for Khabarovsk tomorrow morning."

"Of course, I will, Comrade Major." Nina got up and formally saluted Viktor, who rose from his chair and nodded with approval. "We can leave immediately after I retrieve my gear from the hotel."

"Very well, Comrade Lieutenant." The Major came from around the desk and followed Nina to the door. "Check your weapons and be careful."

Soon, Nina and Pyotr left the precinct and drove away. When Viktor looked at the clock on the wall, it was a quarter to ten. He turned to Private Kapustin and said, "Please contact Captain Nesterenko or Sergeant Darsulov by radio. When either of them answers, let me know."

"Yes, Comrade Major," Kapustin acknowledged and began immediately turning the knob on the radio, tuning to the designated frequency. "It started snowing again. It might affect the reception."

"Keep trying them." Viktor was concerned, and it showed. He was nervously passing back and forth in the room and rubbing his temples with the thumb and the index finger of his right hand.

Katerina couldn't pretend to read the three-day-old issue of Moscow's *Gudok* with genuine interest any longer. She dropped the newspaper back on the reception desk, stood up and quickly approached Viktor, gently grabbing his left elbow, and pulling him to the Captain's office. The Major did not resist. As soon she let go of his arm, he lowered his body, slouching in the chair behind the desk, and closed his eyes.

Katya stood in front of him and studied his face. He had a chiseled, heavy chin with a little dimple, straight nose, and a high hairline on the top of a sloping forehead. His smooth skin was more on the dark side, and his thick hair was pitch-black with touch of white on his temples. Black, curly lashes covered the dark lids of his eyes. He looked younger than his real age, although his face carried the invisible scars of a tormented soul.

Viktor felt the woman's gaze and opened his eyes. His intense brown eyes met her deep grey ones. He smiled, showing a row of rather big white teeth, and pulled his body straight up. Suddenly, he became overwhelmed with joy and anxiety. The mix of those two strong emotions always brought pain, which he hid away from everyone. Viktor slouched back into the chair, wanting to be invisible. Katya understood his intention and tried to leave him alone in the room. But it didn't happen; Private Kapustin stood in her way, signaling to the Major that he had finally gotten connected with Captain Nesterenko.

The line crackled and hissed, as the Major listened intently: "Following your orders, I placed two of my men at Izmailovsky in addition to Sergeant Darsulov. I equipped them with adequate firepower. I called Tynda Headquarters to explain the situation and to request reinforcements but no reply yet, Comrade Major. I'm getting ready to leave, so I will be in New Urgal by two o'clock with more details. Copy."

"Copy. Captain, please do not to leave Izmailovsky yet. I sent Lieutenant Toropko and my driver to return for more evidence. You can come back to New Urgal with them when everything is done. I'll speak with Orlovsky on my own. Before that, I would like to have a chat with your friend Leonid Gordin. Copy?"

"I can arrange that, Major. Kapustin will find him for you. He can assist you if you decide to speak to anyone else. I'll wait for your guys and help them finish their assignment as quickly as possible."

"Great, Captain. I may need to talk with you later, after meeting with Gordin. Good luck, Captain. Over and out.." Viktor turned the microphone off and handed it to Kapustin. "Could you locate Gordin and dispatch him here?"

"Yes, Comrade Major."

The wall clock showed 10:15 when a man of medium height entered the precinct. He quickly passed Private Kapustin, giving him a slight wave and proceeded into the Captain's office. His imported camel shearling coat with white fur collar and his sable fur hat were coated with fresh snowflakes. His demeanor indicated a familiarity with his surroundings. He approached the desk, removed his hat, and offered his right hand for Viktor to shake.

"Leonid Gordin at your service, Comrade Major. Lyubomir has praised you a lot."

For a moment, Viktor was taken aback by the energy and confidence emanating from Gordin. He immediately shook his hand and invited him to be seated.

"Thank you, Citizen Gordin, for coming over." The Major wanted to establish his authority from the outset.

"Why so formal, Comrade Major?" Gordin arched his thick blonde eyebrows. He smiled. "Am I a suspect?"

"Not yet." Viktor mimicked the visitor's joking tone. "That may change, though."

Gordin paused and looked around. He noticed Katerina, still standing at the side of the desk in the least illuminated part of the room.

"Please excuse my rudeness, Katya. I should have greeted you first," Gordin said, changing the subject.

"You are excused, Leonid," Katerina replied rather formally. "Thank you for visiting with Nina and me the other day. Your stories about this settlement and its inhabitants were quite entertaining."

"If you like, I can tell you many more." Leonid smiled, blushing slightly.

"Some other time, Citizen Gordin," Viktor interjected. "I am afraid today we have some official business to attend to. I need to ask you a few questions related to our case."

"I'll leave you here," Katerina announced.

"You don't have to, Comrade Rogozhina," Major said, signaling her to stay. "Please make yourself comfortable, although it should not take long. You too, Citizen Gordin."

"I am perfectly comfortable." Gordin took off his coat and leaned back in a chair. "Go ahead, ask me whatever you need to, but I don't think I know anything concerning the unfortunate death of Citizen Rogozhin."

"I'll be the judge of that," Viktor snapped back but paused and continued more calmly. While he did not care about Gordin's impression of him, he didn't want Katerina to perceive him as rude or irritable.

"Please try to answer my questions as fully as you can, no matter how irrelevant they might seem at first. Every detail can be crucial."

"Of course, I will." Now Leonid sounded very serious.

"Did you know Fyodor Rogozhin personally or otherwise?"

"I only knew of him through my friend Polina and her fiancé Yury Orlovsky. This was last summer." Gordin began slowly. "But I only met him recently, perhaps in early November. Strangely, we met right here in this office. I came to see Lyubomir, as I do almost every day, to complain about something."

"What was your conversation with Rogozhin about?" Viktor came back quickly. "Be very specific, please."

"I wouldn't call it a conversation, exactly. I was doing most of the talking," Leonid chuckled. "I told him that I recognized him from Polina's description and how glad I was to finally meet him. It was rather fascinating to me what Yury Orlovsky and this old man had in common. Fyodor just nodded silently. I asked him why he was sitting in this office alone and the whereabouts of Captain Nesterenko. He explained that the Captain had received a phone call and left to take care of something. Then I introduced myself and explained what my job around here was. Half-jokingly, I asked whether I could interview him sometime in the future. I noticed he became a little bit nervous, so I assured him it was fine if he declined my offer."

"And what happened after that?" Viktor asked.

"All of sudden, Fyodor got up from the chair and left the room. I heard his horse whinnying and his wooden wheels squeaking as Fyodor sharply backed his buggy from a parking spot to the street. I was stunned: no word of explanation, no goodbye. Kind of rude, wasn't it?"

"Why do you think this happened?"

"Listen, I am a journalist, a newspaper reporter for ten years, come this December. I can read people, most of them, like an open book. We are not called 'the engineers of the human soul' for nothing." Now, Leonid felt himself in his element. "Personally, I disagree with this poetic bullshit, you know. I prefer when our second oldest profession is compared with yours, Major. At least the best of us, we are the investigators in the true sense of the word. We are not supposed to change or design human nature, like engineers do, but to observe and honestly interpret it for everyone who reads our writings."

At first, the Major had an urge to stop this philosophical excursion. Obviously, Leonid wanted to impress Viktor or Katya, perhaps both, with his intellectual prowess. But Viktor decided to let him continue. He hoped he could find in Gordin's rambling a golden nugget of information, which might lead the investigation in the right direction.

So, he encouraged Leonid, "I totally agree with you. Katya too, I am sure. We would be interested in discussing this subject later on. I am very fond of journalism and reporters. But for now, can you tell what specifically you observed in Fyodor's behavior that day?"

"I noticed from the moment I met him that he was deeply preoccupied with his thoughts." Gordin returned to the matter of their conversation. "It was on the tip of my tongue to ask him what he was doing in Captain Nesterenko's office, but I couldn't do that. It would be too intrusive on my part. You understand, don't you? So, I thought that small talk would break the ice. Because I have always been a habitual complainer, I started telling him about my post office problems at Listvenny. I thought that he might be sympathetic, as he lived nearby and might've used its services as well."

"What problems?" His intuition told Viktor that he was closing in on something important. "Can you elaborate?"

"Okay. The transfer or delivery of information is another important part of my job as a reporter," Leonid said. "No matter how good or accurate my writing is, if I cannot get it into the hands of my newspaper on time, it might be rendered useless. In this part of the world, communication is highly problematic. Even the telephone doesn't solve all problems: newspaper editors don't like material dictated over the telephone unless it is extremely urgent. They want to work with the reporter's hard copy. It is quicker to edit and safer to avoid factual errors. That leaves only one option as the most reliable and only available around here—the postal service. Almost every second day I have to be at the Listvenny Post Office to mail my materials to the Moscow, Lviv, Khabarovsk, and Birobidjan newspapers, which I am accredited by, and receive their instructions as well as my paid fees receipts."

"How do you get there? Do you have any kind of transportation at your disposal?" Viktor interjected.

"As a matter of fact, I don't. Usually, I hail a passing truck going in the direction of Old Urgal. Drivers know me too well not to refuse a ride," Leonid answered with a sort of pride.

"So, what else did you tell Fyodor about that?"

"Lately, it has become a real pain in the neck for me. Due to work on the BAM, the volume of mail increased exponentially. However, the only post office around here still has just one worker and one supervisor. I don't count, of course, the mail deliverymen or women. To make matters real dire, the worker happens to be a novice, and the supervisor is a lazy bum. In the last three or four months since the old post worker retired and the new girl was hired, they've accumulated mountains of unprocessed mail—envelopes and parcels. It seriously affects my job and frustrates me. So, to feel better, I usually come to my dear friend Captain Nesterenko to whine and complain. That day, I did not find him in his office. Instead, it was my new acquaintance Fyodor Rogozhin on whom I inadvertently unloaded my problems. I guess he wasn't as patient as Lyubomir or had his own troubles, so he ran."

"Do you think the situation at the Listvenny Post Office has improved now?" Viktor interjected again.

"No, it has not. I was there earlier this morning. I think it's getting worse," Gordin said and added. "I did call the District Post Office, though, but did not find anyone with the authority to rectify the problem at Listvenny."

At that point in the conversation, Viktor no longer listened to Gordin. He rushed to the reception room and asked Kapustin to connect him with the Captain over the radio. When Nesterenko's voice came online, Viktor did not waste any time on formalities.

"Captain, are you still at Izmailovsky? How is it going over there?"

"We are almost done with collecting additional evidence and securing the perimeter as you advised, Comrade Major."

"Good, Captain. I need you to do something for me at Listvenny on your way back here."

"No problem. What do you want me to do?"

"I want you to stop at the post office and ask them to check if Fyodor Rogozhin sent any parcels by mail before his death. If he did and the parcel is still there, find out the destination address and ask them to process it immediately. Please insist that they be discrete; no word about it to anyone, period."

"May I ask you what it is all about?" the Captain asked. "I bet you talked to Leonid Gordin."

"Yes, I did. Indeed, he is still talking," the Major replied. "I'll explain everything to you here."

"I think I know where you are going with this, Major," Captain said. "Wouldn't it be safer to remove this package, as evidence, from the post office?"

"It probably would be," Viktor said. "First, I am not sure if that is even legal. And second, let it be *en route* for a while. This way it will be safe enough, as long as nobody knows about it. So, see you soon. Copy that."

The Major handed the receiver to Kapustin and looked at him conspiratorially. "You got it, Private? Nobody is to know!"

Chapter 10

When Viktor came back to the office, he found Katerina and Leonid talking about some literary subject. They stopped and fixed their eyes on the Major, expecting him to explain why he left without finishing the conversation, but no such explanation followed. Instead, Viktor reclaimed the chair behind the desk and asked about what they were discussing.

"Leonid suggested a few new books, especially the latest Russian translation of the novel *One Hundred Years of Solitude* by Columbian writer Gabriel Garcia Marquez," Katerina said with a sparkle in her eyes. "I am familiar with his work. He was influenced by Faulkner and Kafka, but his stories are more magical."

"You are absolutely right; there is a mystique in Garcia's characters and in their relations," Viktor joined in, raising Leonid's eyebrows. "I read this novel a few months ago, and I liked it for the most part. This book is still on my bookshelf at home. Katya, you are welcome to read it anytime."

"Thank you, Viktor. I will take up your offer as soon as I complete the final preparation for my role in *The Taming of the Shrew*." Katya looked a little embarrassed when she realized she had called the Major by his given name for the first time.

"Oh yes, I've heard you were going to play sharp-tongued Katherine," Leonid added enthusiastically. "You will be great in this role, Katya."

"I am not as sure as you are, believe me." Katya tried to avoid further embarrassment. "I never acted in a comedy before, especially one of such calibers. It is tough."

"I am positive you will be great," Viktor reassured her. "Everything can be tough for the first time."

The room suddenly went quiet.

"I wish I could see your premier." Leonid tried to fill the pause, realizing the emotional tension between Viktor and Katya. "When is it going to be? I might be able to come."

Katerina threw an inquisitive gaze at Viktor, as if asking him for a bit of advice. Viktor chose to ignore her plea for help. That didn't escape Gordin.

"If you have a chance, let me know." He tried to defuse the uncomfortable situation for all of them. "As my mamma from Odessa used to say, 'Sometimes, the size of our pride depends on the magnitude of the troubles we are in.' Don't you think, Comrade Major?"

"Your mamma is right." Viktor perfectly understood Leonid's hint, but he didn't want to focus Katya's attention on it. "Did you say your mother is from Odessa? Mine is too."

"She was born and raised there before the Revolution; later on, she moved north," Leonid replied in a sad tone of voice. "She passed away two years ago. This was one of the reasons I took the job in this forsaken land, so far from home."

"What was her name?" Katya asked.

"Her name was Sophia. We called her Mamma Sonya. She was two months short of sixty-two when she died." Gordin paused for a moment. "I came to Kyiv from Lviv a few days before it happened and found her in the hospital, surrounded by my younger sisters Leya and Eva and their family. The doctor told us she had cancer, which was detected too late. She was heavily sedated for the excruciating pain and passed without speaking to us."

"So, before coming here, you lived in Lviv, while the rest of your family resided in Kyiv. Did I understand you correctly?" Viktor wanted Leonid to change this painful subject.

"Yes, you understood it correctly." Gordin nodded and smiled gratefully. "After I graduated from Lviv State University, I was hired as a reporter by the local railroad union newspaper."

"Are you married?" Katerina narrowly squeezed her question in.

"Yes, I am. My wife was here with me for a while," Gordin replied.

"Why is she not with you anymore?"

"Oh, she is still with me." Leonid laughed in a deep, low voice. "She received an offer to teach French in one of Lviv's prestigious specialty schools. We discussed it and decided that she must grab this unique opportunity, you know. In Lviv, we also left our seven-year-old son behind, who just started school. He needs a Mommy, at least—don't you think?"

* * *

From the start, Monday looked like a rather a long day. Leonid kept telling Katerina about his family, his grandparents, parents, and his wife's family. His grandfather, the main accountant for the Kherson Steel Mill, wasn't Jewish. However, he fell in love with a Jewish girl and married her.

It was a bit strange how open this conversation became because just thirty minutes ago, these people didn't know anything about one another. What compelled Leonid to share so many intimate details of his life—as a Jew and as a journalist? Viktor was a bit nervous, but not because of the nature of the subject. His brother-in-law Boris often discussed the situation with the Soviet Jews. But he worried about Katerina's lack of exposure to this subject, and what her natural reaction might be. Who was this Gordin? What drove him to tell deeply personal facts to people he had just met? One thing was for sure—Leonid felt a mutual trust and understanding from Katerina and Viktor. All the same as Major, although he pretended to be preoccupied with some documents in front of him.

"Are you still interested in my stories?" asked Leonid after a short pause.

Viktor said, "If Katya doesn't mind, I would like you to continue."

"Do I mind? I want to know what your story is," Katerina replied without a hint of hesitation. "I remember my dad telling me about the 'chosen people,' the Jews, but only in relation to the Holy Scriptures. One time, he even visited a synagogue in Birobidjan on Yom Kippur, knowing how important Atonement was for every human soul. However, I know very little about the life of the Jewish people in the Soviet Union. Please continue."

Leonid returned to his father's story, a war correspondent in the Great Patriotic War, but he soon concluded the story was too complicated and too long. He suddenly rose from his chair and mentioned a need to be elsewhere.

"I promised my sister Leya to contact her as soon as humanly possible regarding an important decision her family has to make very soon."

Hearing this name again, Viktor suddenly threw a steadfast look toward Leonid. Leonid caught this look and stopped.

"Did I say anything improper? I did mention before that my name Leonid was in the memory of my Uncle Leo. My older sister was named Leya, in memory of mamma Sonya's sister, who perished during the Revolution. Didn't I?"

"Perhaps you did," Viktor replied hesitantly. "It's just that my mom's name is Leya too, full name Leya Solomonovna."

"And what is her maiden name?" Gordin asked right away, taking a deep breath.

"I am not sure. I don't remember Mom ever telling us." Suddenly, Viktor felt an emptiness in the bottom of his stomach, and not from hunger. "But why do you ask, Leonid?"

"I am not sure myself. My mom's maiden name was Shtern, Sofia Solomonovna Shtern. Didn't I also mention this before?" Now, Leonid sounded confused.

A deep silence descended upon the room; everyone was afraid to break it. Viktor returned to his seat and closed his eyes. *Was it just a coincidence?* he wondered to himself. *Many years ago, Mom mentioned a much younger sister she had while growing up in Odessa. She was always sad speaking about her and about their older brother. Too bad she never provided any details. What if I call her right now? Hey, hey, slow down. What if everything is just a coincidence? Then she will be really upset. Let's take it one step at a time.* Viktor glanced at Leonid and found him also deep in thought, most likely very similar thoughts. *I bet he will agree not to rush to conclusions. Wouldn't this mean we are cousins?*

Leonid felt overwhelmed too. His late mother spoke constantly of her lost siblings; her brother, Leo Shtern, even came back into her life after many years, one day in the hot summer of 1961. So why doubt that maybe, just maybe, his Aunt Leya had also survived, living happily all these years with her family at the other end of the country? Why? He could only imagine his Mama Sonya's ecstasy to learn such news. He had no doubts that anything was possible, but he didn't say a word.

Katerina did not fully comprehend what was developing in front of her eyes. Her natural intuition told her that something profoundly important had just happened in the lives of these two men, but precisely what she could not understand.

The silence became unbearable. Viktor was the one who ventured to break it. "So, what happened after your sister Leya was born?"

"Nothing extraordinary." Leonid smiled with relief. "The Gordins lived the life of an average Soviet family: they worked, raised their three children, and hoped for better times. I remember being ten or eleven-years old reading Jules Verne and seeing myself in all those exotic places Captain Nemo visited during his underwater adventures; or fantasizing about helping the Count of Monte Cristo to take revenge on his treacherous friends. I was more of a dreamer and a truant, while my sisters were of a serious type, excellent school pupils and helpers around the house. Unfortunately, our dad began having heart attacks when he reached fifty, seven of them. He eventually died at fifty-seven." Leonid's eyes and cheeks became wet with tears, but he didn't seem to care.

"I must run," he suddenly announced.

"Why don't you wait for Lyubomir and eat with us?" Viktor sounded sincere. "They will be here in a few minutes."

"Thanks, but I do have something important to do," Gordin replied and headed to the exit. "You and Katya were already too generous with your patience. I am sure we'll talk again soon."

"I'll see you off." Viktor motioned to Katya to remain seated and saw Leonid out.

Outside it was snowing. The temperature began falling.

"It will be like that for the next day or two, and then the same snow will be on the ground until April or even May," Leonid explained, shaking Viktor's hand. "I don't know why I told my life story. I never did it before to anyone." He paused and sighed. "Talk to your mom and let me know. I'll come to see you all in Khabarovsk right away."

Leonid waved goodbye and dashed away, disappearing around the corner. Viktor gazed in his direction for a while until he saw two Militia vehicles quickly approach the precinct and park next to each other. Captain Nesterenko got out from his *kozyol* as did Lieutenant Toropko and Sergeant Uvalov from theirs. They looked tired and preoccupied.

"Comrade Major, did you come outside in this cold to greet us?" asked Lyubomir half-seriously.

"Yes, I did." Viktor had already gotten used to the Captain's specific sense of humor and decided to play along. "You must be hungry, aren't you?"

"Honestly, we are starving," Nina interjected.

"Then go directly to the diner," Viktor suggested. "Katya and I will join you shortly. Let's make it quick. It is almost three."

* * *

Even though the regular midday mealtime finished almost two hours earlier, the diner was still busy and noisy. Young people spoke and laughed loudly, trying to warm themselves from the cold before sitting down to eat. It didn't exactly fit the business-like mood of Major Vitus's colleagues. Each of them was preoccupied with their own thoughts concerning the case and personal matters. They ate quickly and in silence, barely noticing the delicious food.

At 15:20, everyone except Sergeant Uvalov gathered in Captain Nesterenko's office. Before starting the meeting, the Major had written some notes in his black pocketbook and put it on the desk in front of him.

"Let's start with Lieutenant Toropko," he said, looking straight at Nina. "Do you have anything to report?"

"I swept a large area around Fyodor's house and didn't find any new material evidence," Nina began. "However, I did come across a bunch of the same footprints we've seen before on the porch, on the planks of the walking path, and in the room where the homicide took place."

"So, the perpetrators were searching in the same area, and for the same thing we were," concluded Viktor. "I think it's too obvious—"

"Yes, it is, but let me tell you what I discovered inside the house," Nina interrupted the Major. She sounded rather excited, so Viktor didn't mind. "Behind the Russian oven, there is a passage to a back room."

"It used to be my room, which Dad built out for me when I was twelve or thirteen," Katerina interjected immediately.

"Yes, yes, I remember you mentioned this before," Nina continued. "I found nothing in that room or in the passage during my first search. But this time I discovered something behind a little door in the middle of this passage"

"That was a concoction my dad came up with." Katya blushed but went on with her explanation. "So that in wintertime I didn't have to go to the outhouse."

"You did not see all this the first time?" Captain Nesterenko joined in.

"I did open the door and understood what was behind it, but I didn't inspect inside it as thoroughly as today," Nina explained apologetically.

"So, what did you find there this time, Lieutenant Toropko?" Viktor asked impatiently.

"I found the pieces of burlap fabric together with the scraps of newspaper," Nina said hurriedly, as she was afraid to be interrupted. "They were stuck to the slimy surface inside the makeshift pipe I mentioned before."

"And how does all this affect what we discussed earlier this morning?" Viktor interrupted her anyway.

"I'm getting to that, Comrade Major," Nina responded with feistiness. "For starters, we now have the inner layer of the material used to wrap our missing package—a sheet of old newspaper—and it has a residue of its contents. And secondly, my discovery proves that

Fyodor did hide the package in a place hard to guess. It means he knew darn well what the murderers were after and how valuable it was."

"Yes, it does prove that doesn't it?" Viktor rose from his seat and exclaimed. "Excellent job, Lieutenant!"

"Thanks, but you thought of it first, Comrade Major," Nina replied with sincere modesty. "It was good that you suggested going back."

"Lets's not pat ourselves on the back yet. We still must figure out many details." Viktor moved his eyes from face to face, stopping at the Captain. "Your report, Comrade Captain, I would like to discuss later. I am sure you would agree."

"I totally agree, Major." Nesterenko replied without hesitation.

"However, please tell me if you've had any news from Tynda about reinforcements," the Major said.

"Headquarters informed me that a company of fifteen servicemen has been assigned to my command for at least one week," the Captain reported. "They will arrive in New Urgal tomorrow morning by train."

"And until then, we have three well-armed men guarding Izmailovsky, correct?"

"That is correct, Comrade Major."

"Regarding the person arrested after the attempt to penetrate the protected house: we must wait until next morning to transport him to Khabarovsk, when additional personnel will arrive. I am sure medical care was arranged to tend to his wounds," The Major sounded confident.

"Why don't we question him as soon as possible? Nesterenko inquired.

"I think that would be a bad idea: we need a good background check on him before interrogation." Concluded the Major. "And now let's take a break and relax a little before we meet with Yury Orlovsky," Viktor proposed.

"Katerina and I would like to go to our hotel room and freshen up. Can we?" asked Nina.

"Certainly," Viktor replied. Then he paused and said, "You know what? You don't have to come back here at all. Have Pyotr drive you to the hotel and stay there. Get some rest. We are leaving for Khabarovsk very early in the morning."

After they were gone, the Major turned to Nesterenko:

"So, Captain, what did you dig up at the post office?"

"As you may know, Fyodor did send a parcel on the same day he visited me—" Nesterenko began.

"Yes, I figured this out even before." Viktor interrupted, "Your friend Gordin unknowingly helped me with this. He recalled step by step his meeting with Fyodor in this office on November 3. It sounded more like a monologue on his part, not a mutual conversation. He complained about the lousy job of the Listvenny Post Office, while Fyodor just listened. Suddenly, the old man stormed out of the precinct, jumped onto his buggy without saying a word. At that point I realized why he wanted to consult with you—listening to Leonid, he had found a solution to his dilemma. So, he ran to the post office and sent away the package that, for reasons unknown to us, was burning his hands like a hot potato. Sorry for interrupting you, Captain."

"You are absolutely right on this, Major! Now, let me tell you who the Old Man designated as the recipient of this package, which was not only valuable but also heavy."
"Hold on, don't tell me yet." Viktor rushed to the door and made sure it was closed tight. "Now, tell me."

"He sent it to Katerina Rogozhina at her Khabarovsky address." The Captain spoke slowly, stressing each word. He expected the effect of an exploded bomb, but nothing happened.

"I suspected that—he sent it to Katerina with instructions for what to do next." Viktor reacted rather calmly. "By all indications, Fyodor didn't have anyone except his daughter whom he could fully trust, so it seems fairly obvious." The Major stopped for a moment. "Too obvious. And why would he put Katya in danger? That is why I suggested leaving the parcel at the post office. It seems the killers didn't realize that Fyodor would do such a thing. It will take a few days, perhaps the entire week, for the package to get to Khabarovsk. That will buy us some time to arrange for all necessary precautions to keep Katya safe."

"I think it is the right course of action, considering one of the killers is still on the loose." Lyubomir agreed. "But sooner or later, he will exhaust the search at Izmailovsky and figure out where to look for this package next. Then what?"

"We have to catch him before that, somewhere around here." Viktor contemplated and then paused. "Or we might devise a plan to lure him to Khabarovsk, using the object of their desperate desire as bait to trap him."

"Again, wouldn't that jeopardize Katya's safety?" Lyubomir expressed his concern.

"I am afraid it would." Viktor shared the same concern. "We have to do everything possible to protect her. I must talk to General Melekhov about that."

"Let's hope we catch this bastard in the next couple of days. The reinforcements should help."

"Yes, let's hope."

* * *

At 17:10, Viktor and Lyubomir heard a ruckus in the reception room. They opened the office door to find a man taking off a sheepskin work-coat, covered with mud and a thin sheet of ice. He then removed his glassy felt boots and baggy overalls, stiff with ice, and left them standing against the radiator. The visitor wore regular fleece pants, a heavy meringue wool sweater, and thick wool socks. He walked right into the office, nodded to the Captain, looked at the Major, and introduced himself in a velvety baritone voice.

"Yury Orlovsky. Sorry for the mess. I am coming straight from the drilling station. You wanted to speak with me?"

"Never mind the mess. Thank you for coming." Viktor took two steps toward Yury and offered his hand to shake.

Yury accepted the offer and shook hands with the Major energetically. Then he waved to Lyubomir as old friends do. The warmth from his hand surprised Viktor, given that he had just come from an 8-hour shift, drilling deep into the permafrost in 45-degree temperatures.

Although Viktor had seen him briefly before, only now could he appreciate his features: a lean and yet muscular body; an elongated face with a straight medium size nose; high cheekbones and deep, wide-seated hazel eyes; and long, wavy blonde hair gathered at the back of his athletic neck. Yury showed no signs of a hangover from his drinking binge Saturday and perhaps yesterday. Still, a few beads of sweat on his large, unobstructed forehead revealed the nervousness that he was trying to conceal. Viktor observed that this person looked like the manly Slavic stereotype depicted in Soviet propaganda posters. Nevertheless, he liked him—his handsome features revealed something rough yet vulnerable.

We must find out what made him and late Fyodor such close friends Viktor thought, looking at Yury. *And how much did he know of Fyodor's intentions before he was killed? But in what state of mind was he? How seriously did this tragic event hurt him personally?*

Similar thoughts occupied Lyubomir Nesterenko's mind. The Captain had known the 32-year-old drilling master Yury Orlovsky since he arrived here. Polina introduced him as her quiet shy boyfriend. Lyubomir always saw Yury in Polina's company, except once, two years ago, when the Captain attended a domestic disturbance call at the dormitory barracks.

It was a typical case of an initially friendly gathering of overworked men turning violent after too much alcohol. Yury Orlovsky, usually the life of the party, ended up in a heated argument with none other than Roman Derenchuk. Yury's peers had always perceived him as a harmless joker and poet who performed *zona*-inspired songs. But that night a few extra shots of vodka revealed a recklessly rebellious and impetuously irreverent young man with a huge chip on his shoulder. His rowdy behavior put him at odds with Roman, who projected the reputation of a strait-laced, career-driven, politically savvy young communist. That night Captain Nesterenko observed a side of Yury's personality that he hid away under usual circumstances.

Soon after this incident, Nesterenko learned that Yury was a subject of interest from Valery Kirsanov, the KGB officer assigned at New Urgal. Lyubomir tried to dig deeper into Orlovsky's past but didn't get far at all. He did come across one important fact: in 1960, at the age of fifteen, Yury spent twenty months in a labor camp for young criminals. Any information about the nature of his crime was redacted from the report, but the Captain could stipulate Yury's strong contempt for authority.

As the Captain recalled, no similar episodes involving Yury Orlovsky ever happened again. His detachment managers and fellow workers respected him as one of their most experienced drilling master and high-impact Socialist workers. His photo was always displayed on the Wall of Honor among the best members of the Ukrainian BAM detachments. However, since that evening, his relationship with Roman Derenchuk hadn't improved—they did not like and did not tolerate each other, period.

How did Lyubomir feel about Yury? There was no simple answer. Polina could hardly offer an impartial opinion of the man she loved since her teenage years. Yet she conveyed to Lyubomir some glimpse into his inner world, his childhood as an orphan and his occasional run-ins with the law. Perhaps it wasn't enough to form a correct impression of him. It wasn't.

Nevertheless, Captain Nesterenko was willing to accept this tormented man with all his good and not-so-good traits. Dealing with him yesterday had proved how right he was: Lyubomir saw not a drunk, but a deeply wounded person who had lost his footing and often looked for the remedy in a vodka bottle, just as so many Russians do. This convinced Captain Nesterenko even more, that what Yury really needed was help, not judgment.

Now, Yury was sitting in front of Major Vitus and Captain Nesterenko, nervously cracking his knuckles, and wondering what this detective from Khabarovsk was expecting to hear from him. He looked at Lyubomir, hoping to get a hint, but the Captain gave none.

"Listen, Yury. May I call you by your first name without all the formalities?" the Major began, trying to put him at ease. "From Polina, we know about your last trip to Izmailovsky. As a matter of fact, she told us in detail what happened after you left to do some animal trapping, and what she heard those two uninvited guests saying. Polina also told us about your host's reaction upon his return to the house. So, we would like you to tell us what you were talking about with Fyodor during your time together in the woods? Did he share any specific information with you?"

"Why do you think Fyodor would share any information with me? And what do you mean by 'information'? Some private information?" Yury sounded a bit irritated. "We were in the *taiga* all day until dusk. We talked about dozens of things: the books I brought for him to read, about his daughter and his life in general, about God. That is what we usually discussed when we met."

"Let me be frank with you, Yury." Viktor felt that this conversation started on the wrong foot and decided to change his tactics. "We're all upset about what happened to a good man and, as I learned, your close friend. But to catch his killers, we must know who they are and why they committed such a heinous crime. I sense you don't trust the Militia very much, do you? But believe me, a lot of good, dedicated people are involved in solving this case. Ask Captain Nesterenko: he will tell you where he spent the entire day today."

Yury suddenly sat up in his seat and started pounding the desk with his fists. "I wish I knew how to help you more!"

"I understand you are upset. We just need you to focus right now. We need to know as much as possible about Fyodor's movements and conversations with other people, even his thoughts before that tragic night."

Captain Nesterenko pulled his chair up and sat next to Yury. "Please don't hold back any details about his behavior."

Yury collected himself and self-consciously leaned back in his chair. "Maybe I need to start from the beginning. Fyodor and I met for the first time in January of 1975, our first winter here. Captain Nesterenko actually let me borrow his .22 caliber sport rifle, so I could go hunting. Remember that Comrade Captain? I had no idea how or what to hunt in the *Taiga*. I was walking through the woods in deep snow for hours when we saw each other in one of those rare clearings. I couldn't recall who struck up a conversation first – most likely Fyodor, who noticed my icy beard and the purple skin on my forehead. When he approached, he looked at my face closer and asked me where I was from. Then he reached into his pouch and pulled a small tin can with thick yellowish lard. He suggested I scoop some of it up and apply it to my face and hands as a thin layer. "Now, you go home and stay warm. And by the way, you don't need a rifle to hunt.""

"The second time we met was a month later when my drilling unit was sent 25km east of here. We had to help the military construction battalion with the widening of the bridge over the Urgal River. We lived in an antiquated passenger railroad car, which was parked on a sidetrack nearby. On one very cold night, the soldier responsible for our accommodations overslept and didn't maintain the stove. By the time we woke up, all the heating pipes in the car were frozen solid, and some had burst. There was no breakfast to eat and no dry clothes to wear, and so no work was done. Our young housekeeper panicked, not knowing what to do. Instead of immediately informing his superior officer by radio, he tried to start a fire underneath the car to thaw the frozen pipes. He almost burned all of us alive.

"By midday, the Army Captain showed up to assess the situation and soon left to look for another available car to replace the damaged one," Yury continued. "Oh, yes, he brought some skimpy breakfast, whatever he could scrounge together in the battalion camp kitchen three hours before dinner. To keep ourselves warm, we put every piece of underwear we had on and we gathered all wool blankets and pillows we could find in the car closet for cover. It helped, but not for long. By four o'clock in the afternoon, the situation became dangerous: some of us fell into hypothermic shock and hibernation sleep. We at least needed hot, hearty food to sustain our body energy. We were praying for someone to come and save us."

"Whom were you praying to? To God?" Viktor couldn't help but ask.

"None of my guys were religious. At least, they wouldn't admit it," Yury replied sharply. "And yet we prayed. Wouldn't you if you'd find yourself in the same predicament?"

"I guess I would," Viktor agreed. "Please go on. What happened after you prayed?"

"We heard someone trying to open the car entrance door. It wasn't easy. The door was frozen shut. It was ripped open by a man with enormous strength. I recognized this man as Fyodor. He brought a few warm clean sheepskin—*tulups. Along with* a few fur hats, and mittens for us to put on right away. He made us stand up and move vigorously so the blood would flow again. Seeing our circulation coming back to normal, Fyodor had each of us slowly drinking fresh warm water from an old thermos. And only after that, he let us eat some hot soup and boiled potatoes with mushrooms, which he also brought with him. We were we were so happy we were saved. When some of my guys joked that the only thing we were missing was a glass of vodka, Fyodor smiled and calmly explained that he couldn't bring vodka, and that it wouldn't be a good idea to drink anyway, considering that we might spend another night in that cold car."

"My question is: how did he learn that your unit was in such a dire situation?" Captain Nesterenko interrupted. "Fyodor couldn't scan the radio waves, could he?"

"I never asked him about that," Yury replied. "He could've accidentally found this out from the construction battalion soldiers passing by Izmailovsky. Maybe this is how he came to rescue us?"

"It is a plausible explanation." Viktor nodded. "How long did Fyodor stay with you?"

"Until nine or ten o'clock at night, maybe even later. I can't recall now," Yury answered after a short pause. "What I do remember is that he was a very good listener and asked everyone including the poor soldier who had caused this trouble, to share a story about their life before coming to this faraway land. He then reminisced about our first meeting in the *taiga* a few weeks earlier. Later on, Fyodor went back to his buggy to cover his horse with a large wool blanket and came back carrying some dry venison jerky. We were chewing it and played cards—a game of Russian *durak*, the fool. The next morning, the new car was pulled to the sidetrack, and we moved into it."

"So, Fyodor didn't stay with you and your crew overnight?" Viktor asked. He sounded a little impatient. "And this encounter was enough to become such close friends?"

"Probably not; as I said already, we became friends gradually," Yury snapped back. "A week later, Fyodor visited us again. He brought more of the dry venison we liked so much, and we gave him back his coats, hats, and mittens with gratitude. After that, his visits became almost regular, like every second night. We were so exhausted from work and so cooped up in that fucking tight railroad car that any guest—especially someone like Fyodor—was welcome."

"What a special man." Viktor said with a profundity in his voice.

"I remember one afternoon we were walking back from the drilling station, tired and covered in a crust of thick ice. At dusk the *Taiga* along the tracks looked like an impenetrable black wall. A dozen yards away from our destination, we heard heavy stomping in the snow, and the cracking of tree branches. We already knew that some grizzly bears awake from hibernation in search of food during winter. Local people call them *shatuns*—the wanderers; they considered the most dangerous animal to come across in the *Taiga*.

This was the first thought that crossed our minds. We wanted to scare the beast off, but how? I pulled the rifle from my shoulder, cocked it, and fired in the direction of the sounds. The bullet went right through a wall of evergreen shrubs and hit something large. It fell to the ground like a ton of bricks. We ran to the car because we had no idea what to do. Fortunately, Fyodor was sitting there talking with our soldier housekeeper. He knew exactly what to do. He carefully led us over to where we thought this bear was, but to our surprise, we found a huge moose lying dead."

"Oh, you were in trouble," Captain Nesterenko noted. "It wasn't the season to hunt those animals yet, was it?"

"It wasn't. Fyodor told us. But what was done was done. We had to hide the evidence of our unintentional crime. Fyodor brought an ax and knives to dress the carcass. With our help, he did it in about an hour. We were amazed. In the process, he taught us how to drain dead animal blood, how to cut the different parts of flesh, and what to do with the bones. For instance, I've considered myself a hunter since I was sixteen, but I didn't know that animals' bones are to be ground and used in feed, which is an excellent source of calcium and potassium. Fascinating, isn't it?"

"So, what happened later? Did you get in trouble?" Viktor asked.

"I don't recall any case of poaching that winter," Nesterenko interjected.

"Of course, you didn't, Comrade Captain. It was never reported. Fyodor assured us it wasn't our fault; it could've been a mad bear threatening our lives," Yury explained with a smile. "But I am confessing now with no regrets. We ate the venison steaks in secret until we completed our assignment at the bridge. Fyodor would often join us at those feasts, occasionally even preparing the meal himself. We all cherished our time during those late suppers."

"It sounds like you became friends?"

"Fyodor and I spent hours talking. He invited me to his home at Izmailovsky, promising to teach me how to hunt without a rifle. To be honest, I was thrilled to accept his invitation. I met Fyodor at his home for the first time in March. We went to the woods, where he showed me different types of traps for marten, mink, water rat, beaver, and wild rabbit. Back in the house, we spoke about our families, books I've read, and the music I play. We touched on faith too. I told him I didn't believe in God. He asked what I did believe in. My answer: pretty much nothing.

"Fyodor refused to take me at my word. He said that humans were unique because of their ability to hold faith. I argued that nobody could expect me to believe in God or hold any faith after what had happened to my grandparents, parents, and uncle. It proves the opposite: they were faithful and loyal citizens, whom God couldn't protect while our so-called system mercilessly destroyed them and millions of others.

"And look at his family history, I told him, from what I'd heard, it was obvious how difficult it was for him to stay faithful. I thought he would agree with me, but Fyodor surprised me by pointing out that this was exactly why I was mistaken. 'All tragedies in the world happen because, unfortunately, people follow false idols. God and his holy scriptures are here to guide and steer us in the right direction, not to protect every one of us individually. I've always followed those teachings faithfully and led other people to do the same,' he said. 'However, I never identified with the Church supported by the State. God is in my heart, not within the Church. That's why the tougher my life got, the stronger my faith became,' he concluded. Frankly, I wasn't convinced, but it sure made me think."

"It sounds like you had very heated discussions," Viktor interjected. "Wasn't it difficult to form a close friendship from opposing sides of the ideological spectrum?"

"I don't know what you are trying to imply, Comrade Major," Yury said with a sardonic hint. "We weren't that far apart in our ideological convictions. We were both victims of the system. Regarding my beliefs, we never touched this subject again, although Fyodor insisted that I tell him more about my family history."

"To be honest, now I am too interested in hearing this story," the Major proposed. "I am sure the Captain will join me in my request."

"I'd prefer not to talk about it," Yury immediately snapped back. "When I did talk on this subject, I got in trouble with the authorities—the KGB, in particular."

Lyubomir turned toward Viktor with an alarmed expression, as if to say *Wrong move, Major. We'll shut him down by forcing him to speak.* Viktor read the Captain's concern.

"First, Yury, we are not the KGB." Viktor's calm voice projected trust and confidence. "And second, we are professionals entrusted with finding the people who committed a murder of a mutual friend. So, you are our friend as well. I can tell you from my ten years' experience that there are no details too small or too insignificant in circumstantial cases like this.

"I'll let you in on a secret, something I learned from my late father," Viktor continued. "At the beginning of my career as a detective, he told me to listen attentively and with a great deal of respect to the people involved in an investigation—to everything they want to share. Their stories, no matter how silly or irrelevant they might sound, always reveal as much about the person as the case in general, like background layers on the canvas of a painting. Trust me on this; we are genuinely interested in your story."

"Yes, Yury, you can trust the Comrade Major," Lyubomir added. "We are not your enemies, so please, speak freely. You won't get in any trouble, and it may help us to catch Fyodor's murderers."

"Okay, okay, I trust you." Yury still felt uneasy. "I'll tell you about my family's misfortune; of course, this is the short version. But I'm not convinced how relevant this is to what happened to Fyodor."

"Perhaps it's irrelevant. Yet, it might explain what made you and Fyodor such close friends," Viktor said with a philosophical undertone. "So please go on."

Chapter 11

In the summer of 1941, the city of Zaporizhe was exceptionally hot and humid. During times like this, thousands and thousands of people spent their days-off on Khortytsa Island, between the two streams of the Old and New Dnieper. This island was an especially attractive place to hide from the burning sun of the southern Ukrainian steppes (prairies). This was due to its wild vegetation, plants, and trees, surrounded by cool, fresh running water.

But it wasn't a normal summer. The country was at war with Germany, and the enemy advance was a few hundred kilometers away. Workers and engineers were busy dismantling the Zaporizhstal Steel Plant and the Dnieper Hydroelectric Station, to send its major equipment east beyond the Ural Mountains, to prevent the occupiers from using these Soviet industrial gems of the first two *pyatiletkas,* Stalin's five-year industrialization plans.

Nikolai and Pyotr Orlovsky, fifteen-year-old twin brothers, desperately wanted to join the effort with their father Alexei Nikolayevich Orlovsky, the shift supervisor of the electric power plant. The senior Orlovsky understood the pride they shared in his work of twenty years, and the pain in knowing that it must be destroyed. Nevertheless, he could not take the boys to work, and he did not want them to stay with their mother Galina, who was busy packing the house goods which the family would need during the evacuation. So, Alexei suggested that they take their small motorboat and go fishing.

This is how on that hot day of August 18, Nikolai and Pyotr ended up at the northern edge of Khortitsa Island in a little bay across from the largest *balka* (ravine) cutting into the island. The boys knew it was the best spot to catch rudd, which the locals called *krasnoperka*, silver *karas*, and *okun*—perch. First, they dug live worms for bait and then settled with their homemade fishing tackle on the trunk of a fallen tree hunched over the water. After casting the lanyards several times, the brothers realized the fish were not biting. On hot days like this, when the level in the river dropped considerably, the fish stayed away from shallow water.

Usually, the boys didn't waste time waiting for the fish to bite, but rather would be turning somersaults, chasing each other, and jumping on top of each other like two wild cubs. Not today, though. Today, they shared the same somber mood as all the adults since that dreadful Sunday, June 22 of 1941. Like all children of the late 1920s and 1930s, the Orlovsky twins knew nothing of war, despite the old photographs on the walls of their house of their father as a young Red Commissar. Their father never spoke of the Civil War. What little they did know came from reading history books and heroic novels, or motion pictures that romanticized the struggle against the oppressive Czarist regime and the White Guards.

Now, they distinctly sensed that something very terrible and dangerous was entering their lives, the lives of their parents, and all the Soviet people. Instead of playing, the brothers sat quietly on the fallen tree and looked at the gigantic dam of the DAZ Hydroelectric Plant.

Their father, together with thousands of Komsomol workers and engineers, had built the magnificent structure in just five short years. Being born in 1925, only two years before construction started, the Orlovsky twins couldn't recall how this place originally looked. They couldn't remember the small, insignificant town of Aleksandrovsk, the precursor of the city of Zaporizhe, or the Porogui—Rapids that prevented trade on Dnieper from reaching all the way to the Black Sea from Kyiv in the far north. This place was like a magnificent dream for hundreds of years. In the 19th century, a self-taught engineer named Mohylko quietly developed the plans to inundate the rapids and open the whole length of the river to year-round commercial navigation. In 1905, his plans were transformed into an idea for a hydroelectric power station. In the beginning of the 1920s, the newly formed State Commission for the Electrification of Soviet Russia accepted the plans for the DnieproHES, designed by well-known civil engineer Ivan Aleksandrov. It was the first among ten proposed as part of the country's Socialist Industrialization Plan.

In 1923 Alexei Orlovsky arrived in provincial Aleksandrovsk, following his teacher and mentor I.G. Aleksandrov. Being only twenty-four, Alexei had left behind three years of the Russian Civil War and four years of studies at Moscow Engineering Institute. He shared Ivan Grigoriyevich's dream of building Europe's largest hydroelectric power station. Hugh Cooper, a retired Colonel of the United States Army Corps of Engineers, was the project's chief advisor, heading a crew of American specialists.

Most of the building machinery, as well as its first eight water turbines and five generators were imported from the United States as well. The projected annual generating capacity was 558 megawatts. They positioned it 10 kilometers upstream of the town, at the narrowest point between the last of the rapids and Khortytsa Island.

The hardest job was to erect the convex dam of steel reinforced concrete, with nine water chambers, 760 meters long, 60 meters high and 56 meters wide. When it was completed, the water level rose nearly 38 meters, creating an enormous reservoir that filled the narrow valley as far as the city of Dniepropetrovsk 140 kilometers to the north. This man-made lake, named the Dnieper Water Reservoir, flooded the rapids, and made the entire Dnieper a high-volume commercial waterway.

For the passenger and cargo boats to bypass the dam, a two kilometer long three-chamber lock was built, flowing downstream along the left bank of the river. Until the beginning of the Great Patriotic War, the DnieproHES operated up to its designed capacity, except during the hot summer months, when the lower water level in the reservoir forced it to reduce its electrical production output considerably.

But on August 18, 1941, none of the water chambers were open; the turbines and generator stood still, waiting to be dismantled and shipped away. Somewhere in the main station building, Alexei Orlovsky was among the crew of engineers and workers carrying out this sorry task.

The sun took on a crimson color as it set behind the edge of the dam. The brothers had not caught any fish, and it was time to return home, so they decided to pick up their father from the station. Pyotr cranked the small outboard motor and engaged the gear as it coughed up a dark cloud of fumes. Nikolai pushed off from the island, and they carefully maneuvered northwest between the small islands of Durnaya Skala and Stolb. As they drew nearer, they saw the outlines of NKVD soldiers bustling across the top of the dam, pushing along massive spools of red insulated wire. Spotting them, a soldier began waving his arms frantically, shouting something inaudible over the dull purr of the motor.

They reached the quay and began to moor when an officer approached them carrying an open notebook. He demanded their names, their reason for being there, and to know what they had seen. Suspicion overcame Nikolai, who turned to Pyotr and shouted "Go! Go!" The officer began screaming profanities, but the boat was already speeding away in the swift current.

In half an hour, as they passed the southern edge of Khortitsa Island, a thunderous explosion split the very air. Giant chunks of concrete flew above the dam and crashed down into the river.

It felt as if the boat was lifted into the air. The explosion sent wave after wave crashing forward, spilling over the banks and sweeping everything there into its angry surge. Looking back at the dam the boys saw a plume of black smoke rising from a 100 by 24-meter hole, through which the Dnieper Reservoir was pouring in an uncontrollable torrent. But the real horror was yet to come. The boat surfed along the city quays, now swollen with black water cluttered with debris pulled from the banks. Suddenly, human bodies emerged on the surface, floating face down and motionless. Many of them wore Soviet Army uniforms. And still the river rose, climbing the hills that surrounded the city.

Only a few people knew what had really happened to DnieproHES at 16:00 hours on August 18, 1941. The NKVD commanders of the Zaporizhe Region had already planned its destruction after the evacuation of its equipment. When they received intelligence that Wehrmacht troops had advanced just a few kilometers west of the city, they hastily decided to blow it up immediately. Unfortunately, they neglected to alert the military personnel stationed in the city, nor did they inform civilians to vacate the zone of possible flooding. These "brave" NKVD commanders were directly responsible for killing thousands of innocent people.

The outboard motor died, and for the next three or four hours, the twins were in shock, aimlessly floating in their boat south of flooded Khortitsa Island until they finally reached the grossly enlarged mouth of the normally small Sukha River at its confluence with the Dnieper. Somewhere here should've been their family home, but now everything seemed to be underwater. It was no longer daylight, and the boys did not have a kerosene lantern to see their way. They had no choice but to find some other place to spend the night. Their only hope was the house of their Aunt Olga, whose house at the foot of a hill had escaped the flooding. So, they steered the boat west, paddling by hand. It took them an hour to reach their destination. Their loving aunt embraced them when they arrived, and they burst into tears. Despite being tall and athletically built for their age, they were still two scared teenage boys suddenly turned into orphans.

Olga, with tears in her eyes, informed her nephews that her husband Kirill had not come home. She was afraid he shared the same fate as the boy's family, swept away by the deadly torrent. And yet, they held their hopes of finding their loved ones or at least find out what happened to them in the light of the next day.

The next morning the flood water receded, and the horrible tragedy fully revealed itself: hundreds of human corpses— men, women and children lay on the street together with their drowned pets. The Orlovsky brothers returned home to find their mother Galina on the floor dead. There was no sign of Alexei Orlovsky either. Aunt Olga did not find her husband. They both might've drowned and been carried by the rushing water downstream many kilometers away.

The moisture and summer heat churned a stinking vapor across the city. That didn't stop gangs of the survivors from the southwestern outskirts of the city to roam the devastation, looting anything left by the flood — canned food, unspoiled medicine, home articles— anything they could pull from the abandoned grocery shops, drugstores, and houses.

There was nobody to chase them away, neither Militia nor military personnel. The local leadership and their security forces had left the city before the disaster struck. So, when at dusk the advanced German 1st Panzergruppe entered the right bank of Zaporizhe, they met no resistance, not a single shot. Reinforced brigades of the Red Army successfully defended the industrial zone on the left riverbank for forty-five days, giving the Soviets the time needed to finish dismantling the equipment to Siberia.

Then the entire city fell under control of the Wehrmacht. With their famous efficiency, the Germans quickly occupied the city administrative buildings, setting up their command headquarters, Gestapo offices, and civilian police forces. *Politsai* recruitment began immediately. They dressed in black uniforms and carried Russian made carbines and

Nagant revolvers. It was amazing how many potential recruits signed up for service. No doubt there were a few NKVD operatives among them, planted as moles for the coming insurgency.

The first business by the new occupational administration was to stop looting and to clean the city of dead bodies. The *politsai* rounded up all able inhabitants to carry out this task with urgency, burying the dead in the mass graves outside the city limits. The second piece of business was to gather all local Jews with their families in one of the large warehouses in the city industrial zone. The Gestapo officers and *politsai* used a lot of civilian volunteers to complete this job rather quickly. Almost eight thousand Jews, who for some reason did not leave Zaporizhe with their evacuated manufacturing plants, were executed immediately at the mass graves, or shipped to the concentration camps.

Nikolai and Pyotr Orlovsky agreed to stay with Aunt Olga for several reasons: her house wasn't damage by the flood; she required help to gather food provision and other life necessities; and the boys needed a nourishing shelter and had to be away from the city central district with its frequent Gestapo and *politsai* sweeps of youngsters as the best source for forced labor.

Soon, the boys took on new interests. They knew that many of their peers, school friends and neighbors were getting weapons, conspiring to kill invaders or disrupt the invaders' everyday life at every opportunity. Sometimes guns and ammunition could be purchased on the black market or from the greedy, corrupted German collaborators and even more often stolen from drunken *politsai* who fell asleep at the tavern. The Orlovsky brothers wanted to join those young freedom fighters as soon as possible, but they had to wait until March of the next year. It happened by sheer chance after one of their school friends arranged a meeting with a mysterious man who might help them with their plan.

The boys recognized this man the moment they were led into a small room in the basement of a house at the southern outskirts of the city. He was the same NKVD officer who had questioned them near the power station just before the dam was blown up and who got upset when they ran away from him. This time, instead of his spunky clean Major's uniform, he was wearing dirty baggy pants and a body-warming jacket—a telogreika of undetermined color, because it was soaked in machine oil that after getting dry gave it a glittery shine. The man, in turn, either didn't recognize the visitors or didn't care who they were. He looked at the brothers with his penetrating eyes and ordered them to be seated.

"I understand from my friend that you wanted to be useful. Do you?" he began, and without waiting for any answer, he continued. "You are brothers, aren't you? What are your names and age?"

The twins kept silent, as they were afraid the man would recall their first encounter.

"Oh, I see. You, fellows are careful. I like that." The man smiled. "At a time like this and in our line of business, we cannot be too careful. But I need to tell you something; made-up names will work. By the way, you call me Uncle Vasiliy. So, how should I call you, comrades?"

Nikolai came to his senses first, realizing that silence wouldn't get them anywhere and that this man seemed quite reasonable.

"We are the Orlovsky brothers. I am Nikolai, and he is Pyotr. We are almost 16," he reported in one breath.

"Your last name sounds familiar. Did I know your father? Or perhaps I have met you before?" The questions followed.

"Our father Alexei Orlovsky was the shift supervisor at the Hydro Station."

"Where is he now?"

"We are not sure," Nikolai replied in a low voice. "He never came home after the blast. Our mom drowned. We found her the next day."

Total silence sat in the room for a few minutes. Everyone lowered their heads.

"On that day, my wife was lost too. Thank God, my daughter Natalia survived," Vasiliy said with a deep sigh. "She is your age, by the way."

"You were there, you must know. Why was nobody warned? So many people died. Why?" Nikolai suddenly exploded with anger.

"Hey, young man, you don't know what you are talking about." Uncle Vasiliy sprung from the three-legged stool he was perched on. "As I said, in war, shit happens. You weren't there, so don't throw blame."

"We were there. We saw who blew up the dam. We saw you there too, Major!" Nikolai shouted.

"Now I remember you, you were the guys in the boat." Vasiliy took two steps toward the boys. "Tell me, why did you run away?"

"We realized we saw something we weren't supposed to see." Nikolai had no choice, but to explain. "I was sure you would arrest us."

"You bet I would." Vasiliy smiled again. "Although you are a little too young and a little too feisty, I like your way of thinking and acting, son. We can use someone like you." His face became serious. "And about that tragic day in August, we might talk again later. So, what is your decision? Do you still want to join our organization to fight our mortal enemy, Nazi Germany? What about your brother? Is he always this quiet?"

"Yes, we do," Nikolai and Pyotr replied in one voice. "Tell us what to do, please. When are we going to get weapons?" Nikolai added.

"Not so fast, boys." Vasiliy returned to his perch and set. "Before any actions, you have to be trained in using weapons and ammo, in reconnaissance techniques, and especially in self-discipline. Our operations are dangerous. I have no doubts about your determination or your courage, but without such training you are as good as dead and very quickly. We don't want this to happen; we need our soldiers to be deadly, not dead. Understood?"

"Are we going to be soldiers?" Pyotr asked timidly.

"Not regular uniformed soldiers drafted by the Red Army, but soldiers, nevertheless, of the invisible front. We are the soldiers of the guerrilla war that disrupts the enemy behind their front lines. So, we must learn how to blend in, how not to raise suspicion, but strike at them blow by blow, when and where they least expected," Vasiliy concluded.

In three weeks, the brothers Orlovsky became members of the insurgency detachment under the command of NKVD Major Vasiliy Arkhipovich Kozinets, who was assigned to stay in the occupied city and to organize a partisan movement. The boys' training began with learning how to use different guns and explosives. They learned about short wave radio communication, basic cryptography and soon became savvy on how to outsmart the omniscient Gestapo and to survive underground life in general. This was when Nikolai met the love of his life Natalia Kozinets, the daughter of his partisan leader. Regardless of her youth, she was an excellent conspirator, a resourceful intelligence gatherer and experienced radio operator. Natalia was the one who taught her new friends, the Orlovsky brothers, how to become skillful guerrilla fighters by being Jacks-of-all-trades. It wasn't a surprise to anybody, including her own father, that she too fell in love with the good-looking, smart, and fearless Nikolai.

The core of the insurgency detachment under the command of Major Kozinets consisted of only twenty permanent members. Often, for more ambitious diversion tactics, the group would engage additional Ukrainian *partizans* located in nearby forests and ravines. Between the spring of 1942 and fall of 1943, they completed more than a thousand operations of industrial sabotage and assaults on German military installations behind the front line. They seriously disrupted the supply of troops by railroad throughout the entire occupation. They killed or took out of service over two thousand Nazi and *politsai* personnel.

The insurgency group that the Orlovsky brothers were members of provided a big help in supplying Red Army headquarters with invaluable intelligence and reconnaissance information on the enemy troops. Nikolai and Natalia were especially crafty at this job.

Over a period of fifteen months, they snatched dozens of low-ranking Wehrmacht officers, who, during their interrogation, spilled a lot of secrets regarding the planning and execution of some major battles. Such secrets put the Red Army in an advantageous position and eventually positively affected the war outcome.

Nonetheless, there were some failures as well. They intercepted intelligence from the headquarters of Field Marshal Erich von Manstein, regarding a visit from Adolf Hitler himself on February 17th, 1943. The Kozinets' insurgency group coordinated an assault with Soviet Air Forces on the location where *der Führer* was supposed to stay. But two days before the operation, the Gestapo arrested almost half the members of Kozinets' group. Whether it was a mole within the organization or an intercepted radio communication, it was hard to say. The arrested *partizans* were tortured and executed, but they never betrayed their comrades.

Von Manstein and Hitler met in Zaporizhe again, one month later; this time the insurgency's operation ended in even greater disaster. The Gestapo captured and executed Kozinets. The youngest members, including Natalia, Nikolai and Pyotr, escaped and found shelter in one of the safe houses deep in the woods, ten kilometers south of the city. They holed up for a month or so, gathering new members and new weapons. By the end of May, the group, now under the leadership of NKVD Major Rodion Sitkarev, reinstated its presence and renewed its commitment to fight the occupational forces.

During that grieving time, Natalia and Nikolai became intimately close. Pyotr and a small circle of friends and fellow conspirators helped the young couple to celebrate their matrimonial union in the hideout. At the end of July, Natalia informed her husband she was pregnant. This news made Nikolai ecstatic but worried at the same time. From this point on, he did everything in his power to keep the future mother away from the dangers of the field operations and direct confrontations with the enemies.

By the fall of 1943, the fight had intensified. The Germans built the fortified defensive line they called Panther-Wotan along the Dnieper from the Kyiv region down to the Crimea Peninsula. At the beginning of October, they pulled the main Wehrmacht forces behind this line. In Zaporizhe they created a foothold over the river using the Railroad Bridge and DnieproHES dam. These were now targets for the Ukrainian *partizans*. The minefields surrounding their objectives made the raids extremely difficult. Many fighters were blown up before they could even approach the fortifications. The solution was to use human guides from among the people who were employed by Germans to lay those mines down to begin with. Some of them did this under duress, and others gladly agreed to help the *partizans*.

On October 9, Natalia received a coded radio message about an upcoming surprise attack by the troops of the Soviet Southwestern Front, and the order to provide its artillery with accurate reconnaissance information of their targets. This required deep penetration into the enemy's installations; it meant that they had to cross the minefields in the dark. Nikolai slowly moved ahead of the group, closely following the man who claimed to know the mines' layout well enough to avoid stepping on any of them.

Everything went smoothly until they had almost reached their destination, a perfect spot for reconnaissance. It was a small patch of shrubs on the hilltop overlooking the main bridge. Perhaps, being too eager to get to safety, the guide stumbled, lost his step, and touched the detonator of one of the mines. In the blink of an eye, the poor man was reduced to bits. His body absorbed the moderate blast, partially shielding Nikolai, who was right behind him. Luckily, Nikolai was thrown a few meters away from the other mines and toward the nearest bush, landing on his back. He suffered a concussion so severe that he blacked out.

When his consciousness returned, he found his comrades hovering over him, trying to assess the damage. Nikolai bled from his ears and nose, but all his limbs were intact. When he tried moving, he realized that he couldn't feel his legs. Warm thick blood soaked the lower half of his trousers where the shrapnel had torn through his legs. At that moment, Nikolai knew he would live, and his group had a job to do. He knew the Germans would have seen the blast and were already moving to capture them.

He ordered his comrades to drag him behind some shrubs and set up the reconnaissance binoculars with the optical system for determining the coordinates of their targets. A full moon illuminated the entire area of the riverbank, so they had to hurry. Nikolai convinced his comrades that the "fritzes" (Germans) most likely attributed the blast to a random animal and wouldn't risk dashing through the minefield to check it out.

"So, let's finish what we came here for and get the hell out," he concluded.

All the way to the underground base, Nikolai bled profusely. They carried no proper medical supplies, like gauze, iodine solution, or bandages to dress his numerous wounds. So, the comrades carried him back to safety as quickly as possible. Nikolai was still alive when Natalia managed to find a local doctor and summon him for help. But there wasn't much this old provincial doctor could help with except to better attend to his wounds by cleaning them up, removing metal particles, at least as many as he could, and slowing the bleeding down. For the next few days, Nikolai barely clung to life, remaining unconscious and running a high fever. Major Sitkarev pulled some strings with his NKVD superiors to get permission from General Rodion Malinovsky himself to place Nikolai in the Red Army field hospital. At that time his divisions of the Southwestern Front had just recaptured the left bank of the city. The military doctors saved Nikolai's life but had to amputate both of his legs above his knees.

* * *

Yury Orlovsky's voice felt weak. He stopped, closed his eyes, and sighed deeply. He seemed physically exhausted. Suddenly, Polina emerged from the reception room and rushed to Yury. She kneeled in front of him, embracing him passionately yet gently.

"Relax, my love, relax," she pleaded with Yury in a soothing voice. "Darling, you don't have to finish your story if it's too difficult."

Yury opened his eyes and kissed Polina in forehead. She got up and waved her hand, prompting Katerina to enter the room. Apparently, the women had been standing behind the door, listening to Yury for some time. They had stopped Private Kapustin from warning the Major about their arrival and were waiting for a chance to enter.

"You are welcome to join us," Major Vitus said, trying to cover up his surprise. "How did you end up together?"

"Polina came to see me in the hotel," Katerina explained. "We went for supper together. She told me about their friendship with my father and spending the last couple of days in the house before he was killed. I was touched. I wanted to meet Yury too. I hope we did not ruin anything."

"Not at all, not at all." Viktor hurried to assure Katerina. "We were taken by Yury's story, but evidently, he needed a break, so you came just in time." He turned to Orlovsky. "Yury, please meet Katerina, Fyodor's daughter."

Yury sprung from the chair and extended both hands toward Katerina. Without any hesitation, she responded to his gesture and stepped right into his gentle hug. They stood like that for a while, with no words uttered. Then he looked at her face:

"Your father loved you so much," Yury said a bit awkwardly. "You are exactly as I imagined from what he told me."

"Unfortunately, my father didn't have a chance to tell me about you, Yury," Katerina replied. "If you are half as good a person as Polina, I will be honored to have you as my friend too."

"I was too young to remember much about the time my parents passed, but lately, I feel like I lost my father again," Yury said in a low vice, covering his face to conceal his tears. "I know how you feel, Katya. I want you to count on me, like I am more than a friend. Like I am your brother. Will you?"

"Thank you, brother. I will." Katya hugged him again and kissed him on his cheek. "But I would like you to finish your story. Siblings should know everything about each other, shouldn't they?" And she looked at Viktor probingly.

What a day! Viktor said to himself. *What life stories, one after another! Honestly, I am exhausted, and I want to know more about the conversations between Fyodor and Yury the day before the tragedy struck. But Katerina is right, we need to let him finish his story.*

"Yes, Yury, you must continue, if you can."

"It is not much left to tell, but the rest of my story happens to be just as sad."

* * *

After the liberation of Zaporizhe, Natalia stayed in the city with the Orlovskys' Aunt Olga, while Nikolai was transported to one of the hospitals in Siberia to recuperate. Pyotr volunteered to join the Red Army, which was steadily pushing the enemy westward. Nikolai returned home at the end of February of 1944; a week later Natalia gave birth to their son, Yury. Despite the harsh conditions in which they had lived the past few years, the baby was rather healthy. But this wasn't the case for the new mother: Natalia's health began to fade before their eyes. Her body refused to hold any food; she coughed blood and sweated from a moderate fever. The diagnosis was acute colitis. Nikolai stayed near his wife, trying to ease her suffering and help Aunt Olga with the baby. But five months later, on a hot July night, Natalia passed away.

Nikolai was devastated, shutting himself off from the world. His old friends from the *partizan* detachment, some of them invalids as well, tried to lighten his mood by making a makeshift wheelchair for him. It was a primitive and rather noisy contraption: a square wooden seat with ball bearings attached to its corners. Nevertheless, it allowed Nikolai to get out of the house. But nothing, not even his child, could pull him out of his grief. Very soon he found relief from his deep depression inside a bottle of hard liquor.

When, in June 1945, Pyotr returned from conquered Berlin, he found a destitute man, a drunk who roamed the streets all day among the other disabled war heroes, begging for a few rubles to buy cheap wine or drugs. Pyotr Orlovsky took control over the family, becoming its guardian and provider. As a member of the Communist Party, one of the liberators of Budapest, Vienna, and Berlin, he landed a good administrative job in the Zaporozhe municipal office. He moved his aunt and nephew to a nice apartment in the better developed left bank of the city. But his hopes of bringing Nikolai back into the family fold, of making him healthy and productive, quickly evaporated. Occasionally, Nikolai would come visit his toddler son and play with him for an hour or so. Then he would ask for money and disappear, only to return a month later.

Pyotr tried everything to break this vicious cycle. He pleaded with his brother, he threatened him with Militia involvement and involuntary hospital treatment, but nothing worked. Nikolai's alcoholism and drug addiction completely paralyzed his will, suppressing any desire for a normal life. In addition to his physical disabilities, he was rapidly slipping into the abyss of mental illness, exacerbated by the drinking and drug abuse.

One cold day in December 1950, Nikolai vanished from the streets, along with all the other homeless people. A few weeks later, Pyotr learned from a former war buddy, now serving in the local NKVD office, what had happened. Although the information was passed as a big secret, and at best was kind of sketchy, Pyotr felt an emptiness in his stomach as he suspected something terrible had been perpetrated on all those poor invalids. An alarm bell went off in his head.[1]

First, Pyotr visited his Party regional office, demanding an explanation into the whereabouts of his brother. The Secretary brushed off his concern, telling him that his brother and the rest of those people would be better off being off the streets and would be well cared for. He received the same cold shoulder treatment in the NKVD office. Moreover, they gave him a hint not to pursue this issue at all; otherwise, he would get in serious trouble as a communist and as a common citizen. Pyotr knew it wasn't an empty threat, but that did not stop him.

---

[1] Stalin never wanted the people of the Soviet Union to know the true number of those who perished in the Great Patriotic War. Even less known is the number of people who survived the war but returned home severely disabled—The estimate was close to ten million. Soviet soldiers and officers of different ethnicities—Russians, Ukrainians, Jews, Georgian, Armenians, Byelorussians, Kazakhs, Moldovans, Uzbeks, and others, returned back to their homes as real heroes. The more fortunate went back to jobs they held before the war. The less fortunate, who returned disabled, would become permanent fixtures on street corners and public transportation in the major cities. The country neglected to take care of those courageous and highly decorated, but damaged heroes. The millions begging for food and money to buy liquor or illegal drugs very quickly became eyesores for the local administration in cities like Moscow, Leningrad and Kyiv.

As always, the solution to this problem was disguised with good intentions. In 1949, by Decree of the Supreme Soviet Counsel of the Karelia-Finnish Autonomous Republic, the first Center for Disabled Veterans was created. However it wasn't located in Leningrad, but on the Island of Valaam in the middle of Lake Ladoga. No official reason was ever given as to why these neglected people were sent to a dilapidated building which was once a 16th century monastery, several hundred kilometers northeast from the closest city.

Special Militia detachments gathered them in nighttime raids, stripping them of their passports and military IDs, and loading them into railroad cattle cars. Just like the political prisoners, they shipped them off to the centers, which, in fact, were typical internment camps. Those camps were run by NKVD and didn't look even remotely like healthcare facilities, with no glimpse of hope for freedom.

But what could his solitary voice accomplish? Practically nothing. His preoccupation with the matter began irritating his friends and work colleagues; some were afraid to associate with him. Aunt Olga, who was getting older and becoming less capable of looking after little Yury, begged him to stop his crusade and concentrate on rearing his nephew. But it was too late: Pyotr was a man possessed, living only to find his brother and bring him home.

In the spring of 1951, his behavior forced the regional NKVD office to add him to the list of local troublemakers and political dissidents. He spent more and more time in their interrogation rooms and detention cells. They stripped him of his Party membership. But this just made him more determined and more zealous. The man had become "an enemy of the State." One morning in May, two security officers brought Pyotr in, just to talk, they said. This time he did not come back home.

Even at the age of seven, Yury remembered Aunt Olga's devastation when his uncle was taken. She had only a meager pension and no child support of any kind. For the next three years, they lived in the misery of deep poverty. Often, the boy had to steal a loaf of bread or box of cheap flour from the corner grocery store. He wasn't alone: there was a gang of young kids who were already accomplished thieves, pickpockets, and con artists. Like Yury, they all came from desperately poor families. The city Militia occasionally raided their hiding places or swept these rascals up from the stores. Most of them would be back on the streets the very next day. Some were sent to the juvenile work camps nearby as an example to others. Many became hardened criminals after two or three years there.

Very likely, Yury would have shared a similar fate. He ended up in a work camp fifty kilometers from Zaporizhe at the age of fourteen. With two years of hard labor and brutal discipline, he grew into a strong, handsome young man. Nevertheless, his future was predictable: no real education, precarious employment, and most likely involvement with a local criminal gang.

But Yury was lucky. At the gate of the camp upon his discharge, his Uncle Pyotr greeted him. Pyotr had been released from the GULAG just one year earlier, in 1960. While no one would consider him a hero, he was deemed a victim of Stalin's atrocities and fully reinstated in his rights, reclaiming his party membership and his old job. Sadly, Aunt Olga did not live to see her nephew again; she died soon after Yury was incarcerated.

Nine years of misery in the GULAG took its toll on Pyotr's health: he developed emphysema and constant debilitating migraines from working in an antiquated coal mine. However, his attitude and demeanor did not change much; he was the same uncompromising truth seeker and a fierce defender of the weak, no matter how often it got him in trouble with the camp commanders and the *pakhans*. But his sense of guilt persisted, both from his failure to find his twin brother and his abandonment of his young nephew. Perhaps it was the guilt that helped him to survive the GULAG.

Pyotr never relinquished his hope to find and rescue Nikolai, but now, when he finally learned about his presumed death and about Yury's misfortune, his efforts were focused on making sure that his nephew would escape his father's fate and would have a better life. For that, Pyotr was willing to sacrifice his own life.

Nevertheless, nothing went easy and as planned. Bad habits die hard, as they say, and some never do. Yury was as headstrong as his late father. While he appreciated what his Uncle sought to accomplish on his behalf, he resisted it in every possible way. He didn't care much about school, but he cared passionately about guitar playing and song writing. At some point, Uncle Pyotr considered a musical education for his nephew, but it required hard work and total dedication, things that Yury wouldn't commit to. So, this idea faded rather quickly. Yet Pyotr did not lose hope that something of interest for Yury would come alone.

One day, the young man passed by a construction site. A big machine pounded the earth in front of it. The machine resembled a huge caterpillar, with a tall metal mast topped by a set of pulleys guiding heavy steel cords. Yury stood there for an hour or more, observing three men drilling a deep hole, in which other workers set a square concrete pole. It looked so fascinating that he eventually approached a burly man who appeared to oversee the entire process and asked him how someone could join his crew. The man was a little surprised, but he glanced at Yury with a smile and asked, "How old are you? You must be eighteen, have a middle school diploma and complete a special training. I can give you the address where you can go to apply. We need strong people like you who would be interested in our job. It pays well too."

This was it. The desire to be a drillmaster became Yury's motivation to go back to middle school and finish it in one year. When Yury reached eighteen, he was accepted to a trade school for drillmaster training, which he completed with distinction in six months. Uncle Pyotr was amazed at such a change in his nephew's attitude. The young man worked so hard in pursuing his goal that for a while he even put away his beloved guitar. Another thing that also pleased Pyotr was the positive change in Yury's behavior toward his numerous female friends. There were no more wild parties with a bunch of floosies. Yury was 23 when he finally laid his eyes on a tiny brunette— the dark-eyed Polina. She was sixteen at the time. They fell in love and stayed together ever since.

*   *   *

Yury stopped and grinned. He had exhausted his memories, with nothing else to add to his story.

"Why are you not married after being together so many years, may I ask?" Katya inquired after a momentary silence. Perhaps realizing that her question was a bit awkward, she blushed and glanced at Polina apologetically. Polina didn't look very comfortable either and chose not to answer.

Yury, on the other hand, didn't shy away from an explanation: "I am not an easy guy to be in love with. I have fought demons all my life; and when the battle is raging, you better stay clear of me. Polina has proven hundreds of times over that she can handle my occasional fits. So, when we decided to get married, I promised to build her a house first, in which we would settle down and start a family, a big family." Yury paused, sighed and then added, "Why do you think we are here? No one ever called me a big patriot to come to this forsaken land; we just needed the money."

Viktor found this explanation sincere and rather straightforward. No wonder, he thought, that Fyodor Rogozhin and Yury Orlovsky developed an affinity toward each other.

"You know what? We have no regrets coming here," Yury continued. "So many great people have crossed our path. I am not sure we would ever have gotten to know them staying where we were." He paused again and turned to Katya. "I would never have met your dad. I guess it was meant to happen. He needed a son, since his was lost in the war. And I needed a father, since my own government took mine away."

Yury gasped as he tried to mask his sobbing. A deep silence hung in the room for a minute or so. Viktor and Lyubomir exchanged glances, indicating that the nature of the relationship between this young man and the old priest didn't need any further explanation. However, there were one or two details that the Major still wanted to explore.

"Sorry to drag you through all this, Yury. We appreciate your honesty and candor. But I need to ask if you can recall your conversation with Fyodor Rogozhin at your last meeting, before you learned about the intruders. Did you notice any peculiarity in the old man's behavior?"

"During our stroll through the woods, we kept quiet most of the time so as to not disturb any animals," Yury began after gathering his thoughts. "But on the way home, Fyodor inquired if I had any news from my Uncle Pyotr, how he was doing in the sanatorium for lung patients, and if the treatment was helping alleviate his troubled breathing. I tried to put him at ease so that he would not worry about my uncle, because I did feel that there was something worrisome on his mind. I asked him if he went to see Captain Nesterenko. He said he did but that the Captain was busy; that it was no longer important."

"So, he was intimately familiar with your life story, and the people close to you," Viktor clarified. "And yet he wasn't as forthcoming with you about the details and problems in his life, I presume?"

"I am not sure." Yury paused. "I guess he told me only what he wanted me to know about himself. I remember early on, he did tell me about his son, who from a very young age lost his way and mixed with the wrong crowd. It caused him a lot of pain, especially after Fyodor learned of his death in the war. He also told me about his own unjust incarceration, during which he got lucky meeting a woman he fell in love with, who later died, giving birth to their daughter." He turned his head to Katya again. "Fyodor always smiled mentioning you. The deep wrinkles on his forehead would disappear; he would look younger and happier. I'd say I knew enough about the man to have him as my closest friend, don't you think?"

Viktor nodded agreeably. "Did you notice any change in Fyodor's demeanor after Polina talked about two men trying to break into the house in your absence? Did he explain what this was all about?"

"He didn't explain anything. He just told us not to be concerned with this unfortunate incident, which he would take care of," Yury answered. "But he seemed preoccupied and worried. I had a strong feeling that he knew something about those intruders. Next morning, we left without hearing another word about it."

Captain Nesterenko was ready to interject with his own question when Private Kapustin's head appeared through the slightly ajar door.

"Sergeant Darsulov is on the line," he reported rather anxiously. "He insists on talking to you, Comrade Major. It's urgent."

Viktor rushed to the radio in the reception room. The connection wasn't very good—the voice crackled and faded in and out, so Darsulov spoke short and clear: "The same man who escaped the other day attempted to gain access to the unoccupied house closest to the edge of the *Taiga*. We surrounded the assailant, but things didn't work out as planned: he managed to escape again. It looks like one of the newly arrived servicemen managed to hit him, but it's hard to say the extent of the wound. We are awaiting your further instructions."

Major Vitus couldn't hide his disappointment. However, he realized that it would be almost impossible to maintain a reliable radio connection any longer. So, Viktor was concise: "Leave half of the personnel at Izmailovsky in case the one who got away comes back. Take the arrested man to the Chegdomyn Hospital to attend to his injury. Watch him like a hawk at all times. Tomorrow, cuff him securely and put him on the train to Khabarovsk, accompanied by at least three service men. I will arrange to receive him at the Khabarovsky railroad station and deliver the perpetrator to the MVD Headquarters. Thanks for your service, Sergeant. Copy that."

Everyone heard and understood what had just happened but did not ask any questions. Viktor dialed the telephone operator and asked for the number in Khabarovsk. Surprisingly, the operator informed him that General Melekhov was on the line waiting to speak with him. *The General must have already received news of the arrest from another source,* Viktor thought. Their conversation was short and encouraging. Although the Major's face still expressed concern, his eyes beamed with satisfaction.

*   *   *

Next morning, Tuesday, November 15 at 7:00, the entire crew and Katerina gathered at the hotel reception desk with their luggage to check out. The woman on duty said, "Your bills are squared away. Comrade Gurevich and Comrade Kulikov are waiting for you at the diner. Captain Nesterenko is there too." She smiled and added less officially, "Have a safe drive home."

Viktor recalled that yesterday Lyubomir had mentioned something about the chief-engineer and local party organization secretary wanting to meet with Major Vitus and his crew before they left. With all the anxiety and excitement of last night, he didn't pay attention to this request and didn't care much about it. But now he realized that they must honor the hospitality of their hosts, especially if this was of any importance to Captain Nesterenko.

The representative of the local administration Semyon Davidovich Gurevich and Communist Party official Vasily Sergeyevich Kulikov both happened to be very well-educated professionals and well-mannered men. During the breakfast, they praised the excellent work of the local Militia, headed by expert detectives from Khabarovsky UVD, in capturing one of the perpetrators of the hideous crime so quickly. They also complimented Lieutenant Nina Toropko and Katerina.

By twenty to nine Sergeant Pyotr Uvalov had the *kozyol* loaded and warmed up, ready to go. Viktor, his colleagues, and Katya hugged Captain Nesterenko, who seemed overwhelmed with emotions.

"Don't you worry, Comrade Major, we will catch the other killer." He sounded reassuring. "This bastard has no place to hide."

"I have complete confidence in you," Viktor replied. "Please, send our regards to Lyuba, and thank you. We'll be in touch."

Chapter 12

Saturday, November 19, 8:00 in the morning. Cleanly shaved and wearing a neatly pressed suit, Major Vitus stood before General Melekhov, who came around his office desk to greet him.

"Good morning, Major," the General started formally but changed his tone right away. "How are you, Viktor? How was your drive back home?"

"It was absolutely uneventful," Viktor answered without any expressiveness in his voice. "Comrade General, I have a request to make. It concerns Katerina Rogozhina, the daughter of the slain preacher."

"Hold on, Comrade Major." General Melekhov waved his hand in the direction of the long conference table. "One step at a time, you know. First, we are going to discuss this case. Colonel Guzyev, your immediate boss, Lieutenant Toropko, and Major Levin, her immediate boss, are on their way here. I called them to this meeting just before you came."

"I need to make my request in complete confidence, Sir." Viktor insisted.

"It seems you took a special interest in this woman. I've heard she is remarkably beautiful." Viktor tried to conceal his smile. "You will make your request after the meeting. They are in the reception room already."

The General opened the door and invited everyone in, showing them to the chairs around the conference table. Colonel Anatoly Guzyev, the Head of the Criminal Investigation Department, moved around the table and took the chair closest to the General's desk. He was a heavy framed man in his late fifties with a large, bald head sitting on a thick, short neck. Next to him was Major Leonid Levin, the recently established department manager for scientific studies and criminal forensics. He was a tall, boyish-looking man, with curly brown hair and a pair of thick glass spectacles mounted on his nose. His rather large Adam's apple rolled up and down under his protruding chin.

Nina and Viktor took their places on the opposite side of the table. Viktor wondered if she was the one who had tipped off the General about Katerina.

Melekhov started the meeting without ceremony, "Comrade Vitus, you may begin."

"Of course, Comrade General. What we have here is a double homicide which happened within a timeframe of ten to twelve hours. The preliminary conclusion of Captain Nesterenko, the local railroad Militia commander, who in both instances arrived on the scene first, was that the two cases were related. And he was correct. Victims Fyodor Rogozhin and the Korean Soldier Kim knew each other and had met on several occasions in the home of the murdered priest. The autopsy conducted by the Chegdomyn coroner Doctor Goldfarb confirmed the use of the same weapons and the same methods in both killings. Circumstantial evidence pointed to the strong possibility that Soldier Kim, who was seeking shelter from the cold, happened to be in the wrong place at the wrong time. He witnessed the killing of Rogozhin inside his friend's house."

"He couldn't escape?" Colonel Guzyev asked. "This soldier Kim was a young fellow and knew the surrounding *Taiga* pretty well, I presume?"

"Initially, he did escape." The Major turned his head toward his boss and continued. "Kim managed to find safety in the nearby Listvenny Militia outpost, where he reported the horrendous crime, he had witnessed to Sergeant Lutsenko. Lutsenko immediately conveyed this information to Captain Nesterenko by radio and tried to detain Kim until someone from the Korean work camp could collect him. We determined from our conversation with the Korean camp commander Riyn Chul-Moo that this young soldier Kim, was selling Japanese watches and Korean moonshine liquor. He likely ran from Lutsenko's custody to avoid being caught with the contraband in his possession. The two killers, whom, by the way, Sergeant Lutsenko noticed standing and smoking at the edge of the *Taiga* early in the morning on route to his shift, were after Kim all night and saw his sudden departure from the Militia precinct. They followed and killed him two kilometers from Listvenny."

Melekhov interrupted, "All right, let's presume we know why this Korean soldier was killed, but what is the motive for killing Fyodor Rogozhin? This is the main question."

"We gathered very important physical evidence and spoken testimonies from the victim's sister, his daughter, his friends, and other acquaintances. They had a chance to observe his behavior or were in contact with him before his demise. Everything has brought us to the conclusion that this wasn't a random crime. Rogozhin knew his killers well, at least one of them. He let them into his own house, perhaps on two separate occasions. We are not one hundred percent sure why he did that, or who the men are and why they killed him with such rage. However, we have a few solid hypotheses." Viktor paused and looked at Nina. "Lieutenant Toropko, would you like to tell us about your findings?"

"Of course, Comrade Major." She glanced at the notes in front of her and straightened her posture. "We collected several artifacts of a personal nature inside the house, where the murder took place. We ran these by the victim's daughter for better identification, and the condition we found them in at the crime scene—everything points to the fact that an interaction between the host and his visitors was very personal and emotionally charged from the start, and yet the violence, which led to the killing, erupted unexpectedly. The uncontrollable rage and intention to humiliate the victim came after." Toropko paused. "Who initiated the lethal outburst we don't know, but hopefully, we'll find out as soon as we interrogate the suspect, who was apprehended and is in our custody."

The General interjected again. "Did any of you have a chance to speak with him yet?"

"No, we have not interrogated him, although I did try," Colonel Guzyev replied soberly, and with a hint of disgust. "He refuses to talk at all, complaining about his medical treatment, although it was obvious that he himself sabotaged the doctors' instructions. So, he's been in and out of KPZ to get medical attention. I am sure he will try to drag this situation out as long as he can."

Melekhov dropped another question. "Do we have any idea about his identity? I saw him briefly; he looked like a real *vor-v-zakone* (a professional thief ordained by his criminal peers). It shouldn't be difficult to identify him. Please photograph him and send his pictures through the proper channels immediately. Is there any news about the whereabouts of the other suspect? He was injured too, as I heard from Captain Nesterenko. Wasn't he bleeding?"

"Yes, Comrade General, he was wounded—twice, as a matter of fact." Colonel Guzyev hurried with the answer before Viktor could open his mouth. "Although his wounds were bleeding, they were most likely superficial. Militia personnel pursued him for about three kilometers through the *Taiga* but lost him."

"How is that even possible?" The General sounded infuriated. "Wounded twice, bleeding, and as I recall from your report, Comrade Major, a middle-aged man with a severe limp— but somehow, he managed to get away. Can anybody explain that?"

"He seems to be a remarkably strong man, Sir. He has a limp in his left leg according to Anna Volkova, the younger sister of Fyodor Rogozhin," Viktor started slowly, afraid to show his emotions. "However, I would take her testimony with a grain of salt. Anna's eyesight is very poor: well-advanced glaucoma and large cataracts on both of her eyes. Although she is not that old, she also exhibited rather serious symptoms of dementia. During our prolonged conversation, she confused me with my late father, whom she claimed she met before. And then Anna even insisted that she recognized her son Dmitry Volkov in this limping man. According to his military records, Volkov was killed during the war. I think the woman wanted to see Dmitry in this man. Still, her delusion was evident—by her own admission, the man never expressed any emotional connection, but on the contrary was rude to her. At one point, this presumed son Dmitry almost let his older and more brutish friend cut her throat."

"A mother's instinct is very strong, Major." Melekhov interrupted. "Perhaps she did recognize him. And his brutal behavior toward the mother he hadn't seen since the war is a totally different story?"

"Frankly, her state of mind is very hard to overlook. Her niece Katerina Rogozhina informed me of how serious her condition is," replied Viktor.

The General nodded. "Comrade Toropko, continue with your findings."

"Thank you, Comrade General." Nina glanced at Viktor, then went on with her report. "We don't have to talk to the suspect in custody to determine what was the initial object of contention between the victim and the perpetrators of this crime. According to Anna Volkova's testimony, the two men brought a heavy package into her house for safekeeping. Several pieces of evidence—a scrap of burlap and shreds of newspaper used as wrapping material—point to its contents: it was unprocessed or perhaps roughly smelted gold. We cannot yet determine with certainty the exact weight of these nuggets or the place they were prospected. However, the collected soil samples from the suspect's footprints may help us to determine the origin of the gold."

"We are running an analysis of these samples as we speak," interjected Major Levin. "After getting the results, we will compare them with the information requested from the different gold mining companies and smaller river dredges in the adjacent regions. It's improbable the gold came from far away."

"So, in a summary, the package of gold, stolen for sure, was the main motive for the homicide." The General looked at Lieutenant Toropko again.

Viktor felt it was his turn to take back the initiative of this meeting.
"I don't think it was the only reason for killing the old man, although it was definitely the motive to confront Fyodor Rogozhin. Rogozhin took the package left by someone who his sister Anna recognized as her son Dmitry and his friend for temporary safekeeping and promised to deal with this matter. When the visitors learned from Anna that she was no longer in possession of their fortune, they grew furious and confronted Fyodor." Viktor paused for a moment to catch his breath. "My guess is that it wasn't the first meeting they had. A few days before, two men visited Rogozhin and asked him to help them with their loot. They couldn't walk around with a pack of gold. It had to be stashed somewhere before they could find a buyer. Fyodor refused to help and threatened to notify the local authorities. That's why the thieves went to Anna for help."

"Why do you think he didn't act on his threat?"

"I have a feeling that during the first encounter, perhaps Rogozhin did in fact recognize one of them, and was hesitant to warn the authorities?" Viktor paused again. "He did try to get in touch with the local Militia. Yury Orlovsky, in his testimony, recalled their conversation about Captain Nesterenko, during which the old man asked if he could trust the Captain with some delicate predicament Fyodor had gotten into. He even went to see the Captain in New Urgal. Unfortunately, Nesterenko was busy with another matter at the time and didn't hear out what Rogozhin wanted to share with him. Instead, Fyodor had a short and apparently meaningless conversation with a local journalist Leonid Gordin about the poorly managed post office at Listveny and then urgently left the precinct."

"So, what light does this information shine on these events?" Melekhov asked in a caustic tone.

Viktor ignored the General's tone. "It gave me a hunch. I asked Captain Nesterenko to visit the post office in Listvenny and see if Rogozhin had been there in the last few days. My hunch was right: the day he was killed, Rogozhin went to the post office and sent a large parcel packaged in a makeshift wooden box to an address in Khabarovsk."

"I assume this parcel was already gone. Otherwise, we would have it in our hands now?" Again, the General asked.

"It wasn't gone yet, but I instructed the Captain not to interfere with its shipment," Viktor replied.

"Can I ask you why you made such a request, Comrade Vitus?" The General could not hide his irritation.

Viktor felt a knot in his stomach but kept his cool. "First, I was sure that the perpetrators were watching our every move. They were so desperate to get the package with the gold back that they attacked Rogozhin's cabin twice. They might have attacked the Captain upon seeing him retrieve the package. Furthermore, wouldn't we need a prosecutor's warrant to retrieve the parcel from the State Postal Service?"

"All right, Major, your argument makes sense. And yet something more important prompted your decision, didn't it?" Melekhov said with a hint of reconciliation.

"Yes, Comrade General, there was another reason not to seize the package at Listvenny and let it continue to travel to Khabarovsk for a few extra days. I thought it would buy us more time to catch these men before they could harm more innocent people."

"Whom would they target, Major?" General gave Viktor a piercing glance.

"Fyodor Rogozhin's daughter Katerina first of all," Viktor answered in one breath and lowered his eyes. "The parcel was addressed to her. That's what I needed to talk to you about earlier, Comrade General."

"You mean about her protection?"

"Yes, Comrade General."

"We'll talk about that after this meeting is over," Melekhov acknowledged. "But now, let's get back to some facts. If you suspected that Rogozhin recognized someone he knew, do you have any hunches about who that person could be, if he is not Anna's son Dmitry?"

"I don't know yet, but I am sure we'll find out soon," Viktor replied calmly, looking straight into Melekhov's eyes. "Judging by the gruesomeness, this murder looks very personal. I have high expectations for the interrogation of the man we caught."

"Don't get your hopes too high, Major," Colonel Guzyev interjected. "You'll need some real incentives to make him talk."

"Or you must have something to throw him off, something to trick him into talking, to play on their pride, maybe vanity. People like that are usually full of themselves," General Melekhov picked up the Colonel's thread. "Research this suspect thoroughly, so he feels naked, with no place to hide. He'll talk."

Viktor didn't doubt the General. He had learned how good an interrogator Melekhov was from his late father.

"All right, comrades, I think we have a good grasp of the case." The General stood up and glanced at his wristwatch. "Let's meet again in 48 hours updates. For now, find out where the gold came from. And have our artist compile a sketch of the suspect still. Distribute this sketch throughout the Krai. Confirm everything about Dmitry Volkov, the nephew of Rogozhin. Search for information on the entire Rogozhin family. Who knows what you may find?" The General paused for a moment. "Get me as much as possible on the man in custody. I am sure he has a long criminal history. And one more thing: what's the link to Roman Derenchuk? I have heard about his father, Myron Zazulya, Rogozhin's protégé, during their time in the GULAG. I would talk to someone in the Zyma settlement who was intimately familiar with both. Everyone is dismissed except Major Vitus."

They gathered their notes and left the room. Viktor remained seated. Melekhov called in his secretary. "Nadezhda Petrovna, be so kind and make some hot tea for the Major and me. Or maybe Viktor would prefer coffee? No? Then, please, two cups of tea and some crackers perhaps."

"I apologize if I was hard on you in there, Viktor," Melekhov began as soon as Nadezhda Petrovna closed the door behind her. "I want to ensure you miss nothing. There are too many unanswered questions, too much history."

"Believe me, I am taking this case very seriously."

"There are too many strange links between what happened thirty years ago and today. I am sure you noticed that in the files." The General abruptly stopped when his secretary entered the room, carrying a wooden tray with two cups of tea and a saucer with a few biscuits on it.

"Thank you, Nadezhda Petrovna. You may take your lunch now." Melekhov took one of the cups from the tray and put it in front of Viktor, as the secretary nodded and left again.

"Indeed, Mikhail Grigoriyevich," Viktor replied without skipping a beat. "I had this nagging feeling when we were driving through the streets of Chegdomyn that I had seen those streets before. And the old woman—Aunt Anna, kept calling me Nachalnik or Commissar Vitus and asking about my mustache."

"You did visit this little town when you were six or seven, Viktor." The General smiled and explained. "I remember your mother, when she had to stay in the hospital for a few days, gave your father a hard time for taking you with him. So, you may actually have memories of that. And you do look quite a bit like your father when he was young. No wonder that half-blind, confused old woman mistook you for him."

"And yet, don't you find all those coincidences strange?" Viktor continued. "It was like revisiting something that happened thirty years ago to someone else, but somehow now it's me."

"Don't overthink the significance of those coincidences. Stay focused on the facts of the case at hand." Melekhov spoke calmly but forcefully. "You cannot anticipate everything that comes your way. Deal with adversities at hand."

"Yes, Comrade General, I'll do my best."

"Then let's discuss some other issues." Melekhov glanced through his notes. "Katerina Rogozhina—is she an actress? We'll need to cover not only her residence but the Theatre too. It will not be easy to set up her security detail in such a busy environment. Station one private and one uniformed officer twenty-four/seven in the hall of her residence, and two plain-clothed agents at the Theatre whenever she is there. Pick smart, experienced people for this assignment. They must realize that Rogozhina is very valuable bait."

"I will monitor her protection constantly." Viktor injected with enthusiasm.

"Of course, you will, Major." Melekhov tried to hide his smile. "Just don't be too obvious."

"Yes." Viktor lowered his head to hide how red his cheeks were.

"Now, reading your reports, I was impressed with Captain Nesterenko as much as you were. His way of analyzing the facts and his actions prove that he has what it takes to be a good investigator. I wonder if the Captain would be interested in being transferred to Khabarovsky UVD. I can talk to his superiors at the Railroad Militia Administration." The General paused and looked at Viktor. "Can you probe his intentions during your next telephone conversation?"

"I can, but I don't think he'll be interested in such a deal." Viktor explained, "As far as I understand, Lyubomir took the job at the BAM to improve his family's financial circumstances. He doesn't intend to stay in our neck of the woods any longer than necessary. As a matter of fact, just two days before our arrival to New Urgal, he sent his school-age daughter and his mother-in-law back to Lviv."

"Ask him, anyway, will you?" the General insisted. "You never know; perhaps his ambitions will change his plans. Although, I can't promise him a comparable salary to what he is getting now from the BAM administration."

"I will ask him." Viktor nodded. "Believe me, it would be great to have Lyubomir as a colleague or even a partner."

"By the way, I am going to write to his superiors a Letter of Commendation and petition for promoting Captain Nesterenko immediately to the rank of Militia Major." Melekhov closed the subject and got up from his chair.

Viktor sprung from his seat as well. He felt relieved that this long meeting was finally over so he could go back to the business at hand and then, perhaps later, go see Katya. He hadn't had one word of communication with her since they had arrived back in Khabarovsk. He had a strong urge to see her.

He was just about to exit when the General's voice stopped him: "Why haven't you visited your mother yet? She is worried about you. I think she has something important to share with you."

Viktor turned around and approached Melekhov's desk. The General looked pale.

"Mikhail Grigoriyevich, I have something important to share with her too." Viktor almost whispered. "But I don't know how she will react. It might upset her."

"Son, are you talking about Katerina?" The General whispered similarly. "Why do you think it will upset her? She will be happy."

"No, no, it has nothing to do with Katya," the Major protested, raising his hands. "It is something I found out talking to Leonid Gordin, the journalist we met in New Urgal. You've read his testimony in my reports."

"Oh yes, of course. It was about Gordin's conversation with Fyodor Rogozhin two days before the old man was killed. But how does all this relate to your mother?"

"What relates to my mother is the story of Leonid's family, particularly his mother." Viktor paused, suddenly hesitant to tell the General about it.

"If you don't want to tell me, then don't." Melekhov stood up and glanced at Viktor with sincere sympathy. "However, I am sure you must tell Leya Solomonovna whatever you have learned."

"I guess I must." Viktor began slowly. "No matter how sad this story is, it might offer my mother some closure. You see, I have a gut feeling that Leonid's late mother Sonja and Leya were sisters who lost each other more than sixty years ago. The problem is, there is no proof."

"Incredible!" the General exclaimed. "I understand why you are experiencing some apprehension. I wish we had more reliable means to check these things out, but I think you should tell her immediately. Don't you agree?"

"I am not sure, Uncle Misha, I am not sure."

* * *

As the huge, heavy entrance door of Khabarovsky UVD slammed behind him, a gust of freezing wind hit Viktor's face. He pulled his coat collar up and closed his eyes against the burst of white flakes. The winter storm had started last night, but only today gathered real strength. The wide city streets and big buildings alongside became wind tunnels, swirling the thick snow up and down. Walking was no small effort, but Viktor didn't have a choice: Freckles had the day-off.

It took him more than twenty minutes to cover the three city blocks to the corner of Muravyov-Amursky St. and Turgenev Street, running parallel to the Amur River. Viktor took shelter under the Museum's portico. He had to decide: to turn right and see his mother or turn left for the apartment building where Katya resided. Viktor wanted to see Katya and talk to her to make sure she felt better.

He turned left onto Turgenev Street, fighting with the stormy wind. By five o'clock, he reached Katya's building. He pulled open the door and rushed in, climbing the stairs to the second floor two or three steps at a time.

As Viktor was about to reach the door, he noticed out of the corner of his eye a Militia officer step in from shadows. He instantly felt the unmistakable poke of a pistol barrel at his back ribs.

"Hurrying somewhere?" the man asked. Viktor slowly turned around. It was obvious this officer did not recognize him in plain clothes. Viktor couldn't recall the officer's name either, but he'd seen him before.

"I am Major Vitus," Viktor said, as he slowly pulled out his badge. The officer examined it but did not put down his weapon. Viktor smiled in approval. "Good job, Captain...?"

"Captain Mukhin, Comrade Major."

"Captain Mukhin. You can lower your weapon, Son." Mukhin lowered his gun, with slight embarrassment. Viktor relaxed his body and continued, "Is everything under control?"

"Yes, all is quiet. Citizen Rogozhina went to the grocery store earlier today. I escorted her. Since then, she hasn't left."

"Again, good work, Captain Mukhin. What time will your partner replace you?" Viktor asked.

"In two hours, Comrade Major. We have twelve-hour shifts."

"Okay, Captain, you can stand down," the Major ordered. "I have to talk to Citizen Rogozhina, so I'll go in."

Captain Mukhin stepped away from the door and sat himself on a chair on the landing. Viktor pushed the buzzer, took one step back so he could be seen through the peephole, took his hat off, and instinctively ran his hand through his unruly hair. In a few seconds, the door opened. She wore a simple dark blue dress and beige wool cardigan. Her hair was tightened in a big knot on the back of her head. She looked stunning and Viktor couldn't help but smile but feeling Mukhin's curious gaze, he wiped it from his face.

"May I come in?" he asked in a formal tone of voice. "I hope it isn't too late?"

"Of course, Comrade Major." Katerina answered in a formal tone, fully understanding the situation, "I just finished cooking, so I hope you won't mind joining me for dinner? I would be happy to invite the Captain too, but I understand he cannot leave his post."

The Captain sprang up and waved his hand, showing Katya that she was right in her assumption. Viktor stepped over the threshold and slowly closed the door behind him.

"I will be glad to join you for dinner, if you insist." He didn't hide his smile anymore.

"Oh yes, I insist." She smiled, taking his coat and hat. "For a second, I did not recognize you in civilian clothes. I have to admit, you look equally dashing in both attires, Major."

Viktor flashed a sardonic smile, but he liked the compliment.

"I'm glad to see your good humor returning, Katya. And please call me Viktor."

"All right! I will call you Viktor when we are alone. Come to the table, please. Viktor…"

Katya led the way into the main room. A white cloth covered a round table under a pretty crystal lamp hanging from the ceiling. "Before we eat, would you like some wine? Red or white?"

"Red, please."

"I prefer red too—even with fish. White wine gives me a headache sometimes." Katya brought a bottle of red wine and set a corkscrew on the table. "I hope you know how to operate this device?"

"Let's find out." Viktor quickly uncorked the bottle. "Do you need any help in the kitchen?"

"You know your way around the kitchen, as well?" Katya called from the kitchen playfully. "Did your girlfriend train you?"

"My *mother* raised me very well. And she even taught me to cook ."

"Really!? My father was the one who taught me. He was a great cook." She stopped.

Viktor went silent too and they both moved from the kitchen to the dining room. Katya brought a glass bowl full of cut cucumbers, raw onions, and radishes. She put it on the table, poured some oil on top, sprinkled some salt, and turned everything several times with a lacquered wooden spoon. But her eyes never left his. Finally, she broke the silence.

"What about your father? Nina told me he is in the Militia, too."

"He *was* in the Militia. My father died about two years ago. He… allegedly committed suicide a few months after his retirement." Katya was visibly shaken by what he had just told her.

Viktor was himself surprised by his sudden frankness. He tried to diffuse the awkwardness by pouring the wine.

Katya took a sip and kept looking at him in anticipation. Viktor continued.

"In 1937, my father investigated your father in response to an anonymous letter alleging his involvement in anti-Soviet activity. Even though she was confused, your aunt was correct in recognizing my father in me. She had known my father, Commissar Vitas, back in '37."

"Why was she so hostile to you?"

"I don't know. My father's investigation concluded that the accusations were baseless. He closed the file. Actually, in the process of his investigation, my father and your father became quite good friends."

"Your father had mentioned their relationship?!" Katerina asked in amazement.

"He did not, But I came across some notes confirming that they saw each other a few times over the following years. When your father was investigated again in 1949, and eventually incarcerated, I did not see any proof of my father's involvement at that time."

"You said your father 'allegedly' committed suicide. You think it wasn't a suicide?"

"At first, I was sure someone forced him or even helped him take his own life." Viktor spoke slowly, in a low voice. "I investigated all the circumstances and went through all the documents my father left behind, including - by the way - your late father's case files. There were no direct or indirect connections, no obvious reason for him to kill himself. At least, I could not find any."

"And then what?" Katya put her hand on top of Viktor's.

"It was a difficult time, both personally and professionally. Eventually, my new commanding officer, General Melekhov, closed the case. And he was correct."

"So, you are satisfied with the results of your investigation?" Katerina asked.

"I don't see any evidence of foul play. But…" Viktor took a deep breath.
They went silent again, sipping their wine. Katya went back to the kitchen and returned carrying a large pot. They filled their plates with *Zharkoye* (a hearty meat stew) and began eating. Viktor smiled and raised up his thumb up in approval. Katya blushed. He couldn't tell if it was the wine or something else.

The bottle was almost empty, when Katerina excused herself, went to her bedroom, and soon re-emerged with a hefty yellow envelope in her hand.

"Remember, I promised to let you read my aunt Dasha's letter." Katerina handed the envelope to Viktor. "Here it is. It is quite long but it will give you a good idea who my parents were, as people."

Viktor took the letter carefully and tried to open it up. Katya immediately objected by gently and yet forcefully grabbing Viktor's hands.

"Please, not here, not now. You can have it for as long as you need it."

"All right." He put the envelope in the inner pocket of his jacket and looked into Katya's eyes. "I think it's time for me to go. Thank you for a delicious meal, delightful wine, and your abundant patience with me. I hope we'll do it again soon, if it won't interfere with your private life." Viktor paused for a moment, waiting for her reaction, although none followed. "There is also something important I need to mention: you will be receiving a postal notice for an incoming package. Let your security detail know the minute you receive it. They will alert me immediately. Do not tell anyone else about it, and do not go to the post office…"

"Do you mean this notice?!" Katerina interrupted, jumped up, ran to the kitchen drawer and ran back holding a little green piece of rigid paper. "I received it today and didn't pay much attention. I am used to receiving packages of nuts and berries from my father. What so important about this one?"

"Your father sent this the day before he was killed," Viktor explained as delicately as he could. "Tomorrow, I will personally go with you to the post office. We have to get this parcel as soon as possible and as discreetly as possible. You will understand everything later, I promise."

"Yes," Katya agreed reluctantly. She moved toward the door, pulled Viktor's winter coat from the hook, and handed it to him. She suddenly looked tired.

"You did not answer me, Katya, if we could repeat this evening again." He felt a little embarrassed, like a schoolboy, but it didn't matter.

"Maybe we will. I don't know," Katya replied hesitantly. "It is late; I must be at the Theater very early. I'll see you tomorrow anyway, Major."

The door closed slowly behind him. Captain Mukhin sprang to his feet. The Major glanced at his Japanese wristwatch. It read 11:15.

"Be vigilant, Captain." Viktor patted Mukhin's shoulder. "We have someone very precious to protect."

* * *

The freezing wind burned his face as Viktor walked out into the empty street. In seconds, his mouth was full of snowflakes. He spat them out, pulled up his coat collar, and made his way toward his home. He thought about Katya, about the case, and about tomorrow.

Approaching the corner, Viktor caught a long shadow in his peripheral vision. He first thought it was his own shadow, but then it moved rapidly in the opposite direction. Instinctively, Viktor stepped sideways. It was too late! Someone very large crashed into him, trying to grab him around the waist and tackle him to the ground.

Viktor trained in Sambo and Jiu-jitsu since he was 12, and though he has neglected the gym for many months now, the instincts kicked in. He spun around quickly, using his attacker's inertia, and flipped him over his hip. The man went down hard; letting out an animalistic groan as he hit the snow. But, for a man his size, he was agile and quickly regained his footing.

Viktor reached for his gun, but the buttoned-up coat and scarf slowed him down enough for his attacker to reach him first. *'Damn it!'*. The big man grabbed Viktor by the lapels and swung him into the wall. The impact knocked off his hat and the wind from his lungs. The big man followed up immediately with a powerful punch to Viktor's midsection. Viktor blocked most of the force of the blow with his right hand and immediately countered with a right elbow to the man's throat. The elbow landed closer to the chest, but the big man still staggered backwards a step, giving Viktor a chance to follow up with a vicious kick to the knee. The big man buckled. No time to go for the pistol now. He'll have to finish this with his hands. Viktor stepped in with a left hook aiming at his attacker's temple. He made good contact, but the effect was minimal. The big man tried for another tackle, but this time Viktor felt a simultaneous blow to his upper back. Knife! Viktor cursed himself again. I'm done!

The attacker grabbed his coat collar again and slammed him against a wall. Viktor's head began to spin and he felt warm and sticky blood running down his back as he slid down. That was the last thing he remembered before losing consciousness.

* * *

Viktor had no idea how long he was unconscious, hunched against the wall. It must've been at least ten or fifteen minutes, judging by the hefty layer of snow that covered his hair and his coat. He looked around; the street remained deserted. His fur hat was lying in the middle of the walkway not far from him. The Major reached for his hat without feeling any restriction in his movement. There was a pounding sensation in his head and some nagging pain in his shoulder. He straightened his upper body, put his hat on, and tried to get up. It took some effort, so he leaned against the wall before attempting to walk further.

Was this a random attack by some thug trying to rob a lonely pedestrian? Viktor thought to himself, inspecting his pockets. *A crime of opportunity? My money is gone, but my ID, the envelope with the letter inside and the postal notice are here. And where is my pistol? Oh, no!*

The Major reached for the shoulder holster under his coat. The thick rawhide holster was wet, practically soaked in his blood, but empty; his standard-issue Makarov pistol was gone. He panicked—it was a punishable offense for a Militiaman to lose a service weapon. But this wasn't what scared him the most.

Katya! His mind screamed. *This bastard is here, in Khabarovsk. He knows where she lives. He watched me leaving Katerina's building. He recognized me from Izmailovsky!*

Viktor rushed in the direction of Katerina's building, overcoming the pain and dizziness. The possibility of encountering this dangerous man again, now armed with Viktor's gun, crossed his mind, but just for a second. He brushed it off and kept on running. He flew up the stairway, where the piercing eyes of two men in plain clothes stopped him cold. Captain Mukhin recognized the Major right away but seemed somewhat puzzled.

"I am being relieved from my duty by Captain Shostak, Comrade Major," he reported. "Has something happened?"
The Major suddenly felt very weak and grabbed the railing with both hands to stop from falling. Both officers immediately came to his aid and helped him to sit down.

"I was attacked on the street right after I left." Viktor was breathing heavily. "I think he stabbed me in the back. He took my pistol."

"Did you see him? Who was it?" Mukhin asked.

"I couldn't see his face. He was big and tall. He could be our suspect. I was afraid he had come back here." The Major looked like he would faint again. He slouched against the rails and closed his eyes.

"I did not see or hear anyone entering the building after you left, except Shostak, who arrived just five minutes ago," Mukhin whispered into Viktor's ear and then turned to Shostak, raising his voice. "Captain, we need to call an ambulance. He is bleeding. We might lose him. Do something!"

At that moment, the door opposite Katerina's apartment slowly opened with a nasty squeak. The face of a middle-aged man with a gray and balding head appeared in the crack: "May I ask what this commotion is all about? I have the right to know!" He demanded in a voice as squeaky as his door.

"Don't worry, *Papasha,* we are the Militia," Shostak replied. "Better tell me, do you have a telephone in your apartment? Our comrade needs urgent medical attention."

"You must be crazy. Who would give a telephone to a retired accountant? I am nobody," the man answered with sarcasm. "Knock on another door. I am sure that pretty young actress has one. That big shot benefactor of hers would definitely get her a telephone to be in touch all the time."

"Thank you, citizen; what is your name, *Papasha*?"

"Samuil Evseyevich Shatski, if you must know. Is he wounded, your comrade? He doesn't look good at all."

"Okay, okay, Citizen Shatski. You can go back to sleep." Captain Shostak was ready to turn around and ring Katerina's door when the old man moved from behind the door and approached Captain Mukhin, who continued to hold and comfort Viktor.

"I must tell you something else." The old man sounded very secretive. "This afternoon, just before I saw you hanging around here, I had a visitor. He did not show me any ID but introduced himself as a Militia officer"

The Major summoned the last of his strength to listen to what the old man was saying. "What did he want from you and how did he look?" Viktor interjected anxiously, just barely audible.

"You wouldn't believe it; I couldn't. This man wanted to rent my apartment for a day or two. And when I laughed in his face, he became mad and said that he would temporarily appropriate my apartment from me by power of decree. I laughed again and suggested that he return with a court order. He wasn't happy but he left reluctantly, threatening me with his return."

The Major and the Captain exchanged glances.

"Can you describe this man?" Viktor asked with effort.

"He was very large, but he didn't look like a Militia operative; he wasn't dressed like you. Oh yes, I also noticed something strange when he was walking back to the door. He was limping heavily with his left leg, like it was shorter than his right one."

"What about his face? Can you describe his face? Was there anything unusual in his features?"

"Yes, he had a long thin scar on his right cheek going all the way to the corner of his eye socket. And some word or just a few letters tattooed on the side of his neck. A rather small tattoo, I must say." The old man went silent, waiting for a reaction.

The Major's pale, tortured face smoothed out. He almost smiled.

"Do you mind, Comrade Shatski, if I bring our artist to you tomorrow and you can help him sketch the man's face you have just described to us so well?"

"I don't mind."

"Thank you for your help, Comrade Shatski." Viktor was losing his strength again.

At that very moment, Katerina opened her door and looked at Captain Shostak with sleepy eyes.

"Who are you?" She couldn't hide her displeasure. But then she noticed Mukhin hunched over Viktor and almost screamed. "What is happening? What's wrong with Major Vitus?"

"He is wounded and needs medical attention." Captain Mukhin replied. "Do you have a telephone?"

"Yes, yes, I do. Come in, Comrade."

"Captain Shostak is my name. Where is it?"

"It is next to a sofa in the big room." Katya rushed toward the Major, forgetting that she wasn't holding the flaps of her robe with her hands any longer, revealing her silk nightgown underneath. "Bring him inside. We must help him now. Who knows when the ambulance will come?"

Once again, Viktor gathered all his strength and stood on his feet with Mukhin and Katya's help. He even managed to produce something that resembled a smile when she placed her hands under his elbow to support his steps. Slowly, they reached the sofa. Before putting Viktor on it, Katya carefully removed his heavy shearling and his suit jacket. It was obvious how much blood he had lost. The entire back of his grey shirt and his gun harness were soaked in blood. The bleeding needed to be stopped as soon as possible, so Katya decided not to bother with unbuttoning the shirt; she grabbed scissors and cut it around the collar and along the sides. She saw the wound right on the top of his left shoulder blade. She dipped the blood-free portion of the shirt in vinegar and cleaned around the open cut. It was so painful that Viktor fainted again. He would not remember the arrival of paramedics, nor his ride to the hospital.

Chapter 13

Morning, November 20. Almost nine o'clock. Viktor lay in a large hospital ward with white tiled walls and ten narrow metal frame beds. Only one of the beds was occupied. He'd been awake since six, waiting for a surgeon to visit him at his hospital bed. The nurse reluctantly informed him that he was brought to this hospital by ambulance after midnight with a bleeding laceration in his left shoulder blade. They operated immediately, cleaning the wound and closing it with seven stitches.

The door opened. Instead of a doctor, a short woman rushed into the room, wrapped in a woolen shawl and holding a heavy coat and a large sack in her hands. She landed right on Viktor's bed. He wasn't surprised at all—this woman was his mother.

"Mom, why are you here?" Viktor realized how stupid his question was and shut up.

"Because. You could've called me and told me you were alive. I had to bother Mikhail Grigoriyevich to find out what happened to you and where you were." Her trembling voice was full of worry. "He just told me that you were fine, and you stayed overnight in this hospital."

"I am fine, Mom. I really am, so don't worry and go home." Viktor took his mother's hand and kissed it. "I'll try to see you tonight. Okay? I have to go to MVD headquarters. The General and other people are waiting for me there. You understand, don't you? Now, the doctor must discharge me."

At this moment, a tall, lanky man in his early sixties dressed in washed-out green surgical garb, with *bahils* over his shoes and a transparent cap covering his wavy grey hair, silently glided into the ward.

"You are the patient, Viktor Raymondovich Vitus?" the doctor asked in a deep, pleasant voice. "And this is your mother, I presume?"

"Yes, I am his mother," Leya Solomonovna replied immediately. "And you look familiar..."

"My name is Boris Andreyevich Bolshakov, the Head Doctor and Surgeon of this hospital." He reached his right hand out to the woman and gently shook her hand. "I am the one who fixed your son's wound."

"Will I live, Doctor?" Viktor interrupted him jokingly. He was afraid his mom would learn the gruesome details of the incident. "Seriously, Doctor, can I leave this place immediately? I feel fine."

"Let me look at your bandages, and if they are still snow-white, I will discharge you." Bolshakov helped Viktor to turn on his belly. "I think your mom should wait in the hall, please."

Viktor appreciated the doctor's discretion and nodded in agreement that his mother should leave the room. Leya Solomonovna stood up and headed to the door, but not before throwing a reproachful glance at her son.

After a thorough examination of the wound, the doctor pulled a small notebook from his pocket and began writing. It gave Viktor a little time to indulge himself in his old habit. He loved to observe and analyze people's body features, like the size and shape of their hands and fingers, noses, ears, or lips. He found their bodily habits especially revealing: the twitch of their eyes, pulling at their ears, stroking their eyebrows, or any other manifestation of their unique personalities born of nervous stress. He had this compulsion ever since he could remember, from early childhood. When detective work became his profession, Viktor realized the benefit of such an uncanny ability and learned how to control it and use it. It wasn't always clear-cut in connecting people's idiosyncrasies with human kindness, honesty, loyalty, sensitivity, human courage, or lack of them. God knows how often he was wrong in his conclusions. However, it was always a productive exercise to evaluate people he met and even predict their actions and reactions.

Observing Doctor Bolshakov, Viktor made a note of his hands, especially his fingers. They were long: people of his profession and musicians usually possessed hands like that. But his were exceptionally elegant and sensitive. This was obvious by the way he held his pen and applied it to the paper. Something else Viktor noticed: the doctor's chin with its deep dimple looked as if it was sculpted by some ancient Greek artist. Perhaps the chin protruded forward a little bit too much; nevertheless, it did not make the face any less attractive.

Boris Andreyevich felt his patient studying him closely. He stopped writing and raised his eyes from the paper.

"I have to tell you, young man, you were lucky. Your leather gun holster minimized the damage, preventing deeper penetration from the attacker's knife. Otherwise, you would have kept bleeding profusely, and I wouldn't have had time to stitch you up."

"Thank you, Doctor. This means I can leave now, doesn't it?" Viktor sat up and turned sideways with his feet touching the cold concrete floor. He began looking for his clothes.

"Yes, you can go home now. However, you must promise me that you will take it easy for at least a few days until everything heals." Bolshakov left the room as silently as he had entered it before.

Seeing him leave, Leya Solomonovna rushed back to her son's side. Viktor found his socks and pants but couldn't see the rest.

"Let me help you with this." His mother reached into her sack and pulled out a fresh white shirt. "Your driver told me that you lost a lot of blood. I am sure the doctor instructed you to stay home for a few days. I want you to stay with me. At least, you'll eat properly and gain your strength quickly."

"Not now, Mamma. I must run to the office. I must talk to my colleagues. The General is waiting for me too. I am in big trouble, Mamma. The bastard took my pistol." Viktor spoke rapidly, jumping from one thought to another. "I promise, after I am done, I'll stay with you. You will feed me some nice dinners, a few of my favorites, you know. And we'll talk. Okay? But now I must run. And you go home – Freckles will drop you off."

He hopped on one leg as he finished pulling on his pants and then glanced at his wristwatch. It showed 9:45. There was no time to waste. He could forget about shaving or any other grooming. His tie was nowhere to be found either. Overcoming the pain, Viktor grabbed his mom's sack and headed downstairs impatiently, stopping on each landing to wait for his mother, who breathlessly tried to catch up with him. They hurried out to the hospital entrance, where they found Sergeant Uvalov wrapped in a cloud of his own breath, pacing in front of the frost-covered *kozyol*. Of course, the engine was running. When he saw Viktor, he smiled.

"You don't look that bad, Comrade Major. They fixed you well, didn't they?"

"They did, they did." Viktor was in a hurry to leave this place. "After dropping me off at Headquarters, you are going to take my mom home. Please see she gets in. Let's go!"

In twenty minutes, Viktor was behind his desk on the third floor of the UVD Administrative Building, going through a pile of messages on small yellow and orange papers. A few of those messages immediately drew his attention. One asked him to come to the Forensic Lab and see Lieutenant Toropko. Another note was from Nadezhda Petrovna, summoning him to General Melekhov's office as soon as possible. Also, a special Internal Investigation form was needed to report the status of his missing 9mm Makarov.

After a little hesitation, Viktor decided to take care of this issue right away. He took off his winter coat and rolled the chair up to the desk. But no matter how hard he tried to concentrate on filling out the form, he couldn't write a word. Fragmented thoughts and images swirled in his feverish mind, like a kaleidoscope: the wry face of Captain Mukhin catching him from falling down the stairs, replaced by the worried face of Katya leaning over him. Then his mother's sad face as she tried to kiss his forehead, and back to Katya's face and the feel of her soft, warm hands on his cheeks.

Viktor couldn't understand what it was. Perhaps he was hallucinating from all the medications in his system. He rested his head on the desk and closed his eyes, breathing deeply and slowly. A relaxation began to descend upon him. Then suddenly, it dawned on him. Viktor sprung up, reached into the inner pocket of his civilian jacket and pulled out the old yellowish envelope and the little green postal notice.

He called to the two plain-clothed field agents watching a muted TV in a small room adjacent to his office.

"Take this notice." The Major handed it to one of the agents. "Ask my driver to drive you to the Central Post Office. But have him drop you off on a side street, away from the building. You must do all this very discretely. Understand?"

"To do what, Comrade Major?" The agent sounded a bit confused.

"Go straight to the manager's office and present this notice." The Major curbed his impatience and spoke slowly, placing emphasis on each word. "He must give you a parcel, a relatively small but heavy wooden box. Try to carry it to the car without drawing any attention. When you arrive back here, bring this box to the Evidence Room and deposit it under the 'Izmailovsky murder' case. No tampering with the box, and don't forget a receipt. Take the receipt to Lieutenant Toropko or directly to me. Is everything clear?"

"Yes, Comrade Major. Should we go right away?"

"No, today is Sunday. Go first thing tomorrow morning." He looked at the agents with a patronizing gaze. "Okay?"

Viktor turned his attention back to the paperwork for his lost weapon. He stared at the form for a moment or two before getting up with a strong intention to do something else. *Let's see what Nina has to report,* the Major whispered to himself.

He headed to the lab, on the same floor of the building. Lieutenant Toropko, in a white lab coat, was leaning over a device that looked like a microscope with some unfamiliar contraptions attached to its base and lens bracket.

Nina noticed his curiosity and rushed to explain. "It is our spectral analysis equipment. It helped to determine the composition of the residue I found on the porch of Rogozhin's house, with the highest degree of accuracy. We discovered the same residue all over the shoes of the perpetrator in our custody."

"And what does it mean?" Viktor sounded a little foggy.

"This is why I left you a note. I wanted to speak to you before writing an official report of my findings." Nina looked at the Major worriedly. "Are you okay? I know what happened to you. Go sit down. Do you need help?"

She gently grabbed Viktor's right elbow and led him to a nearby chair.

"I am fine. Really," Viktor insisted, but he slowly lowered his body into the chair and closed his eyes for a moment. "Those damn pain killers they fed me this morning are making me lightheaded."

"It's all right; just relax." Nina pushed the chair closer to a wall, so he could rest his head against it. She rushed to get him a glass of water.

"Thanks; I feel better now." Viktor was sincerely grateful. "So, tell me about your findings, but do it a bit slower."

"Okay, I will." She realized the Major was joking and smiled. "Your hypothesis regarding the place where they stole the gold from was correct."

"I hoped it might be proven already," Viktor replied impatiently. "I expect the package with the gold in our evidence room by tomorrow morning. You will be able to inspect it much closer and…"

"But I already know where those two men came from." It was her turn to interrupt. "The spectral analysis gave me the full composition of the sand in the footprints they left behind. I compared the mineral composition of the silica and heavy metals in our collected samples with existing geological records. Again, you were right: they couldn't have come from too far. The same sand is typical for the region adjacent to the Buriya River Valley of the Khabarovsky Krai, but only on the Blagoveschensk side, where there are quite a few small gold mines and river dredges."

"How far from Urgal is it? Have you checked?" The Major became more alert. He even tried to get up from the chair. Nina wouldn't let him.

"No more than 150km, I think," she replied.

"That is totally possible to cover on foot." Viktor paused for a moment. "We have to contact Blagoveschensk UVD immediately. I am sure there will be some information about crimes committed recently at one of their gold mining facilities."

"We must report all this to the General. A personal inquiry from him will speed up the process," Nina concluded.

"Would you accompany me now? He is expecting me already." Viktor managed to stand up.

"Of course, Comrade Major!" Lieutenant Toropko replied enthusiastically. "Just let me collect some notes, so we will be better prepared for any questions the General might have."

"Good thinking, Lieutenant."

When they arrived at his office, Nadezhda Petrovna informed them that the General Melekhov had someone important in his office; nonetheless, she didn't let them leave but insisted they take seats in the reception room. She approached Viktor and sat next to him.

"How do you feel, dear?" Her voice was full of genuine concern and sincere compassion. "I've heard your mom visited you in the hospital. She was worried sick, the poor woman."

"Yes, she did," Viktor almost whispered. "I am fine, so I sent her home."

"Really?" Nadezhda Petrovna exclaimed doubtfully. "You lost quite a bit of blood from what I heard. Judging by your looks, you should've taken a break for a day or two. What do you think, Comrade Lieutenant? The Major would never admit it. I know him too well."

Viktor got up from his seat and tried to protest, so Nadezhda Petrovna gently pulled him down back into his chair and signaled him to shut up. He felt embarrassed in front of his young subordinate, but he obeyed.

"I agree, Comrade Major would benefit greatly from a couple of days' rest." Nina tread lightly at first, but then revealed: "He almost fell from a dizzy spell just half an hour ago, Nadezhda Petrovna."

"I see. I'll talk to the General about that." Nadezhda Petrovna touched Viktor's forehead with the back of her left hand, as a nurse checks a patient's temperature, and then returned to her desk. "I'll definitely talk to Mikhail Grigoriyevich."

The office door swung wide open. A short, balding man emerged, wearing the insignia of a Militia Colonel on his epaulets. General Melekhov followed behind him. He seemed preoccupied. Although Viktor was never formally introduced to this officer, he knew him as Colonel Malinin, Head of the OVIR, the Department of Visas and Registration.

"Please keep me informed on this matter, Comrade Colonel," concluded the General. He then waved to Viktor and Nina, inviting them into his office.

"I asked my secretary to leave a note for you, but, in fact, I did not expect you, Comrade Major, to be at work for at least two days," the General began as soon as he was back behind his desk. "I see you disregarded your doctor's advice and ignored your mother's plea. I am sure you will not obey my order either, would you?"

"So then, please don't make me disobey you, Comrade General." Viktor tried to kid his way out of this predicament. "There is too much happening for me to be away from the case, you know."

"I assume this is why you and the Comrade Lieutenant are here, isn't it?"

Nina took the initiative. "Yes. The data collected at the scene, samples of the sand in the footsteps, clearly point to its origin. It is the Blagoveschensk Region area adjacent to the Western Khabarovsky Krai near the Buriya River Basin."

"In this area, there are many small gold mines and river dredges," Viktor picked up after noticing that Nina nervously stumbled with her words. "The perpetrators did come from one of those places. By the way, Rogozhin's package will be delivered to our evidence room tomorrow morning."

"So, your theory about how Rogozhin got rid of the package by mailing it to Khabarovsk has proven to be right, Comrade Major?" General interrupted. "I just hope that the safety of Citizen Katerina Rogozhina isn't compromised."

"It shouldn't be. I got the postal notice from her yesterday. Two plain-clothed operatives will retrieve it discreetly," Viktor said confidently, but not without some concern in his voice. "She still must work at the Theater with our security details."

"Okay, but let's go back to what you were saying."

"Yes, Comrade General, what I was saying." Viktor tried to concentrate on his previous thoughts. "It would take a long time to research all those places, especially given the fact that we still don't know the names of the suspects, neither the one in our custody nor the one still at large, running around with my Makarov."

"We shall talk about that later, Comrade Major," the General interjected. "Please continue with your point."

"My point is, we need to make an official inquiry with Blagoveschensk UVD regarding any crimes being investigated at locations nearby." Viktor slowed down and exchanged a glance with Nina, soliciting her support.

"So, what is the problem? I think it is a very logical thing to do." Melekhov threw an intense gaze at Viktor and then at Nina.

"We don't want to sound presumptuous, but we think that such an inquiry might have more weight and garner a response much quicker if it came directly from you, Comrade General," Viktor answered in a single breath.

"I see the merit in your request, comrades. We are pressed for time," the General concluded and made some quick notes in a ledger in front of him. "I promise this request will go out immediately. Anything else?"

"That's it for now, Comrade General. Thank you for your help," Viktor replied and slowly got up. Nina quickly followed.

"Then, Lieutenant, you can go back to your lab. You, Major, remain here. We need to talk. Please, sit down," the General ordered.

Nina closed the door behind her as she left. Walking from around his desk and taking a chair next to Viktor, the General said, "First, tell me, how do you feel?"

"Honestly, I feel fine—a little lightheaded, but I can work."

"Nadezhda Petrovna did not think so. She insisted on sending you home." Melekhov sounded sincerely worried. "Perhaps it would be a good idea for you to rest a couple of days."

"I can't, Mikhail Grigoriyevich," Viktor pleaded hopelessly. "We have to hurry. An armed killer is on the loose."

"Yes, yes, and with your gun." Melekhov gently touched Viktor's shoulder. "I understand your anxiety. Are you sure it wasn't just a random attack, a crime of opportunity? The attacker did steal all your cash as well as your weapon, didn't he?"

"That just shows his desperation," Viktor answered after a few moments. "What if the underground network of outlaws in Khabarovsk did not accept him, or just didn't trust a newcomer without any verified *bratva* credentials? They would shelter him, provide him with some minimal clothes and food, but that's all. Therefore, he desperately needs money and a weapon. He knows where Katerina lives—he attempted to get closer by bullying his way into her neighbor's apartment. So, it's only logical that he attacked me when he had an opportunity, when I was leaving her building last night. I did not anticipate such a daring move, and he got what he wanted."

"What you are saying makes perfect sense," the General agreed, although there was a little hesitation in his voice. "Nevertheless, do not blame yourself. No one could've seen it coming. You did well to survive, with some thanks to your holster, according to your doctor's opinion. But did you have a chance to see your attacker?"

"No, I did not. I just noticed the person was big and strong. I could barely get away from his grasp. I got lucky, Uncle Misha." Viktor recounted the traumatic event only as he would with someone very close. "Now, it's up to me to fix this unfortunate situation. I must find this bastard before he can cause more harm."

"Do you have a plan?"

"Katerina's neighbor, who I mentioned earlier, is supposed to provide a detailed facial description for our sketch artist. This is first and foremost." Viktor's voice projected resolve and determination. "And then—"

"Then you have to be armed," the General interrupted with authority. "Have you filled out the required form? If not, you must do it right away, so I can sign off on it and request an immediate replacement for your weapon. And something else: you will need additional resources in manpower at your disposal. You have my order to invoke as many operatives and plain-clothed agents as you deem necessary."

"Thank you, Comrade General. Permission to leave?" The Major got up and brought his stretched wrist to his temple in salutation, entirely forgetting that he wasn't supposed to do so while in civilian clothes. The General paid no attention to this deviation in protocol.

"And last, but not least, Son—" Melekhov got up too and gently embraced Viktor, whispering in his ear, "Be careful out there, I beg you in the name of your mother and in my name as your godfather. Oh yes, I order you at least two days of rest in your mom's home, starting now!"

Walking through the reception area, Viktor looked at Nadezhda Petrovna and smiled gratefully. She smiled back and waved her hand.

Back at his desk on the third floor, Viktor couldn't help but think about his late father, General Vitus. How would he handle a situation like this? How would he organize the citywide hunt for a killer who was smart, strong, daring, and resourceful? He didn't know, but he was determined to find this killer who would stop at nothing to harm the woman for whom Viktor cared. He would bring him to justice. One way or another.

Viktor was just finishing filling out the form when a Lieutenant from the Armory Department approached his desk, carrying three wooden boxes.

"General Melekhov ordered me to deliver these to you so you can select the weapons of your choice." The young man tried to be as formal as possible. He placed all three boxes on the desk in front of the Major and opened them one by one. "You can have the powerful single-action Tokarev pistol, the 'TT' for short, the Makarov semi-automatic pistol you are well familiar with, or this old reliable six-shooter Nagant revolver. Or any combination thereof."

"You mean I could have all of them if I wanted?" Viktor wondered somewhat jokingly.

"I don't think you will need all of them, but two, one primary and another secondary, would make sense," the Lieutenant explained very seriously. "So, which one do you choose?"

"Let me have the Nagant as the main and the Makarov as the spare. It looks smaller and may be more easily concealed."

"Very well, Comrade Major. Please sign here; and good luck with these babies." It was his turn to crack a joke, but then he finished on a serious note. "And may I have your report form? I will deliver it to the appropriate hands for approval."

"Of course, Lieutenant. I appreciate you saving me a trip downstairs."

The moment he was left alone, Viktor stuck the revolver in the holster under his jacket. He then fixed the Makarov to his right leg above the ankle using electric insulation tape, just the way he saw many detectives do it in the movies. He put the extra magazines and loose ammo into his jacket pockets and placed the empty boxes away in the lower drawer of his desk. He felt much more confident and ready to go back to work. There was no question in his mind where he must go first, but first he had to find the department sketch artist to take along with him.

Viktor grabbed his winter coat and fur hat and rushed down the stairs to the holding cells and interrogation rooms. There, in a small office next to one of the 'torture chambers', as they were called, he found a skinny, middle-aged man with receding curly hair, wearing large glasses and thorny dark eyes behind them. This man was the only sketch artist for the entire UVD, Anatoly Silvestorovich Zelenin.

Ever since he had been a student of the Academy of Arts, people who knew him remembered him as a talented young painter. His teachers expected him to become a great portraitist. However, it never happened. Who knows why? So, Anatoly Zelenin eventually became a great sketch artist capable of compiling incredibly accurate portraits of wanted criminals or missing persons just by listening to descriptions of their facial features and physical attributes. He was a well-mannered man with a happy disposition, who considered himself fortunate that his artistic skills were put to good use. At the same time, the professional lives of most of his peers from the Academy amounted to nothing more than copying the ageless portraits of Party leaders.

"My greetings, honorable Anatoly Silvestorovich!" Viktor addressed the artist with exaggerated dramatic pathos. He had known Zelenin for many years and always admired his talent. They were friends. "Am I glad to see you, Maestro! Sorry to bother you on Sunday, but your invaluable services are required again."

"Dear Comrade Vitus, you have saved me from boredom," Zelenin replied, matching Viktor's dramatic tone. "So, I am at your service, and my toolbox is ready. I presume we are to drive somewhere, aren't we?"

Five minutes later, Freckles sped his two passengers down the main city drag in his frosty *Kozyol*.

He turned down Turgenev Street toward Katerina's building. Viktor glanced at his wristwatch again. Its phosphorus-coated hands, glowing in the pale interior of the car, read five after four.

Katya will be home in thirty minutes, Viktor noted in his thoughts. *It will give me enough time to set Zelenin up with Shatski for a sketch session before I can see her.*

When they approached their destination, Viktor noticed an unmarked black Volga across the street with two plain-clothed operatives inside, in addition to a Militia sentry posted at the building's entrance. The additional precautions to assure Katya's safety were in effect already.

The Major hurried up to the second floor, followed by Zelenin. He found Captain Mukhin there, who sprang to his feet and took a position at Katya's door, just as he had the day prior.

Noting Viktor's surprise, Mukhin explained, "I drove Citizen Rogozhina home ten minutes ago. I don't know why, but today she left the Theater earlier. She seemed nervous," the Captain concluded hesitantly.

"Thanks for warning me, Captain." Viktor sounded sincerely grateful. "I'll talk to Katerina later. Now I want to check on our friend Citizen Shatski. Comrade Zelenin will work with him on the suspect's sketch."

"I am so glad you are well, Comrade Major. She will be too," the Captain said in a lower voice. "We were worried about you. I told her about your condition; she went from pale to red and back to pale."

"I am fine. The wound happened to be superficial. Thanks to you guys, I didn't lose all my blood." Viktor didn't know what else to say, so he knocked on Citizen Shatski's door and quietly disappeared behind it together with Zelenin.

In a few minutes, the Major emerged back on the landing and instructed Captain Mukhin, "When Comrade Zelenin finishes his job, take him downstairs. Ask the driver of the black Volga parked across the street to drive him to the office and immediately come back here. We cannot let the suspect penetrate this building at any time, day or night."

"Understood, Comrade Major." The Captain straightened up and saluted.

Viktor waved at him to relax and rang the bell to Katya's apartment. The door opened almost instantly, as if she was waiting for him.

* * *

Viktor wasn't sure whether Katya was genuinely happy to see him or just politely concerned about his wellbeing. Her apartment hallway was poorly lit, so he couldn't determine the true nuance of her smile, but it was enough for him to see that smile. Today, he had a chance to see something else: following her to the main room, Viktor glanced inadvertently at the woman's back realizing that until this moment, he had never seen her figure in its entirety. Even last night, during their first informal meeting, he was so nervous that the only thing about Katya he could recall was her lovely face, piercing eyes, and luscious hair. But today, the dark blue knitted wool dress she wore was so tight that every curve of her body underlined her feminine beauty and sex appeal. Viktor stumbled for a moment before regaining his composure.

Katerina felt his intense stare on her back. However, she did not want to turn her head and witness his embarrassment. She was accustomed to those glances from men, so their admiration didn't bother her, but didn't inflate her ego either. It was a part of life Katya had to accept, whether she liked or not.

The room they entered looked messy: an overturned chair, a pile of blankets and pillows on the sofa; shreds of a white shirt with bloody stains on the floor nearby.

"I couldn't do anything after the paramedics took you away," Katya began to explain. "You had lost a lot of blood. I was worried."

"You don't have to be worried now. I am fine. I was worried about you." Viktor was bumbling a little. "We can clean up this mess in no time."

"No, no, I'll do it myself. I just came from work and haven't gotten around to it yet," she interrupted. "Please sit down and tell me what happened after you left. Nobody would explain to me how you got wounded, Viktor."

"Katya, why do you want to know?" Viktor replied after a few moments of silence. "It doesn't matter anymore. A vicious man attacked me, but I survived. I happened to be luckier than your father. That's all."

"I knew it. I could feel it!" Katerina announced. "I am not a dummy. I see what is going on, all those people around— following me, protecting me. The killers are here aren't they? They did this to you! But what do they want?"

"Katya, you must not be afraid." Viktor took a step closer and gingerly embraced her. She did not move, just became a little stiff. He whispered, "My dear Katya, I won't let even one hair fall from your head. I swear. Do you hear me?"

She stood quietly, putting her hands around Viktor's waist. She started sobbing, though not for long. The doorbell rang, and then again and again. Someone was very inpatient. Katerina let go of Viktor, wiped her eyes, and moved towards the door. He caught her hand, stopping her cold.

"Wait, I'll check it out. Stay here," Viktor commanded in a low voice. "Never be in a hurry to open the door unless you know for sure who is behind it. Please?"

"I was sure when I opened it for you, Comrade Major?" Katya smiled and looked straight into his eyes.

Viktor smiled back, and unexpectedly for both, gently kissed her forehead. He pulled open the door, expecting to see Captain Mukhin. To his surprise, it wasn't him. A rather tall, round-shouldered and yet youthful looking man stood across the threshold. He wore an imported Italian shearling coat, more fashionable than practical, complemented by a colorful, oversized scarf carelessly wrapped around his neck and the lower part of his face. Only his purple earlobes were visible between the edge of his frosted scarf and a pointy fur hat sitting deep on his head. His dark beady eyes emanated nothing but anger. In his left hand, the man carried an elegant brown leather briefcase; in his right hand he held a key with which he had just tried to open the door.

"What the hell is going on here?" the man muttered after pulling down his scarf. "Why in the world would anyone change this lock? Dear, did you do it? Have you been robbed? And who are you?"

"I am the one around here who asks questions!" The Major exclaimed with authority. "You are?"

"My name is Alexandre Garanin, the Artistic Director of Khabarovsky Theater." The man couldn't hide his confusion. He stepped into the hallway and tried to look over Viktor to see Katya, who was still standing in the middle of the main room. "And may I ask, who I have the privilege of speaking with?"

Viktor introduced himself. "I am investigative inspector, Major Vitus, Khabarovsky UVD. And may I ask you what the purpose of your visit is here today?"

"I kind of live here… on occasion." Garanin now sounded bewildered. "Perhaps I could speak with Kseniya Krylova."

"Who is Kseniya? You mean Citizen Katerina Rogozhina?" It was Viktor pretending to be confused. He wasn't. The second he saw Garanin's face in full light, he recognized him from one of the photographs in the apartment. He had just put the image and the name together. He turned sharply to Katya and gave her a long look.

"Citizen Rogozhina, would you like to speak with your boss, who by his own admission, lives here occasionally?"

Viktor couldn't help the caustic tone in his voice. Naively, he had expected no such turn of events. Just a few minutes ago, he was in seventh heaven, and now he felt hurt. Memories and forgotten emotions started pouring in, filling him with an all too familiar sense of anxiety and anger. The only hope was that Katya would say something to make all this go away before his panic took over and he ran.

But Katya stood silent. She had never been in a situation where she felt so desperately helpless. She didn't know what to say or do.

Captain Mukhin, whose face appeared within the door frame, broke the silence: "I'm sorry, Comrade Major. While I took Comrade Zelenin to the car outside, as you requested, he entered the building and told our private Militiaman that he was a tenant here; he even showed his key." Mukhin sounded apologetic. "Do you want me to remove him from the premises?"

The time it took Captain Mukhin to explain what had happened was enough for Viktor to take hold of his growing anxiety and look at the situation rationally. How much did he know about Katerina Rogozhina's private life? Not much. Maybe there wasn't enough time, or maybe he had been afraid to know more. What was the difference? Perhaps he had experienced all these feelings for Katya due to wishful thinking? A longing for a deep and meaningful relationship. Or perhaps it was a genuine infatuation with this exciting woman? It didn't matter now.

"No, Comrade Captain. Citizen Garanin may stay." The Major grabbed his coat and headed to the door. On his way out, he intentionally and somewhat forcefully bumped into Alexandre, who remained in the same spot. "Let them talk. Your main objective, Captain, is the same: to protect Citizen Rogozhina at any cost. This can never happen again." Even in the staircase's relative darkness, Mukhin noticed the wry, pain-stricken expression on the Major's face.

"Don't you worry, Comrade Major. I understand. It will never happen again," the Captain replied.

Again, a gust of cold, thorny wind blew in Viktor's face as he left the building and stepped into the street. However, this time he paid no attention to it. Freckles kept the *Kozyol* just a few steps away, with the engine running so it was quite warm when Viktor got inside the car. Viktor settled into the front passenger seat, took off his hat, and closed his eyes. For a few moments, he didn't want to think about any of the pressing matters at hand. Pyotr, his loyal Sancho, didn't interrupt the deep silence with his usual questions either.

So, they just sat there, but not for long. An impatient tap on the front passenger window forced Viktor to open his eyes. Viktor could see nothing through the thick frost covering the inside of the glass. Instinctively, he reached for his gun and asked loudly, "Who is it?"

Sergeant Uvalov also readied his weapon and turned the windshield wipers on, so they could take off at once. Realizing they couldn't be seen from inside the car, the person knocking tried to peer through the windshield. Viktor recognized Garanin right away by his funny hat and the gigantic scarf around his face. *What could've happened?* This question ran through his mind and made him nervous. *I left this guy in Katya's apartment just a few minutes ago.* Viktor reluctantly rolled down the window.

"What's going on, Gararin?" Viktor shouted.

"I'm sorry to bother you, Major." Garanin paused to collect himself. "Katya kicked me out."

Viktor had little pity but listened on.

"I could not make any sense of it. I just returned from Moscow and here she is, crying and saying something about my 'betrayal'. And something about her father," Garanin whined, and annoyingly fixed his attire. "I asked the officer who was hanging around, and he referred me to you, Major. I'm glad I caught you. Would you be so kind as to give me a ride home? It is not far from the Theater. Maybe you can fill me in on what's going on?"

"For starters, we do not provide such services. I'm afraid you'll have to use public transportation. And, secondly, because I oversee the official investigation, I cannot reveal any facts related to the investigation. However, as a private citizen, Katerina Rogozhina may inform you of the nature of the crime committed. So, my suggestion is to go back to where you ran from and kindly ask her again about the tragic misfortune that happened to her father, Fyodor Rogozhin."

"She said she didn't want to see me. It happened so suddenly. I didn't even have time to retrieve the briefcase with my ID and my money. You see, there are no decent pockets in this bloody coat."

"The best I can do is to lend you five kopeks for a bus or three rubles for a taxi. Take your pick, Citizen Garanin."

"Okay, I must take you up on your generous offer, Comrade Major. Thank you. I'll pay you back as soon as possible." Garanin sounded miserable.

"You'd better." Viktor procured from his pants pocket a flat bundle of cash and pulled the smallest bill out. It happened to be a five-ruble banknote. "So, hurry up before you freeze your ass off."

The moment the Major jumped back in the car, Pyotr shifted the transmission straight into second gear and pushed the accelerator pedal almost to the floor. They shot off, leaving Garanin behind in a cloud of steam from the exhaust pipe.

"Let's make a quick stop at the office," Viktor instructed cheerfully. "I need to talk to Anatoly Silvestorovich, our sketch artist, and see what he came up with. Then you will take me to my mom's home, and after that, you may rest until tomorrow morning. Okay, my Sancho?"

"Okay, Comrade Don Quixote!" Pyotr was happy to see his boss in a good mood again.

*   *   *

Vitus found Zelenin in his tiny office behind a makeshift tabletop easel with double-sized drawing paper attached to it with a few headpins. The artist was holding several lead pencils and charcoal sticks in his hands. He moved his head slightly, mostly his eyes, back and forth from an open notebook to the easel, laying down precise lines of different thickness and shape. Every so often he stopped to pull translucent sheets with partial images from an old vinyl portfolio standing upright against his easel, testing them against his image until he found the one he needed. Then he would put it aside and go back to his drawing, changing it or adding new details. It was a very meticulous and slow process, which required sharp artistic skill and tremendous concentration. Zelenin noticed the Major when he showed up at his office door but didn't express any reaction. Nothing could disturb him or redirect his attention when he was engrossed in his work.

Viktor had observed this process many times, and he knew damn well not to break the artist's concentration. He quietly and carefully squeezed behind Zelenin and glanced at the drawing over his shoulder. Although it looked finished, the artist continued correcting some areas by rubbing his fingers against the surface and blurring existing lines or adding tiny new details to accentuate the dimensions of the image.

"There is a limit to how big a piece of paper I can use for my sketches," Zelenin explained. "Unfortunately, our new Xerox machine wouldn't accept originals bigger than the standard sheet. Too bad: on a larger scale, I could've put much more facial details. Don't you think?"

"It's good enough for me," Vitus replied. "This face looks real even if it is not life-sized. Excellent job, Anatoly Silvestorovich!"

"Thank the old man. Is his name Shatski? His visual memory and verbal descriptions were so vivid and so precise. Not often do I come across people with such observational abilities," Zelenin admitted with in an assured manner. "It makes my job so much easier."

The Major leaned over the easel to study the sketch more closely. He then straightened up suddenly.

"The guy on your sketch has an uncanny resemblance to our victim Fyodor Rogozhin." Viktor exhaled and then paused, thinking. "Or perhaps, the same male facial features run in all of Rogozhin's family."

"It is very possible—even distant family members can share a close resemblance," Zelenin agreed.

"I must show this sketch to someone. So, what is the next step, Maestro?" Viktor asked.

"I am afraid the next step shall wait until tomorrow morning," Zelenin replied casually. "Our Xerox copy room is closed until then. Lieutenant Zykov, who is in charge of it, went home an hour ago."

"You're kidding me, aren't you?" Viktor was in disbelief. "Are you saying no one else has the key to that room?"

"Not anymore," Zelenin replied after a moment of hesitation. "I used to have access to that room around the clock. Anytime I needed to make a copy of my work or pretty much anything, I would go in there and do it."

"What changed?"

"About six months ago, they acquired three newer, faster Japanese Canon copiers. So they made the room a restricted area, installed a secure lock on the door, and put this Lieutenant Zykov in charge." Zelenin sounded quite upset. "He decides now who can make copies, how many, and of what kind of documents. This Lieutenant is not one of our officers. He was sent from regional KGB."

"Do you mean to tell me you are not trusted enough? Are you in trouble again?" Viktor lowered his voice almost to a whisper. "Anatoly Silvestorovich, you know you can level with me."

*   *   *

A few years prior, Zelenin was caught Xeroxing a book written by Alexandre Solzhenitsyn after his release from the GULAG. When the popular Moscow literary magazine *Novi Mir* published the novel *One Day in the Life of Ivan Denisovich*, it was like a bomb exploding in the face of the Soviet leadership. Only the personal blessing of Nikita Khrushchev allowed it to be published in the first place; in the midst of a wave of anti-Stalinism, he thought the revealing novel would strengthen his own grip on power. However, it didn't take long for the country's political situation to turn 180 degrees. Khrushchev was ousted in 1964, and all the people who had dared to criticize Stalin found themselves under investigation. The publishing of Solzhenitsyn's books stopped, and the original manuscript of his *Gulag Archipelago,* finished in 1967, was confiscated. Solzhenitsyn himself became *persona non grata* in his own country.

Fortunately, one typewritten copy of *Gulag Archipelago* had made its way to the West, where the book was published in its entirety. In 1970, its author was awarded the Nobel Prize in Literature. The Soviet press didn't even mention this highest honor, pretending as if nothing had even happened. Solzhenitsyn was refused a visa to go to Sweden to receive his award. A year later, there was a failed attempt to assassinate him by poisoning. Finally, in February of 1974, Solzhenitsyn was arrested and soon expelled from the USSR to Germany, where he was finally able to receive his well-deserved Nobel Prize.

This spurred new interest in his book, especially among the young people who had previously heard very little about this courageous man. But his work was hard to come by—only typewritten copies were secretly circulated from hand to hand. Zelenin had rare access to a Xerox machine at MVD Headquarters, a relatively new technology brought to the USSR from Japan. He used it to duplicate the prohibited book, given to him by a fellow artist. The risk he took could not have been higher.

When the Khabarovsky KGB office investigated the incident, Viktor involved himself first as a character witness and then later as counsel for the defense. He pointed out one mitigating circumstance in favor of his friend: the pages he had tried to copy were torn from the original magazine publication twelve years earlier, so technically it did not constitute an act of underground publication to advance anti-Soviet propaganda under the Soviet Penal Code. Viktor successfully argued that the legitimate publication of the original precluded prosecution on such grounds. The only fault on the part of Zelenin was using office equipment for private gain.

With some pressure from Viktor's father, the Head of the Khabarovsky Krai UVD, the investigators found no criminal intent in Zelenin's actions; they recommended only administrative punishment. Raymond Vitus reprimanded him with a two-week suspension, without pay. Zelenin knew darn well how lucky he was; by any Soviet standard, it was a slap on the wrist. Ever since, the artist was deeply grateful to Viktor and his late father.

* * *

Zelenin interrupted Viktor's recollections. "No, no, Comrade Major, I am not in any trouble. I'm just concerned that my sketch of this dangerous criminal will not be available for distribution until midday tomorrow."

"It looks like there is nothing we can do," Viktor concluded. "Just make sure the copies go directly to the Telex room and to the operatives on the streets. Please put a few copies on my desk too."

"I'll make sure, Comrade Major."

"See you tomorrow, my friend," Viktor said, touching Zelenin's shoulder as a sign of goodbye.

.

Chapter 14

Viktor opened the door of his parents' home and quietly stepped into the dimly lit entry hall. He wasn't sure whether his mother was asleep or not, although it wasn't late yet, twenty to nine. Viktor was hanging his coat when he heard her steps right behind. He turned around and, with a smile, embraced the little woman, his dear mother. The tip of her head hardly reached her son's chest. He lifted his uninjured hand and gently stroked her silver hair; it felt silky and warm.

"How are you, Mom?"

"I am fine. How are you, Vitin'ka?" Leya Solomonovna addressed her son with a term of endearment. "You just missed your sister and niece. They stopped by to check on me but couldn't stay longer."

"How are they?" Viktor's concern was sincere. "Everyone is healthy, I hope?"

"They are well, just busy with work and school." Leya Solomonovna replied and then paused. "Let's talk about it later, while you eat."

Viktor didn't insist on hearing an explanation. He was hungry, so he followed her into the dining room and took his usual spot. Since he was a little boy, he had always sat at the chair on the left side of his father's place at the head of the table. For the last two years, that chair had remained empty. Mother and son exchanged sad glances; their open wound had never healed.

"Remind me later: I have to show you something I found the other day in a box with your father's private documents," Leya Solomonovna dropped in casually as she headed into the kitchen adjacent to the dining room.

"What did you mean, a box with private documents?" Viktor asked cautiously. "I thought I saw Father's entire archive during the investigation, to the last shred of paper. Are you telling me there is more, Mom?"

"I was cleaning the armoire in our bedroom. You know that monstrous piece of antiquity I dragged with me from my home in Moscow after I married your father and joined him here." Leya Solomonovna put some utensils and napkins on the table in front of Viktor. "I expected you earlier. You looked hungry, but please be patient; your favorite food is heating up. It will take a couple more minutes, my starving boy."

Viktor swallowed, anticipating the dishes he loved from childhood: the cabbage and potato soup in real beef broth, the garlicky chicken cutlets, mashed potatoes with butter and chopped raw onion. His mom was an excellent cook and always knew how to please her children and grandchildren. Leya Solomonovna wasn't as energetic as she was before her husband's death, so her children didn't expect the regular gatherings in their parents' home with three course dinners and homemade desserts, but her skills in the kitchen were still legendary.

But something else had also changed. The Vitus widow had lost the privileges of using the special retail stores, to which her late husband, as a member of the Khabarovsky Krai Party Committee, was traditionally entitled to. Now she relied on her neighbor and friend Alyona, the wife of General Melekhov, who succeeded Raymond Vitus as Head of the Khabarovsky UVD. Even though General Melekhov wasn't yet a member of the local Party Committee, he enjoyed the generous privileges of the elite Soviet *nomenclatura (State and Party officials)*. From time to time, Alyona invited Leya Solomonovna to shop with her for the fresh produce, meat, and fish that were rarely available in the ordinary stores. However, Leya Solomonovna didn't feel comfortable using her friend's kindness that often, so she learned to shop like a common citizen of the country, and to get by on whatever she could purchase in regular shops or at the local bazaar. Nevertheless, she never mentioned these inconveniences to her children.

It took Leya Solomonovna two trips to bring all the hot food from the kitchen and place it in front of Viktor. She then rested in her chair across the table. Viktor closed his eyes for a moment, inhaling the flavors, familiar since his childhood. Then he slowly began eating. The silence was broken only by the occasional sound of the spoon scraping the bottom of the plate with soup, and by the sighs of pleasure that Viktor couldn't hide.

"Do you want another helping?" asked Leya Solomonovna. "There is more."

"No, no, Mom. It's enough soup," Viktor mumbled, finishing the first dish, and reaching for the cutlets. "I can't wait to start this."

"I am so glad to see that you still enjoy my cooking. I couldn't help but notice your lack of such appetite for a long time, my son," Leya Solomonovna proclaimed full-heartedly. "You know, heavy drinking can do that to you—"

"Mom, where does this come from? Who told you I'm drinking?" Viktor was genuinely surprised by the direction this conversation had suddenly taken.

"It doesn't matter, Son. I didn't have to be told. Mother's heart: her intuitions rarely lie." Leya Solomonovna spoke slowly, looking straight into Viktor's eyes. "I hope it is behind you; isn't it?"

Although Viktor didn't expect to have this conversation with his mother now, he felt relieved it had happened. He and Leya Solomonovna were too close to hide anything from each other, and Viktor knew that he would need to face the truth sooner or later. So why not tonight?

"Mom, I promise you, as I promised Uncle Misha." His voice trembled a little. "I haven't had a drink in two weeks. I swear."

"You don't have to swear. I believe you, Son. Finish your food, and let's talk about something else."

Viktor glanced at his mother with gratitude and concentrated on emptying his plate. The silence hung for a minute or two. Then he pushed the empty plate away, wiped his lips with a linen napkin, and turned his entire body toward Leya Solomonovna.

"So, what do you want to talk about?" Viktor asked, this time rather joyfully. He was happy that the tough subject seemed to be over.

"It is about Raya and Boris. They have decided to leave—"

"Where to? Did Raya send her job application to the Moscow Symphony again?" Viktor questioned, although he had some idea what the answer would be.

"No, Raya and Boris are getting ready to submit their request and all necessary documents to OVIR for emigration." Leya Solomonovna sighed. "They are waiting for my decision."

"What decision are you talking about, Mom?" This time Viktor was truly confused. "They are asking for your blessing, aren't they? But how come they never talked to me about all this?"

"Because they realize it might affect you, Son. Raya was planning on talking with you." Leya Solomonovna paused again. "Of course, only after I tell them whether I am leaving with them or not."

"Mom, you are seriously thinking of going too?" Viktor hardly expected this turn of events and sounded flabbergasted. "I'm not asking you this because you all are leaving me behind. I am just worried about you, Mom."

"Believe me, I will be heartbroken if it comes to that. I will be even more miserable staying here, worrying sick about how they are over there and knowing I will never see them again—those cute kids' faces." The woman pulled a napkin from the table, covered her face with it, and began sobbing.

At this moment, Viktor noticed how much older his mother looked after the last two years. He jumped up and rushed around the table to hug her slumbering little body. He gently patted her back, comforting her. She grabbed his hand and kissed it. They remained like that, silent for a while.

"I love you, Son." Leya Solomonovna began slowly but rather firmly, as a person whose mind was made up. "You are strong like your father was. If you stay, you will survive here. Raya and her children need me more than you do—"

"I am sure Boris's parents will be going with them too," Viktor pointed out.

"Oh yes, they will. Their documents are already filed. However, Raisa is not their daughter. I am her mother. No one will replace me," Leya Solomonovna replied with conviction.

"So, it looks like you have decided, Mom. Haven't you?" Viktor asked her hesitantly.

"It looks that way, doesn't it?" She took a deep breath and pulled the napkin to her eyes as if getting ready to renew her sobbing.

"Please don't cry, Mom. No matter what, you all have my support. Don't worry, I'll find a way to deal with this situation," Viktor concluded. "I just hope Uncle Misha and Aunt Alyona will understand."

"My Son, they are good people and good friends, but they are not Jewish." Leya Solomonovna looked closely into her son's eyes. "If they will at least understand my decision, it is fine, but if not, so be it. I am not going to change my opinion about them. What I really hope is that one day soon you, my son, will join us."

"Who knows, Mom? Perhaps, one day I will see all of you again." Viktor sounded philosophical. "Today, I don't feel like a real Jew, though. I don't feel Latvian either. I know one thing; this is my country. I have to stay here."

"But you are a Jew, my Son. You are. One day you will feel it and accept it."

This last statement hung in the air in silence, before Viktor found the courage to move on to another touchy subject he had to bring up.

"Mom, listen. Speaking about our heritage, you never told us much about your side of the family." He threaded carefully. "I just remember your maiden's name was Shtern, wasn't it?"

"Yes, my family name is Shtern. I never hid it from my husband nor my children." Her voice became more confident. "It's just that the story of my family was so tragic I kind of blocked it from my memory, and I didn't feel like burdening you with it."

"I think, Mom, now it is time you tell me this story, if you are not too tired after such a long and troublesome day, of course."

"No, I am not tired. Why do you want me to do this now?"

"Mom, you will find out, but later."

* * *

Solomon Shtern was born into a wealthy merchant family of the First Guild in the southern Ukrainian City of Odessa at the end of the 1870s.

Before the First World War, his own family lived with an abundance of parental love and affection between siblings. Leo, the oldest son, was born in August of 1900. He had a good character and many talents, the strongest of which was the performance of humorous *kalambours* and practical jokes, very often to the point of annoying his unwitting audience. However, he became more serious and mature when his sister Leya was born in September of 1910. Leo was very protective of her, and being several years older, he actively participated in the girl's rearing. Four years later, the youngest child Sonya came into their life, becoming the center of attention and admiration of the entire family. But the older siblings didn't mind and loved this spoiled little creature with all their hearts.

Everything changed in 1917. The First World War, one of the bloodiest in history, was winding down. The nations that had participated in this nightmarish struggle were exhausted and financially broke. Social unrest was brewing with exceptional intensity in Germany and Russia. The tired soldiers abandoned the front trenches and returned home with their rifles, mad as hell at their commanders and their governments. They were mad about the death and misery they had gone through for the sake of the rich getting richer while the poor becoming poorer. The situation wasn't sustainable, and the Revolution was imminent.

In February, sailors and soldiers overwhelmed the Czarist security forces in Petrograd, Russia's capital, taking total control and demanding that Emperor Nikolai II abdicate his throne.

The different political parties formed a provisional government, including the largest coalition of Social Democrats with the three major factions of Communists, the Cadets, and Anarchists. However, deep discord and constant fighting over the ways and means by which the new Russia would build her future made this government ineffective, even anemic, and eventually irrelevant. And so, the first truly democratic government in Russia's history never graduated from provisional to permanent, finally collapsing on October 25 of 1917. Vladimir Lenin brilliantly took advantage of the situation, mounting a successful assault with the well-organized Bolsheviks (the largest part of the Socialist forces) under his command. Immediately following their victory, they exercised extreme terror upon the real and imagined enemies of the Marxist ideology. The country and its families were divided right down the middle, brothers against brothers and sons against fathers. In the next four years, bloody Civil War pushed the country to the brink of extinction.

The Shtern family experienced its own turmoil. Leo joined the Red Army. His parents opposed his decision, not solely for ideological reasons, but mainly because Leo had just turned eighteen. His younger sisters couldn't understand why their mother, who usually had a sunny disposition, was constantly crying, or why their kind and gentle father looked angry and irritable most of the time. For six months they received no news of Leo's whereabouts, or even if he was alive.

That summer, the family got a glimpse of their son and brother when the Red Army took temporary control of Odessa. Only eight years old at the time, Leya still remembered Leo in his leather pants and hat, his shiny jacket and high boots. On one hip he carried a big Mauser pistol in a polished wooden holster, and on the opposite hip a slightly bowed saber in a leather and bronze sheath. Leo looked much older than his real age, very mature and handsome.

Leo stopped at the house at dusk, dismounted his white horse under the side portico, and entered through the back door, avoiding the possibility of being seen by neighbors. During his unexpected but very joyful visit, he informed his parents that he had become a Commissar of the Red Cavalry Army under Semyon Budyonny. He also informed them that he was well fed and had enough warm winter clothes, and that they shouldn't worry about him at all. Everyone was happy. Solomon Shtern closely studied his son's magnificent uniform and menacing weapons, rattling with each body movement. His wife couldn't move her teary eyes away from her firstborn, who looked like a grown man. She treated him with hot tea and homemade cookies, smiled, and asked silly questions that only a loving mother could ask.

But the happiness didn't last long. Leo got up in an hour or so, kissed his parents, hugged his little sisters, and left as quietly as he had arrived. Leya never saw her older brother, whom she had always adored, again. A few days after Leo's visit, rumors circulated around the city that the Reds had left, pushed out by the White Volunteer Army.

From the beginning of the Civil War the situation in Odessa was very fluid.

Control over the city very often changed hands between Red Militiamen organized by the local Bolsheviks supported the Red Cavalry brigades of Semyon Budyonny; Cossacks of the numerous factions of the National Ukrainian Government led by Ataman Semion Petlura; and the White Volunteer Army of Generals M. Alexeyev, L. Kornilov, and P. Wrangell, reinforced by the international forces of Entente Alliance, whose French Navy battleship anchored in harbor in December of 1918. Obviously, this city with its sunny shores of the Black Sea had strategic importance to all players in this bloody war. And yet, the emotional dimension was no less important.

Although he wouldn't be considered an extremely wealthy man, Solomon Shtern hired a couple of armed guards from the Jewish Defense group to stay at his house with the family around the clock on Reshelievsky Street.[2] For a few months, everyone felt safe—until one dreadful day in December.

*   *   *

Leya Solomonovna interrupted her story, clutched her chest, and reached into one of the kitchen drawers. She pulled a small aluminum tube and tried to unscrew its top with shaking hands. Viktor knew darn well what it meant—his mother's angina. He rushed to help.

"Don't worry, Son. I can handle it." Leya Solomonovna finally got a big white tablet out of the tube and placed it under her tongue. "It's my usual palpitation. I am a little nervous. This pill should work fast."

"Mom, we can do this another time, you know." Viktor hugged her and kissed her forehead. "There is no need to stress yourself."

---

[2] The years of the Russian Civil War were especially tumultuous for the Jewish population living in the city's poor districts, like Moldovanka or Peresyp. Every time control of the city would change hands from Reds to Whites or to Ukrainian Nationalists, the Jews would be the first target of the next spiral of terror and violence. Tired of constant pogroms, people began organizing their own self-defense groups, often consisting of well-armed and well-trained Jewish gang members. Notorious gangster Mishka Yaponchik was the most popular and successful protector of the people. For hefty fees, he supplied bodyguards to the local synagogues, easy targets for desecration, as well as the Jewish inhabitants of wealthy neighborhoods. At the end of 1918, members of Odessa's upper class, predominately Jewish, often became victims of vicious attacks from Bolshevik mobs or directly from Red soldiers, whoever for a while happened to take the city. Such attacks were always painted as acts of Marxist class warfare.

"No, no, it's fine. This tragic part shouldn't take that much longer. I was too young to remember all the gruesome details anyway."

"You can continue when you feel better, Mom."

"I do feel better." She closed her eyes for a moment and sat calmly. Her breathing steadied, becoming deeper. "I wasn't even nine yet when it happened."

* * *

That day began much like any other. Right after breakfast, Solomon Shtern situated himself in a comfortable armchair by the living room fireplace with thick spectacles on his nose and the local daily newspaper in his hands. His older sister, Buzya, who served as the family's live-in nanny and was never married, took little Sonya back to the children's room. Young Leya went upstairs to the music room where she practiced her violin, followed by her mother Hava Shtern. They both enjoyed the musical exercises and cherished the time they spent together.

Hava had been born into a wealthy family in Kishinev, the capital of Moldavia. At seventeen, she graduated from the Conservatory of Music as an accomplished piano player. However, her parents never planned any professional music career for Hava. One year later, they welcomed a marriage proposal from a mature bachelor Solomon Shtern, the successful merchant. He arrived in Kishinev accompanied by the famous matchmaker Madam Tsiperovich, famous for connecting the young and not-so-young men of well-to-do Jewish families with brides from the neighboring Bessarabia Region. The common opinion was that the most beautiful women who ever lived came from there. Judging by the fortune Madam Tsiperovich had amassed; matchmaking services weren't cheap but apparently worked quite well.

Although Hava was a well-educated modern woman, she freely accepted the life of a good wife and devoted mother. And yet, she had one undying ambition: to pass on her musical talent to her first-born son, Leo. It had to be said that despite the turmoil caused by World War I and the Revolution, the country had not lost its eternal love of music. No matter what was going on in the city streets, the Odessa Opera House never closed its doors to the best singers in the world and their fanatically dedicated audience. Likewise, fans always filled the halls of the city's numerous nightclubs: Army and Navy officers, soldiers and sailors, bourgeois society and blue-collar workers, even the poor; anyone who loved popular music, Gypsy romances, or French *chanson* would come if they could afford the price of admission.

Teaching their children music was another craze among rich and middle-class families. No other place in the world had so many private music schools and tutors. Ten months out of the year, the people strolling through the streets each night became the unintended audience to the sounds of pianos, violins, cellos, and voices flowing from the open windows of the city. It seemed like every kid in Odessa was learning to sing or to play an instrument and enjoying every minute of it.

But not quite every child. To Hava's chagrin, Leo adamantly refused to have anything to do with the piano. The boy was stubborn and had totally different interests in life, so she waited more than ten years before trying to realize her dream with her second child. Although she knew the girl was likely destined to become a wife and mother as well, Hava simply could not disregard her ambition.

And she wasn't disappointed; her daughter Leya's musical prowess became evident at only three years of age. At five, she picked the instrument she wanted to learn: the violin. In less than a year, Leya easily surpassed her peers in her ability to tame this rather complicated instrument, even to creatively express her emotions. She never missed a single lesson and was always eager to learn something new. Hava was very happy, at times ecstatic, to see her daughter's progress, to observe the seeds of knowledge fall on fertile soil.

That early December morning, Leya and her mother were anxious to immerse themselves in the magnificent world of musical sounds when they heard a frightening noise downstairs, and unfamiliar voices laced with profanities. Hava signaled to her daughter to stay put and rushed out of the room to the second-floor corridor overhanging the living room and entrance hall. At that moment, Leya heard several gunshots, followed by shrieks. Living in a big city, she had heard gunshots and shrieks before, but never this close and never so loud.

Without even realizing it, she walked to the door with the violin and the bow hanging in her hands. The first thing she saw in the corridor was her mother hanging over the balustrade of the staircase.

Leya stood frozen, trying to figure out what could've happened. Only the lower part of her body was visible, but she knew it was her mother. It was her dress. So, she snuck down the stairs until she could see the upper part of the body hanging upside down. And her mother's face: it was distorted, with the eyes wide open in horror. A thin stream of blood flowed from her right temple down along her dark wavy hair.

Leya wanted to scream, but no sound came out. She ran down the stairs, not understanding the danger. She crossed the living room on the way to the main entrance, hardly noticing the commotion in the dining room. Strange men, in grey military overcoats and fur hats, rummaged through the drawers of the China cabinets, stuffing their pockets with silverware. Lucky for the girl, they paid no attention to anything else around them. Their long rifles leaned against the dinner table. It looked to them as if no one else was left alive in this house.

Leya abruptly stopped when she noticed her father lying in a puddle of blood, not far from his favorite armchair in a puddle. His right hand still clutched a two-barrel shotgun he had purchased recently. She didn't see his face, only the back of his head with its round bald spot. Three more bodies were on the floor in front of him, closer to the door. One of the men in the grey overcoats had his face completely blown off. Two were in plain clothes with handguns in their hands. Leya knew them: they were the guards hired to protect the family. Evidently, the attack was so sudden and sneaky that they had no chance of preventing it.

When the girl finally reached the entrance, she discovered it was partially blocked. The motionless corpse of a huge man in the same grey Ukrainian National Army uniform was wedged against the door, shot by the guard at the beginning of the attack. Leya jumped over the body and ran from house, still clutching her violin and bow.

The next thing she remembered was a crowd of people surrounding her, speaking a strange tongue. A woman with a pomp of black hair threw a warm wool shawl around her trembling body and picked her up from the ground. Leya closed her eyes and fell into the abyss of unconsciousness. A day or two later—she wasn't sure—Leya awoke in a dark tent, dressed in unfamiliar but comfortable clothes. She was alone, hungry, and frightened. Leya looked around and noticed several children of different ages sleeping on bare straw mattresses. The memory of her horror started coming back. She began crying, quietly at first, then louder and louder so that someone would hear her. The same woman with magnificent black hair slid into the tent and gently hugged the girl to calm her down.

"Shush, my beautiful girl, shush." The woman almost whispered in Russian with an unusual accent. "No need to wake those kids up. They are tired. You must be tired too. Why do you cry, my precious?"

"My mommy, she is not alive anymore. My daddy, he did not move." Leya was talking slowly, mixing Russian and Yiddish words, and swallowing her tears at every pause. "Sonya, where is Sonya? I didn't see her."

"Who is Sonya?" the woman continued in a whisper.

"My little sister Sonya—she is only four." Leya, with her huge round eyes, stared at the woman, as if in disbelief. "You don't know my sister Sonya?"

"I didn't see her. You were alone when we picked you up. And what is your name, precious?" the woman asked. "How old are you?"

"I am Leya Shtern. I am almost nine." Leya abruptly stopped sobbing and began searching around in the dark with both hands. "My violin! Where is it?"

"Girl, nothing happened to your fiddle. It should be here somewhere." The woman made an effort to look for the violin. "We'll find it in the morning. Do not worry."

"I want it now. Find it now!" insisted Leya in the tone of a spoiled child.

"There is no light, my precious. We have no kerosene for the lantern. You'll have your fiddle tomorrow. Understood?" The woman didn't leave any doubt that this subject was over.

"We must go and look for Sonya, then." Leya continued sobbing. "She is alone and frightened."

"Okay, I'll send Nikola to look for her. Does she resemble you?"

"Nothing like me. Sonya has long blond curly hair. She is button-nosed. Why can't I go and look for her too?"

"Because it's dangerous. They might take you away."

"Who might take me away?"

"Police, gendarmes, soldiers. I don't know, my precious. Anybody." The woman didn't sound very convincing, but it stopped the questioning.

"Then Nikola must go now!" Leya ordered.

"He will, he will. But you go back to sleep. Promise, my precious?" The woman helped Leya lie down and covered her with a warm blanket. "You are my daughter now; I'll take good care of you."

The girl felt emotionally exhausted. She closed her eyes and quickly immersed herself into a long, deep sleep filled with nightmares. The next day, as if nothing had happened, she played with the rest of the kids, picking up their strange dialect. Only once or twice, mostly in passing, Leya remembered the horrible events of the past few days; then she would search with panic-stricken eyes for the woman who had blanketed her with love and protection. When she found her washing clothes nearby or stirring some steaming stew in a big pot over the open fire, her sudden fear would dissipate, and she would go back to being a little girl again with her beloved violin.

In the next month or two, the images of Leya's family members, especially her sister Sonya, visited her less and less, and then almost never. Isn't it amazing how fast children can block the pain and tragedy of personal loss and begin a new life?

Her new life was different indeed. Leya and her new siblings were not properly fed or warmly clothed every day. She forgot the last time she'd had a hot bath or washed her hair or used a warm water closet. But it wasn't something she thought about. Leya felt safe and loved here among these rough, loud, and very affectionate people. By now, Leya knew the names of every man, woman, and child sleeping in those old, dirty and tattered tarpaulin tents, living as one close family—a community of totally free people.

They called the woman who became her new mother Zara. She had four children: the ten-year-old boy Val, five-year-old twin girls Zoya and Leila, and the toddler Roman, another boy. The young man named Nikola, who was always around Zara, wasn't the father of her kids. Leya soon learned he was the woman's brother. In this small tent city called a *tabor*, there were three more women with kids and five men, another eighteen people altogether.

The eldest, Zach, had unruly gray hair and a beard, only one leg and a wooden stump for the other. He seemed to be their leader, and projected strength and confidence despite his advanced age, giving his orders in short, exact sentences. Later, Leya learned that Zach was the father of Zara, two more women, and four younger men. The rest of the adults were the children of his younger brother Georg.

Zach liked Leya from the moment he heard her playing the violin. He would sit down in front of the girl and listen for hours to the music she made. Then he would pull his harmonica out of his pants pocket, cover it with his enormously large hands, and put it to his lips.

Leya could hardly believe the sounds the man managed to extract from this simple little instrument, and she wanted to learn how to play it too. And soon, she did. He was a great teacher, who could produce a sound from almost anything—a leaf, a wooden chip, or a string—creating a magnificent piece of music for his people to carry in their souls.

He told her about these people as well. He hated when anybody called them gypsies. "We are Roma people. We are Arians, descendants of the ancient Indian tribe. We are freedom-loving people who will never kneel to anybody. We are people with a rich history, a great culture, and unwavering pride."[3]

---

[3] The Traveling Gypsies were another minority of the Russian Empire, treated poorly for hundreds of years. They were banned from residing in major cities, and they could purchase neither land nor property. They were consequently forced into a nomadic life and surviving through borderline or fully criminal activities, shuttling across the country and crossing borders without permits. The Czarist governmental agencies never included them in the Census and therefore couldn't record or process their identities or other related information.

Although most Gypsies claimed to belong to the Russian Orthodox Church, the common population neither trusted them nor accepted them as brothers and sisters in the Faith. They often considered their women as witches and their men as *Vardoulakis*, a cross between vampires and werewolves. They blamed them for snatching domestic animals and even children, or for inflicting them with illness and other misfortunes. This prejudice led them to ostracize and persecute the Gypsies, even the occasional mob lynching.

Soon, Leya began to believe she was truly one of them, even if she looked different.

One more thing drew this refined but totally illiterate man to the little girl from another world. She could read and write, and besides Russian, she spoke French and understood Yiddish. Perhaps this was why it took Leya less than a year to learn their native Roma tongue.

Life in the *tabor* was not only music and fun. While the younger women looked after the little children and did the cooking, the others went out to earn their collective living. It was all predicated-on crafts they had perfected over the centuries of living their nomadic lifestyle. Originally from the Bessarabia region of Moldavia, the Zach and Georg Mauri families would pitch their tents outside Odessa every spring, at the start of the tourist season.

There they entertained people on the streets with singing, dancing, and fortune telling. The Gypsy women mesmerized spectators with tarot or palm readings, while the kids would pick the pockets of unsuspecting passersby. Before the theft was discovered, the perpetrators would be long gone, moving on to other tourist areas of the city. This unsavory activity required many special skills that had to be taught from a very young age. Perhaps one must be born into it. Leya, for the life of her, couldn't learn those skills, so her job was to play the violin.

For Gypsy men, summer nights were the times they could steal the horses grazing in open fields away from their owners' barns. Their ability to snatch the animals, in the blink of an eye and without a peep, was uncanny. In the next few days, those horses showed up at local fairs hundreds of kilometers away and sold for a cheap price, only to be stolen again and moved to another part of the countryside. This was a dangerous enterprise. Local farmers forced the gendarmes to chase after the thieving Gypsies, or they formed their own militias

---

And yet, Gypsies were always a subject of interest, even fascination, to the Russian upper classes; they romanticized the exotic beauty of their women and their musical talents in general. Many exclusive restaurants and officer's clubs in St. Petersburg, Moscow, Kharkov, and Warsaw featured companies of Gypsy singers, dancers and musicians, whom they considered the real *charm*. However, the stars of these shows were the subjects not only of admiration, but also sexual exploitation on the part of the patrons. Before the Revolution, it was very fashionable among members of elite society to keep a young, pretty Gypsy singer as a concubine. The classical literature of pre-revolutionary Russia reflects this fascination with the Roma people and the abuses inflicted upon them, for instance in the poems of Alexandre Pushkin and Mikhail Lermontov and in the novels of Leo Tolstoy and Fyodor Dostoyevsky.

to catch and often kill them on the spot. Nevertheless, it was quite a lucrative business and therefore worth the troubles.

Many things changed with the First World War, and even more with the Civil War. The Mauri *tabor* continued to migrate to Odessa every spring, but tourists no longer came to enjoy the seaside with its sunny beaches. The armies requisitioned all the healthy horses, leaving very few to steal. And now, for the second year in a row, the *tabor* found itself between opposing forces in this vicious fight, struggling to make even the minimum needed to survive. Danger might come from anywhere.

The spring of 1919 came and went without a drop of rain. It was so dry and hot in the middle of April that the birds would not fly or sing, hiding all day in the dusty trees. The Odessa city boulevards along the seashore were empty; the beaches were abandoned except for the stray dogs staying cool in the surf.

The battles of the civil war raged on, and it became evident the Red Army was prevailing. The battleship Entente left the harbor, and French sailors no longer strolled along Primorsky Boulevard. The elite of the city occupied Odessa's ports with mountains of suitcases, trying to board one of the few commercial vessels sailing for the Romanian Port of Constance or Turkish Istanbul. In this they competed with the demoralized White Army officers seeking to flee the country.

Leya and her new family worked these desperate crowds waiting for days on end. Many women welcomed the fortunetellers and paid them generously, hoping to hear about their future life in an unknown land. The girl played sad melodies on her fiddle, setting the mood and distracting the naïve clients. From time to time, Leya recognized friends and acquaintances of her parents among them, but she said nothing.

The fleeing troops idling at the docks also enjoyed the young Gypsy musicians, though they had no money to pay and very little to be stolen, except their winter uniforms and warm overcoats. So, the gendarmes did what they did best: chased those Gypsy rascals away, threatening to shoot them. Sometimes, it wasn't an empty threat. One day, Zara's eldest son Val and Georg's grandson cleaned out the pockets of an officer sleeping on the pier. They were shot in the back as they fled, and both died on the spot.

These two poor kids weren't the last to lose their lives that summer. Leya remembered waking one sultry night to a loud commotion outside the tent. She saw three men on horses rush into the camp. Two of them quickly dismounted and pulled the third from his horse and laid him on the ground. Zara recognized this man right away and ran toward him, wailing. It was her baby brother Nikola, bleeding profusely from several wounds. His companions told their story. After days of finding nothing worth stealing, they came across a stable of horses grazing outside a hamlet. A dozen Free Cossacks from the remnants of Ataman Semen Petlura's Ukrainian People's Army were drinking heavily in one of the houses, and it seemed nobody was watching. But when they jumped on the three best horses, some guards hiding in the bushes nearby opened fire.

Nikola died the next morning, and they buried him in a shallow grave behind Zara's tent. Leya took his death as hard as Zara. She had befriended this strong and handsome young man who, despite the danger, had searched for her sister Sonya.

With this tragedy, the *tabor* abandoned any hope of surviving the bloody war. By unanimous agreement, they took down their tents, loaded their wagons, and started out for their native Bessarabia. When they reached the outskirts of Tiraspol, the largest city on the Dniester River, it became evident that crossing into Moldova would be impossible. Red Army regiments held one bank, and German soldiers held the other, locking the border so tightly that not even a field mouse could sneak in. Nor could they remain there: armed bandits roamed the land, or Red Soldiers might confiscate their horses and belongings in the name of the Revolution. So, Zach decided to move east to Central Ukraine, where the war was dying out, and relative peace and order were gradually taking hold of everyday existence.

In less than a week, their caravan reached Yekaterinaslav, later Dniepropetrovsk, with no trouble. After all their tragedies and losses of the last two years, they hoped to return to normality, at least in the sense that Gypsy people perceive. However, the entire country stood on the threshold of the untested reality of the new Soviet Russia, and Ukraine was a part of it.

Newly formed *soviets* of People's Deputies, consisting of uneducated members driven by propaganda, ruled by decree. Most old social institutions were intentionally destroyed, and the new ones were of little help or relevance. The Bolshevik Communist Party presided over the whole mess, and local Party Committees became the arbiters of the people's daily life.

The situation in Yekaterinaslav wasn't any different. Several pressing issues were on the agenda, including reviving the local economy, supplying the population with food and other basic necessities, and establishing at least a semblance of law and order.

Crime had flourished amidst the chaos caused by the Revolution and Civil War. Gangs terrorized the workers and bourgeoisie in the city and robbed the rural peasants blind. So, the government created the *VeCheKa* All-Russian Special Emergency Commission, the secret police arm of NKVD and precursor to all subsequent institutions of the State Security apparatus.

Thousands of proletarians, former police, and low-ranking veterans were recruited and trained on the job. Its agents pursued and often executed on the spot anyone deemed a criminal element, counterrevolutionary, saboteur, or other foe of Soviet regime. The *VeCheKa* forces proved more effective in cleaning up the country's urban areas than the Worker's and Peasant's Militia. Quite often they swept up petty thieves but also innocent people in their dragnets, prosecuting them just as harshly.

VeCheKa raids took several members of the Mauri family in the first years after settling their *tabor* near Yekaterinaslav. They disappeared without a trace. Two teenage boys and their younger sister, Mara, were caught and shipped off to the colonies for stray children, which were little more than juvenile work camps. A few times, Leya narrowly escaped these roundups while playing her violin on the street for small change, perhaps because she did not look like her siblings.

These losses weighed on the family patriarch, Zach, as he grew older and weaker. He became gravely ill in the spring of 1922, coughing blood and burning with fever. All Zara could do was apply a cold, wet rag to his forehead and give him lots of water; that was the only medicine she had, but it didn't help much. The old man passed away one foggy morning. Leya sat quietly with the other children at the foot of his smelly, small mattress, patting the man's wooden leg. They played the violins and flutes, and sang sad songs as they buried Zach, the way he would prefer to leave this world.

Zara was never the same after her father's death: no more singing or dancing, no more fortune telling in the city squares. Her proud, glossy black hair—which always reminded Leya of the shimmering ebony surface of the grand piano in her parent's house—turned lumpy and grey. She began drinking heavily, spending away the loot Zach had left behind, and then the jewelry she had inherited from her mother—gold and silver necklaces and beautiful rings with precious stones.

Soon Zara neglected the children, even little five-year-old Roman. So Leya and the twins took Roman out on the streets with them, playing and dancing for the crowds. The people rewarded them generously, considering the hard times raging through the country. Perhaps even the presence of young Roman spared them the persecution of the police.

And yet, the situation turned from bad to worse. Often the kids returned to find their mother in a stupor while some strange man, most likely the one who had sold her cheap moonshine, ransacked the tent. Awaking the next morning, she would expropriate every last kopeck the children earned to cure her terrible hangovers. It did not matter to her anymore that she was leaving them cold and hungry. And those men kept coming and drinking with Zara.

In the late spring of 1924, one such man became a frequent visitor to the *tabor*. Zara called him Grishka, and he was especially scary. Curly hair covered his round head like black tar, and a grey-tinged beard hid his whole face except for a crooked nose that protruded like an eagle's beak. He wore a patch of soiled brown leather over his left eye, and his huge Adam's apple rolled up and down every time he swallowed his saliva.

Grishka not only looked mean; he was mean. More than once Leya intercepted his glances at her and the twins, and even at her age she recognized his undisguised desire. The lust that emanated from his one eye frightened her. One night she caught him fondling one of the girls on his lap. She ran toward him, screaming at the top of her lungs to leave her little sister alone. Grishka just laughed, until their half-drunken mother realized what was going on and grabbed her daughter from him. The children ran and hid, as Grishka chased after them, raging like a bull. When he could not find them, he unleashed his anger on Zara, knocking her out cold with one blow of his hammer-like fist. Then he dropped on the ground next to her motionless body and began gently stroking her hair, whimpering like a child.

After this incident, Leya hoped that Grishka would leave and never come back. Unfortunately, he stayed and cared for Zara while she recovered. Two days later, he brought a wagon filled with his personal belongings, bread and sausages, and bottles of molted rye drink that the locals called *kvass*. How did he acquire all these provisions when the young Soviet Russia suffered from a long drought and devastating famine? It was only possible if he had robbed one of the local Party elite's secret food stores. Every big regional center in the country already had one or two of those.

As a gesture of his goodwill, Grishka invited all the Mauri family to an unexpected feast, during which he announced his intention to become the new head of the clan, promising to protect and provide for it. Everybody but Zara reacted to his promise with enthusiasm. No matter how badly this family needed a man who would take on this role, she knew that Grishka was not such a man. He was a liar, a brute, and a hardened criminal with no loyalty but for himself. However, Zara didn't say a word. She was too weak, too dependent on his booze.

Leya didn't trust this horrible man either. After a sleepless night, Leya decided she must take her twin sisters and little Roman and leave this place forever. Of course, it would break Zara's heart, but it was better than living under the thumb of a monster. The following day, Leya secretly collected the children's clothes and blankets and her violin. Grishka drove his wagon out to collect more provisions and would not return that day. At midnight, she awakened the kids, dressed them, and sneaked out of the *tabor* in total silence. She planned to walk that night far enough beyond Yekaterinaslav so that their mother or Grishka could not find them.

At eight o'clock in the cool, foggy morning, Leya and the kids finally stopped to rest. Each of them ate a piece of dry bread, bundled up in the blankets, and slept until dusk. They continued their journey under the cover of night, avoiding small villages and little towns but occasionally visiting tiny hamlets to beg for breadcrumbs and fresh water. Leya lost count of the days they had traveled when, one morning, they reached the outskirts of the city of Kharkiv. She understood this was a good place to blend in and earn a few kopeks, so that day Leya and her siblings joined the army of two million homeless children living throughout Ukraine.

In December 1926, Kharkiv's NKVD agents swept up her and her partners in crime. It wasn't their first arrest, and Leya had often wriggled out of such jams by telling some of her unbelievable fables. This time was different. Perhaps she had grown tired of the heavy burden of caring for three kids not much younger than herself, or perhaps she was just scared of another brutal winter. So Leya agreed when NKVD Inspector Maslov offered to arrange for her to join the Gorky Colony. On one hand, Leya felt good that she would from now on have a permanent roof over her head and three meals a day, every day, something she hadn't had for almost seven years. On the other hand, she felt guilty because her siblings couldn't go with her. Roman and her twin sisters were too young to be admitted to this type of colony, but she was smart enough to realize the arrangements would be best for all of them.

Leya spent that winter learning the rules and customs of the Gorky Colony. Strict discipline and executing responsibilities were the two fundamentals of everyday life. The colony was economically and socially self-sufficient in every way. The colonists milked the cows, fed the pigs, and harvested all the vegetables from the gardens. And yet the most important task was attending school classes. Leya worked hard to fill the gaps in her education: math and science, Russian language and even literature. Of course, she excelled in music, becoming first violin in the colony's orchestra. She rediscovered classical music, which reminded her of those long-forgotten exercises with her late mother.

One day Leya was called in to meet Anton Makarenko, the founder and inspirational leader of the Gorky Colony. Anton Semyonovich informed Leya of his plan to form a new colony on an old aristocratic estate near Kharkiv, allocated by the Soviet government. He explained that he planned to use his best pupils at Gorky as young mentors, and that Leya had made the list.

So Leya returned to Kharkiv at the end of 1927 to live and study at the Felix Dzerzhinsky Colony. Though everyone believed in the effectiveness of Makarenko's methodology, that first year proved difficult: many teenagers refused to be rehabilitated, and some used the colony continue their criminal activities hidden from the NKVD. But eventually those "bad apples" were weeded out. By 1929 life in the colony had become as normal as it could be. Leya remembered those years as happy and very productive.

In 1932, she graduated with distinction from the *RabFak,* the Worker's Faculty. After passing several auditions, Leya was accepted by the Moscow State Tchaikovsky Conservatoire under the famous violin professor Abram Yampolsky. Leya said goodbye to the Colony and the city of Kharkiv, to start a new chapter of her life.

* * *

Leya Solomonovna paused, took a deep breath, and closed her eyes. Viktor jumped from his chair and once again gently put his hands around his mother's shoulders.

"How do you feel, Mom? Do you need your medicine?" He sounded worried. "You can continue your story another time. It is rather late, almost midnight."

"It's all right, Son. Everything is fine. I am done with my story anyway." Leya Solomonovna smiled, freed herself from Viktor's hug, and got up. "You look tired too. Let's go to sleep."

"Tell me, Mom, how come you never told us about your youth before?" Unable to help himself, Viktor then asked, "Did Father know this story?"

"For the most part. He was the one who actually used his NKVD connections in getting all my ID papers in order," Leya Solomonovna explained. "Don't forget, for many years I was just a homeless kid without any family roots. Your father contacted the Odessa municipal archives and received confirmed information about my parents and younger sister. The only problem was that under the name Shtern we were all recorded as deceased— killed by the house fire in 1919. Evidently, no one knew I had survived."

"Couldn't it have happened that somebody else survived?" Viktor sounded very curious. "You know, mistakes like that often happen."

"Frankly, I blocked that tragedy out of my memory, or at least I tried. But I know for a fact my brother Leo wasn't there. He was away, fighting in the war." The woman looked a bit confused.

"So, did they adjust the records?" Viktor held his breath but insisted. "Did you make a follow-up inquiry about your brother?"

"Raymond told me that, according to the Red Army archives, Leo Shtern went missing in action. And I left it at that. Does it mean he could be alive?" Leya Solomonovna looked at Viktor rather strangely, as if she felt something.

It was on the tip of his tongue, and yet Viktor didn't dare say what had become obvious. He had a better proposition.

"I tell you what, I'll call in tomorrow and stay with you all day. Wasn't it precisely what Doctor Bolshakov suggested, and Uncle Misha ordered?"

"That's a good idea, Son. You need to rest."

Several minutes later, Viktor was in his old bed under a heavy comforter. He couldn't recall the last night he spent in the room where he grew up in, but it felt good, especially with his beloved mom sitting next to him. His bedroom hadn't changed much: a few personal things collected over the years and some books, mainly in jurisprudence, had migrated from here to his own apartment. The rest remained in the same place since he had moved out.

"Mom, there is one more thing before we say goodnight. I would really like to hear how you and Dad met. I don't believe you ever told me that one."

"It's not a short story, but I can tell you if you want to hear. I'll try to make it quick."

* * *

Leya dedicated her very existence to playing the violin. Professor Yampolsky and her other conservatory teachers praised her talent and work ethic. Yet they noted her lack of ambition, without which no one would climb to the top of the profession. Frankly, Leya didn't care much about this; in her mind, she was grateful just to accomplish what seemed impossible only a few years earlier. Her life in Moscow opened new horizons, and Leya intended to take it all in.

Besides music, she developed a real passion for modern poetry. One night someone from the dormitory invited her to a reading in a private flat near Sadovy Boulevard. She remembered very well the relatively small room with fifteen or eighteen people, primarily young women, sitting on the couch, chairs, or just standing and listening to a lanky young man with thick, round glasses, reading rather exaltedly from a cramped piece of white paper:

Is this century really worse than those before?
Perhaps in that dazed by fear and grief,

It touched the blackest sore.
It could not heal.
In the West, the earthly sun shines yet,
And city roofs gleam in its light,
But here, the white one marks doors with crosses,
Summons the crows and the crows are in flight.

It was an excerpt from a poem of Anna Akhmatova, famous poet of the Silver Epoch written in 1921. Leya smiled as she recognized it; she was quite familiar with this work. At that moment, she noticed a handsome young man in his late twenties with neatly cropped black hair dressed in a custom-made grey suit. He was sitting on the piano stool in the corner and moving his eyes from face to face. When he met Leya's eyes, he froze up. They looked at each other rather intensely for a minute before the young man flinched. His face turned red. Leya smiled again.

For the next fifteen minutes, they exchanged glances a few times, and every time he would lower his head and blush. It was so cute that Leya instinctively moved closer to the corner where he was perched.

This move didn't escape his attention. The young man got up and inconspicuously waved his hand in the direction of the door. Leya let him pass her and followed him out of the room. The entrance hall was almost dark, but she noticed that he was a head taller than her. She was just about to ask him his name when the man touched his lips with his finger.

"Let's leave this place," he whispered. "I am sure you are familiar with this poetry."

"What if I don't want to?" she whispered back. "I rather enjoy this poetry—"

"I understand and respect that, but we must talk," he insisted. "It is for your own sake."

Leya sensed this was more than some clever line or joke. They quickly left the apartment and soon found themselves across the street in a small city square. They found an empty bench and sat apart from each other in total silence.

He spoke first. "Sorry I dragged you out of that lovely party." He sounded a bit sarcastic but concluded on a serious note, "You have to trust me; it isn't a safe place for a girl like you. By the way, my name is Raymond, Raymond Vitus."

"How do you know it isn't safe? And why in the world do I have to trust you, Raymond Vitus?" Leya couldn't hide her irritation. "Although you speak perfect Russian, you are not Russian, are you?"

"You are very perceptive. What is your name?"

"Leya, Leya Shtern," she quickly replied. Something was very trustworthy in the demeanor of this young man. "You didn't answer my question."

"I am Latvian. My parents are from Riga," he explained. "My mother passed away a few years ago. My father lives and works in Leningrad. I am a Muscovite for the last four years. You are not Russian either. Can you tell me about yourself, Leya Shtern?"

"I have very little to tell. And why do you want to know?" she asked with some degree of playfulness.

"First, it would be a sign of common courtesy; after all, I did tell you who I am, didn't I? And second, I would love to know you better." He blushed again.

Laughing, Leya sprang from the bench and rushed back to the street. He hurried after her.

"I wonder if the trams are still running?" Leya pondered. "I hate to walk all the way to my dormitory that late. It is pretty far."

"Oh, don't you worry; I am not going to let you walk alone. Or we can flag a taxi."

"Thank you, Raymond, but it's not necessary. I usually get around the city without a bodyguard, you know, and on foot. Taxis are rather expensive for my taste." She looked straight into his eyes and smiled again.

"You're right. I am not your bodyguard, though I wouldn't mind being one; it would be my pleasure to accompany you on this journey. If you agree, of course." Raymond jokingly bent his upper body forward and ceremoniously waved his right hand first across and then toward Leya, as a knight would ask a lady her permission to follow. She curtsied slightly, and with a big smile offered her right hand. They began laughing loudly, then hopped carefree down the street, hand-in-hand.

By the time they arrived at their destination two hours later, they knew almost everything about each other. Raymond told her that he had completed his training in NKVD school just six months ago. Tonight, was his first individual field assignment as an operative: to observe and take notes on people unlawfully participating in secret, unauthorized social gatherings. Pretending she was scared, Leya asked him if he would arrest her. It wasn't funny, but they laughed at the idea of her being arrested. He explained why he pulled her out of that apartment: he had an urge to protect her from any harm.

He was too shy to admit how deeply he was struck by her beauty and poise. It had never crossed his mind that this could happen to him. Then he remembered the words of his favorite writer, O. Henry: "It is an undisputed fact that some time woman and man instantly fall in love the moment they lay their eyes on each other. It is a risky proposition the love from first sight when she didn't see his checkbook yet, and he has no idea how she looks in the morning. Nevertheless, it happens in life." Raymond's inner voice screamed victoriously, *yes, indeed!*

In turn, Leya told Raymond what she had gone through before lady luck smiled on her. She told her sad story as a matter of fact, without complaint or regret. Listening to her, Raymond understood where this young woman's inner strength came from. It was a revelation for him, who until then had lived a comfortable and uneventful life. It also confirmed his initial impression: this girl is amazing, and she must fall in love with him as much as he was in love with her.

Nevertheless, it didn't happen right away. Although Leya liked this handsome and funny young man from their first encounter, she was concerned about his occupation, especially the fact that some of his daily assignments were to uncover and arrest enemies of the State. This was a dangerous job. Would she be strong enough not to have a nervous breakdown knowing that he was in constant danger? It took her some time to realize that it didn't matter, that she loved him so much she could face anything that would come with this love.

For the next four months, they saw each other at least three days a week, talking about films they had seen or books they had read, or their lives before they met. Their growing love became evident to everyone around them. The conservatory teachers often pointed out to Leya that she was neglecting her studies, and Raymond's NKVD superiors caught mistakes in his paperwork. Frankly, the young lovers didn't care, but they should have.

In late October, Raymond was called onto the "red carpet," as the agents of Lubyanka Square headquarters called it. The NKVD Head People's Commissar Genrikh Yagoda informed Inspector Raymond Vitus of his immediate transfer to Khabarovsk. There was no mention of his occasional lapses; rather, Yagoda read a personal message from Comrade Stalin, which praised Raymond's service and commended his invaluable knowledge and experience for the establishment of an exceptional Soviet law enforcement outpost in the Russian Far East.

This news frightened Leya. Did it mean they would never see each other again? She couldn't bear the thought. Raymond was very upset too, yet as a military man he had to comply with the order, especially one presumably issued by Comrade Stalin himself. He tried to calm Leya, saying that it was only a temporary setback, and that he would come back for her as soon as possible.

Leya didn't cry; she just convinced herself that whatever happened did so for the better. Their unexpected separation would allow her to graduate on time, and Raymond was better off with no distractions in a new, unfamiliar place. But how long would they be apart?

Two days before his departure to Khabarovsk, Raymond asked Leya to marry him. She said yes. They married the next day in a small ceremony at the regional Soviet of Deputies. That night, Leya's roommate went to sleep in someone else's dormitory room. The next day, the newlyweds said a tearful goodbye to each other, and Raymond Vitus boarded the train to Khabarovsk.

Leya was right; everything worked for the better, just not as quickly as she expected. A year later, Raymond returned to Moscow for a training seminar. The happy young couple didn't have much to pack to start their new life in Khabarovsk: just some old furniture Leya kept in her dormitory room, to be shipped by train later.

* * *

Leya Solomonovna noticed Viktor fighting to keep his eyelids open, so she went silent.

"No, no, Mom. Do not stop." Viktor forced himself to react. "I want to know the end."

"What end? After that, it was our life of forty years." Leya Solomonovna sighed and gently put her right hand on her son's forehead. "Sleep now. We are both tired. We'll talk tomorrow. Remember, you are staying home."

Chapter 15

M onday, November 21. 7:30 in the morning. Viktor opened one eye and saw his mother's face. She looked like he remembered her twenty-five years ago, young and beautiful. He drifted back into his shallow dream but could hear her pleasant voice clearly.

"How do you feel, Son? Did you sleep well?"

"Yes, Mom," Viktor muttered in response.

"Yesterday, you wanted to tell me something. Didn't you? I could feel it."

Viktor began breathing heavily, but his eyes remained shut. Leya Solomonovna knew her son was still asleep. She patiently waited. After a while, he muttered out again, not quite coherently: "What do you want to know first?"

"Who dressed your wound right away? The captain who came with you in the ambulance told me it wasn't him."

"Katya Rogozhina. You might know her as Ksenia Krylova, the actress from Drama Theater." His speech continued to be slurred.

"I do recall this name. What was an actress doing there?" Leya Solomonovna inquired in a deliberately calm voice.

"She's the daughter of the murder victim in my current investigation." Viktor paused and sighed in his sleep. "She is under my protection. I was checking on her."

"Checking on her? You like her, don't you?" She sounded concerned. "Isn't it prohibited to get involved personally with any subject in a case?"

"Yes, Mom. What do you want me to do?"

"You must stay away from this woman. She is definitely vulnerable now."

"But I do like her, Mom. I haven't felt this good for a long time—almost forgot."

This time, Leya Solomonovna paused and sighed. She didn't know what to say; yet she knew quite well how Viktor felt.

"Is she pretty?" Her voice lost any color. "She is not married, I hope."

"Katya is wonderful," Viktor answered. "She is not married, but she has a boyfriend. I am not sure how serious it is, though."

A smile crossed his lips. Leya Solomonovna was sitting in total silence, watching her son fall back into a deep sleep. She knew that when he woke, he would not remember a word of this conversation.

It was a mother's little secret she had discovered and guarded since Viktor's childhood. When he was four, Leya Solomonovna noticed how deep her son's sleep was. This condition most likely contributed to a very common disorder among boys of that age: bedwetting. The problem wasn't very serious, but it required getting him up to go to the bathroom to avoid such mishaps. Doing just this, she discovered her son would communicate freely and without reservation while still asleep, remembering nothing afterwards.

Ever since, Leya Solomonovna used this peculiar ability to find out what was really going on in her son's life when he wouldn't reveal it any other way. Many situations warranted such measures during Viktor's teenage years, when he was a free-spirited, stubborn, and secretive lad, much like his father had been. Nevertheless, the mother never compromised her son's trust nor took advantage of the information to which she would not otherwise be privy, with one exception.

In 1969, Viktor came home from his senior year at Leningrad State University. Leya Solomonovna immediately observed her son's poor mental state. Of course, everyone in the family knew of the tragic, untimely death of Viktor's fiancé, Yulia, but perhaps not how hard it had hit him. The grieving young man cut himself off from the outside world, staying in his room all day, pacing back and forth until late into the night. He refused any interaction with his parents or friends, often avoiding eating in the dining room. But knowing her son so well, Leya's biggest concern was the crazed look in his eyes.

Leya Solomonovna felt she had to intervene, so she plied her little spell early one morning. Viktor revealed his strong suspicion that Yulia's death was no accident, that whatever happened was staged. Most distressingly, the local prosecutor squashed Viktor's every attempt to pursue the matter and even threatened him with physical harm. This frightened her so much that she broke their unspoken confidence and shared the information with Raymond Vitus.

Raymond reacted a bit strangely, as if he may have known about it already, but he agreed that they had to address the problem as soon as possible. They broached the topic the next day when his mother lured Viktor into joining the family for supper. Viktor became visibly upset when confronted with information he thought nobody in his family should've known. He angrily expressed that he had no intention to discuss the matter, and he even hinted that his father might have a hand in it after all.

Leya Solomonovna jumped in before the senior Vitus had a chance to reject the accusation. She confessed to Viktor how yesterday morning she tricked him into revealing what had been bothering him, and that her concern for her son's mental state prompted her to share this disturbing information with his father. All three stared at Leya Solomonovna in disbelief.

Viktor's sister Raisa broke the silence first, asking in slightly exaggerated horror if her mother ever used the same technique on her. Raymond smiled cunningly, commenting on some of his mother's gypsy skills and hoping that he wasn't a victim of a similar psychological experiment. Thankfully, the children didn't register his inside joke. Leya Solomonovna reassured everyone that it only worked with Viktor because of his unique ability to communicate in his sleep.

Viktor continued looking flabbergasted. Raymond managed to convince his son to put his suspicions aside, to go on with his life and honor the memory of his late fiancée for who she was: a loving, beautiful, and intelligent young woman. In turn, his mother reminded him that tragedies like this were a part of life and should strengthen his character, not destroy it.

Viktor listened to all these arguments rather calmly, agreeing to leave the matter alone, but hoping deep inside to discover the truth, with or without his father's help. Leya Solomonovna had promised herself never to use her son's "weakness" again, and she had kept this promise until now.

* * *

By 10:30, Viktor was up, his face shaved, and his hair neatly combed. He looked well rested and energetic. Leya Solomonovna waited for him in the kitchen with his favorite food: fried potatoes, a couple of poached eggs, a veal sausage link, and a cup of piping hot black coffee. He hugged his mother and eased his body onto the bench between the kitchen wall and the small breakfast table—his usual place since he was a little boy. No words were spoken until Viktor pushed away the empty plate with the fork and knife on top.

"Thank you, Mom. That was great! I've missed your food a lot."

"I am glad you liked it." Leya Solomonovna smiled and asked, as only a mother could. "Would you like another helping? I have more of those links."

"Oh no. I've had enough. Thank you, Mom."

"Then have more coffee while I bring Father's box I mentioned yesterday, okay?" She poured more coffee in his cup and left the room.

After a few minutes, Leya Solomonovna returned with a relatively new shoebox in her hands and put it on the table in front of Viktor. He started to lift the lid to see what was inside, but he instantly put it back in place and looked at his mother.

"May I go through all this later? There are a lot of papers, aren't there?"

"Not that many, but you can do it whenever you want. I don't think there is any urgency."

"Thank you, Mom." Viktor swiped the box off the table and put it on the bench next to him. "I still have several questions to ask you in relation to your life story, if you don't mind?"

"Why would I? Hopefully, I will be able to answer them."

"But before we begin, I have to call my office and alert them about me taking the day off." Viktor got up to go to the entrance hall where the telephone was.

"I have already called your boss, Colonel Guzyev. He told me you could stay home more than one day." Leya Solomonovna looked at her son victoriously.

"Mom, you are always one step ahead of us, aren't you?" He smiled and handed her his empty breakfast plate.

"What happened to your Gypsy siblings?" Viktor got right to it. "Did you find them?"

"I did eventually. After a few months at Gorky Colony, I received a letter from Inspector Maslov, informing me, as he had promised, both locations where my twin sisters and our younger brother were placed," Leya Solomonovna replied. "Unfortunately, they were separated from each other; the girls were sent to some orphanage near Kyiv, and little Roman went into foster care with a family in Chernigov."

"And how did their lives turn out?"

"Not bad at all. I did mention the sisters' musical talents, especially their singing abilities, didn't I? They both went through *RabFak* and were accepted to the Moscow School of Performing Arts and Music. Roman, who happened to be a wonderful dancer, had a different career path. Interestingly enough, all three of them reunited at the same place, the Moscow Gypsy Theater. I found out about it a few years later."

"Did you have a chance to meet them again?"

"Oh yes, and rather incidentally. One day in the fall of 1935, Raymond came home, waving two tickets in his hand and shouting, "Guess where we are going tonight? We are going to see a Gypsy show." She paused. "It was a musical variety show with Gypsy musicians, singers and dancers dressed in colorful ethnic costumes. From the start, I was nervous, but I got even more emotional when, in the second act, I recognized my Gypsy sisters on stage, singing a beautiful duet. After the show, we managed to go to the actors' dressing room. The reunion was very moving. Roman was there too. I didn't recognize him at all; he grew up to be a strong and handsome young man."

"Have you kept in touch with them after that meeting?"

"We exchanged letters with Roman regularly until the war broke out. He was drafted, despite being an actor. Usually, actors, singers and performing artists in general were used to entertain troops. I never found out why he wasn't retained by the Theater Company during those tough years." Leya Solomonovna paused again.

"Perhaps he volunteered? That would explain how he ended up in the regular army," Viktor speculated.

"Perhaps he did. The truth is, no matter how this happened, I never heard from him again. Only in 1947, I received a letter from one of twins, Zoya. She informed me that she and her sister Leila were back in Moscow doing the same thing they were doing before the war," Leya Solomonovna continued. "And there was no word about Roman's fate."

"A bit strange, don't you think?"

"Son, life is full of things you can call strange and often mysterious."

Silence settled in over the kitchen table for a few minutes. Leya Solomonovna got up to carry Viktor's plate and utensils to the sink. He broke the silence first.

"Mom, I know we've gone over a lot, but…" Viktor hesitated for a moment and then spit it out. "Why did you and Father wait for so long to have me? When I was born, you had been married for six years, right? And you decided to have me in the middle of the war?"

"First, we had been married for seven years. Secondly, you don't always decide these things, Viktor. You are a grown man; you should know that by now." Leya Solomonovna stopped for a moment and sat down to catch her breath. "For the same reason, I should tell you something rather delicate too. You weren't our first child. It—he was a boy supposed to be born in March of 1938. But it didn't happen. Thirty days before the term, I had him stillborn. Raymond wasn't home at that time. The new NKVD chief Nikolai Yezhov had called him onto the red carpet in Moscow. I was worried sick, not knowing if my husband would come back or not. Those ten days in January almost killed me. We were lucky, I guess; Raymond did come home alive, even with a big promotion. But we lost our firstborn son. That's the truth. I suppose this was the right time to tell you."

Leya Solomonovna covered her eyes with both hands and leaned her body against the table. She looked physically and emotionally exhausted. This made Viktor regret he had prompted such heartbreaking memories.

"Mom, I am sorry you had to revisit those dreadful events. You didn't have to tell me all that." He moved to the other side of the table and sat next to his mother, putting his arms around her trembling shoulders. "It's okay, Mom. Would you like your Valerian drops?"

"No, just give me a few moments, Son. I'll be alright. Tell me something pleasant and interesting about your life."

The first thing that came to mind was Katya. Yet he hesitated, afraid to reveal more than he already had. For a while, they continued sitting at the kitchen table close to each other silently. What in the world could be more comforting and reassuring for a mother than a warm hug from her son?

Neither of them realized how long they had been sitting like that. The sound of the door lock being opened came from the entrance hall. Raisa entered and closed the door behind her.

"Mom! Are you home?" she shouted, taking off her fur coat and hat. "It's me, your daughter."

"We are here, in the kitchen!" Leya Solomonovna replied energetically but with a slight hesitation. "And you don't have to shout. I can hear you well enough."

The young woman rushed toward them with a big grin and embraced them both at the same time. She smelled like wintry air, fresh and cold. There were a few snowflakes on her long eyelashes.

"Oh, my God. Am I glad to see you, Brother! When was the last time we saw each other? Lilya and Alex were asking about their favorite uncle, wondering how soon they could see you." Raisa spoke at the speed of a hundred kilometers per hour before she pushed herself up on her toes, trying to reach her brother's cheek with a kiss. Viktor graciously leaned forward to let his baby-sister express her affection. Ever since he could remember, they were always close, loving each other and caring for each other like only siblings could.

"How are you, Sis?" He kissed her on the cheek in response. "It has been a long time, indeed. The kids are getting bigger and smarter every day, aren't they? Tell them I have missed them, too."

"I'll tell them, but you could stop by to visit us someday. Are you that busy?"

"As a matter of fact, I am extremely busy lately. I was out of town for two weeks," Viktor explained apologetically. "How is Boris doing; swamped as always with his cases at the Public Defenders' office, I presume?"

The smile left Raisa's lips. Her expression became rather grim. She glanced at her mother as if to ask: *Did you tell him anything yet?* She slowly lowered herself on the bench and searched for something to wipe her eyes. As always, Viktor hurried to offer his handkerchief.

"What happened? Did something happen to your husband?" He sounded really concerned and turned to Leya Solomonovna. "Mom, do you know what happened to Boris?"

"I told him— I told you about their decision to leave the country." There was some anxiety in her voice. "I also told you that Boris's parents already filed their documents at Moscow OVIR. That is all I know. Oh, yes, and that I have decided to join you Raisa and your family."

"Mom, you did decide to go with us! That is great!" Raisa ecstatically jumped out of her seat and hugged her mother. She turned to Viktor, "And what about you, Brother?"

"What about me? Are you asking if I am going too? I already told Mom I am staying here. There is nothing for me to do anywhere but here. End of discussion, Sis." Viktor was upset. "You and Boris can do whatever you consider to be the best for your family. And if Mom decides to follow you, I am not going to object."

"Sorry, I didn't come to trouble you," Raisa apologized. "In fact, I didn't expect you here, but Mom told me over the phone that you were hurt, so I had to know if you were fine."

"I am fine, Sis. Thanks. Mom convinced me to take the day off. That's all." Viktor sounded conciliatory. "Just before you came, Mother and I were talking about her life with our father. I bet you have no idea how brave our mom was and what a romantic our dad was. You should hear her stories, but for now tell me what happened to Boris; why are you so worried about him?" He glanced at his wristwatch.

"Actually, there is nothing wrong with Boris. He is just depressed and mad about what is happening with his job. Yesterday, after Boris informed his boss about our decision to apply for exit visas, he was fired. When he asked for a reason for such a sudden dismissal, his boss shouted in his face in front of all his colleagues that he couldn't tolerate any person under him who betrayed the Motherland." Raisa's speech was again stuck in high gear. "How do you like that? My Boris is a traitor now. I am afraid when I go to my orchestra rehearsal tomorrow, our conductor will accuse me of the same crime and fire me too."

"Hold on, Sis. Don't get so worked up." Viktor had to calm her down, at least for his mother's sake; she was taking this news especially hard. "There is no doubt Boris's boss is covering his ass, but I don't think he has the right to dismiss anybody just on a whim without proper procedure. I am sure Boris can file a formal complaint with a higher authority and be reinstated. After all, he is a lawyer and knows what channels to use. You don't have your request for exit visas approved yet, do you?"

"Of course not. But we just learned my in-laws did." Raisa began sobbing. "So, instead of complaining and trying to hold on to our jobs, we have to do everything possible to speed up the approval process. We need help. Vitya, you must know the OVIR supervisor; what is his name? Colonel—"

"Colonel Malinin. I know of him, but I don't know him, and I never spoken with him." Viktor stopped and took a big breath. "Listen, why don't you ask Uncle Misha for help? Isn't General Melekhov your godfather as well? He adores you and will help you more than I ever could."

"I thought about talking to Uncle Misha, but I was afraid he would not approve of our decision." Raisa stopped sobbing and concluded, "You know how he is."

"You think he hasn't learned about your decision already? Don't be naïve." Viktor suddenly recalled seeing Colonel Malinin leaving Melekhov's office yesterday but said nothing about it. Instead, he said, "Trust me, he will be willing to hear you out. I can prop him up a little before you speak to him. You know, test his mood about it, if you want me to."

"If you feel it will work, of course, you can prepare him." Her voice became more optimistic. "Thanks, Viktor, my true protector."

"Don't mention it, Sis. And your husband should be your true protector. Remind him of that and maybe he will stop being depressed? In times like this, when you can't even imagine what lies ahead of you, he must be especially wise and strong, as I have always known him to be since he joined this family." Viktor realized how rather patronizing his statement was, so he paused for a moment. "I'll talk to the General tomorrow. I promise."

"I was also going to talk to him and Alyona," said Leya Solomonovna, as she looked at both her children with sadness in her eyes. "Anyway, I have to explain my decision to them. After all, they are our longest standing, and closest friends. They deserve to know the truth."

"Well said, Mom! I agree." Viktor felt relief that this painful subject was seemingly over, at least for now.

It was in Viktor's nature to avoid any family conversations on subjects he wasn't comfortable with and today was no exception. Lately, after the death of their father, discussions on governmental policies regarding the Jewish population and their rights to reunification of the families in Israel or other countries of the West happened more and more often. Usually, Raisa and Boris initiated these conversations, offering solid and convincing arguments for leaving the USSR. Leya Solomonovna didn't reject those arguments but never showed her enthusiastic support either. Viktor, on the other hand, didn't agree with them at all, although he knew darn well the history of anti-Semitism coming directly from Kremlin after the victorious ending of the Patriotic War against Nazi Germany.

He knew about the killing of the famous director of the Moscow Yiddish Theater Solomon Michaels, and the following prosecution of the rest of the members of the Soviet Anti-Fascist Committee in 1947. The people still remembered the notorious Doctors' Plot of 1952 against the mostly Jewish medical professionals of Moscow, which in truth was cooked up by the MGB Ministry of State Security. Then there were the well-substantiated rumors of a plan born in the mind of Stalin himself, just before his demise, to resettle the entire Soviet population of Jews to Siberia and the far-eastern regions. Nikita Khrushchev revealed those plans during the Communist Party XX Congress in 1956.

Unfortunately, the anti-Semitism sponsored by Soviet leaders flourished with greater intensity after Israel had achieved a convincing victory over its Arab neighbors who attacked the young Jewish State in 1967. The Kremlin sponsored and militarily supported those attackers, and could not accept such a failure, so they did whatever they could to punish Israel for it.

Viktor was very aware of these facts, and deep inside was very sympathetic to the Jews who wanted to be reunited with their ancestral homeland and join in celebrating the victory of their newly revived country, under its white and blue flag. However, no matter how often he thought about that, it always depressed him a lot.

Suddenly, he saw a window of opportunity to bring up the subject he was holding back. Raisa's presence looked like a perfect opportunity too. "Now that this matter is settled, can we talk about something else?"

"What do you want to talk about?" Leya Solomonovna asked, looking at him anxiously as if there wasn't enough excitement for one morning.

"Yes, what is on your mind, Brother?"

He felt the eyes of his mother and sister piercing through him like laser beams.

"Mom," he began slowly, searching for the right words. "A few days ago, I heard a story that made me think differently about your lost brother Leo and sister Sonya."

"What about my sister Sonya?" Leya Solomonovna sounded surprised but calm. "What did you hear? Who could've told you about her?"

"His name is Leonid Gordin. He is a journalist working as a correspondent for some newspapers in Moscow and in his city of Lviv in Western Ukraine." Viktor deliberately didn't rush his answer, giving his mom extra time to prepare for the information she was about to receive. "I was taking his statement for my investigation. I don't know why, but he decided to tell me his life story. I was hoping to stop him at some point, but I couldn't."

"What does this story have to do with my sister Sonya and brother Leo?" His mother's question was with doubt. And yet her voice was full of anticipation.

"Leonid told the story about how his father met and married his mother during the war. Her name was Sonya Shtern." Viktor stopped and looked at his mother attentively. Leya Solomonovna was motionless. Her face lost all color. Raisa noticed it too and sprang from her seat.

"Mom, Mom! Where is your 'Validol,' Mom?" she shouted and went searching for the medication.

"It is in my pocket. Relax—I am fine. Don't interrupt him, please. Go on, Son!"

"Honestly, I didn't catch it right away, although it sounded like your maiden name, Mom. So, I asked Leonid to elaborate, and he repeated: his mother Sonya's maiden name was Shtern, and she was born in 1915 or 1916."

"Where is she now?" Leya Solomonovna asked anxiously. "Does she live in Lviv?"

"No, she lived in Kyiv. Although for the last eight or nine years, before going to work on the BAM, Leonid resided with his wife and son in Lviv. Two of his sisters also live in Kyiv with their families," Viktor explained, moving closer to his mother in anticipation of the next obvious question.

"You said she lived in Kyiv; so, where does she live now?"

"Mom, she died two years ago from cancer." He felt like he had delivered a blow and had to protect his mother by putting his arms around her shoulders.

"So, you are sure this guy's late mother was my sister Sonya and not some other woman with the same name?" Leya Solomonovna freed herself from her son's hug and looked straight into his eyes. "I hope you realize such coincidences do happen."

"I understand, Mom, that you don't want to believe she is gone before you could even talk to her, but this is the unfortunate truth. And now I am quite sure: her paternal name was Solomonovna, just like yours. I don't believe it is coincidence." Viktor embraced her again. This time his mother started crying, without any sound, just shedding her tears.

There was very little to say to stop those tears. Leya Solomonovna buried her face in Viktor's chest and kept weeping quietly. Raisa moved next to them and put her arms around her mother too. A deep silence descended upon the kitchen. It was hard to say how long it was before the old woman straightened her body and wiped her tears with the lower part of her apron. Her entire demeanor indicated her intention to find out all the details about her sister.

"So, let me get all the facts straight: my little sister somehow survived that terrible tragedy at our home. Who saved her? Where did she live before getting married? What about her husband? Is he alive?"

"Mom, listen." Viktor interrupted her barrage of questions. "Sonya married a journalist whose name was Yefrem Gordin. He died from a heart attack in 1968, if I remember correctly. I do not know how Sonya survived when your home was ravaged or what happened to her after. Leonid didn't touch upon this when he told his story. I am not sure he has this information either. However, I recall him saying that his parents named their youngest daughter Leya in the memory of Sonya's sister who presumably perished during one of the pogroms in 1919."

"Oh my God!" exclaimed Leya Solomonovna, grabbing her apron and bringing it to her teary eyes again. "It all comes together, doesn't it? It's no coincidence—this woman was my baby-sister!"

"It does look this way, Mom. Although you will never get a chance to see her, at least we found her children—your nephew and nieces, and their children. Isn't that worth being happy about?" Viktor tried to console her.

"Yes, Son, I am sad and happy at the same time. I am looking forward to meeting all of them as soon as possible, but how do you know they have any interest in finding me and our family?"

"Oh, they have. You should've seen the face of this fellow Leonid when he tried to connect the dots: it lit up like a New Year Tree! He is our cousin!"

"I must speak to him right away," Leya Solomonovna said anxiously. "Can you call him?"

"I'm not sure he has a private telephone." Viktor paused for a moment, thinking about how to reach Leonid. "I guess the best way is to call Captain Nesterenko. I was going to discuss our case with him anyway. The Captain can ask Leonid to call us back. Maybe even today."

"Who is this, Captain Nesterenko?" Raisa asked.

"He is the head of the local railroad Militia office at the BAM. He helped me with my case in Urgal—a great guy!" Viktor explained, rushing to the phone in the entrance hall. "I'll call him immediately. He should be in his office now. What time is it, quarter after one?"

Leya Solomonovna also got up from the bench and hurried to the stove. "I forgot about dinner. Rayechka, will you stay for dinner with us?"

"I wish I could, Mom," Raisa replied with sincere regret. "The children will be home from school in an hour. Boris is at home too. They will ask me for dinner, which I haven't even started to prepare yet."

"I understand. Kiss all of them for me." Leya Solomonovna followed her daughter to the door and helped her put on her heavy fur coat.

Noticing that Raisa was leaving, Viktor covered the telephone mouthpiece with his hand and leaned toward his sister to kiss her goodbye.

"I'll call you as soon as I talk to Uncle Misha," he said in a low voice, and then locked the door behind Raisa.

At that moment, Viktor heard someone on the line.

"Yes, yes, I am waiting to be connected with Captain Nesterenko. Thank you." He paused, but only for a few seconds. "Is this you, Lyubomir? Please speak up so I may hear you better. Now it's better. Good afternoon, Comrade Captain. Before we exchange any information, can you ask the Militiaman on duty to call your friend Leonid Gordin to the office? Yes, right now. No, it is a private matter. Thanks."

Viktor covered the mouthpiece again and turned to his mother, who remained in the entrance hall.

"They will try to find your nephew and get him on the phone. It may take some time, though. Please go start dinner. I'll call you."

"It is fine, Son." Leya Solomonovna smiled and hurried back to the kitchen.

In a minute or so, Viktor heard the voice of Nesterenko on the telephone telling him that Gordin was in the village and would come to the precinct as soon as possible.

After a short silence with subdued static in the background, Viktor heard Leonid's voice and immediately replied, "Hello, Cousin! You were right; your mother and my mother were sisters who lost each other when they were young children. Everything I've learned supports this. Understandably, Mom is very upset that your mother is no longer with us, but she is very happy to find you, your sisters, and the entire family." He stopped breathing heavily and listened to Leonid's reaction. "Oh, yes, of course, she has many questions and wants to see you as soon as possible. I'll let you speak with her, but please consider she is rather fragile right now. Mom! Come here and talk to the nephew you didn't know existed."

Leya Solomonovna rushed from the kitchen and grabbed the phone from her son's hand.

"Is this Leonid? You are the son of Sonya Shtern?" She was visibly nervous, so Viktor pulled a chair and gently forced her to sit. He stood behind her and put his arms on her shoulders. "I don't know where to begin. I have so many questions. I understand. We must meet. I would love that."

She handed the telephone back to Viktor and started crying, covering her eyes with the soft edge of her apron. He couldn't remember seeing his mother like this, not since his father's funeral.

"Leonya, I apologize, but Mom is too emotional to speak. Thanks for understanding." Viktor carried on, but his voice was also quivering. He paused for a moment to get a hold of himself. "You must come over soon. When would it be possible? In two weeks? Very well. Call me so I can send my driver to pick you up. Of course, you will recognize Pyotr. He was with me in New Urgal. Okay, till then."

Viktor hung the telephone up and turned to his mother.

"Soon you will get to see your long-lost nephew. Too bad you'll be moving away."

Afterwards, mother and son had a quiet dinner at the kitchen table. Together, they washed dishes, put everything away, and retired to their rooms without a word to each other. Leya Solomonovna lay down on her bed, feeling exhausted, physically and emotionally. She closed her eyes, hoping to take a much-needed nap, but she could not. Her head swirled with thoughts about what had just transpired.

One particular thought nagged at her again and again: how did her baby sister Sonya—whom Leya Solomonovna remembered only as a four-year-old child—look later in her life? She hoped Leonid would have some pictures. At least this brought some solace to her aching heart and a smile to her lips.

Each time she started to fall asleep, her mind turned to a new set of worries, and her wide-open eyes stared at the ceiling. Was she making the right decision to join Raisa and her family, leaving their Motherland for a distant, unknown place? How would Raymond react to such a move if he were alive? What would Viktor's life look like after the family left? What was she going to tell the Melekhovs? What would their reaction be? There were many questions—tough questions—and no answers.

At the same time, Viktor grappled with his own dilemma. He did not consider himself Jewish, but he never denied some connection to his maternal roots. He respected that his sister felt differently and had become more in touch with their Jewish heritage, perhaps under the influence of her husband. He also dearly loved Raisa's Jewish in-laws; they were honest, decent, hard-working people—qualities that had become foreign to Soviet society as of late.

Although Viktor, like many Soviet people, was aware of this situation, it had not touched him on a personal level until now, when his own mother, sister and her family had become affected by such perverted policies. He had no doubts they needed his support and his help. *How could he help them?* Viktor asked himself. *The only hope was getting Melekhov involved. After all, OVIR was under his direct command. Even a little nudge to Colonel Malinin could make a huge difference.*

The General's personal connection to the Vitus family was well known within the circles of the local power structure. So, it would be in his interest if this matter were resolved expeditiously, without drawing attention from the Party bosses here or in Moscow. *And the sooner the Vitus widow left, the sooner Melekhov and his wife could take over Mom's flat. Nothing was wrong with that*, he thought turning red face. *Life goes on. I'm sure uncle Misha would agree to help.*

His optimistic mood didn't last long, though. A new wave of thoughts filled Viktor's mind; thoughts that made him panic. How would he survive without his close-knit family around? In his darkest days, his devoted mother and his loyal sister were his source of strength and confidence. Was it possible that he would never see them again? Viktor's heartbeat faltered and his body shivered at the notion. He grabbed his chest and inhaled as much air as he could, holding it all in until the fluttering gradually stopped. It was unbearable.

He considered how volatile his professional life might become. *Probably not right away, as long as General Melekhov was in power. Uncle Misha would not let anything bad happen to his godson,* Viktor honestly believed. *But what if circumstances changed, and there was no one to watch his back?* He also believed that his late father's legacy might protect him, at least while it still lived on. *But how long would that be?*

This last thought made him reach for the shoebox his mother gave him at breakfast. Viktor lifted the lid off and took out a rather thick, standard-sized yellow envelope lying on top. He examined it carefully before looking inside. There was a round seal stamped over the open flap in smudged ink: *Top Secret*. Viktor recognized the seal from past correspondence with the local KGB office. Only three words marked the envelope's front side: *To Comrade Vitus*. There was nothing else—no postage stamp, no return address, no name of sender.

Inside, he found a handwritten letter on several pieces of paper ripped from a notebook. On the top of the first page, Viktor read *2nd of September 1975*, and underneath, *Dear Raymond*. The date shook him—his father received the letter just a few days before he committed suicide. Viktor rushed to the last page to see who signed it: "Yours always, loyal Vartan A."

At first, the name didn't ring a bell, and he returned to the beginning of the letter. The author apologized for sending the letter by courier rather than the regular mail service. The letter made the standard polite inquiries concerning Leya and the children and then asked if Viktor had ever recuperated from the "events" in Leningrad.

At this point, Viktor figured out who had written this letter. Of course, it was Ivan Artemovich Arutyunov, his father's oldest friend and classmate at the Leningrad NKVD Academy; General Arutyunov had signed it with his Armenian birth name "Vartan." *Apparently, there is a reason for that,* Viktor caught himself thinking. The peculiar timing of this letter struck Viktor again. *Was there a possible connection between this letter and Raymond Vitus's suicide?* Viktor's intuition told him there was. *I must read it in its entirety—but not now*, he concluded, already physically exhausted and emotionally drained by the events of the day.

Viktor stuffed the pages back into the envelope and put it aside. A small stack of old photographs tied together caught his attention. Some of them had turned yellow more than the others. He pulled the top photograph out. In its right lower corner, there were two lines of embedded print: *Atelier Broussard, Riga. September of 1914.* A young man with a long mustache, dressed in the uniform of a low-ranking officer of the Russian Czarist Army, stood next to a seated woman with light hair and a little blond boy on her lap. Viktor saw a definite resemblance between this man and his late father, so he guessed it was a family picture taken before his grandfather Alfred Vitus went off to World War I. Another photograph captured the same woman with the boy in a gymnasium jacket, about 8 or 9 years old. A date was written in lead pencil on the back of the photo: *October 1917.* Viktor looked intensely at the face of his grandmother, trying to recall her name. He couldn't, and that vexed him. *How come Dad rarely spoke about his own mother? One time*, Viktor remembered, *he told me that his mother was a schoolteacher, and another time, in passing, mentioned something about her unfortunate premature death.* That was it—no details, though it was known to the family that Alfred Vitus didn't live long enough to see his son get married either. *How had that happened?* Again, it was a subject never discussed in front of the children.

"Perhaps Mom knows more? I have to ask her," Viktor decided, and pulled another old photograph from the shoebox. In it four people sat at a long table, all looking into the camera. The picture had been taken from a distance and was so deteriorated that it was almost impossible to distinguish the faces. Viktor pulled a magnifying glass from the drawer and studied the photo more closely. He recognized two faces: his grandfather Alfred Vitus, and the other—he could hardly believe—was Felix Dzerzhinsky, the legendary creator and head of *VeCheKa*. On its back he found written in faded black ink: *Meeting*

with "Iron Felix," J. Vatsetis, and L. Trotsky. Petrograd, April of 1918. Viktor had no idea that his grandfather was so close to Dzerzhinsky.[4]

Viktor pulled out another old photograph; it depicted twelve men in early Red Army uniforms with tall Russian rifles at their hips. From the previous photo, he recognized his grandfather and J. Vatsetis, dressed in the typical leather suit of a Soviet commissar. On the back of the photograph there was a description in faded pencil writing: *Red Latvian Riflemen. Lenin's personal security detail. Petrograd, January 1918.* There it was— another surprise staring at him.

He knew that his grandfather was one of the original volunteers of the famous Latvian Riflemen Battalions established in 1915 by Czar Nikolas' Decree to defend the Baltic territories of the Russian Empire from Germans in World War I. In one year, this regiment grew to forty thousand troops. By October 1917, more than half of those soldiers and some officers had joined the Bolshevik Revolution, serving as the building blocks of the future Red Army. What Viktor could not know was that later, J. Vatsetis was appointed as Deputy to Leon Trotsky, the Soviet People's Commissar of the Army and Navy. Vatsetis became his trusted right hand during the most difficult years of the Civil War. Also, Viktor did not know that Felix Dzerzhinsky drafted almost all the men in the photograph, including his grandfather Alfred Vitus, as the foundation for the future Soviet state security services— first *VeCheKa*, and later NKVD.

---

[4] Apparently, this photograph was taken shortly after the signing of the Brest-Litovsk Peace Treaty, which in practice removed Russia from the First World War. This did not come without major sacrifices in territory that previously belonged to the Russian Empire: Finland, Poland, part of Ukraine, and all the Baltic States— Lithuania, Latvia, and Estonia. All those countries immediately proclaimed their independence and allied with Germany.

From the beginning of the negotiations with the Germans, Lenin's trusted advisor Leon (Lev Davidovich) Trotsky headed the Soviet delegation. He soberly analyzed the dire situation in which the young Russian Soviet Republic found itself: only two and a half months removed from the Bolshevik Revolution, the country was vulnerable, with a badly equipped and poorly trained army, and in need of a peaceful diplomatic solution to the war inherited from the Czarist regime. But Trotsky encountered strong opposition to his assessment from Party Central Committee members and V. Lenin himself. Trotsky only managed to convince Lenin to sign the treaty by the beginning of March, faced with the viable threat of a renewed German advance and the capture of Petrograd in particular. This gave a desperately needed reprieve to the Red Army and allowed it to turn its attention to the fight against its counter-revolutionary foes.

As Viktor looked at the photograph, the telephone suddenly rang loudly. Viktor jumped at the sudden noise, then dashed to the entrance hall to keep it from waking his mother. There he found Leya Solomonovna already answering it. Her son's frantic entrance startled her, and she dropped the receiver from her hand. Viktor caught it before it hit the floor.

"Who is there?" he whispered to her.

"Mikhail Grigoriyevich," she whispered back. "He was asking for you."

Viktor lifted the receiver to his ear. Trying to sound calm, he said, "Comrade General, I am listening."

"Viktor, why are you breathing so heavily? Are you all right?" His voice expressed genuine concern.

"I am fine, Mikhail Grigoriyevich. I was just in a hurry to pick up the phone before it's ring disturbed my mother's rest." Viktor explained. "But she is still quicker than me, Uncle Misha, can you believe it?"

"Oh yes, I can," the General laughed. "Please tell her I am sorry for interrupting her rest. I figured she would be up at this time."

"You figured right, Mikhail Grigoriyevich," Viktor assured him. "Did you want to speak with me, Comrade General?"

"Yes, indeed. We need you in the office tomorrow morning, Major. Of course, if you feel well enough. We have received all the necessary information about the man in custody. It's time to start his interrogation."

"Understood, Comrade General. Any response to the sketch of my assailant?" Viktor asked.

"I don't think we have any." The General paused. "But you haven't told me yet about your health. Are you fully recovered? I can give you another day?"

"It is not necessary, Comrade General. I am totally fine. I will see you tomorrow morning at—"

"Be at my office at eight," the General jumped in. "We have to discuss something else."

Viktor heard the line click and then total silence. He slowly put the receiver back on the hook and turned his head. His mother stood a couple of steps away from the telephone. She had listened to his conversation with the General. *This is odd*, Viktor thought. *She has never done that before. She must be worried.* Without a word, he hugged her and kissed her on her temple.

"I must go home, Mom," he said, almost whispering in her ear. "Uncle Misha insists on seeing me very early. He wants to talk to me before the official meeting. Please try to get a hold of him and Aunt Alyona tonight. They ought to hear from you first."

"Yes, I know." Leya Solomonovna replied in a low voice and then kissed Viktor on the cheek. "Let me feed you before you go."

Chapter 16

Early morning of November 22. For the last few minutes, General Melekhov and Major Vitus sat across the conference table, looking at each other in silence. Neither of them knew what to say, though both knew what it was all about.

Leya Solomonovna had spoken with Uncle Misha and Aunt Alyona last night, telling them of her decision. How had the Melekhovs taken it? Not very well, Viktor imagined. The General's eyes expressed only one question, to which Viktor's eyes seemed to reply: *I am not going anywhere. My life is here.*

The General broke the silence. "It has to be done quickly and quietly. If the decision has been made, there is no reason to attract unnecessary attention to this matter, either here or in Moscow. Don't you agree? I'll make sure Colonel Malinin understands this."

"I agree, Comrade General." Viktor nodded. "Thank you, Uncle Misha."

"Then let's start our office meeting. Everyone is in the waiting room already," the General concluded with a sigh of relief. He went back behind his desk and pushed a button on the intercom. "Nadezhda Petrovna, please ask everyone to come in."

People trickled into the room, taking chairs around the conference table. Viktor remained sitting, greeting his colleagues with a smile in response to their inquiries about his health. Colonel Guzyev took the chair closest to the General, followed by Major Levin and then Lieutenant Colonel Burykin, the supervisor of the KPZ (preliminary) holding cells. Finally, Lieutenant Toropko sat next to Viktor and gently touched his elbow, letting him know she was worried about him and that she wanted to talk with him about something important. Viktor copied her gesture in acknowledgement.

Skipping any formalities, General Melekhov asked Burykin: "What is the physical condition of the suspect arrested in Izmailovsky?"

"According to the infirmary medical report, his condition is satisfactory, Comrade General."

"So, he can undergo questioning without any restrictions?"

"There are no restrictions, Comrade General."

Melekhov marked something in his notebook and dismissed the Lieutenant Colonel. Burykin stood up, saluted, and marched out of the office.

"Okay, Comrades, let's now review the latest developments of this case and discuss interrogation tactics with respect to the perpetrator in our custody." The General turned to Colonel Guzyev. "First, what do we know about him, Colonel? I am sure you have digested all the information gathered on him."

"He and his partner—who is still at large—are wanted by Blagoveschensk UVD under the names of Grigori Burda and Ivan Stepanov, respectively. There is a warrant for their arrest for the murder of Kirill Mazur, the shift manager of Beloretsk Dredge Co.," Guzyev reported.

"Do we know when the killing in Beloretsk took place?" the General interrupted. "Are there any connections between the homicide there and the one in Izmailovsky?"

"The homicides took place approximately ten to twelve days apart," the Colonel answered after glancing at his notes. "There is a definite connection between them: these killings were committed by the same perpetrators."

"I meant, did one killing perhaps trigger the other?" the General specified.

"If I may jump in?" Viktor offered. "It doesn't look that way. The killing at Izmailovsky wasn't premeditated; it looked more like a crime of passion, so to speak. I am sure Lieutenant Toropko will support my opinion."

"I agree," Nina added. "And from what I saw in the report from Blagoveschensk UVD, it looks like the killing of the shift supervisor Kirill Mazur wasn't planned either. It was seen as necessary to cover another crime—perhaps the theft of the gold."

"This is my opinion too," Guzyev interjected. "Both killings were extremely sloppy done in the heat of the moment. However, all details need to be confirmed during the interrogation."

"Understood. What else do we know about the perpetrators?" the General asked. "We must be armed with the most reliable information before questioning."

Guzyev looked at his notes before answering. "Grigori Burda is not his real name. The State Administration of Penitentiaries and Labor Camps identified him as Grigori Kondratenko, a former resident of the City of Fastov, initially retained by the Juvenile Correction Center, near Kyiv. He is of Gypsy descent, although separated from his parents at a very young age. He lived on the streets of Kharkiv and Kyiv, eventually ending up in the dragnets of the NKVD. He escaped in 1934, at the age of fourteen, but was recaptured three months later while committing an armed robbery with a few other young gang members. For his participation in this crime, he was sentenced to fifteen years of hard labor at Lagopunkt №17768, located in the Magadan Region."

"When did he complete his sentence? And how in the hell was Kondratenko hired by the State gold mining company?" General sounded furious.

"He never fulfilled his sentence. One hot day in the summer of 1940, when he was twenty years old, Kondratenko successfully performed his disappearing act." He paused dramatically; Colonel Guzyev obviously enjoyed telling this story.

"The guards missed him while counting prisoners at the end of the work shift. They called in the special canine security team, but prisoner Kondratenko had vanished into thin air. An escapee in labor camp garb could not go far without attracting attention unless supplied with civilian clothes, provisions, and an escape route through the treacherous permafrost swamps surrounding the Lagopunkt №17768. An investigation confirmed that Kondratenko did receive such help. However, I have no more information on that."

"Okay, okay, Comrade Colonel, I do remember this unfortunate and somewhat unique incident from a report circulated at that time through all Departments of the Commissariat of Internal Affairs," Melekhov noted. "It seems that information of this nature doesn't have any bearing on the case at hand. So, please, continue. Nevertheless, I will contact the

Commandant of that camp and find out as many details as possible. It might give us some leverage—perhaps a trump card in getting the truth from this guy?"

"After 1940, Grigori Kondratenko ceased to exist." Colonel Guzyev did have a knack for the dramatic. "There is no military service or other war records under this name. Instead, a person with the same face but the name of Grigori Burda appeared among the living—in 1944, at one of Sverdlovsk's local building projects. Six months later, he registered as a construction worker on a payroll list in Novosibirsk. He stayed put until the fall of 1946 and then he disappeared again for two or three years."

"So, is there any record of Grigori Burda before 1944?" Viktor asked, using the pause in Guzyev's story. "Has anyone with this name participated in war activities? Perhaps, we can look in some hospital records."

"It is hard to say. Such inquiries would take years to process in the State archives," Guzyev replied. "So far, our search hasn't produced any information on Grigori Burda before 1944."

"That would mean the new credentials that escapee Kondratenko had managed to obtain were fake, don't you think?" Viktor asked rhetorically.

Everyone was silent. Only the General replied. "Most likely, after a few years in the GULAG, Kondratenko surely could develop close connections among professional criminals. Those guys know well where to get fabricated documents."

"It is very probable, Comrade General," Guzyev hurriedly agreed.

The General changed the subject. "We'll see about that—we'll see. And what do we know about the other suspect?"

"The other, Ivan Stepanov—his name is real," the Colonel continued. "He was born in Sarnovka Village, southeast of Moscow—the Oryol Region in September 1923. In August 1941, he volunteered to join the Red Army and was sent to the Moscow Front. In the winter of 1942, Private Stepanov participated in the battle for Stalingrad. And here is where this story has a weird twist..." Guzyev paused again for dramatic effect.

"Please don't do that, Comrade Guzyev. We are not in the theater." The General smiled. "Just give us the facts."

"Oh, I am sorry, Comrades. I didn't mean it, but the story gets rather interesting," Guzyev explained apologetically. "During a nightly reconnaissance operation deep behind the enemy frontline, Ivan Stepanov was seriously wounded. Yet he still managed to save the life of Lieutenant Komarovsky, his gravely injured superior officer, by dragging him back to our trenches under heavy fire. They both ended up at different hospitals and never had a chance to see each other again. Even if they had met, it would be impossible, because Lieutenant Komarovsky was blinded."

"That is a great, albeit sad, story, but where is the twist you mentioned?" Melekhov sounded puzzled.

"I inquired into the incident, which was well documented; it even received some press coverage at the time. The other soldiers in his platoon didn't survive that covert operation. Going through their records, I came across a copy of the official notification sent to the family of one of the fallen soldiers… by the name of Ivan Rogozhin." Guzyev stopped, glancing at the people around the table victoriously, one after another.

For a minute or two, there was total silence. Viktor felt like his jaw might have hit the floor. Melekhov looked quite flabbergasted too but took hold of himself.

"That is a twist, all right. So, the son of our victim Fyodor Rogozhin, Ivan happened to be in the same company with the future killer of his father at the time of his death? What a coincidence!" the General exclaimed and paused. "Or maybe not. I do not believe in coincidences like this, you know."

"I don't believe it is a coincidence either," Viktor concluded confidently. He turned to Melekhov. "I have a gut feeling that this detail is the key to the entire case, Comrade General."

"Perhaps, Major Vitus, perhaps." Melekhov replied philosophically. "Comrade Guzyev, you did well, but we have to dig even deeper. We must figure out how a presumably good guy, a war hero, partnered with a professional thief and murderer? I think we have enough ammunition to start the interrogation of Kondratenko—or whoever he is today—Comrade Major. And keep me in the loop. If he does not talk, let me know. Everyone is dismissed."

* * *

One hour later, Viktor sat on a slightly elevated wooden chair in a small room with no windows and bare walls painted dark green. There was a metal table screwed to the floor and a steel chair of regular height in the middle of the room. A burly man with a heavy complexion occupied it. Although Viktor had seen him once from a distance, this was Viktor's first chance to study his features closely. He had a narrow forehead and protruding jaw, with shortly cropped hair. A thick beard, black as tar, covered his entire face. A steel chain wrapped across the enlarged knuckles on his hands, bonding them to a steel ring on the table. His demeanor gave all the indications of a brutal and ferocious man. However, Viktor was not intimidated. He had seen plenty of specimens like this from the GULAG.

On the contrary, unexpected thoughts of Katya filled Viktor's mind, and now he had to suppress a strong urge to grab this animal by his hair and smash his face against the table. *Stay cool, stay cool, Comrade Major*, Viktor calmed himself. *To find out the truth, you must outsmart this thug. Let's see who this guy really is.*

Kondratenko perhaps guessed the emotions of his interrogator, judging by the contemptuous smile that formed on his crooked lips. He decided to test him too; his eyes squinting with hostile impudence: "Aren't you the one I saw at that godforsaken hamlet? You are so young and careless."

"Cut it out, Citizen Burda, or better yet, Kondratenko— the "Gypsy." Isn't this your real name, and your *pogonyalo (criminal nick name)*?" Viktor realized he had to take charge from the start. "So, stop wasting my time by being cute and tell me what happened first in Beloretsk and later at *khutor* Izmailovsky."

Kondratenko seemed unimpressed. He made the same impudent face again and leaned back in his chair.

"Who is Kondratenko? I don't know anybody with such name, Nachalnik," he muttered through his teeth. "You asked me to tell you what happened, where? In Beloretsk? I have no idea."

"Where can we find your buddy Stepanov?" Viktor decided to reveal Stepanov's name right away, ignoring his last statement. After a short pause, he continued. "I am sure you know that he is in Khabarovsk now. Don't you?"

"I don't know anyone with this name either, Nachalnik. Are you trying to hang something on me that I didn't do?" His voice turned louder, more obnoxious.

"What did you do, Citizen, if you are not Kondratenko?" Viktor tried to stay calm. "I am sure that those leaded pellets in your behind won't let you forget under what circumstances you were arrested. So, tell me, what business did you and Stepanov have at Izmailovsky, trying to get inside that particular house?"

"We got lost in the *Taiga* and hoped to get some sleep when this crazy guy began shooting at us." Kondratenko explained vaguely, like he had just come up with a story. "That's all, Nachalnik."

Viktor realized that this nut needed a little nudge to start cracking. Kondratenko was not motivated to open up—unless it was in his interest to stall the investigation—especially if he wasn't sure if he was the only one who had been captured. *We need to bring in the big guns to shock this guy, as the General suggested,* he thought.

Viktor closed his notepad, put his pen into the front pocket of his uniform jacket, got up, and walked to the door. He then heard, "How did you dig out my real name, Major?" Kondratenko leaned forward, pushing against the table with his chest. The tone of his voice revealed sincere curiosity and real concern at the same time.

"Well, I am glad you asked, Citizen Kondratenko." Viktor felt the window of opportunity open, and he had to be very careful not to let it be shut again for good. "I may tell you about that, only if you tell me where Ivan Stepanov can be found."

"Dear Nachalnik, what in the hell gives you the idea I know where this monster is?" he replied with a short delay and a smirk, hinting at his real intention to say something after all.

Could it be that the proverbial black cat has crossed the road between them? Viktor thought. *Or is it just typical for career criminals to act in self-preservation. I must let him reveal more about that.* With his eyes only, Viktor silently expressed his interest.

Taking notice, Kondratenko continued, "He is a madman. Never listened to me. It is because of his stubbornness that I am here while he is free as a bird." He sounded irritated. "Everything was so simple until he went crazy and put us in a real mess."

"What did he do to deserve such respect from you, Grigoriy?" Viktor couldn't avoid some sarcasm.

"He decided to murder everyone in his path when we had a chance to get back our loot and quietly disappear instead. And then, in Izmailovsky, he went berserk and mutilated that poor old pastor. What for? If I hadn't interfered, he would have cut the throat of the old lady who mistook him for her son." Kondratenko poured all this out in one breath in a low voice while staring at his hands. "And now, I am sure he is after this young hussy, believing that the loot is in her hands. I personally doubt it. However, he may kill her anyway."

"Then help me to stop him," Viktor interrupted him, pleading. He became visibly nervous and impatient.

Kondratenko sensed it right away. He raised his head and looked straight into the Major's eyes. "Ah, this is personal for you, Nachalnik." He smiled with his crooked lips like before.

"She doesn't have to become another victim of this monster—like Mazur, like her father, Fyodor Rogozhin, or like that Korean child-soldier. Did I miss someone?" Viktor decided not to hide his emotions, hoping it would affect Kondratenko. It did not.

"Who knows, maybe you did miss someone. I am not talking anymore." Kondratenko almost whispered, turning serious. "I will tell you one more thing, Nachalnik: Ivan isn't going to last long on his own. He put me here, and now without my word, the local *bratki* (*criminals*) won't accept or help him. They don't trust him. Without me, he is a stranger, an outsider—dead fish, understand?"

"So, why wouldn't your *bratki* help us to catch Stepanov before he does something really stupid again?" Viktor reasoned.

Kondratenko remained silent. Viktor hesitated to reveal that Stepanov had attacked him and taken possession of his service pistol. Deep in his gut, Viktor wasn't sure about the veracity of anything this hard core criminal had told him so far. What if this was all an attempt on his part to put all the murders on Stepanov and limit himself only to theft charges? Everything had to be checked and re-checked before arriving at the truth. In the meantime, this line of communication had to be maintained.

"What do you say, Grigoriy? Will you help us? It is in your best interest; I hope you understand?" Viktor kept pressing. "You are smart. You have been in situations like this before. You shouldn't pay for something you haven't done. Am I right, Grigoriy?"

"I don't know, Nachalnik. I really don't. Let me think about it. But now, I am tired. I want to go back to my cell. I have to sleep." Kondratenko tried to stand up. He looked pained and exhausted. "Please have the guards unchain me. Sitting on this fucking chair is killing me. I must lie down, Major."

Viktor remained alone for a few minutes after Kondratenko was led from the interrogation room. He gathered his thoughts while writing down the unexpected information he had gathered. The more he thought about it, the more he believed that Kondratenko told the truth—perhaps not in its entirety, but nevertheless, the truth. Next time, he must convince him to provide additional details on how all three killings happened and motivate him to put the Militia in contact with the local underground world to lure Stepanov into a trap.

*   *   *

Nina stopped Viktor on his way to the third floor, and led him to the Forensic Lab. After she closed the door behind them, Nina said, "It's Katya."

"What? Did you talk to her?" Viktor asked.

"No, I actually went to the Theater to see her yesterday before her evening performance," Nina explained rapidly. "She called me in the morning two or three times. I missed all her calls, so I decided to go and see her in person."

"So, what's going on?" Viktor got right to the point, trying to conceal his concern, though not very successfully.

"She just seemed like the stress of everything is crushing her," Nina continued.

"Did she mention anything specific?" Viktor insisted.

"She seemed rather upset with her director, Garanin, who has become overly demanding, almost impossible to work with. And she expressed her worries about your well-being, constantly repeating that you had saved her life and she wasn't grateful enough. This is what I got."

Viktor turned defensive. "First, I didn't save her life, at least not directly, and second, it is my job to protect her."

"It seems you take it very seriously, don't you, Comrade Major?" Nina smiled, gently touching his wounded shoulder. "By the way, how are you today?"

"Fine, fine, Lieutenant," Viktor replied, turning his blushing face instinctively away from Nina. It was an awkward moment, and yet it felt good.

"Go see her. Ask her yourself about what she meant," Nina concluded, walking away from Viktor. "I am sure she will be happy to explain."

"Maybe later tonight. Now I must see General Melekhov about my first encounter with Burda."

"How did it go?" Nina turned around and asked. "Did he talk?"

"Oh yes, he talked. The question is how much of it was bullshit?" Viktor didn't want to be more specific yet.

"Sure, Comrade Major. I am glad I had a chance to speak with you today."

"Me too, me too. Thanks." Viktor lowered his voice almost to a whisper. "You are a real friend, Nina."

* * *

When Viktor arrived at the office of General Melekhov, his secretary Nadezhda Petrovna let him know that the boss was in a meeting and couldn't be disturbed for another hour. It was disappointing, but Viktor didn't mind returning to the third floor. He had just remembered to call Captain Nesterenko, so he rushed upstairs to his desk as quickly as possible.

An operator connected him with New Urgal quickly. After one ring, Viktor recognized the voice on the other end of the line:

"Sergeant Darsulov, here. What is the nature of your call?"

"Hi, Sergeant Darsulov. This is Major Vitus. Can I speak with Captain Nesterenko?"

"I am afraid not," Darsulov replied. "How can he reach you when he returns, Comrade Major?"

"He knows how, Sergeant. Just tell him it's urgent. Do you expect him soon?"

"I don't know, Comrade Major. He didn't inform me about his whereabouts or what time he was expected back in the precinct."

"Isn't that against regulations, Sergeant?" Viktor asked with some irritation. "What if any serious emergency should arise, and you, the person on duty, have no idea where your superior officer is or how he can be reached?"

"I understand your concern, Comrade Major," Darsulov replied after a short pause. "The Captain left the office rather in a hurry without telling me anything. He didn't take his radio unit with him either—it is on his desk."

"So, you cannot contact him in any way?" Now, Viktor did sound genuinely concerned. "I think you must do everything to locate him. What about his vehicle? Did he drive or go on foot?"

"I do see his vehicle through the window. He walked. Then he must be somewhere in the village. I'll find him, Comrade Major, right away."

"Okay, go ahead, Sergeant! I'll be expecting his call soon." Viktor put down the mouthpiece and smiled. *What a fearless man. Single-handedly repelled the attack of those two thugs!*

He decided to stay put until Nesterenko called him back and began to study the paperwork received on Burda and Stepanov from Blagoveschensky UVD more closely. His attention was drawn to a couple of unsolved cases near the Beloretsk urban settlement in the last three years. In both instances, missing-person reports triggered the investigations.

One case from April 1974 was about a man by the name of Pavel Ivanovich Kulikov. The Blagoveshchensk State Department of War Veterans sent inspector Kulikov to some nearby villages for routine meetings with the recipients of war pensions. It was a common practice to check and see if those recipients were still alive or if their relatives or neighbors were fraudulently collecting their benefits after they were deceased. Citizen Kulikov hadn't come back from this business trip. After visiting several veterans residing in Beloretsk, he vanished without a trace. An investigation was triggered but they couldn't arrive at any definite conclusion regarding his disappearance.

The second case was from February 1977 when a thirty-five-year-old woman named Nastya Frolova didn't return home from work at the Beloretsk Dredge Co. Again, an investigation found no conclusive evidence of foul play; the possibility of homicide was not ruled out, although no bodies were ever found.

As Viktor read through the witness's transcriptions, his telephone rang. He knew who was on the other end of the line.

"Lyubomir, hi, my friend. Darsulov told me you left the office in a rush. Is everything under control?"

"Oh yes, yes, Comrade Major." His voice seemed calm. "No problem. It was my fault for not telling Darsulov where I went. Our local Party boss needed to see me right away."

"In this case, please convey my apology to Darsulov."

"It is not necessary, but if you insist, I will." Lyubomir changed the subject. "Better tell me what's new."

"Last time we spoke, I told you about my encounter with Stepanov, didn't I? Who is he? Ivan Stepanov is the name of the perpetrator who attacked me and got away with my Makarov, you remember?" Viktor began slowly and then gained more steam. "The other one, who is in our custody, goes by the name of Grigoriy Burda. He assumed this last name after his successful escape from a labor camp in 1940. His real name is Grigoriy Kondratenko. We received all this information yesterday. We continue to dig deeper into his past, though. Today, I conducted his first interrogation."

"I bet you he wasn't very forthcoming."

"He wasn't. Nevertheless, he admitted to the killings at Izmailovsky, but claimed Stepanov committed them, not him. It remains to be seen how much truth there is in his statements. We need more ammunition to completely crack this son-of-a-bitch, and more importantly, to make him help us locate and arrest Stepanov before he kills again."

"Any more developments? I understood you wanted to talk to me about something. Didn't you?" Nesterenko asked casually.

"Yes, Lyubomir, I have something to tell you on behalf of General Melekhov." Viktor's voice sounded rather formal. "Nina and I told him about our joint work at the crime site. He is very impressed by your investigative skills and professionalism, and he wants to offer you a permanent position as a detective here in our UVD. If you accept, it will trigger your promotion to the rank of Major, of course. Would you consider making such a career move?"

"Thank you, Comrade Major, for such high appreciation of my work, and many thanks to Comrade General for his offer. Honestly, I don't know what to say right now."

"I am not rushing you. I understand you must discuss it with Lyuba, with the entire family. For what it's worth, I would be honored to have you as my partner. Think about it, please."

"I will, I promise," Lyubomir answered with confidence. "Now I have something to tell you. Leonid shared the news regarding your mothers. He is so excited. He is getting ready to travel to Khabarovsk to meet all of you. Lyuba and I are very happy for you."

"We are all excited too, believe me. My mother couldn't sleep all night. Please tell Leonid we are waiting for him to visit us as soon as possible."

"Okay, my friend. Bye for now. Talk to you in a couple of days," Lyubomir replied. The line clicked as it disconnected.

Viktor glanced at his wristwatch. It showed 14:05. The General's meeting must've been over. Viktor picked up the receiver and dialed Nadezhda Petrovna.

"You can come down and see the Comrade General. I'll let him know you are on your way."

After hearing the detailed report of the first interrogation, General Melekhov couldn't hide his satisfaction, and yet he let Viktor know his expectations were much higher.

"The moment he started talking, you should've pushed him for more details," the General explained. "Apparently, he is not dumb. He realized very quickly that we had done our homework."

"I did as much as I could," Viktor insisted, but it sounded more like an excuse. "Perhaps his wound hasn't healed completely. I didn't think he was pretending that sitting in that steel chair did hurt. He begged to stop the questioning but promised to consider my proposal."

"You see, here is where I disagree with you," the General insisted. "You should have continued to press him precisely because he was weak and vulnerable. This is one of the basic rules of successful interrogation. But it's okay, Major, you did well. Next time I would push him much harder, though. I am sure what I learned from Commandant Bogdanov this morning will make Burda, or rather Kondratenko, more agreeable."

"How so, if I may ask?" For a moment, Viktor had forgotten the formalities of a subordinate.

"It is hard to believe, but Major Serguey Bogdanov is the son of the Commandant Ivan Bogdanov who managed the Lagopunkt №17768 at the time when Kondratenko escaped." It seemed the General didn't mind such informal décor between subordinates and superior officers. He even sounded a bit excited. "Serguey is familiar with the whole story of that escape. He admitted it was strange receiving an inquiry about someone who had been presumed dead for thirty-five years. Nonetheless, he got really anxious when I told him we had captured this long-standing fugitive."

"Did you get the whole story, Comrade General?"

"Yes, I did, and what a story it was," Melekhov replied. "You see, retired Major Bogdanov Senior is still alive and lives with his son Serguey in the same house outside the camp. His wife, Serguey's mother, was there too for some time, although inside the fence. She was incarcerated in 1941 after being discovered as the one who organized Kondratenko's escape."

"Why would the wife of the camp Commandant do such a thing?" Viktor sounded puzzled.

"Are you ready to find out why?" The General paused. "Love. The young wife of the Commandant of a forsaken Lagopunkt in the middle of frozen Magadan Tundra fell madly in love with a young, good-looking camp prisoner. Isn't it corny?"

"So, she helps him escape. But what about her husband? He missed it all, letting this affair happen on the campground, right under his nose? It's hard to imagine, don't you think?" Viktor speculated.

"Look, Kondratenko was not only young and handsome at that time but also very clever and manipulative. He turned the head of the credulous young woman, and she did everything to help him survive in the wilderness. You have to give her credit—she prepared a hand-drawn map of the safe passages through the swamp. She secretly did a dry run herself, creating several hiding places with appropriate clean clothes, rubber boots, and non-perishable food, of course. Such thorough preparedness was the main reason our lover boy was never caught. Very quickly, he was pronounced dead. Obviously, it was the easiest way to close the case and avoid additional inquiries from Moscow."

"But what happened to the loved one who Kondratenko left behind? I am sure she didn't go through all the troubles without expecting anything in return."

"Of course, she did not. Soon after the escape, she began asking her husband's permission for a seat on a plane flying to the "mainland." Her explanation? She wanted to visit her sick mother." The General continued after a short pause. "Precisely, that drew Bogdanov's suspicions. His rather harsh interrogation of his wife proved he was right. In tears, she owned up to her actions and revealed the plan to join her lover in Rostov as soon as she could get away from her husband. In a fury, he beat her to a pulp, but she survived."

"Did she get her day in court?"

"She did not. Bogdanov's first impulse was to shoot his unfaithful wife dead right on the spot, but he decided not to." Melekhov slowed down. "He threw her into the general camp population just like any other prisoner."

"Without a formal investigation, without any legal due process?" Viktor was sincerely shocked.

"Dear Son, I hate to hurt your sense of justice by reminding you that your vision of how law and order must be administered is not shared by the people who run the GULAG." Melekhov leaned closer to Viktor and lowered his voice to a minimum. "Don't be naïve; those commandants at Lagopunkts, especially the remote ones, do not follow the same rule of law that we do. They honestly believe they are local rulers with the unrestricted right to judge and execute everyone who is incarcerated, as well as every person living around the camp."

"That is disturbing." Viktor tried to mask his shock at the bluntness with which General Melekhov, his Uncle Misha, revealed his honest opinion about the country's entire judicial system. "So, what happened to the poor woman?"

"A few years later, Marina—that was her name—hung herself when she was assigned to work in the camp laundry room." The General was brief. He realized that he had inadvertently made Viktor uncomfortable.

Total silence set in the room for the next few moments before Melekhov spoke again.

"We have an advantage over Kondratenko. He doesn't know what we know. It will throw him off when he finds out. Trust me, Kondratenko never forgot the camp rules, and under no circumstances would he want to be returned to the custody of Major Bogdanov, neither father nor son."

"We just have to convey to him how eager they are at Lagopunkt №17768 to put their hands on him," Viktor continued the General's thought. "So, when do you want to take your own shot at the interrogation, Comrade General? Tonight, perhaps?"

"No need to rush, Major. Tomorrow morning, let's say at 10:00, would be appropriate," the General replied. "You are dismissed. Go home, get some more rest."

"Thank you, Uncle Misha." Viktor couldn't help calling Melekhov by his first name. For the first time today, he looked straight into his eyes.

"Oh, Viktor. By the way, regarding your personal matters…" The General also sounded informal. "Tomorrow afternoon, I am having a meeting with a big shot from the KGB office. Then I will talk to Colonel Malinin at OVIR. Tell your mom and Raisa everything should be resolved soon.

Viktor nodded gratefully, saluted, and left.

He quickly returned to his desk. It was a quarter to four. He had only a couple of hours to go through the paperwork he was studying before Nesterenko's phone call and his meeting with the General. He had a strong feeling he would find something important within all those investigative protocols and interrogation transcripts. It took Viktor a few more minutes to focus on the task at hand and pull back the thoughts he had when he was interrupted. What was the common denominator in both these cases? Was there someone who had crossed paths with both victims but got overlooked? Viktor perfectly understood it could've easily happened considering the time gap between the two seemingly unrelated events.

Another thing was that two different investigators, who would never share their findings, handled those cases. So, it was perhaps up to him to rectify the problem. Viktor mentally separated himself from the outside world and dived into reading and making notes on a separate sheet of paper: names of people questioned, timestamps of the events being touched upon during those conversations, other details.

Time flew, and Viktor lost track of it. So far, the common denominator was out of his grasp. However, he was sure he stared at it but could not recognize it yet. He needed a fresh look, a clear mind—then it would reveal itself. Viktor leaned back in his chair and closed his eyes. What else did he need? He needed a break from all of this—his job, his fellow officers, all those pitiful felons, wretched arm robbers, and delusional murderers. He suddenly realized where he would like to be at this moment: next to Katya, to hear her husky voice, to smell her wavy hair, to feel the warmth of her body, and to make her believe that only he could be her true protector. He had to see her immediately. Viktor dialed a guard at the info booth downstairs and asked for his driver. Pyotr was still there waiting for his instructions. Viktor blew a sigh of relief and reached for his overcoat and hat. While putting them on, he looked at the paper he had just read one more time and then froze.

The missing piece was staring him right in the face. Of course, Ivan Stepanov had crossed paths with both presumed victims, Kulikov and Frolova. Kukilov came to Beloretsk to meet with Stepanov—and only with him—although Stepanov might deny that. And Frolova happened to be a girlfriend of Stepanov for a while before her disappearance, according to the statement given by her mother. Was it a coincidence? "No way!" Viktor exclaimed out loud, he became so elated. He took off his hat and returned to his chair, feverishly writing down his thoughts. Suddenly, he stopped.

"I'll continue this tomorrow; it requires more digging," he said to himself. "Now I must go to see Katya!"

Chapter 17

A few minutes later, Viktor sat in the car warmed up by his loyal Sancho. Viktor couldn't hide his good mood, and Pyotr didn't need to ask his boss where to drive. The *Kozyol* sped up, pushing through the wind tunnels of the deserted streets, passing from time to time the slow-moving city trolleys.

It was pitch dark in front of the car windshield. Swirling crystalline snowflakes caught in the headlight beams performed their fairy dance. Viktor closed his eyes and imagined himself somewhere—he wasn't sure exactly, but he felt warmth and serenity. Nothing else mattered.

Flashing his ID, Viktor quickly passed the Militia private at the building's entrance. He flew up, skipping one or two stairs at a time, until he almost bumped into Captain Mukhin, who stood on the edge of the landing at Katya's apartment door.

"Oh, it is you, Comrade Major!" exclaimed Mukhin, and he let the Major pass. "I wondered who would rush upstairs that fast. I am glad you feel healthy enough to run."

"Thank you, Captain. I couldn't do it without your help." Viktor couldn't conceal his good mood. "Is everything in order? Has anything suspicious been going on lately?"

"There was nothing out of the ordinary, Comrade Major," the Captain replied. "Citizen Rogozhina came back home from work accompanied by the man who claimed he lived here. You must remember him from the other day?"

"Yes, yes, I know who you are talking about." Viktor jumped in hurriedly. "Citizen Garanin, if I am not mistaken." He tried to hide his sudden nervousness. "Is he still here?"

"No, he is no longer here," Mukhin answered. After a short pause, he continued, "I noticed Katerina Fyodorovna wasn't happy about Garanin following her home, but she let him in. I couldn't help but overhear that they were arguing, pretty loudly, for about ten minutes. Then he stormed out, slamming the door behind him. His face was red, and his eyes were blood-shot. I thought he would have a stroke or something."

"How long ago did he leave?"

"I would say almost two hours ago, Comrade Major."

"Have you seen Katerina since she returned home?" Viktor asked cautiously but then clarified. "In your opinion, was she okay after this incident?"

"It's hard to know. She hasn't come out. But I bet she is fine. Katerina Fyodorovna is one tough lady, I must say."

"Understood. I appreciate your assessment, Comrade Captain." Viktor felt a bit awkward. He couldn't find anything better to do but to grab Mukhin's hand and shake it. "Thank you for your service. You may relax now, Captain."

Then he knocked on the door. The silence behind it was unbearable, so he knocked again. This time, a weak voice asked, "Who is it?"

"It's Major Vitus."

After a rather prolonged silence, which seemed to Viktor like an eternity, the lock clicked, and the door opened. Katya stood there in her blue silk nightgown with a thick beige wool robe over it, warm socks, and white fuzzy slippers. Her hair was pulled up and tightened into a ball. Without make-up, she looked younger, although he noticed that her eyes were red and puffy from crying. Viktor had never seen Katya like this before, so homey, and so vulnerable. He timidly stepped back, thinking his unannounced visit might upset her.

"I am sorry. I didn't expect any guests. I was ready to go to bed," Katya said apologetically. "If you don't mind seeing me like this, please come in."

Viktor regained his confidence the moment the door closed behind him. After all, it wasn't that late, and he was here in an official capacity.

"Katerina Fyodorovna, I need to ask you a few questions." He elaborated, "I am not going to take too much of your time."

"It is okay, Major Vitus. I understand," she replied and then smiled. "Really, I am glad to see you, Viktor."

He took this as encouragement, stepped toward her and reached for her hands. She didn't resist; on the contrary, she led him to the couch.

"Sit, please sit. Would you like a cup of tea?" Katya asked. "How stupid of me—you must be hungry. I can make you a sandwich or something."

"Oh, no. I am not hungry." Viktor was happily surprised. "Tea would be enough."

While she was busying herself in the kitchen with a kettle and teacups, Viktor took his shearling off and situated himself on the couch with a notepad and a pencil. In his Major's uniform, he did look quite formal, and he felt hot. Perhaps it was from anxiety, but Viktor became sweaty and panicky. When Katerina returned to the room holding two cups of piping hot tea, she noticed that Viktor wasn't comfortable. She put the small saucers with cups on the coffee table and insisted that Viktor unbutton his uniform jacket.

"It is too hot in the entire apartment building," she explained, "Our maintenance guy is pumping steam in the radiators like crazy. We complained, but he doesn't listen."

"Let me do it, please." Viktor sounded a little embarrassed, so he tried to cover it with a joke. "I bet Captain Mukhin is happy as a clam. It is rather warm on the stairway landing as well."

"You are right." Katerina pulled back. It was not clear if she referred to the joke, or she meant unbuttoning Viktor's jacket. "You don't have to suffer from this heat, Major. Please, take it off."

Viktor followed her suggestion and took off his uniform jacket, gladly shedding this ultimate symbol of formality. Immediately, he relaxed. She sat on the couch at an arm's distance from him and carefully brought the teacup to her lips. After first sip, she looked at Viktor, encouraging him to do the same.

"Go ahead, drink your tea before it gets stale," Katya insisted. "I am sorry I didn't buy any pastries today. I was returning from work in the company of someone who I had asked to stay away from me, so I couldn't stop at the store."

"Mukhin told me that Garanin escorted you home." Viktor decided not to pretend he didn't know about what transpired before his arrival. "Listen, next time he bothers you, let the Captain or me know. We will stop this once and for all."

"Thanks, but that is not necessary. I can handle it on my own. Besides, Garanin didn't make me cry. I just remembered my dad warned me about him, and I didn't listen." Katya sounded irritated but resolute. "After tonight, I am sure I will see him only at the Theater. And still, that will be too often."

Viktor nodded in agreement. "I have no doubt you can take care of your personal affairs, but please, don't refuse my help in anything. Promise me!"

"All right, I promise," Katya replied after a short pause. "I haven't seen you for a couple of days. Did you have a good time off? What is happening with your investigation?"

"Let's start with my time-off—it was useful and enjoyable. I spent two nights in my old home, sleeping in my old bed, listening to my mom's family stories, and talking with my sister about her husband and children." Viktor caught himself being so open, but it felt quite natural, so he continued. "I spoke on the phone with Lyubomir and Leonid. They said hello to you."

"Nice. If you speak to them again, please return my greetings to them." Katya reacted with a smile and then asked. "By the way, did you relay Leonya's story to your mom?"

Viktor never imagined that Katerina had paid attention to the exchange between him and Leonid when he told his story, and she definitely did not hear their short conversation outside the precinct. Her perceptiveness took him aback.

"As a matter of fact, I did." He announced with genuine excitement in his voice. "It is hard to believe, but it looks more and more probable that my mom did find her long-lost sister and brother, and the nieces and nephews she didn't know before. So, it makes Leonya my cousin, doesn't it?"

"Yes, it does. Congratulations!" Katya exclaimed. "Your mom should be ecstatic. I am sure Leonid will come to visit Khabarovsk."

"Soon, very soon," Viktor replied. "My mom is happy and sad at the same time, you know. She'll never get to meet her sister, but she will meet her sister's son."

He fell silent, suddenly feeling exhausted. Katerina reached to him with a handkerchief and gently wiped the beads of perspiration from his forehead. Viktor didn't protest. On the contrary, he smiled gratefully, took her other hand into his, and slightly squeezed it as a sign of gratitude. She didn't protest either. For a while, they quietly sat close to each other. Katya broke the silence first.

"You didn't drink your tea; now it is cold and stale. Would you like a fresh cup?"

"Thanks, Katya, but no." Viktor tried not to ruin such a magical moment by letting her hand go, although he did feel thirsty. "I still have to tell you about the progress of the investigation."

She nodded as Viktor finally pulled his hand away from hers and pulled out the notepad, ready to begin.

"My report is not going to be a long one. Today, we are in the phase of getting as much information as possible about the suspects, their true identities, their latest residence and employment, and so forth." Viktor paused to take a sip of tea. "How much have we learned? Quite a lot, but unfortunately there is very little I can divulge at this point. Sorry, it's a rule." He took another sip. "One of them is in our custody, though. He happens to be a hardcore criminal living under a false identity. We have begun questioning him, but so far it's been tough sorting out the truth from the lies in his testimony."

"Does he know where his partner is hiding?" Katerina asked.

"Apparently, he didn't share with his partner any knowledge about Khabarovsk's underground hideouts, so he claims he doesn't know."

Viktor stopped abruptly; afraid he had said something he shouldn't. "Nevertheless, you are right—it is a very pressing issue. First and foremost, we have to find this dangerous killer before he commits another murder."

"So, how are you planning to find him if you don't know where to look?" Katya asked in a worried voice. "This is not a little city we are talking about, you know."

"We do have a few ideas." Viktor sounded a bit evasive. "Our field officers are pretty familiar with some of those hideouts, but before going in, they need to know how the suspect looks, his facial and body features, his habits, and traits. Therefore, I need to ask you a few questions."

"I don't see what relevance to this matter my answers can have, but go ahead, ask me," she replied, though her uncertainty was evident.

"You might not see any relevance. However, any additional information will help to connect the dots, as we say. Please trust me." He had no choice but to be evasive. "Remember, you took several family photographs from your father's house. Can you bring them over?"

"Of course, I have them right here." Katya leaned toward the coffee table and pulled out a little drawer. "Which ones, specifically?"

"Let me see the old ones that were taken before the war."

The stack of photographs was not that big, so it didn't take long for Katya to separate the three in which Viktor was interested.

"Here they are." She handed the pictures to him and added, "Will you explain to me what significance these pictures have with the case?"

"Okay, as you recall, your Aunt Anna mentioned several times that she recognized her son Dmitry as one of the men who visited her. Considering her severally impaired vision and senility, we questioned the validity of this statement—you remember?" Viktor treaded lightly, simultaneously studying the photographs.

"What if it wasn't an indication of her delusional mind? What if she did recognize or thought she recognized her boy? He was her youngest child, wasn't he? It didn't matter that this man was crude to her, bad-mouthing her and threatening to kill her. She believed it was her son who had vanished in the war but finally returned to his mother after all those years." Continued Viktor.

"It is possible!" Katya exclaimed, covering her mouth with her hand in shock. "How could I doubt my poor Aunty? It could've been Dmitry. Oh my God! Does it mean my father was killed by his nephew?"

"There is another plausible scenario. What if we were correct in our initial assessment, and your aunt mistakenly took the man for Dmitry just because he resembled her son or someone else in her extended family? Therefore, I need these photographs; they might help us prove or disprove either of the theories. I am sure at least one of them—the one where your Aunt Anna is shown with her husband, daughter, and son—can be compared with the sketch of the man, who tried to get near your apartment and who attacked me."

"Now I understand," Katya said with a sigh of relief. "How else may I assist you with your investigation, Comrade Major?"

"For example, can you recall anything else your father told you about his son, your half-brother Ivan? Anything?" Viktor asked, putting aside the photographs, and preparing to write in his notepad.

"I already told you that my father discussed Ivan only once," Katya answered without hesitation. "I had asked him who the young man was in the photograph I had found between the pages of his prayer book. He brushed it off. I asked again. I remember he gave me a stern look as to not bother him again. But you know I was a teenage girl who wouldn't take no for an answer. So, perhaps just to get rid of me, Dad reluctantly explained that the young man in the photograph was his son Ivan who perished at Stalingrad battle during the war. And that was all."

"You never found your father's attitude a little bit odd?"

"At that time, I did not." Katya paused for a few seconds. "Come to think of it, after what I learned lately from Aunt Anna's story and from Dasha's letter, I would agree it might be odd. I am guessing you have read her letter, which I gave to you. Did you?"

"To be honest, I haven't had a chance to read it through yet." Viktor replied apologetically. "I have it with me, though."

"Read it now! Of course, if you have a little more time to spare? What do you say, Comrade Major?"

Viktor seemed a bit embarrassed: it had slipped his mind to red this potentially important letter. He tried to downplay it.

"Please do me a favor—you read it, so I can make some notes. Is that okay?"

"No problem. I just hope not to break into tears." Katya unfolded the letter and looked for a proper page to restart the story of her mom and dad.

"Don't worry—if you cry, I can wipe the tears off." Viktor touched her shoulder gently. "Please begin."

* * *

It was January 1951, the Eve of the Russian Orthodox Christmas; Olecya Zozulya had already lived outside Lagopunkt №4382 a couple of months. Earlier that day, a soldier had delivered a short note from Commandant Major Listov, promising a six-hour conjugal visit with her husband the next day. Suddenly, she became nervous, like getting cold feet before a wedding. She could not sleep. Lying in bed, Olecya watched the moments of her life flicker before her eyes, as in a movie.

Olesya's childhood, as she remembered it, was happy and unclouded by strife. She and her brother Roman grew up in a close-knit family, the children of a local county doctor and a schoolteacher. Their small village Obroshyno was only a dozen kilometers from Lviv, and yet it had that unmistakable flavor of provincial life. Everyone knew everyone, and everyone knew what was going on under every roof of Obroshyno. Poles, Jews, and Gypsies lived alongside the Ukrainian population of ten thousand inhabitants. There were all kinds of shopkeepers, professionals, craftsmen, horse breeders, and traders. To say they loved each other would be an exaggeration; however, there was peace in their coexistence.

At least, it was like that until that dreadful September of 1939. Everything changed when the Soviets, after signing the Pact of Non-aggression with Nazi Germany, took control of Poland. The words of Olecya's father still rang in her head: "We are on the verge of another bloody war." Doctor Yaroslav Peskiv wasn't that old, but he remembered the First World War quite well and the devastation it had brought to his land. His prediction became a reality in less than two years. The new war caused suffering and pain for millions of families, and the Peskiv family was no exception.

The first blow came on the third day after the Germans occupied Western Ukraine in July 1941. Early in the morning, the shouts of men and the laments of women awakened Olecya. Through the window of her second-story bedroom, she saw a young Nazi officer and two Ukrainian *politsai* forcing their neighbors from their homes. They led Mr. and Mrs. Ginzburg, and their two daughters to a truck. The girls were still in their pajamas. A few other Jewish families already sat in the carriage, clutching their scanty belongings. Apparently, the women's lament came from there.

The sight shocked and dismayed Olecya. The Ginzburgs weren't just neighbors, they were her family's closest friends. Yaroslav Peskiv and Moisha Ginzburg were colleagues of sorts: one was a doctor, and another was a pharmacist; Sara Ginzburg taught the Peskiv children music together with her own daughter, Faina, who had the voice of an angel and a heart to match. Everyone called her Feigale, a Yiddish word for a little singing bird. She was Olecya's closest friend, her only friend. They loved each other like sisters. They were always together at school and at home, until that morning.

Still in her sleeping attire, Olecya dashed downstairs, trying to join her friend Feigale to protect her from any harm. Her mother, Maria Peskiv, abruptly stopped her at the door. She embraced Olecya tightly and covered her daughter's mouth, about to explode in a shriek.

"Shush, baby, shush. There is nothing we can do," her mother whispered in her ear.

"Why are they being taken away by those soldiers?" Olecya whispered back. "They didn't do anything wrong, did they?"

"They did not. You see the Ginzburgs are not alone on that truck."

"Then why are they being arrested? Olecya insisted.

"Because they all are Jews, my dear child," her mother replied. After a long sigh, she added, "The Germans are afraid of the Jews. I don't know why."

They stood at the window, clasping each other, crying profusely as they said goodbye to the people they were so close to for so many years.

By this time, Yaroslav Peskiv had joined them too. He was visibly upset. "For the last few weeks, I kept begging Moisha to pack his family and evacuate to the East while there was a chance. This stubborn man didn't listen. He preferred civilized Germans to the savage Soviets. His Rabbi in Lviv told him not to worry. Can you believe it?"

Soon, they couldn't see their neighbors anymore. The German truck pulled away, leaving only a cloud of dust. Olecya didn't know then that after the war, she would be reunited with her best friend Faina Ginzburg.

In a month's time, the Peskiv family suffered another blow. The doctor learned through a network of his colleagues that his son Roman Peskiv had been gravely wounded. Right after the German invasion of the Western provinces in the summer of 1941, Roman joined the Organization of Ukrainian Nationalists of Stephan Bandera and his Insurgency Army.[5] He was wounded in a skirmish with SS troops and secretly taken to a hospital in Lviv to avoid the wrath of the Gestapo.

Yaroslav headed to Lviv without hesitation, to personally oversee his son's care. He found Roman in a coma; his young body riddled with bullet holes. For fear of the Germans, the medical staff could not procure fresh blood. Neither could his father. A few days later,

---

[5] In 1934, the Organization of Ukrainian Nationalists (OUN) organized several successful terrorist acts against Polish authorities. Its leader Stephan Bandera was arrested several times and received jail sentences. From 1939 he and his followers became the mortal enemies of NKVD, but when the Soviets retreated from the Western Front, Bandera immediately turned his attention toward the fight against the Germans, who had rejected an alliance with the OUN. As soon as the Nazis realized that the situation could get out of hand, Bandera was captured and sent to one of the concentration camps in Germany where he was incarcerated until 1944. However, the numerous military units of OUN continued their insurgency without the presence of their famous leader.

Yaroslav returned home with his first-born child in a casket. The entire village gathered for the funeral to pay their respects to Roman and the devastated Peskiv family.

* * *

Katerina stopped reading and closed her eyes for a moment. She sighed before speaking out.

"Although I had read this ten years ago, I wasn't actually aware of what my mom's family, and people in general, endured back then."

"Don't blame yourself; you were too young to take all this in," Viktor commented with the conviction of an older person.

However, he silently admitted that he never thought about the last war in the same terms either. He knew why: his and Katerina's families, like all those who survived that terrible war in the Far Eastern part of the country, hadn't had firsthand experience of the Nazi occupation and bloody battles taking place in the European part of the Soviet Union. They did lose many of their fathers and brothers in those battles, but he, as very few, had never fully realized what it was to deal with a mortal enemy face to face.

Katya continued on with the letter.

* * *

Yaroslav and Maria were never the same. The doctor quit his practice, and his wife did not step onto the school ground again. The neighbors stopped seeing them outside their house as their deep depression completely took them over. Olecya became the center of their attention and the only purpose of their existence.

At the end of the winter of 1942, Maria accidentally cut herself with a kitchen knife while preparing dinner. The wound wasn't deep, but it became infected, nonetheless. She applied a folk remedy, rather than bother her husband with it. But soon the inflammation spread all over the woman's body, poisoning her blood. Doctor Peskiv used all his skill to reverse the sepsis, but he succeeded only in postponing the inevitable for a few days. Maria passed away, tormented by the unbearable pain and guilt of leaving her devastated husband and young daughter alone.

Her mother's death forced Olecya to mature fast. She now had to care for her emotionally incapacitated father and their dwelling, which crumbled with neglect. It was then that Myron Zozulya, the older brother of her school friend Dasha, came to her rescue. Myron was a strong, handsome, and very handy young man. He and Olecya quickly grew more and more fond of each other as they fixed the house and cared for the old man together. But Doctor Peskiv didn't live long enough to see better times. He developed pneumonia in the harsh winter of 1943, passing three weeks later.

Olecya and Myron married in May of 1945, the day after the Great Victory over Nazi Germany was officially pronounced. Early in the morning, they visited the local Greek Orthodox Uniat church to be wed in secret by a priest, witnessed only by their sister Dasha. Then they repeated the ceremony at the City People's Counsel to receive a state-issued marriage certificate.

Not many guests attended this ceremony either, but one was very dear to Olecya: her lost neighbor and closest friend Faina Ginzburg. Faina arrived in Obroshyno a few days before the wedding, liberated by Soviet soldiers from the Terezin concentration camp in Northern Bohemia. She was the only member of her family who lived through the terrible ordeal. In 1943, her parents were transferred to Auschwitz and perished in the Nazi gas chamber. Her younger sister remained with her at Terezin but succumbed to the lung illness only two months before their liberation.

Although happy to see her, Olecya barely recognized Faina. She looked at least twenty years older. Her personality had changed too; she had become bitter and caustically sarcastic. She refused to play piano or sing anymore: "I have entertained my mortal enemies long enough," she told Olecya. "That was how we survived."

She shared with Olecya another secret of her survival—a story of a handsome young SS officer fell in love with a beautiful Jewish girl on the first day of their arrival at the concentration camp. For the next two years, he did everything to keep her from harm, and to help her family avoid extermination. Needless to say, she couldn't help but to accept this officer's love.

Even with his secret protection, the Ginzburg girls, like the rest of the prisoners, suffered unimaginable hardship and humiliation. Their musical talents, and particularly Faina's singing ability, made their everyday existence a little more bearable. After all, Germans were always known for their love of classical music, and they could fully appreciate her talent even if a Jew possessed it.

The tender love between Faina and Gunter fueled her determination to live. Unfortunately, this love couldn't have a happy ending. In the middle of 1944, her lover transferred to the Eastern front, where he was killed in the battle for Budapest. Faina learned about his demise from a letter received by one of Gunter's friends. She was devastated and ready for the worst. However, it was her sister, not she, who didn't live to see freedom.

A month after Olecya's wedding, two men in MGB uniforms paid Faina an unexpected visit, whisking her away in their traditional black soviet made *emka (MK)* car. She didn't have a chance to say a final goodbye to her best friend. Ever since, the fate of Faina remained a mystery to Olecya.

Precisely nine months after the wedding, Olecya's son Roman was born. Myron received the position of the head carpenter with the local State Construction Company. His salary allowed Olecya to stay home with their first child. The happy couple was planning to have another one in two or three years, but life had different, more sinister plans in store for them.

In August 1948, Myron Zozulya was arrested, accused of treason, and soon found guilty. To serve his prison time, he was sent to Lagopunkt № 4382. Olecya found him there two years later, a crushed and broken man. He was so frightened, so emotionally frozen, that he wouldn't even let his wife near him. He didn't even ask about his beloved son Roman.

And so Olecya lay in bed, staring at the sooty log ceiling, and thinking. Tomorrow she may see her husband, most likely for the last time. How could she thaw this human block of permafrost? How was she to bring him back from this state of absolute despair? How would she turn him back into her old Myron? She had no idea.

It was always possible to refuse this long-awaited conjugal visit, but would it sit well with Olecya for the rest of her life? What would she say to Roman when he grew up and asked about his father? Olecya didn't know what would happen in the morning, and she had no choice but to make the best of it.

Then totally different thoughts took over the woman's feverish mind. Olecya couldn't pretend anymore that Fyodor, whom she had met just a few weeks earlier, meant nothing to her. Every encounter with this fascinating man made her quiver to her very core. She had never experienced anything like that before. What was it? Is this what was called crazy passion? Olecya considered herself a passionate woman. She did love her husband, and she always enjoyed their intimacy, but not like this. Olecya would never forget the night Fyodor visited her for the first time. Every touch of his gave her an immense electric shock; every kiss by him sent her into a spin she wished would never stop. Three unforgettable hours—the only time he could be with her before returning to the *zona*—passed in the blink of an eye. And now, lying on this hard, squeaky bed, one overwhelming desire consumed Olecya: to spend just one more moment with Fyodor.

"Am I a terrible wife and bad person?" she asked herself and answered, "Only God can be the Judge!"

That dreadful day had begun with a problem: heavy snowfall blocked the doors of many houses, including the one where Olecya stayed. It took her and Babka Yelizaveta almost two hours to dig their way out. When Olecya reported to the guard post at the visitor's building near the camp's gate, the Lieutenant on duty informed her rather spitefully that the time of the approved conjugal visit would be cut short because she was late.

He led her through a tiny entrance hall to a door with a round hole covered by a sliding latch. A private sprung from his chair and opened the door. It was a small room, with no windows and a dim, naked bulb hanging from the wood-paneled ceiling. This illuminated a metal-framed bed with a flat straw mattress covered by a green military blanket.

Olecya saw Myron as soon as her eyes adjusted to the poor lighting. He slouched in the corner of the bed, his feet bare. When he recognized his wife, a strange wailing sound emitted from Myron's mouth. Olecya froze in place in the doorway, not daring to take another step.

The Lieutenant pushed her from behind, and in an irritated voice said, "Are you going to waste your precious time, Citizen Zozulya, or what? Get comfortable and give a kiss to your husband. He is the lucky dog today. Isn't he? Ha-ha."

Olecya inched closer to the bed. When she touched its metal edge with her leg, the entire frame shook. Myron's wailing became more intense. He buried his head between his knees and stretched both his arms out, as if to hold her at bay. Olecya intuitively accepted his wish and stepped back, feeling frozen again.

The Lieutenant left, closing the door behind him. Olecya heard the cover slide over the peephole. She took off her winter coat and thick wool shawl, dropped them to the floor, and took a step toward the bed again. Realizing that the guards had left the room, Myron stopped wailing and straightened his body. Olecya took it as a silent invitation to sit near him. She did so rather carefully.

Myron shuddered a bit but didn't change his position, remaining in the corner and now glancing at his wife apologetically, as if to say, *please don't judge my misery: I am not the same man I used to be.*

Olecya nodded in understanding. No words were uttered for five minutes. They just sat across from each other and quietly shed their tears, staring at each other intensely. Olecya quickly noticed that, unlike their meeting in the Deputy Commandant's office, Myron didn't smell bad; his nails weren't dirty, and the numerous scrapes on his skin didn't bleed. The garb he wore was clean. However, his demeanor remained the same. Olecya's heart was engulfed with acute pain and pity. She began sobbing loudly and reached for his hand. He met her halfway, grabbed her palm, and brought it to his lips. She moved closer and embraced him, feeling now that his unnaturally thin body was shaking uncontrollably.

She had to find words to calm him down, to make him trust her again. Olecya began singing a Ukrainian lullaby and patting his back very gently like a mother does to a baby who is having a hard time falling asleep.

After a while, it started working. His trembling subsided, his body was more relaxed, and he responded with a firm hug. Olecya decided to comfort him even more, so without forcing Myron to loosen his grip on her, she rubbed her feet against each other and pushed her heavy *valenki* (felt boots) off her legs. Then she tried leading him to change their position from sitting to lying down. He strongly resisted and interrupted her singing by putting his right hand over her mouth.

"Shush, they can hear us." He whispered right into Olesya's ear, "Why did you come here? You didn't expect to see me like this, did you?"

Olecya tried to answer, but Myron evidently wasn't interested in her explanations. It was his chance to talk.

"What did I do wrong? Why is God punishing me?" He was still speaking in a very low voice, but Olecya could feel his anger. "This is my punishment, isn't it? But why is that? These people, bad people, broke me. I am not a man anymore. They are killing me every day, little by little. I have tried to stop it myself, but I am too weak. I'll be dead soon anyway. You will not need to come to this hellhole ever again. Leave, go home, and take care of our son. Go! Do you hear me?" He pushed Olecya away.

He ranted like this for some time, revealing the disturbing details of his punishment. Olecya didn't keep track of it—they were sickening, but she didn't stop him because she knew he had to let everything out. So, Myron kept talking and talking until suddenly he stopped and broke into an uncontrollable rage.

And then he went totally silent, and this frightened Olecya the most. He reminded her of a trapped and gravely wounded animal which desperately wanted to end its suffering. The poor man rolled from one side of the bed to the other, banging his head against its metal frame from time to time. Then he would spring up to his knees and begin to rock his body in a frenzy until losing balance for a moment and hitting the wall, falling flat on his back, and laying there just for a moment, after which he would repeat everything again.

Olecya hovered above him in total despair, not knowing what to do or how to stop this horror. Myron eventually exhausted himself, curling into a fetal position in the corner of the bed. Soon, she realized he had fallen into a deep sleep. It was a relief. Olecya lay down next to her poor husband in the same fetal position and pulled the thin green military blanket over their bodies.

Three hours later, the Lieutenant entered the room and found the couple just like that, quietly laying on the bed next to each other. Their farewell was short and wordless. Myron looked confused and disoriented, like someone brought back from the abyss of a crazy dream. Olecya felt sad and philosophical; she was sure this would be the last time she would ever see her husband and the father of her child again.

Back in the room rented from Babka Yelizoveta, Olecya sat on a three-legged chair, tearfully thinking of leaving this place. Yes, it brought her so much pain and anguish, but at the same time, an incredible sense of happiness and serenity. She realized that none of it would last, but she wasn't going home unless she spent at least one more evening with Fyodor. So, she ran to the village store, hoping to see him there. Fyodor was there and looked as if he were expecting her.

The next day, he entered her room at 18:00 sharp. He had a little white flower in his hand again. She didn't ask him where he found it in the middle of winter; she just gratefully smiled and kissed him on the cheek. For the next three hours, they not only made passionate love, but they also talked. Knowing full well that this might be their final meeting. They shared all they could of their past and their hopes for the future.

Fyodor told Olecya of his greatest heartache—his son Ivan, whom he could not save from falling into evil. Although he considered Ivan's death in the war as some redemption, Fyodor still blamed himself for his son's sins, and he prayed every day to save his eternal soul. Even in his dreams he saw Ivan refusing to speak with him, which caused constant pain and despair. However, he hoped one day this pain would go away.

In turn, Olecya told Fyodor about her greatest worry, her husband Myron, whom she had come so far to support, only to find him in such a terrible state. She described her last visit with him, his erratic revelation of the horrific mistreatment he had to endure, his psychotic behavior, and her fear of him attempting to commit suicide. Fyodor expressed his deep sympathy for her husband's circumstances and promised to help in changing those circumstances for the better in whatever way he could. His promise put Olecya somewhat at ease; she knew in her heart if a man like Fyodor promised, he would keep his word.

At 21:15, Fyodor regretfully donned his inmate garb and made ready to leave. Olecya stood close to him at the door, holding his hands. She felt like crying, but she wanted to be strong and didn't shed a single tear. He kissed her forehead, acknowledging her incredible courage. Uncharacteristically for him, his knee felt weak and almost buckled; he trembled inside but fought hard not to show it. He didn't want to leave, but he had to. They embraced and shared a long, passionate kiss. There was nothing to say to properly express their feelings, so they said nothing. Fyodor gently pushed her away and stepped into the darkness, closing the door behind him. Olecya sat on the bed and began crying soundlessly.

Ten days later, Olecya arrived in Lviv by train. Her sister-in-law Dasha met her on the platform, holding young Roman by the hand. Olecya dropped her luggage on the pavement and ran toward them as fast as she could. She picked up Roman in a swift embrace and pulled his little body close to her. The boy didn't make a peep.

"Look, he didn't forget me!" Olecya exclaimed. "Hi, I am your mommy!"

"She is my mommy," Roman replied in a low voice and stretched his hand in Dasha's direction.

"No, no, baby. I am your mommy. Dasha is your aunty," Olecya held back tears, continuing to hold the boy as tight as she could.

Roman didn't resist; however, one of his hands was still extended toward Dasha.

"Don't you worry, dear. He hasn't seen you for three months. He is a little confused." Dasha herself sounded unsure. "Give him a few days, and he'll be alright. He is a sweet boy."

All the way to Obroshyno, Olecya held Roman on her lap, facing her. The boy looked at his mother with the curiosity and genuine interest of a child. Not even once did he try to reach Dasha for comfort.

Back home, Olecya began to feel safe and secure again. Dasha was right: it took only a few days before Roman fully accepted Olecya as his real mother, although every time his aunty was around, he would become a little bit excited.

It didn't bother her at all; Olecya appreciated very much what her sister-in-law had done while she was away. As a matter of fact, their relationship was getting stronger and stronger. Olecya didn't hide from Dasha the truth about the terrible condition she found Myron in and her doubts about seeing him ever again. Two months later, when Olecya realized she was pregnant, she told Dasha about Fyodor and what had happened between them. She was sure it was his child she carried inside of her this time. Dasha never expressed any resentment toward Olecya, nor did she bear any grudge on her brother's behalf. On the contrary, her entire life from this point on was a testament to her unwavering commitment and dedication to Olecya. She promised not to get married, although she had several suitors who pursued her rather vigorously.

Olecya's troubles with her pregnancy became obvious in her seventh month. The local doctor, who happened to be a pediatrician, couldn't explain the bleeding Olecya was experiencing quite regularly. Then Dasha took her to a specialist in Lviv. Upon thorough examination, the obstetrician prescribed some medication, advised Olecya to spend the next two months in bed, and return to his clinic when she will be ready for delivery.

Did she listen to the doctor's advice and stay in bed? Of course not, and as a result, the labor began prematurely, with serious complications. Dasha couldn't take Olecya to Lviv to deliver the baby in a well-equipped clinic as was suggested. The local physician did everything he possibly could to save both mother and newborn, but Olecya finally bled to death during the four-hour delivery. Fortunately, the baby girl was born alive—a bit underweight, but healthy.

Caring for the family she had suddenly inherited left little time for Dasha to mourn the death of her best friend. She found a job close to home, demanding but well paid, allowing her time in the morning and evening to cook and clean for the children. The neighborhood women helped when they could. She learned to be a good mother, fulfilling her promise to Olecya.

However, there was one dying wish from Olecya that Dasha could not abide. Olecya had asked her not to write to Myron, but to tell Fyodor of his daughter. Instead, she wrote a letter to her poor brother, revealing the whole truth about his wife. Dasha did this soon after the tragedy, when her emotional state was shaky. Perhaps she did it out of still lingering resentment, or perhaps out of fear in the face of an uncertain future.

Did Dasha regret it? Yes, she did, but what was done was done. Later, she tried to clear her conscience and wrote a letter to Fyodor, as Olecya had wanted. She received a reply full of sadness and excitement. Fyodor wasn't shy about what Olecya's love meant to him and how deep his grief was when he learned of her untimely death. He also let Dasha know that he, too, had kept the promise he had given Olecya to help Myron. Her brother was now under his wing and doing well, although the unfortunate letter she had written him shook him to the core.

Their correspondence continued until 1954, when Fyodor was freed from the labor camp and returned home. In his last letter, he informed Dasha of his decision to visit her and Katerina at Obroshyno as soon as he could get back his proper documents, including his passport.

For Dasha, the day Fyodor showed up at the door of her home came too soon. She had to admit that she liked him a lot. He was a handsome, mature, and sensible man, just as Olecya described him. The moment he crossed the threshold, Fyodor looked as if he was at home, getting involved right away in helping Dasha with the kids. It was amazing how unmistakably he recognized things, which had belonged to Olecya, even little trinkets. He picked them up carefully, holding them in his huge hands as if he was trying to somehow establish a connection with her.

Even more amazing was how he related to the children. No matter how excited or unruly one of them became, his gentle touch to the head or shoulder would immediately calm the child down. He had many interesting stories to tell, and they listened with a great deal of attention even if he spoke in Russian. Roman was more cautious and reserved in his emotions toward the man, while Katya became infatuated with him from the first moment they met. She wouldn't let go of his hand until Fyodor calmly reminded her that it was time to eat, or sleep, or go to kindergarten. Katya, who usually never listened to anyone, especially Dasha, obeyed his every order without arguments or tantrums.

Since very early in life, Katerina demonstrated character traits which were hard to ignore and even harder to tolerate. She was independent to a fault, stubborn to the point of rejecting any authority, and bossy with everyone around her regardless of age. And, if this is not enough, all those qualities were magnified by the sharpness of her mind and her ability to express herself.

Roman was the easiest target of her authoritarian terror, her shrewdness, even cruelty. He had missed his chance to establish the superiority of an older brother, and he was too weak and too gullible to stand up to his smart baby sister. No wonder that he not only was afraid of her but despised her with every fiber of his rather large body. She was a difficult child; extremely difficult, indeed. The more Katerina grew, the bolder she became; Dasha had no clue what to do about it.

Two weeks passed before Fyodor announced his decision to return home. While Dasha enjoyed the sense of peace and serenity he brought to her home, she wanted him to leave. She only feared the agonizing dilemma keeping Katerina or letting her go to live with her biological father, who had developed such a strong bond in such a short time. For his part, Fyodor encouraged her to accept that Katerina would be better off with him, but he would not force the issue.

In the next day or two, Dasha decided to let Katerina go. Soon, the happy father and his little daughter left Obroshyno for good, promising to write. A few years later, Dasha finally accepted a marriage proposal from one of her most persistent suitors, a forty-year-old print shop foreman from Lviv named Vasyl Derenchuk. The man moved his new wife and adopted son to the city and provided for them well. Roman grew up as a fine young lad.

Dasha never wrote to Katya until that letter, but she never forgot the little girl who caused such mischief. From the occasional letters from Fyodor, she knew her niece was doing well, surrounded by love and God's grace, and this always warmed her heart up. When Katerina reached her sweet sixteen, Dasha finally decided to write this letter and tell her the story of her late mother. "Happy birthday, my dear niece Katya!"

Katerina put the last page down and looked at Viktor with her teary eyes. "When I received this letter ten years ago, it went right over my head. I was too young," she said and sighed. "But, today, everything is different. Thank you for making me read it again."

Chapter 18

Next morning at 8:30, November 23. Viktor was heading to General Melekhov's office when he heard a commotion behind him and the voices of two low-ranking officers mentioning a shooting. He immediately turned around and hurried back to the first floor, where the officer on duty sat behind a telephone switchboard. Usually, whatever crime or security threat in the city had taken place was reported first to this station before any initial information was forwarded to the appropriate UVD department.

Another unwritten rule was that the officer on daily duty who received the initial information wouldn't divulge it to anyone but whoever was in command at the time. Major Vitus was one of the commanding officers, and an explanation was in order. The young Lieutenant had an expression of great concern on his face.

"A shooting occurred early this morning during a robbery of a drugstore," the Lieutenant reported to Viktor. "It's in a residential neighborhood around the meat processing factory on the north side of the city. Artema street. "

"What kind of weapon was used by the robber or robbers? Were there any casualties?" inquired Viktor.

"According to the divisional Militia Inspector who originally reported the incident, two 9mm bullets were fired before the perpetrator got away empty-handed. The pharmacist on duty was struck once. He is listed as not seriously injured," the Lieutenant replied.

"Does it say where did they took the pharmacist?"

"I don't have this information at the moment, Comrade Major."

"Then get it, and fast, Lieutenant. It is extremely important."

While the Lieutenant feverishly made phone calls, Viktor continued thinking to himself. Even based on limited and somewhat sketchy details, he had a strong hunch it was the work of Stepanov armed with Viktor's pistol. The fact that he did it rather inefficiently and unsuccessfully indicated that he acted alone. *Hey, Kondratenko was right*, he thought, *his former partner wasn't getting any help from the local underworld crime professionals.*

Stepanov's ill-conceived operation pointed to another fact: he was also wounded during the confrontation with Sergeant Darsulov at *khutor* Izmailovsky. Perhaps he wasn't injured as seriously as his friend, but many days of neglect had finally caught up with him. This explained why Stepanov hit the pharmacy rather than a grocery store. And he had done it early in the morning because he didn't need money or food. He was in desperate need of medical supplies.

Viktor looked around for Pyotr, who was already standing nearby in anticipation of the Major's next move. At Viktor's signal, he ran outside to start the engine. The Major was just about to follow his driver when the Lieutenant handed him a piece of paper with the name of the hospital and announced, "Captain Golovin is looking for you. He has an urgent message from Comrade General."

Captain Golovin was the Adjutant to General Melekhov. He wasn't one who could be ignored. However, Viktor was sure that this conversation could wait. Right now, it was far more important to get to the hospital. Viktor continued out the door, yelling to the Lieutenant: "Please tell the Captain I have already left to investigate the shooting. I'll be in the General's office in two to three hours at latest."

Viktor arrived at the hospital and was led to the wounded patient. Serguey Stepanovich Shumov, a man in his early fifties with a large balding head, was the pharmacist on Artema Street. He lay in the bed with the upper part of his body slightly elevated. The bullet shattered his left arm, which rested in a sling, wrapped in bandages.

Shumov was fully alert and smiling, perhaps due to being so lucky. He took his time looking at the composite sketch Major Vitus presented to him before concluding, "It does resemble the man who shot me this morning. Only I couldn't see the top of his head; he was wearing a hat. But those eyes. Oh, yes, that's him."

"What things did he ask you for?" Viktor asked.

"He wasn't talking. He just held the gun pointed at me. The woman did all the talking."

"What woman?"

"I don't know her name, Comrade Major. She looked like she was in her late thirties. Quite attractive. Dark eyes and dark hair. I think I saw her in my pharmacy before, a few times maybe."

"So, what did she want?"

"She demanded hydroperoxide solution, bandages, sanitary napkins, cotton balls, and rubbing alcohol. I told her I hadn't seen any of these items for many months, except 3% hydroperoxide in a small bottle. But she didn't believe me and began shouting at the top of her lungs. The man with the gun quieted her and threatened to shoot me dead if I didn't comply with the woman's demand right away. I tossed her the bottle of hydroperoxide and told them, again and again, I didn't have anything else. At that moment, the man suddenly fired his gun twice in succession. I felt a sharp pain in my arm and fainted. I woke up in this bed."

"Did you notice what kind of weapon he had? What hand, right or left, did he hold the gun?"

"I am not sure what gun it was." Shumov answered after a few moments. "Weapons are not my thing. However, I noticed he held it in his left hand."

"Did you notice anything else about this man? How was he dressed?"

"He had the usual short sheepskin coat and earflap wool hat. Under the coat, he wore a brown, heavy knit turtleneck and military-style cotton teasel pants; he wore *valenki* too." Shumov then added, "When they walked in, I noticed he was limping. Not just a little bit— I mean serious limping."

"Which leg was he favoring?"

Shumov paused again, frowning before answering. "Honestly, I couldn't say. Sorry, Comrade Major."

"It's okay, Comrade Shumov. You were very helpful. Please get well soon. We'll be in touch if more information is needed."

"Any time, Comrade Major, any time. I am at your service." Shumov couldn't hide his smile again.

The entire visit took less than half an hour. Viktor was very satisfied with the information this one fortunate pharmacist had provided. This proved his earlier hypothesis without any doubt—it was Ivan Stepanov. In total desperation, he committed yet another crime. And something else: Stepanov had a new accomplice this time, some young woman he had picked up and befriended when he arrived in Khabarovsk. Most likely, she was sheltering him and trying to nurture him back to wellness. There was a strong probability that this shelter was in the same neighborhood where the shooting incident had occurred. It may help tremendously to shrink the area of the hunt for the fugitive and speed up his capture. All these deductions and speculations played in Viktor's head while returning to UVD Headquarters. Melekhov should be pleased with the report.

* * *

Melekhov was not pleased with the report. For some reason, the General sounded irritated and upset, snapping at everybody, especially Viktor. Major Vitus tried to construct the most plausible scenario of Stepanov's next moves following the botched heist. He had discussed his theories with Lieutenant Toropko and Colonel Guzyev before the meeting, receiving their full support.

Surprisingly, Melekhov didn't show an interest in Viktor's theory, particularly in its details. He hurried the Major, almost forcing him to skip all the details. It didn't take long for Viktor to guess that the General either was short on time before his next scheduled meeting or someone had spoiled his mood during a previous engagement. There were only two options: to find a pretext to postpone this presentation until a later time when the General would be more attentive or skip all the details and jump right into planning for all possible actions to catch the fugitive sooner than later.

It was clear the first option wasn't realistic, so Viktor paused, took a deep breath, and proceeded with the second.

"Ivan Stepanov is hurt and needs urgent medical help," Viktor began in a confident voice. "He is desperate and will try another attempt to get medical supplies. Perhaps it will not happen today—he knows the entire city Militia is on high alert looking for him—but it may possibly happen tomorrow."

"He won't try another pharmacy," Melekhov interjected spitefully. "He knows by now he can't do that again."

"Perhaps he will attempt to hit a nearby hospital?" Viktor concluded, as everyone around the table nodded in agreement.

"I agree, Comrade Vitus; it is a viable option." The General nodded and turned to Captain Golovin, who sat quietly at the end of the conference table. "Comrade Captain, please make sure the necessary Field operations personnel secure all city hospitals, especially the one in the north of the city."

Viktor interrupted Melekhov before he finished his instructions. "But there is another option. It may be more convoluted, yet less risky and easier to pull off."

"What is it, Vitus?" the General asked with visible irritation.

"Stepanov and his accomplice might rob a grocery store, possibly a larger one with more cash on hand." Viktor tried to sound calm and collected. "Then with the stolen money, his girlfriend will be able to buy everything needed on the black market. Everybody in the city knows where to find it."

"I find this scenario more plausible, and more dangerous. More people can get hurt, and it will be more difficult for us to prevent," the General concluded after a moment of silence. "However, we have no choice but to try to figure out what stores are the most probable targets and secure them tightly. Comrade Guzyev, would you be so kind and do an analysis. Please do it quickly, so we can dispatch the necessary contingents."

"I am on it, Comrade General," the Colonel replied without delay. "I hope we'll get lucky and catch them red-handed."

"Comrade Colonel, luck doesn't factor into our line of work. You should know that by now." Everyone had heard the General's favorite slogan before, but no one smiled. "Everyone is dismissed except for the Major.

Everyone cleared the room, and the General pulled up next to Viktor. Viktor knew what was coming, so he decided to step on the firing line before Melekhov even had a chance to say anything.

"I know, I know, Mikhail Grigoriyevich, I jumped the gun without consulting with you," Viktor said, lowering his eyes. "I was too anxious to speak with this pharmacist…"

"It doesn't matter how anxious you were or even how important it was." The General was emphasizing every word. "If you are summoned by your superior officer, you don't ignore it, especially in the presence of Captain Golovin— he is a son of some local big shot. He is watching my every step like a hawk, this son-of-a-bitch." Obviously, it was bothering Melekhov, and he needed to get it off his chest. "I knew why they insisted on assigning him as my Adjutant, and I couldn't say no." You should've seen the expression on his face when he informed me that you refused to answer my call."

"I am really sorry for my foolishness, Comrade General. I had no idea. Nothing of the sort will happen again." Viktor sounded apologetic.

Viktor sat there speechless. For the second time in the last few days, he discovered a vulnerability in Uncle Misha—-something he was trying desperately to hide. This aging career professional, a commanding officer in the State power structure, expressed his deep distrust and open displeasure with the system. Although Viktor hadn't heard similar complaints from his late father, this didn't mean it never happened. It would be interesting to ask his mother if she recalled Raymond Vitus's attitude toward his local bosses or Moscow.

"I'll be more careful, Uncle Misha, I promise." That's all he could say in this awkward situation.

"All right, son. Let's leave it at that." Melekhov also felt like he had suddenly stepped onto thin ice. "Now, wouldn't you rather hear about my conversation with Kondratenko this morning?"

"When did you talk to him? I thought we would do it together." Viktor couldn't hide his disappointment.

"Me too, me too. But you took off this morning before consulting with me, didn't you?" the General replied, smiling. "So, I decided not to waste time."

"Did your plan work?"

"The situation did require much extra persuasion, I must say. Eventually, the full prospect of falling into the hands of Bogdanov's, who have never forgotten the man that ruined their family, dawned on Kondratenko," the General explained. He handed Viktor a piece of paper torn from a notepad. "Here he is, the local *vor-v-zakone* who goes by the name 'Petukh.' I remember him well from at least twenty years ago when he was freed because of a massive amnesty and settled here in Khabarovsk. Soon, we knew 'Petukh' gathered under his command many criminal elements, big fish and small fish, causing serious problems for city law enforcement. Nevertheless, he was never implicated directly in any cases. A smart bastard— very smart."

"Is he still active?" Viktor asked, studying the piece of paper with crooked letters and numbers written in ball point pen on it.

"I doubt it, although five or six years ago, his name came up in an armed robbery case," Melekhov recalled. "Again, nothing stuck. I still think he went into retirement, being at least in his seventies."

"Do we know his real name?" Viktor asked.

"Oh yes, his real last name Petukhov. Very trivial, don't you think?" The General burst out laughing. "It does explain his prison nickname."

"I guess it does." Viktor smiled for the first time today, putting the precious information in the chest pocket of his uniform jacket.

"Please be careful and smart while contacting this old man. The bastard can read through you—smell the cop in you and refuse to talk."

"I'll do my best to fool him. However, how do we know that he will cooperate?" Viktor sounded concerned.

"First of all, show him his scribbles—he must believe you were referred by Tsygan (gypsy), whom he knows quite well but has no idea about his present whereabouts, of course. Secondly, you will need to convince him it is in his interest to help locate Stepanov as soon as possible."

"I understand. May I be dismissed, Comrade General?" As soon as Viktor heard the name Stepanov, he immediately felt an urge to return to his desk.

"Yes, you are dismissed."

A few minutes later, back at his desk, Viktor found a yellow sticky note attached to his telephone: "Your mother called. Please see me. Nina."

Why would Mom call Nina? She doesn't know her, Viktor asked himself. *What was so urgent to look for me at work? Mom usually doesn't do that unless it's a real emergency.* He was worried about her—too much excitement lately, troubling her heart condition. Viktor put down the notepad he had brought from the meeting, grabbed his leather document pouch, and rushed to the Lab.

Nina met him with a barrage of questions in rapid succession. "What did the General want? Did you get reprimanded? Did you call your mom? Is she okay?"

"What do you want to know first?"

"Doesn't matter."

"By the way, how come my mom called you? She doesn't even know you," Viktor demanded.

"She didn't call me. I was passing by your desk when your phone rang and rang," Nina began slowly. "I assumed it was important, so I picked it up."

"Next time, please do not pick up my phone without asking. What did my mother say?"

"She sounded overexcited and wanted to speak with you right away. I told her you were in a meeting with the General. So, did you get beat up?" Nina asked again.

"A little. It doesn't matter. I deserved it." Viktor decided not to go into details. "Better tell me why she was looking for me."

"I have no idea. She didn't seem upset."

"If you don't think it's an emergency, then I'll call her from my desk. Now, I must see Zelenin, the sketch artist."

"Do you have another job for him?"

"No. Remember the small photograph of Rogozhin's son?" Viktor reminded her and continued. "Katerina gave it back to me at my request. I want Zelenin to look at this photo and compare it with the sketch he made. He has a good eye for things like that."

"You think it wasn't Dmitry who killed Rogozhin." Nina paused to catch her breath. "Are you positive?"

"Of course not, at least not yet. It's just a theory that I haven't shared with anyone except you. So, please be discreet," Viktor insisted. "I still need to check a few details, make another inquiry. Understood?"

"Understood, Comrade Major." She nodded and then changed the subject. "How is Katya? You did see her yesterday, didn't you?"

"I did indeed. Katya is fine. We had a nice conversation. Thanks for warning me. Now, I have to hurry to see Zelenin before he goes home. Bye, Comrade Lieutenant. We'll talk again tomorrow."

Viktor rushed downstairs and found Zelenin at his drawing board. Armed with a huge magnifying glass, he studied the photo of Ivan Rogozhin for several minutes, moving his eyes to the sketch lying on the board next to him from time to time. Viktor was patiently waiting behind him. Finally, Zelenin turned to him, handing back the photograph.

"I cannot be entirely sure, but the main facial features of the teenager in this photo have an uncanny resemblance to the features of the older man in the sketch," Zelenin concluded.

"If I could get hold of a larger picture, I would be able to say this with a higher degree of probability. However, even under existing conditions, it is obvious to see the similarities between these two images."

"Thank you, Comrade Zelenin. I fully trust your expertise." Viktor put the photo into his pouch, shook Zelenin's hand, and hurried back to his desk on the third floor.

* * *

Back at his office desk, Viktor dialed his mother, but there was no answer. It began to worry him. *Where is Mom? Why is she not picking up the phone?* He glanced at his wristwatch; it was five to four in the afternoon. What was happening at his mom's home? Viktor was just about to hang up and call Pyotr to drive him there when he finally he heard her voice on the other end.

"Mom, is everything fine? You are breathing heavily like you were running away from someone. Why didn't you answer my call for so long? You scared me, Mom." Viktor couldn't decide whether to sound concerned or angry.

"Nothing to worry about, son. I did run as fast as I could when I heard the telephone ringing, but otherwise I am fine," Leya Solomonovna replied after a short pause to catch her breath. "I was in the pantry looking for some products when you called. It is quite a distance, you know."

"So, everything is fine." Viktor sighed with relief. "And your urgent call to my office earlier was in regard to what?"

"I wanted to tell you we are going to have a guest tonight," Leya Solomonovna declared in an almost formal tone of voice. "My nephew, your cousin Leonid, called before noon. He just arrived in Khabarovsk, and I invited him to come as soon as possible. He will stay here."

"This is wonderful, Mom!" Viktor couldn't hide his excitement. "But promise me to take it easy. You know darn well what it can do to your heart, don't you?"

"Yes, son, I promise. I have already asked Raya to pick up some "Validol" tablets for me on the way here. She is coming with Boris and the kids. I want you to be on time too. And now, I have to begin preparing dinner for all of us."

There was a question on the tip of his tongue that Viktor wanted to ask his mom—if he could bring Katya with him. After all, she knew Leonid, and she knew his parents' story. She would enjoy such an unexpected family reunion. This would be therapeutic for her as well to help her with her grieving and healing. But then he decided not to.

"Okay, Mom. You go and cook your best meal. I am looking forward to seeing all of you tonight," Viktor said in a low voice and slowly put the receiver down. *What a great event it will be for Mom and for the entire family,* he thought. And at the same time, how inconvenient it was for him. All his plans to find support for his hypotheses and write a request to the local Militia precinct for the available information on Ivan Stepanov and to see Katya again must be postponed. Of course, he could've invited Katya to this important event, but he chickened out.

It was too late now. Viktor glanced at his watch: there was not much time, but if he stayed focused, he could at least write the letter of formal inquiry to Oryol Regional UVD. At six o'clock, Viktor put the envelope in a special bin and left the building with the intention of going to his mother's home. The moment he took the front seat in *the Kozyol*, he changed his mind.

"All right, Sergeant, you know where to drive, don't you?"

"Yes, Comrade Major, I do."

Less than ten minutes passed before Viktor arrived at Katya's building and he rushed to the second floor, skipping again every other stair. He was stopped by an unfamiliar young man in plain clothes at the door to Katya's flat. His grey thick wool coat wasn't buttoned up, so Viktor noticed a shoulder holster with his Militia standard-issue service revolver.

"Where is Captain Mukhin?"

"He is off tonight. He left one hour ago. I am his replacement. Lieutenant Lavrov at your service, Comrade Major." The young Militia officer saluted the Major.

"Is everything under control, Comrade Lieutenant? Is Citizen Rogozhina inside? Is she alone?"

"Yes, Comrade Major, she is. At least since I assumed my post. Captain Mukhin didn't tell me about any visitors."

"Very well. I must see Citizen Rogozhina now. It shouldn't take long." Viktor stated in an informal tone of voice and proceeded to knock on the door.

The door opened momentarily. It seemed tonight Katya was expecting him. She was neatly dressed in a dark blue skirt and an elegant beige wool blouse, which accentuated her slenderness at the waist. Viktor caught himself thinking how it would make him happy to put his hands around Katya and pull her close to him. She most likely figured out his thoughts and smiled. This made Viktor blush. He didn't want the Lieutenant to see it, so he quickly stepped inside and slammed the door behind him. Katya didn't want to embarrass him any further and began helping him with his coat. Then she gently pushed him into the living room.

"Come sit down, Comrade Vitus. You look tired. Want some hot tea? I have some pastries."

"No, no. Thank you. I actually came to pick you up. We're running late, so I thought I would explain in the car," Viktor uttered in one single breath.

"Where are we going, may I ask?" Katya's voice was rather firm, almost official.

"I wanted this to be a surprise, but I should probably explain," Viktor admitted reluctantly, seeing her reaction. He sat down on the couch and continued. "Leonid Gordin is in town. I am sure you remember him, don't you? I thought you would be interested in seeing him too."

"Why didn't you bring him here? Where is he now?" Katya asked. It was obvious she was a bit excited.

"He is at my mom's apartment. After telling his story to her, we both realized that my mother and his late mother were sisters who had lost each other during the Civil War. I let

Leonid speak with my mom and confirm some additional details to support this fact. There are no doubts he and his sisters are my mom's nephew and nieces. Which makes my sister and me their first cousins. Imagine that!" Viktor took a long pause and looked at Katerina.

She stood in the middle of the room motionless. Her face didn't show any emotion. If she were asked at that moment, she wouldn't make sense of her feelings. It was a subconscious resentment of someone who was still hurt by her own tragic loss—or possibly something else, which was impossible to explain. And yet, it immobilized her for a moment, but only for one short moment. The next thought that popped into her head was why Viktor wanted her to be a part of this family celebration. Katya didn't have the answer to this question either, at least, for now.

"I am so happy for your mother, for all of you." She eventually got hold of her strange emotions and smiled. "But I don't feel right to join your family for such an occasion. Who am I to do such a thing? Yes, Leonid does know me, but your mom and your sister have never met me."

"I told my mom about you. And it wasn't in any connection to my investigation."

"Why?" She insisted on an explanation.

In response, there was silence. Viktor wasn't ready yet to ask even himself why he mentioned Katya to his mother. He didn't expect such a question, and he panicked. However, this time, it felt different from what he had experienced dealing with women lately—fear of commitment, lack of confidence, or simply fear of getting hurt again. Rather, Viktor realized more and more that Katya was constantly on his mind, from the moment he woke up to the end of the day. He couldn't wait to see her. There was a problem, though: he hadn't had the guts to tell Katya about his feelings because he was afraid of rejection. However, things could not go on like this—he had to break the silence.

"You want to know why, don't you?" Viktor began slowly gathering his courage. "Because I care about you, Katya. Very much so. Now you have it."

Now it was Katya's turn to go silent. Continuing to stand in the middle of the room, she looked so unprotected and so vulnerable. Viktor jumped from his seat and embraced her as gently as he possibly could, still afraid of frightening her. She didn't protest his sudden impulse. On the contrary, she moved closer to him and put her head on his chest. She did it effortlessly, without a word. Who knows how long they were standing like that, refusing to let go of each other and yet forbidding themselves to use any deeper acts of affection? Again, Viktor was the first to break the silence.

"You haven't told me how you feel about me yet."

"Come to think of it, Comrade Major, I care about you too. I really do." Katya sounded genuinely sincere. "So, what are we going to do now?"

"Now we are going to put our coats on and hurry to my mom's apartment. We are awfully late."

"No, I have another proposition. You go without me. And tomorrow, you will tell me all about it." She gave Viktor a quick kiss on the lips and wiggled her body out of his hug. "Please, no more arguments. Promise?"

"I'll promise if you'll give me at least one valid reason for not going with me tonight." Viktor tried not to sound upset, but he was well aware of how strong-minded this seemingly delicate woman could be.

"The reason is the same as before — no matter how much I care about you, I am not ready to meet your family, especially your mom. I hope you understand." Katya didn't leave any doubt that this was her final decision. Viktor had no intention to argue, especially now.

*   *   *

Approaching his mother's apartment and holding the keys in his hands, Viktor heard a chorus of muffled voices behind the heavy door. The sound of laughter and excited screams of children was music to his ear. It symbolized his family's happiness and gave him a sense of security.

Only one thing missing was Katya, but after what had happened between them tonight, Viktor's heart was full of hope.

He unlocked the door and stepped into the flat, which had the familiar ambiance of home. It was *his* home for most of his life. Viktor found everybody on the couch or nearby with Mom and the guest seated in the center, going through a stack of photographs, and then passing them around. Each photograph was triggering a loud reaction, gay or sad. Viktor smiled and made himself noticed with a greeting and enthusiastic apology for being late. The first who acknowledged his arrival were Alex and Lilya. They ran to him and jumped into his arms, covering both cheeks with their smooches.

"Hi, Uncle Vitya! We couldn't wait to see you!" they screamed over each other.

"Hey, hey, kids, be careful. Don't hurt your uncle. He hasn't fully recovered from his wounds." Raisa got up from the couch and rushed to her brother's rescue.

"What wound?" The children quietly climbed down off him to the floor, looking up at Viktor with genuine concern.

"Oh, do not worry, kids. It was just a scratch. I am fine. I'll tell you more about what happened another time. Now, let me say hello to your other uncle, the one you never knew until today." Viktor approached Leonid and hugged him. "Welcome to the family, my newly discovered brother!"

"I am happy to be here!" Leonid couldn't hide his nervousness. "Even when I saw you in New Urgal for the first time, my intuition prompted me to tell you my family story. I felt the connection."

"Me too, me too, but not right away," Viktor admitted. "Only when I heard your mom's maiden name, you know. It's so sad she is not with us today."

"She is looking down from above. She is so happy I found you all." Leonid got teary and turned to Leya Solomonovna, who sat alongside him with her eyes full of tears. "We are not going to lose each other again."

Leya Solomonovna, Leonid, and Viktor put their arms around each other in a tight and rather long embrace that was eventually broken by the woman: "It is time to eat, children!" She pointed to the dinner table. "This is not only for you, Alex and Lilya. You all are my children. And I am going to feed you now."

Everyone laughed and hurried to the dining room while Leya Solomonovna and Raisa rushed to the kitchen. Viktor and Leonid sat down next to each other.

"Did you have enough time to tell my mom everything about your family?" Viktor asked. "I am sorry I had to attend to something very important and was late."

"It's all right, really. I understand," Leonid replied. "I did the best I could telling Aunt Leya about how her little sister Sonya survived. After her nanny, aunt Buzya had heard the shots from the rifles, she hid them both behind a trapdoor under the stairs leading to an attic. Only when flames engulfed the entire building, did they escape through the back entrance. There is more to tell, but we have our whole life ahead of us, don't we? The photos I brought with me should help a lot to tell the story of my family."

"I would like to see them."

"Of course."

"How did you like your cousin Raisa and her family?" Viktor continued.

"What a lovely family she has." Leonid sounded sincere. "Boris seems like a great guy, a good husband and father. Their kids are terrific. I am sure they will be close friends with my boys. I can imagine how excited my wife Mila will be to see you all when she comes here next summer."

"Is she coming just to visit you alone, without your kids?"

"Yes, this time alone. The kids will stay with her parents for a month or two," Leonid went on explaining. "If the offer to teach in Lviv will come through, Mila returns home before September, and I will follow her a month or two later.

"I see, that makes sense. Did Raisa or Mom tells you about their decision to emigrate?" Viktor decided not to beat around the bush.

"No, they did not." Leonid responded after a long pause. "Is this final?"

"I think so. They should get their exit visas in two weeks. Boris's parents and sisters are leaving the country from Moscow very soon." Now it was Viktor's turn to pause. "I am staying here."

"Forever? Or just for now, may I ask?" Leonid was treading carefully.

"I don't really know." Viktor sounded upset. "I guess for now."

"I hope you realize how tough it will be on you, my cousin. I can see how much your family means to you. There must be a real good reason for you not to join them?"

"There are several, and they are all valid," Viktor concluded, hinting he didn't want to talk about the subject anymore.

The supper went just as Leya Solomonovna planned. It wasn't heavy but refined and delicious. As an appetizer, they had traditional *gefilte* fish prepared from scratch. This was followed by chicken, meat-stuffed cabbage, and homemade cooked dumplings, (*vareniki*), stuffed with cherry preserves. Of course, there was wine on the table too. At the conclusion, everyone, including the kids, had hot tea with Mom's famous apple strudel. During the meal, there were questions about the guest's family members, especially the children. Alex and Lilya wanted to know what their newly discovered second cousins did after school and their interests and aspirations. The adults, in turn, wanted to know more details about Leonid's spouse, his two siblings, and their families. As much as he could, Leonid tried to satisfy the curiosity of his newly discovered relatives. It seemed this lovely feast would never end. But it did.

While everyone was leaving the table, carrying their plates and teacups to the kitchen, Leonid tapped Viktor on his arm, asking him to remain seated.

"I must tell you something, brother. Please let me refer to you as the brother I never had, not the cousin you are," Leonid began. "Your sister and your mother's decision didn't surprise me at all, although I couldn't read clearly how you felt about it, and therefore I was holding back with my reaction at first. I must confess to you; since I was sixteen—in fact, since I met our uncle, Leo, whose name I inherited, and who lived in Paris since 1920— my deepest and most persistent dream has been to leave this country. Believe me, I am not a dissident or enemy of the State. I just never felt that I belonged here. I felt my destiny wasn't here, but somewhere else, perhaps in France, even better in the United States. Please don't laugh; I am telling the truth."

"I am not laughing, brother. I am not laughing. I understand your desire and sympathize with your dream." Viktor didn't expect this confession at all. Still, he reacted with sincere conviction but cautiously. *Who could blame me?* he thought to himself. *Relative or not, you must be careful to avoid a possible setup.* And yet he was ashamed because it didn't sound right. "I just feel differently right now. Honestly, I am not sure what I feel anymore. Tell me, what does the rest of your family think about it?"

"We had a chance to emigrate back in 1972. My mother-in-law supported me, but my wife and her father weren't ready for such a drastic change," Leonid explained with some degree of regret. "Lately, they are warming up to this idea more and more. I suspect they see a lot of people coming to the same decision for the sake of their children."

"I guess it is very personal. Indeed, different people have different opinions about what is best for them and their kids. Don't they?" Viktor, one more time, tried to hide behind a generic philosophical statement, but he couldn't help asking, "So, you think you see this move in your near future?"

"I do. I do. Both of my sisters and their families are already doing whatever's necessary to obtain exit Visas. My family is still at a crossroads, though." Leonid tried to wind down this uneasy subject. "I am sorry I started it. It wasn't my intention to make you uncomfortable. Please forgive me."

Soon, everybody gathered back in the living room. Leonid sat on the sofa between the women. The kids were next to them, and Viktor and Boris pulled chairs in front. The pictures began changing hands, and new questions flowed, one after another. The stories related to these images were long, even for Leya Solomonovna, who was almost exhausted. Halfway through, Leonid realized this himself and stopped.

"I think we need to postpone this until our next meeting."

Viktor scanned the room, trying to find out whether everyone enjoyed the stories as much as he was. Evidently not— nine-year-old Alex seemed bored and restless, constantly looking at his father with the voiceless question: *May we go?* Boris, so consumed by this exciting family gathering, didn't pay any attention to his son.

It seemed to be the perfect time for an intervention. Viktor got up, giving the sign to Leonid for a short intermission, and kneeled next to his little nephew.

"What would you like to do, Alex?"

"I would play chess if I could," the boy said apologetically, understanding that his impatience had interrupted something important.

"But you would need a partner to play with, wouldn't you?"

"It's okay, Uncle Vitya. I can play by myself, making moves for Whites and Blacks in turn. I do that all the time. Really, it's fine with me. I cannot find anyone to beat me anyway." Alex sighed and glanced at his father.

"It is true—Alex is way ahead of all his peers. And not only in chess."

"Then, Alex, I'll take you to Grandpa's room, and you can use his chess set. Do you know which one?" Viktor took the boy's hand and led him to the office where the late Alfred Vitus loved to play chess.

"Yes, I know, Uncle Vitya, the one with marble figurines. Thank you, Uncle."

"My older son plays chess very well too." Leonid proclaimed in a rather low voice, more to himself, following Viktor and Alex with his eyes. "It has been a long time since I have played with him."

Leya Solomonovna gently touched his arm and said, "I am sure you'll see all your family soon."

The moment Viktor emerged from the office and closed the door, Leonid promised again to resume his stories at another time. Viktor heard a gasp coming from the disappointed audience. The large clock on the wall was showing five minutes to midnight. The kids needed to be in bed long ago.

It was getting late, and everyone seemed tired, including Leonid. He reached for his glass of water while Raisa and Boris rushed into an adjacent room. A few minutes later, they returned, smiling.

"Imagine, poor Alex fell asleep right next to the chessboard. We put him on the sofa. He didn't even react," Boris explained. "It looks like we have to leave him here overnight, if that's fine with you, Leya Solomonovna?"

"It's all right, but what about school?" she asked.

"He can skip school." Raisa laughed, coming back to her seat. "It doesn't matter now, does it?"

The room went silent for a few moments until Leya Solomonovna said, "Speaking of Leo Shtern and his life, what happened to him?"

"This would be a long but fascinating story," Leonid reacted with hesitation in his voice.

"I must know about it…" Leya Solomonovna insisted regardless of the late hour.

Leonid still sitting on the couch has straightened his posture and began his story.

* * *

At the beginning of the sixties, after several petitions to President De Gaulle and to the National Assembly, Leo Shtern received French citizenship and a French passport. Finally, he could realize his intention of returning to the Soviet Union to find his sisters. For the next three years, he made numerous inquiries with the Red Cross and Soviet archive offices, trying to locate them to no avail. Finally, in 1963, one of his business associates in Moscow forwarded Leo some information that mentioned several people named Shtern residing in Odessa and Kyiv. They could've been relatives of his immediate family. Soon after, Leo's first journey to the USSR was set.

On a hot summer day of 1963, Leo landed at Sheremetyevo and was met by a young woman named Masha near the passport control booth. She introduced herself as a representative of "Intourist," the official organization that serviced foreign tourists and businessmen visiting the Soviet Union. Masha spoke decent French and was extremely polite. She led him to a black Volga, where he sat in the back seat. On the way to Hotel Moscow, she went into more detail about her role as his interpreter, tour guide, and in-country public relations assistant. Strangely, none of these services were needed in Leo's case.

Leo was about to say as much, when he remembered what many of his associates who had visited the USSR before him has said: the drivers and interpreters who surrounded you on your trip, all received their orders and were closely supervised by the KGB. In some instances, these were KGB agents whose goal was to weed out potential spies, shield foreign tourists from excessive interactions with regular citizens, and avoid any possible international incidents. None of this really mattered to Leo, since he had no plans to jeopardize his first visit to the Motherland since his youth; besides, he had a very important business assignment and a tight schedule. He spent the next three days visiting different ministerial offices, introducing his company's capabilities, and trying to land some deals with the Soviet government.

While Khrushchev's policies of *détente*—the thaw in the relationship between East and West—were in full swing, Western businessmen flooded into Moscow. The inefficient Soviet economy needed various new technologies, and these visitors were ready to provide them. But what Leo and his company had to offer was quite different and somewhat unique considering the rigidity of existing socialist industries. His expertise lay in taking an existing industry or segment and making it work much more efficiently, with higher productivity and lower cost. Several governmental agencies found this proposition very attractive, so Leo managed to sign preliminary cooperation agreements with the two largest Siberian timber-processing enterprises. With this, the business part of his trip was done.

His Russian guide Masha immediately presented him with a few options to explore other parts of the country, mostly the popular tourist attractions around Moscow, Leningrad, and the Crimean peninsula. Leo politely declined those options and told her that he had different plans for the remainder of his visit. He wanted to fly to his native Odessa and meet a distant relative who might know the whereabouts of his sisters. Masha promised to get the authority's permission to do so and make all the necessary arrangements as soon as possible if Monsieur Shtern would provide the name and address of his relative.

Three hours later, she returned to the hotel with an official reply to Leo's request. She informed him that Mikhail Shtern had admitted that he was, in fact, related to the late father of Monsieur Leo Shtern; Solomon was his fraternal nephew. Unfortunately, due to his official position, the meeting between Citizen Shtern and the foreign guest couldn't take place. Nevertheless, Mikhail conveyed his warm greetings to his newly discovered cousin Leo and passed along the address of another person for whom he might be looking for. The name was Sonya Solomonovna Gordin. Her maiden's name was Shtern, and she was born in Odessa. She didn't have a telephone, so there was no way to contact her. So, they would have to fly to Kyiv, where the woman and her family resided.

Leo became so overwhelmed with this news that he couldn't help but hug the young woman who delivered it. Masha didn't mind it at all; she was genuinely moved by what had unraveled in front of her. The next morning, they arrived in Kyiv and checked in at the local Intourist hotel. At four o'clock that afternoon, Masha knocked on the door of an apartment Gordin's family had recently occupied. Sonya answered the door, having no idea what kind of unexpected and precious guest was sitting in the car fifty feet away, trying to calm himself down.

* * *

Leonid stopped and looked at Leya Solomonovna somewhat apologetically. "I wasn't home, and I missed the moment they met. Later, my father told me it was intensely emotional. There were a lot of tears."

"I can imagine," Leya Solomonovna mused in a low voice. "They actually knew each other very little. Sonya was a toddler when they last saw each other. I doubt she could remember Leo, could she?"

"She often talked about him. She named me after him, for God's sake!" Leonid insisted. "She did remember him."

"So, what happened after that?" Raisa jumped in.

"The usual." Leonid was poised to elaborate. "When I came home, my parents and my oldest sister were sitting around the table with sweets and a steaming tea kettle, talking to a well-dressed but unfamiliar man. They were weepy, their faces red from crying."

"Much like tonight!" Boris exclaimed.

"Yes, a little shocking to me at that moment, to say the least," Leonid agreed and continued. "Mom introduced me as her son Leonid and explained to me with happy tears in her eyes, 'This is your uncle Leo, my brother. He found me after all these years.'
The man got up from his chair and approached me with vigor. He embraced me and said to me in perfect Russian, 'It is great to meet you, my dear nephew. I can't wait to get to know you better.'"

"Did he seem like a foreigner?" Raisa asked rather casually.

"In fact, from the first moment, I identified him as such. In my French studies, I had some experience dealing with Western tourists, from France in particular. His very slight accent gave it away," Leonid explained. "So later, when we were drinking tea and exchanging some details about our daily lives, I asked our guest in French about his home in Paris. He didn't show any surprise at all and immediately switched to French. After that we bonded. He seemed vivacious, genuinely funny, and physically fit, despite being a chain-smoker. Leo smoked those awful, strong, unfiltered French cigarettes, Gaétans, one after another.

"Taking advantage of the absence of his "Intourist" handler Masha—who he insisted stay in the car—he told us the latest anecdotes about Soviet leaders and their often-outrageous behavior at home and overseas. Honestly, my parents were a little uneasy but laughed at every joke. It was a magical evening."

"Was that the only time you met him?" Leya Solomonovna wondered with a deep sigh.

"No, we had one more meeting the very next afternoon, when we all gathered at the Kyiv Intourist Restaurant on Lenin Street," Leonid replied. "This time, it couldn't be very intimate, though. Masha wasn't sitting at the table, but she was hovering nearby, just in case. Despite that, we had a wonderful time. After a very generous and classy feast that lasted two hours, Leo informed us that he was leaving that night for Moscow and returning to Paris the next day. We were all sad. He expressed his hope to come to visit us again the following year. He also encouraged me to study French and promised to write to me in French if I promised to reply to him in Russian."

It was Viktor's turn to ask, "Did he ever visit you again?"

"No, he never visited us again, although I knew he was in Moscow for three days a couple of years later. It was most likely a follow-up business matter. But he kept his promise and wrote to me regularly until the era of *détente* ended," Leonid replied.

"Do you have any information about Leo in later years?" Leya Solomonovna asked cautiously, as if she were almost afraid to hear an answer.

"Unfortunately, none. From Leo's letters, I knew he had some health problems in his lower extremities—varicose veins disease, I believe. Otherwise, besides his bad smoking habit, he took good care of himself," Leonid speculated. "I recalled him talking about some painful but very effective treatment for his circulatory condition he was getting once a year, every year, at a specialized clinic in Switzerland. It cost him a fortune but kept him alive and active. Mom was very worried about his health. I received his last letter around the summer of 1970, after which we had no idea what happened to him."

"Did you have his Paris address?" Viktor asked.

"Yes, I do. I'll forward it to you if you wish."

As the long, emotionally charged evening was winding down, Raisa, Boris, and Lilya gathered their things and said a heartwarming goodbye to this newfound member of the family. Their son Alex stayed behind, sleeping soundly in his beloved grandfather's office. Viktor decided to also stay with his mom and Leonid, sharing his old room with his cousin, which allowed them a couple of extra hours to talk. Taking turns, they touched upon various events in their lives and exchanged some philosophical perspectives before they both fell asleep. However, the last thought in Viktor's head this night was about Katya, and how much she would have enjoyed herself had she come with him.

Chapter 19

Thursday, November 24th. Eight in the morning. Viktor, in full uniform, stood outside General Melekhov's office, waiting for the signal from the intercom speaker box on the desk of Nadezhda Petrovna. Such unusual formality wasn't incidental. An important guest was paying the station an unexpected visit—The Inspector General of the Ministry of Internal Affairs from Moscow,

They had already been outside the General's office an hour or longer. Major Vitus did not wait alone: Colonel Guzyez, Major Levin, Lieutenant Toropko, Captain Mukhin and even the sketch artist Zelenin—they had all been summoned to the meeting by Captain Golovin, Melekhov's Adjutant. Finally, the General called Nadezhda Petrovna to invite everybody inside.

General Melekhov sat in his chair behind his desk. His guest from the Capital sat at the opposite end of the conference table, flipping the pages of a thick notebook wrapped in a brown leather binder. When everyone took their appropriate places, the guest stood up and introduced himself as Lieutenant General Anatoly Ivanovich Firsov. He was a rather small-statured man in his late fifties with a smoothly shaved head and an elongated face, covered by wrinkled skin with multiple bumps and birthmarks. His closely set, watery blue eyes pierced through his thick glasses.

"As you all should know, I, as the Inspector General, report directly to MVD Minister Comrade Shchelakov Nikolai Anisimovich. My job is to make sure that all ministerial departments in Moscow and all local UVDs are functioning properly and at their best capabilities." The visitor spoke with a sense of confidence and self-importance. "Now, let me explain why you are all gathered here. The homicide case your team is investigating has another aspect—the alleged theft of a very precious property: gold. Gold that belongs to the Soviet people and our government. Thanks to your heroic efforts, this property was recovered. And today, it will be going back to the Treasury. That is why I am here. Now, on behalf of the MVD Minister, I would like to take this opportunity to congratulate all of you—particularly Comrade Major Vitus—for the successful recovery of such a large amount of Socialist property."

Firsov began clapping and approached Major Vitus and shook his hand. Then he went around the table and repeated the handshake with the rest of the team.

After returning to his chair, he continued, "Before letting you go back to work, I would like an update on the latest status of this case." He paused for a moment. "Of course, I could've gotten it from General Melekhov, but he suggested you might do it better."

Lieutenant Toropko raised her hand and then stood up, "Everything our investigation compiled so far is a mix of scientific facts, logical deductions and numerous personal testimonies." She continued, a little more nervously, "However, we haven't received solid confirmation on the origin of the gold in question. So, I think removing it from our investigation prematurely is not the best course of action right now."

Firsov contorted his face and scanned the faces around the table. "Does anyone else share the Lieutenant's opinion?"

Viktor and Major Levin both raised their hands immediately. A moment later, Colonel Guzyev raised his hand too, but rather cautiously. The Inspector General waved his hand in his direction, prompting him to answer first.

"I think Lieutenant Toropko has a valid point," Guzyev replied hesitantly, getting up from his chair. "We would need a few more days to tie everything up."

"And you, Comrade Vitus, what do you think?" Firsov turned to the Major.

"I must agree, Comrade General, it is a little premature to remove this evidence. We may need it to lure the perpetrator—who is still at large and dangerously desperate—into believing that he has a chance to still obtain it." Viktor made an effort to talk calmly. "This way, we will be able to capture him without risking any more lives. Our plan is to…"

"I don't care, Comrade Major!" Firsov could not hide his irritation. He sprung up from his chair and almost screamed. "Your investigation is taking too long. It lacks aggressiveness and clear vision. And what about all this security detail for the victim's daughter? We cannot waste such valuable resources."

"It is necessary, Comrade General." Viktor jumped in impulsively. "The killer is still at large and a definite threat to her."

"Well, maybe you should've caught him the first time and closed this case a long time ago? Don't you think, comrades?" Firsov addressed everyone, letting them know he was tired of this discussion. "You go ahead with your plan, but I'll stick to mine. The gold is coming with my people today. I will continue to monitor the progress of your investigation. This meeting is over"

He dismissively waved his hand, and the officers began trickling out the office in a stunned silence. When Viktor reached the door, he heard Melekhov's voice.

"Comrade Major Vitus, please return. We must discuss something important with you."

Viktor. The General and Melekhov walked to the office's back room, where a private lounge was located.

"Major, we have received reports of you visiting the daughter of the man who was murdered." Firsov took control of the conversation immediately.

"Yes, I have visited her." Viktor answered shaken by the surprise question.

"There are multiple reports here. Why are you visiting her so much?"

"Just making sure she is okay." Viktor failed to come up with an adequate answer. Melekhov and Firsov looked at one another.

Viktor attempted to save the situation. "It seems as if there were always new questions pertaining to the murderer that I believed she could help ascertain."

Firsov straighten himself and looked directly into Vitus' eyes. "Just to be clear, Major— there will be in no way any funny business during this investigation. Because of the high monetary value involved in the recovery, we have eyes on us. Do NOT jeopardize this case."

"Of course, Comrade General." Viktor seemed in shock.

"There is a report here that you were in Citizen Rogozhins apartment for more than three hours. What was that all about?" Firsov asked, with anger.

"I was questioning her, and she had an emotional episode which pertained to her feeling guilty about my getting stabbed, sir."

"I see. And that neccissated you are being there that long?"

Suddenly Melekhov interrupted, in a seeming attempt to subvert the conversation. "Major Vitus has a very important day, General. Today he is going undercover to see if he can dig up some info on where this murderer might be holed up. As I remember, you are going to see Petukh, one of the local bosses today—weren't you, Major?"

Viktor nodded his head. "Affirmative."

"After this week, the investigation should be wrapped up so there will be no need to visit Citizen Rogozhin moving forward." Melekhov continued, almost not permitting Firsov from saying another word.

"Major…" Melekhov put his arm around Viktor and began walking with him to the door. "…You have a scheduled session with our wardrobe and make-up specialist this morning, don't you?"

"Yes." Viktor replied in a low voice.

"Well get to it— it will take some time. Just be very careful; this son-of-a-bitch Petukh has a nose for fakes. Understood? And keep me abreast, will you? Now go."

Viktor left the office in a daze. Soon afterward, he slipped away to the safe house. Once there, the makeup specialist would decorate his body with just enough tattoos that Viktor would be accepted as a real *Vor*. In five hours, he was transformed into a man with a grey peppered mustache, bushy eyebrows and dressed in common, undistinguished clothes— dark, thick-wadded pants and a padded *telogreika*. The whole time, Viktor couldn't stop thinking about the exchange that just took place. Was he out of line with his feelings for Katya? He decided that whatever just took place wouldn't affect him because his feelings for Katya were sincere. Finally, he put on a winter felt hat with long ear flaps, knee-high cowhide boots, and an oversized wool scarf wrapped up to his eyes. It was time to put away all his thoughts and focus on the matter at hand. Perhaps it was good that he was preoccupied with these thoughts and not overthinking his meeting which was about to take place? He walked out to the frozen, windy street and hailed a taxicab. He was sure even his mother wouldn't recognize him like this.

Victor wasn't surprised that this meeting was set in one of the numerous city bathhouses: guys like Petukh usually liked to conduct their clandestine business in crowded places with mostly naked people—no hidden weapons, and no distinguishing marks to remember.

A huge fellow wrapped in a white linen sheet met Viktor in the reception hall. He nodded to a woman attending the door and then led Viktor to a long corridor with lockers on both sides. Without a word, he signaled Viktor to get undressed and put his clothes in one of the open bins.

The man watched closely as Viktor shed his clothes; he couldn't help but smile when he observed Viktor carefully untangling his warm, cambric booties worn on his feet (instead of socks) and shoving them into his boots. The smile quickly disappeared as Viktor pulled off his heavy sweater, exposing the tattoos covering his neck, shoulders, arms, and wrists. The giant scrutinized these for a moment, then revealed his own arm, with tattoos marked "BK-240/2," the designation of the colony for extremely dangerous criminals in Solikamsk, Perm Region, on the Kama River.

"White Swan Prison? When?" the giant grunted.

"I was brought in at the end of 1968. You?"

"Got out in 1962. Did you know Colonel Gavrilov?"

"No, I missed him. He was transferred in 1967." Viktor was sure this guy was checking him out. So far, everything was going as planned. He was gaining his trust. One problem remained, though. He had yet to find an excuse not to go into the steam room—nobody knew how all those fake tattoos and his make-up would behave in the steam. "Listen, man, I cannot go in there. Heart problem, you know. Can we talk somewhere else?"

"Oh boy, you are so young. Is it serious?"

"Yes. In 1973, I barely survived a heart attack. Five years in that shitty hellhole can kill anyone, you know. But, thanks to that, I was released."

"I wouldn't call it luck, man." The giant sounded quite sincere. "My name is Denis. I am not the boss here. Let me go and ask Petukh what he wants to do. Stay put. I'll be right back."

Viktor sighed with relief: his story seemed credible. He looked around and saw a small table and a couple of chairs at the end of this corridor. *This could be the place to talk. But let's be patient. This is definitely Petukh's playground. He will decide,* Viktor speculated. A few moments later, Denis came back with a serious face.

"What should I call you, *bratok*? What is your *poganyalo*?"

"*Sapog,* (meaning the boot)," Viktor replied in a hurry.

"Well, Sapog, go sit at that table." Denis pointed to the end of the corridor. "Petukh needs some time to dry himself up and get dressed. You, too, can put your pants and your sweater back on. It is rather chilly in here, isn't it?" The giant smiled and disappeared again.

Viktor didn't waste any time sitting at the table. Judging by the numerous nicknames carved into its plywood top, this table was Petukh's favorite place to hold meetings with his partners in crime. The faded bloodstains splattered all over its painted green surface proved that many of those meetings hadn't ended amicably. So, Viktor carefully inspected the table, tapping his fingers across its top while inconspicuously running his right hand under it. He checked his own side first, and then, making sure no one was around, the side opposite him.

"Hey, what do we have here?" Viktor murmured when his hand touched something cold and ribbed. He quickly released a leather strip holding the thing in place and pulled it into his lap. It was a gun. Adrenaline pumped through his veins, but he tried to stay cool and collected.

What should I do? He spun the barrel and found five bullets in it. *If I leave everything as it was, I am risking being shot. Who knows what temper Petukh has and what assessment his bodyguard Denis reported to him? It might not be a high risk, but still a risk. And, if I render this gun inoperable, the consequences could be even more unpredictable.*

Viktor had only a few seconds to decide. He emptied the bullets into his pants pocket, put the gun in its original place, and returned to his initial seat. Denis appeared at the door of the steam room. A much older man walked in lockstep right behind him.

This man was Petukh. Viktor admitted to himself that the description given by Melekhov was pretty accurate. He looked old but not frail, short but with an oversized head, with grey hair sticking up from front to back like a cockscomb. Like his bodyguard, he wore a fleece tracksuit and imported white sneakers. He didn't bother to introduce himself or ask the visitor his *poganyalo*. He sat on his chair, facing the corridor, and waited.

"I have a message for you," Viktor said calmly, stretching his words like chewing tobacco.

"From whom and what does it say?" Petukh asked without turning his head.

"Tsygan sent me to see you. He needs help." Viktor reached into his pocket, which made Denis move hastily toward him. Seeing a piece of paper in Viktor's hand, he relaxed. "This may explain."

"What prevented him from showing up in person?" Petukh became more animated. "What, he is now? The Ace of Spades or something? Since when?"

Petukh took the note from Viktor. He turned to Denis, who handed him a pair of glasses, and then began reading. Finished, Petukh put the piece of paper on the table in front of him.

"I recognize his scribbles, but it doesn't say much. What happened to him? Where is he now?" he asked with some agitation in his voice.

"He is hurt—couldn't come himself. My *bratki* are taking care of him. In a week or so, he'll be all right, I guarantee." Viktor tried to sound as convincing as possible.

Petukh nodded approvingly. It gave Viktor extra confidence, and he continued with his story.

"The problem is not with Tsygan, though. It is our incidental partner Stepanov who can mess the whole thing up."

"Wait a minute," Petukh suddenly interrupted him. "I know nothing about any partners. A few weeks ago, he sent me a *telega* (message) about some shiny loot for a quick sale, and him coming to Khabarovsk soon. He didn't mention any partners. Tell me about it."

"There were three of us working at that dredge," Viktor treaded slowly. He realized that the original story he and Melekhov had agreed upon might have a few holes because Kondrateko, whether deliberately or accidentally, had left out some important information regarding his dealings with Petukh. So, he decided to improvise, although there was a danger in doing it on the fly. "I was hired for office duty, you know, bookkeeping, correspondence. But I knew what Tsygan and Stepanov were doing on the riverbank."

"Hold your horses, bratok. I've known this son-of-a-bitch for many, many years. He's never trusted anyone," the old man interrupted. "How did you know each other, and how did the three of you get together? You are much younger than Tsygan, and he has never been to White Swan."

"With me, it is a long story," replied Viktor, trying to bide time.

"It's all right, I have no place to be." Petukh threw a quick glance at Viktor.

"I knew him since I was eleven or twelve, back in Kharkiv. After the war, it was a tough time, a hungry time. I had to hunt for food and warm clothes," Viktor began. "One day, I was caught stealing boots. Tsygan, who was my mother's come-and-go boyfriend, took pity on me, and bailed me out of the local juvenile detention center. I called him Uncle Grisha. For the next three or four years, he was my mentor and teacher. He's the one who named me Sapog. And then, he disappeared." Viktor paused for a moment. "I went solo until I was caught again—two years of prison at Korosten near Kyiv. I moved on to more serious stuff and spent some time in Rostov. After I was released, there on the street, I bumped into Tsygan, just by chance. Again, he took me in. I worked with him almost every day. He and his *bratki* trusted me so much that had me manage their *obschiak (Kassa)*— their little private bank. That's how I learned bookkeeping." Viktor paused, indicating he needed a drink.

Denis immediately brought a glass of water from the entrance hall and put it on the table in front of him. Viktor took a few slow sips before he resumed his story.

"There were a few happy years, and business was booming. We were making money hand over fist. However, everything comes to an end, I guess."

"What happened?" Petukh was becoming impatient. "Did Tsygan get arrested?"

"No, he didn't. A long time before, he told me that he could not be arrested at any cost, even death. He shielded himself masterfully from any possibility of being caught by the *menty (Militiamen)*. He possessed an amazing premonition for danger. On that day, at the last moment, he did his usual disappearing act. Four of us, I included, were arrested, convicted, and eventually ended up in White Swan. But we kept in touch all those years. When I was released, Tsygan rushed to my aid again due to my failing health. He called me to come to Beloretsk— the Blagoveschensk Region, where he recommended me for a bookkeeper's job at the Gold Mining Co. It was in the late fall of 1973."

"And what about the other partner? What is his name again?"

"Stepanov. Ivan Stepanov. Honestly, I do not know much about this guy and how he became such close friends with Tsygan. He had been there at least five years when I arrived." Viktor deliberately sounded unsure. "From the beginning, he struck me as a strange dude, you know. He is huge, physically strong, and handsome, but a paranoiac, easily explosive, and violent. He can kill in one blow with his enormous fist. I was always afraid of him. He never liked me either."

"Hmm. So, you have no idea when and where they met?" Petukh sounded puzzled. "You may go on."

"By observing the company's production practices and procedures, we found ways to steal and, most importantly, safely move those precious nuggets off the premises." Viktor paused to sip some water. He needed time to think where he was going with his story.

"Over a two-year period, we gathered in our possession more than a kilo of gold, and we had no intention of stopping. Everything was going great. A couple of months ago, Stepanov suddenly became obsessed with the idea that one of the foremen on the dredge had discovered the theft and was closing in on him and Tsygan. He got so paranoid and agitated that he would pretend to be sick and skip work. One day, this foreman stopped by Stepanov's cabin to find out what was wrong with him. Evidently, they had a quarrel, and Stepanov killed him. I remember that unfortunate night Tsygan ran to me for help to bury the body before dawn. Stepanov refused to help him for some reason."

"Wow!" Petukh exclaimed. "Was he right to be suspicious of this guy?"

"Who knows? I was never convinced that this poor foreman had any idea about our illegal activities. But after what happened, we had to drop everything and run from there as far as possible and as fast as we could." Viktor paused again. "We needed a safe place to weather the storm, and to find a buyer for our loot. Stepanov had a solution: hiding at his family hamlet in the Buriya district of Khabarovsky Krai. It was not far from Beloretsk, less than two hundred kilometers or so, and nobody would look for us there."

"That was your plan too?"

"In part. The full plan was to split until we found a buyer." Viktor continued with more confidence. "I would go to Birobidjan to see my buddy from White Swan, Leibel Katz. He settled there a few years ago and had some connections. Uncle Grisha would head to Khabarovsk to see you, I am assuming. Stepanov would hide with his family at *khutor* Izmailovsky until we got back. To move around with our loot wasn't safe, you know. At the last moment, Tsygan changed his mind and decided to stay with Stepanov. I presume he couldn't trust him enough."

"And something bad happened at that fucking *khutor*, I guess?" Petukh was getting impatient.

"I wasn't there. I was already in Birobidjan when I got the *telega* from Tsygan begging me to come back to Izmailovsky right away and pick him up because he was seriously wounded." Viktor was on a roll with his story. "I found him alone with a huge hole in his buttock, weak and hungry, in one of the empty, dilapidated houses close to the edge of the *Taiga*. He and Stepanov, who also got shot, were separated. Tsygan didn't know where his partner was at that moment, but he was sure if he survived, he would definitely go to Khabarovsk."

"I want to know who was after them. Who shot them?" Petukh insisted. "Had someone taken your loot from them? And why was Tsygan so sure this guy Stepanov would end up in Khabarovsk?"

"I, myself, was confused." Viktor deliberately sounded a little inconsistent in laying down the facts.

"Listen, this is what Tsygan told me: first, they visited the big man, a local priest, who suspiciously looked like Stepanov, only bigger. This priest was very upset after talking to Stepanov and refused to help, threatening to report them to the authorities. They retreated and went to see the old woman who lived in a neighboring house, who happened to be the priest's sister. She, on the contrary, was very happy when Stepanov showed up at her doorstep, calling him 'Dima' and 'my Son,' and trying to please him in every way. The woman agreed to hide the package without even asking what was inside. They stayed in her house for two full days sleeping, eating, and drinking as much as they wanted. Then, they were gone for a day, visiting the store in a nearby village to buy more vodka. But when they came back and had another feast with vodka, the woman informed them that she had handed their package over to her brother for safekeeping. Stepanov got so enraged he almost killed her."

"So, what's the big deal to get back something that belongs to you! Am I right?" Petukh exclaimed.

"Hah, this is where the troubles began," Viktor replied with dramatic flair. "Just like during the first encounter, the conversation between the priest and drunk Stepanov didn't go well. As Tsygan recalled, the priest refused to return it under any circumstances. The priest called Stepanov a devil and showed him a photo of the young girl who was, according to him, his daughter. He began praying, holding her photo close to his chest." Viktor suddenly realized he, in fact, was rehashing his investigative scenario of Rogozhin's case in front of a semi-retired underground criminal boss. He paused for a moment before continuing,

"It infuriated Stepanov so much that he grabbed an ax lying near the stove and, with one quick blow, plunged it into the man's skull. But the priest didn't fall. He turned around with a roaring sound and charged at his assailant, who stood petrified in disbelief. The priest, in turn, hit him with his fist so hard that Stepanov, who was much younger, fell down. Tsygan was trying to protect his crazy partner. He jumped on the wounded man and slowed him enough to let Stepanov get back on his feet. At that moment, Stepanov pulled his knife and stabbed the priest repeatedly until the old man crashed heavily to the floor, dead."

Petukh turned his head to his bodyguard. "I haven't heard anything that horrendous for a long time. Have you, Denis?" Looking back at Viktor, he asked, "So, they searched the house after being done with the killing and found the loot?"

"They did search the house but didn't find the gold, not even a trace of it." Viktor sighed deeply and looked at Petukh. "Here is why we need your help."

"Explain, please."

"You see, someone unexpectedly became a witness of that massacre." Now, Viktor felt he must be especially credible and convincing. "This someone was a young Korean soldier. It wasn't clear what he was doing that evening peering through the window of the priest's house. Nevertheless, he saw what happened. Tsygan and Stepanov went after him and eventually caught up with him in the *Taiga* the next morning, but not before he reported the crime and their descriptions to the local Militiaman. Stepanov cut the throat of the kid anyway. However, the hunt was already on, during which they both were wounded."

"And how does this in any way involve me?" asked Petukh.

Viktor apologized. "Sorry, I got off track. Before they got separated, Stepanov insisted on his version of what happened to the loot, being sure that the old man somehow transferred it to his daughter, who permanently resided in Khabarovsk, so this city should be their destination."

"And you know for a fact that this crazy guy is in Khabarovsk as we speak?" Petukh sounded genuinely concerned. "But you mentioned before that he was wounded too, wasn't he? What is the extent of his injury? Do you know?"

"Judging by what Tsygan told me, his wound shouldn't be very serious. However, it could've become badly infected without proper care, especially if the bullet fragments or pellets were never extracted. I know this from my own experience, believe me," Viktor explained in a matter-of-fact tone.

"Hey, I believe you." Petukh ran with this thought. "Now it makes sense what I have heard on my short-wave radio scanner—I always keep a tab on what our glorious defenders of law and order are discussing on their mobile radio. When was it, Denis?"

"I think yesterday, around ten or eleven in the morning," Denis replied right away.

"Oh yeah, precisely. There was some commotion at an *apteka* up north. Gunshots were fired, according to what I heard. Armed robbery, I assumed," Petukh speculated. "It could've been your buddy Stepanov looking for some medical supplies to mend his wound. Wait a minute, where did he get a gun?"

"Good question, Boss," Denis reacted. "It is not easy to get one if you don't know who to ask."

"You see, it makes him even more dangerous. This way, you must help us find him before Tsygan comes back," Viktor interjected. He didn't want any speculation about the gun. "If it was Stepanov, the local *menty* could be on his tail already. If we get him first, there is a chance to recoup our gold. Otherwise—"

"Otherwise, say goodbye to your precious loot. You're right," Petukh finished Viktor's thought rather sardonically—it seemed to be his nature.

"And a hefty cut for you." Viktor pointed out.

"Oh yeah, my cut. Let's talk about that," the old man replied slowly. "If you want me to help you, I expect a nice chunk of change. Of course, a commission on the sale of your gold must be separate."

"Understood." Viktor deliberately made a long pause as if he was mulling this demand out. "Tsygan authorized me to tell you that if Stepanov didn't survive, we'd split the proceeds three ways. But if he is alive—a more favorable scenario because he already knows where to find the loot—everyone gets one quarter. What do you think, is that fair?"

"Perhaps not..." Petukh began slowly. "In my book, whether Stepanov lives or not, I get the same cut, one-third plus commission. It is your problem to get back what belongs to you. Understood?"

"Listen, I personally have no problem with your demand, but I am not sure what Tsygan will say," Viktor didn't want to draw the slightest suspicion by agreeing too quickly.

"Again, it's not my problem. I need your answer now, or bye-bye, my friend." Petukh insisted forcefully.

Viktor took some time to answer, looking straight at Petukh without blinking. Then he sighed rather dramatically and blurted out, "Alright, alright—you get one third. But do not try to catch Stepanov. Let us deal with him. Just find him and keep an eye on him while informing me. Okay? And promise me to do this without any delays and quietly. Agreed?"

"Agreed," Petukh replied and stretched out his right arm to shake hands. "Let's do this one step at a time. Tell Denis how to reach you. It was a pleasure to do business with you, Sapog."

He got up and disappeared behind the door to the steam room, leaving Denis and Viktor at the table, exchanging all the relevant information. Before seeing Viktor to the exit, Denis grabbed his elbow.

"Now, you can give me back my bullets," he said in his low, raspy voice, smiling. "You think I didn't see what you'd done? Smart move, though, I must say."

"Sorry, I couldn't take chances." Viktor smiled back, pulling the bullets out of his pocket.

* * *

Outside, it was dark, windy, and very cold. Viktor pulled his hat flaps down and glanced at his wristwatch before hailing a cab. It was quarter to eight. He was desperate to see Katya, but first, he had to go the safe house to transform back to his normal self. Then he had to stop by Melekhov's office to let him know everything had gone okay. It looked like there was not enough time. Hopefully, Freckles hadn't gone home yet.

Back at Headquarters, he found Sergeant Uvalov hanging around the office, wondering where in the hell his boss had disappeared to for half the day. However, he didn't ask Viktor about that. He just drove him back to the building that had become so familiar to both of them. The whole way there, Viktor looked at Freckles in an odd way, which bewildered the young Sergeant.

Katerina looked especially lovely, in a long black skirt and blue jersey top, with her shimmering hair pulled all the way back. Without asking permission, he immediately took off his shearling coat and his fur hat, hung everything on the coat rack, and turned to Katya, smiling. She was close enough that he could inhale her natural fragrance, see every little imperfection of her smooth skin, and feel the heat from her every breathe. He seized the moment and kissed her moist lips. It wasn't a raw, wildly passionate kiss unleashed by the crazy desire of two lovers. It was a gentle kiss—-an expression of adoration and deep affection between a man and woman who were only at the beginning of their road to passion, taking their time to know each other better. It caught them both by surprise. Viktor didn't want this moment to end; neither did Katya.

The next two hours passed in quiet conversation while drinking tea with pastries. Katya listened with a great deal of interest as Viktor told her about the visit with his newly discovered cousin. At one point, Katya expressed genuine concern regarding the health of Viktor's mother under all the emotional pressure. Katya told Viktor about the challenges during rehearsals for the Shakespearian play she was starring in and the general mood in the theater. Nothing was said the entire evening about the status of the investigation. Nor did Viktor mention anything about the upcoming emigration of his mother and sister. It was a lovely, quiet evening, which they both badly needed.

Viktor returned to his apartment at ten minutes to midnight. He was so exhausted that he crashed on his bed and fell asleep, still in his uniform. It was a shallow sleep full of strange but familiar dreams and illusive images, a sleep that caused more distress than relief.

* * *

Viktor felt tired at six the next morning when his alarm clock rudely awakened him. So, he refreshed himself by splashing cold water on his face. Later, Viktor took a warm shower and shaved. Then, he searched for food and found none, not even instant coffee. Yet, he didn't feel hungry.

Indeed, he felt good: he finally got to kiss her. To taste her sweet lips. *Just take it easy, don't push too hard. She's not the kind of woman you can rush into anything with, especially when she is so vulnerable.* He was not ready for a real relationship either; too many disturbing things were happening in his life. Viktor might end up alone in this world, with no family. It frightened him. Only Katya could potentially save him.

A knock on the door interrupted the thoughts swirling in his head—It was loyal Sancho, who came to drive him to Headquarters. A few more minutes, and he might snap or go insane, like what happened in Leningrad. It was time to focus on the long, crucial day ahead. Viktor threw on his coat, opened the door and stormed through it without inviting Pyotr in.

"Come on, no time to spare, Sergeant!" he exclaimed, slamming the door behind him.

"Yes, Comrade Major!" Uvalov saluted his boss and rushed downstairs to start the car.

The day began with a short meeting in General Melekhov's office. Evidently, the high-level guest from Moscow was gone or was busy somewhere else in the building. Viktor knew he had to be careful around Firsov, although the idea of removing such important evidence from custody didn't sit well with him, especially now that he had established close ties with the criminal underground. This might eventually lead the Militia to a whole network of illegal dealings, and they needed this confiscated gold as bait.

He shared this thought with Melekhov; however, the General didn't seem overly enthusiastic about the merit of such a plan.

"I think it is premature to talk about that now, Comrade Major," he explained somewhat reluctantly. "The point regarding the evidence is well taken. I am working on it."

At that moment, Melekhov was more preoccupied with catching the fugitive. Nevertheless, he was pleased with Viktor's report about his meeting and admitted they had to be patient and wait for the information Petukh promised to dig up.

"In the meantime, we have to be vigilant to prevent any new shootings in the city," Melekhov concluded. "Hopefully, we'll catch Stepanov red-handed if he dares to attempt another robbery."

For the next hour and a half, Viktor sat at his desk, filling out paperwork on his undercover operation. He checked the mail that had piled up in a bin on his desk and found an envelope that gave him a jolt. His request for information he had sent to the Blagoveshchensk Regional War veteran's affairs office was answered with a copy of Ivan Stepanov's personal registry card. There was no photograph attached to it, but it was a concise list of his physical attributes: height, weight, hair and eye color, scars, etc. Such a description most likely was recorded in the hospital where Stepanov had his rehabilitation before his military discharge. After studying this information, Viktor concluded that these attributes almost perfectly described the person who had attacked him and assaulted the clerk in the *apteka*. It looked like his crazy hypothesis—that Ivan Stepanov was really Ivan Rogozhin—had just hit a wall.

Around noon, after he shared this new discovery with Colonel Guzyev and Lieutenant Toropko, Viktor prepared to leave for his mom's place for an hour. He wanted to see Leonid and have a meal with him. Leonid planned to leave for New Urgal the next day, and Viktor wasn't sure he would have enough time to spend together before his departure.

When he stopped by his desk for his coat and hat, he found a sticky note from the Department of Field Operations and knew immediately that his lunch had to be postponed. He rushed to the first floor and received a message from Marusya, the housekeeper of an undercover "rendezvous" point up north. "Denis is waiting for Sapog to exchange some info." Such expediency was unexpected but promising. *Petukh must have bought the story without any reservations and jumped into action to get his money as soon as possible,* Viktor concluded in his head. *I have to hurry—Denis may not wait that long.*

There wasn't enough time for a full transformation and for all the tattoo placements. But the meeting was not in the bathhouse; one tattoo on the upper neck and another on the wrist would be sufficient. Of course, he could not forget the mustache and grey peppered sideburns. Regarding dress, a heavy turtleneck sweater would work fine, and the rest of his attire would be the same.

Thirty minutes later, Viktor arrived at the meeting by cab, where he found Denis waiting for him. Denis was sipping tea with a big, honey-flavored *pryanik* (cookie), glancing at his wristwatch. It was obvious he was getting nervous. He greeted Viktor, visibly relieved.

"Hey, Sapog, another five minutes and I'd be gone. This darned *pryanik* is very good, though. Thank you, Marusya, thank you." He sprung from the chair, inadvertently hitting the lampshade above the table with his balding head.

With one hand, Viktor stopped the lampshade from swinging and, with the other, gently pushed Denis back into his seat.

"It's all right, Denis, it's all right," Viktor said calmly and pulled another chair close to the table. "Enjoy your cookie. Sorry for keeping you waiting. I had to stop someplace. I cannot get used to this brutal cold. How can you live in this fucking climate?"

"Easy, Bratok, easy," Denis replied with a crooked smile. "Let's not waste any time, Sapog."

"Let's not. Marusya, can you bring me some tea? Was anyone besides this big fellow asking for me while I was out?" Viktor detected some tension and tried to put Denis at ease. "So, what have you guys found out?"

"Before I give you everything you need to catch this crazy bastard, I have to ask for a favor." Denis paused while Marusya was serving the tea. He leaned closer to Viktor and lowered his voice almost to a whisper. "It shouldn't be difficult for you to do, Nachalnik."

The blood rushed from Viktor's head. Although he always expected the possibility that his cover might be blown, he didn't expect such boldness from this fellow. He felt dizzy, but he didn't let a single muscle in his face move. Reaching for his weapon would be foolish; he had no doubt Denis was armed and ready. So, he remained calm.

Any aggressive reaction on the part of Marusya wouldn't help him in this situation either. Moreover, it could be lethal. With his peripheral vision, Viktor noticed that she, being an experienced field operation officer, had drawn her weapon and repositioned herself closer to the exit. It wasn't clear if their adversary was aware of her move.

"Come on, Nachalnik. I'm not going to do anything stupid." Denis smiled, revealing his ugly yellowish stumps for teeth. He leaned back and took a more relaxed pose. "I figured out right away you were a *ment*. I didn't say a word to Petukh, though."

"May I ask why you let my act go on?" Viktor sounded genuinely curious. "Why would you let Petukh, your boss and *vor-v-zakone*, be fooled by an undercover Militiaman?"

"Please hear me out!" Denis pleaded conciliatorily. "Neither Petukh nor I play any role as underground crime figures anymore. We retired a long time ago and have since lived quite comfortably, thank God. The Militia has nothing on Petukh and even less on me. Why would I be afraid of you, Nachalnik? Besides, I understand that coming to us for help, must mean this is very serious. Petukh may have his own motivations for helping you. If you were telling the truth about Stepanov, I can understand why this monster must be stopped."

What Denis was saying seemed to make sense to Viktor. There wasn't much choice, anyway. Viktor had to play along.

"Okay, what I can help you with?" he asked with a sigh of relief.

"It's about my nephew—My sister's son," Denis began slowly. "She raised him alone. I was helping her as much as I could, you know. My poor sister, she fell on really bad times."

"What happened to her?" Viktor interjected, seeing how emotional the guy became.

"You're the first person I've shared her story with. Sorry." Denis paused for a few moments before continuing. "About eleven years ago. Galina, my sister, had a good man for a husband and their seven-year-old son Kolya. Vasily, his father, worked at the aircraft factory as an electrical engineer. Galina had a good-paying administration job as an office manager. They lived in a nice three-room apartment. One day, Vasily didn't come home from work. Galina didn't hear from him for the next 72 hours. She didn't panic, but it was very unusual even if he had been sent to another city on a business assignment. When she went to the factory with an inquiry about her husband, the head of the personnel office delivered very disturbing news to her: Vasily Kulaguin had been taken away by KGB officers, and his present whereabouts were not known."

"Did she have any idea what could've prompted his arrest? Perhaps she was aware of any undesirable activities by Vasily, or something he said in front of strangers?"

"As far as I knew, my brother-in-law was a Communist Party member, a trade union activist, and all-around straight-as-an-arrow guy. But how can anyone be sure of anything?" Denis replied quickly. "It happened rather long ago."

"And your sister? Did she try to find out why he was arrested—what charges he faced?" Viktor kept pushing for details.

"She did try, and this led to new troubles." Denis stopped, pulled a cigarette from the pack on the table in front of him, lit it, and inhaled the first puff. "The KGB told her to lay off if she didn't want serious consequences. Galina was too stubborn to listen. Soon, she was fired from her cushy job and demoted to cleaning the offices at night— the same ones she used to manage. Thank God, they didn't incarcerate her or take Kolya away"

He took another deep drag and slowly blew smoke in sequential white rings. It gave him time to control his emotions. "I couldn't help Galina much, not as a provider for my sister nor as a role model for the boy. I had just been released from the White Swan Prison. Nevertheless, as soon as I got on board with Petukh, they never went hungry. As a matter of fact, I've doubled my financial help for the last five years, because Galina developed a lung disease. The problem is Kolya. At eleven, and without a father, he always wanted to be like me—emulate me. I couldn't let that happen; I didn't want him to repeat the same mistakes. So, I stayed away from him as much as possible until Galina began spending more and more time in the hospital. The boy needed everyday care and constant attention, which I couldn't provide. Left to his own devices, my nephew got involved with the wrong crowd. By the age of fifteen, the Militia already arrested him a few times for disorderly conduct, being under the influence, petty theft, you know, rebellious teenage stuff."

"And you, big guy, couldn't knock some sense into him? It would teach him a lesson."

"As I said before, I never was a positive role model for this boy. I couldn't bring myself to lay a hand on him. So, I kept talking to him, but all my preaching fell on deaf ears." Denis still sounded a little emotional. "Galina and Kolya are my only family. I loved this boy like my own son. I tried desperately to steer him on the right track, but I failed. Now, Nikolai is no longer a little boy, and he is in big trouble this time."

"So what can I do?" Viktor asked.

"The problem is they won't let me near him. And his public defender is a real jerk. He doesn't give a hoot about him. And he wouldn't speak with me either. I don't know what to do." Denis looked at Viktor with teary eyes. "This is why I need you to help me, Comrade Nachalnik. I promise I will be useful to you, going forward."

"Let me see what I can do," Viktor replied rather hesitantly. "I can't promise anything, but I will try to find out about his case. Now, about our business—I believe you brought something for me, didn't you?"

Without saying a word, Denis pulled a piece of folded paper from his pocket and tossed it on the table. Then he grabbed his pack of cigarettes and turned toward the exit.

"What is this?"

"Two addresses where you should find your perp. You told us not to touch him." Denis said, moving toward the door and Marusya. "So, we didn't. Be careful—he has a gun. Don't know where he got it, though. Not from our *bratki*, that's for sure."

"Hey Denis, thanks for the information." Viktor hurriedly replied before the big guy was gone. "I will try my best to help your nephew. Come visit Marusya soon. She'll tell you what to do next."

On his way back to the office, Viktor tried to sort out what had just taken place. On the one hand, it was rather upsetting that his undercover performance was a dismal failure. On the other hand, he was glad how things unfolded. He obtained the information he needed, although it had yet to be verified. He had gotten himself a potentially valuable informant deep within the local criminal network, albeit Denis's story seemed a bit flimsy. Yet, for some inexplicable reason, Viktor seemed to believe him. He'd have to do some digging—perhaps request the file on Kolya's father through his KGB contacts? Or go directly to the UVD Juvenile Crime Department? But getting Stepanov, his real nemesis, came first.

Chapter 20

Viktor switched his attention from Denis directly to Lieutenant Colonel Bakhtiyar Faizulin, the Head of Field Operations. By four o'clock that afternoon, all the people necessary for carrying out the sting to capture Stepanov gathered in Faizulin's office.

He instructed the field agents to secure the area around the addresses Viktor obtained. Colonel Faizulin placed Major Bogdan Oleinik in charge of the advance team: he was to contact Major Vitus via mobile shortwave radio once establishing visual confirmation of the target's whereabouts. Additionally, The Colonel ordered the team not to rush into any actions that might unjustifiably jeopardize their lives—the fugitive was armed and extremely dangerous.

Viktor returned to his desk to await Major Oleinik's first report. In the meantime, he looked into the arrest of Denis's nephew, Nikolai, Kulagin. Major Vitas needed something to distract him from worrying about the upcoming operation; and for some reason, this bratok Denis fascinated him. Viktor found no record of anyone with the last name "Kulagin" in the arrest and detention log? Did this mean Denis had fed him a bogus story? The question remained—for what purpose? Viktor refused to accept it. With some further digging, he found a few kids in detention with the name Nikolai. However, only one of them was seventeen, who carried last name of his father— Burlak.

Viktor was just about to request this young man to be brought from the cell to the interrogation room when he heard a crackling voice come through the speaker of his portable radio. "Comrade Major, do you read me? Respond, respond." It was Major Oleinik.

"I can hear you, Major. Please report!" Viktor shouted into the receiver of the portable short-wave radio.

"There's not much to report, Comrade Vitus," Oleinik replied. "Everything is quiet. No sign of our target so far. He is, most likely, inside the apartment drinking tea and watching TV. I am kidding, Major, but still, how much longer can we maintain our stakeout in such brutal cold?"

"I share your concern, Comrade Oleinik. It is brutal." Viktor sounded sympathetic. "But we have to give it more time. It's only a quarter to seven now. We cannot risk raiding an empty place. I think Stepanov and his girlfriend are still out trying to get access to some medical facility. They must be coming back soon. Copy that."

"Understood. Copy out."

Viktor returned to the business at hand. He requested the officer on duty to deliver Nikolai Burlak to the interrogation room. In the meantime, he reviewed the arrest protocols and the initial interrogation in the detainee's case folder. What struck him the most was the totally arbitrary decision by a patrolman for the arrest and, following it, the lack of probable cause for the prosecution. Reading those protocols and a few contradictory testimonies of the witnesses, Viktor developed the strong opinion that the poor kid had nothing to do with the crime. He just happened to be in the wrong place at the wrong time. So, this misunderstanding could've been easily cleared up if there weren't two unfortunate aspects: Nikolai's previous not-so-stellar record, which the case officer apparently put in front of the facts, and the disgraceful indifference of the public defender assigned to the case. The thought of how little it takes to ruin someone's life appalled Viktor, and he was determined not to let this happen to Nikolai Burlak.

In ten minutes, the guard led in a good-looking, quite tall, and skinny young man with thick, and unruly blonde hair on his rather large head. He wore sweatpants, an oversized sweatshirt, and heavy high ankle boots with the laces removed. Judging by his half-opened eyes and wrinkled clothes, Viktor was sure he'd been asleep when they came for him.

"Please take a seat." The Major pointed to a metal chair screwed to the floor on the opposite side of the table. "Your full name and age?"

"You know damn well my name, Nachalnik. It's in the folder," the young man replied offhandedly, spitting on the floor.

"Don't get fresh with me, kid!" Viktor got up from his chair and banged on the table with both hands.

"What do I care?" The lad continued with an attitude, unfazed by Viktor's gesture.

"Do you want me to talk to your Uncle Denis?" Viktor said in a hushed but stern tone.

"You know my Uncle?

"Yes, I know your Uncle. And he is very disappointed with you. But you're lucky. Because he wants me to help you." Viktor leaned in slightly. "I'm the only thing between you and freedom. Understood?"

The kid paused for a moment, locking eyes with Viktor. "Does my Mom know I'm in here?"

"She doesn't. Again, thanks to your Uncle. So right now, you need to cooperate with me so we can get you out of here. Got it?"

The young man nodded his head with slight hesitation.

"All right, Kolya. Better tell me how the hell you got mixed up with those hoodlums. You knew what they were about to do, didn't you?"

For the next twenty minutes, Nikolai shared the details of what had happened on that unfortunate evening and how he and his closest friend Gennady were in the wrong place at the wrong time—how Nikolai was arrested, and his friend got away. Viktor took some notes for the investigator. He would try to persuade them to dismiss all charges. He felt optimistic it was possible.

"Now, you can go back to your cell. But do not talk to anybody about your case—Nothing about your uncle or about our conversation. Got it?" The kid nodded oafishly, and the guard came in and escorted him out.

When Viktor returned to his desk, it was almost eight. There was no news from Major Oleinik. What if he was right, and all that time Stepanov and his girlfriend were inside while his guys were freezing their asses off? He'd give it a half hour more and then they had to act. Viktor pulled over the microphone and began calling.

"Major Oleinik, do you copy me? Please reply. Do you copy?"

"I copy, Major Vitus," the voice on the other end finally came through the airwaves. "Sorry I was silent. There was nothing to report. You decide what our next move is. Copy that."

"At 22:00 sharp, you have my go-ahead to penetrate both addresses simultaneously. Report the results immediately. Copy." Viktor ordered.

"At 22:00 sharp we will descend on both locations. Copy." The voice in the speaker responded with confidence.

"Please be careful and good luck. Over and out." Viktor put the microphone in its nest on the black box and looked at his wristwatch. It was five after ten. He looked around, picked up the telephone and dialed a number. After several rings, he heard a click and a sleepy "Hello."

"Katya, you are not asleep, are you? I am sorry if I disturbed you. Is everything okay? I had a crazy day, so I couldn't stop by."

"I understand. Don't worry about me, I am fine." Katya didn't seem to sound upset. "I was reading and almost fell asleep. I had a tiresome day too. Tomorrow I must be at the theater very early. Wasn't Leonid going to leave today?"

"No, he will leave tomorrow. I didn't get to see him either. I'll call Mom after I talk with you. Leonid is still there." Viktor felt some discomfort, yet he was happy to hear Katya's voice. "Sorry again for interrupting your rest. Have a good night. I'll see you."

"Yes, Viktor. Thanks."

After a short pause, he glanced again at his watch and dialed another number. Leya Solomonovna answered almost immediately.

"Is it you, son? I have been expecting your call since seven. What happened? Why are you not here? I hope you didn't forget Leonid is leaving tomorrow morning. It would be nice to spend more time with him, don't you think?"

"Yes, I do. Mom, the problem is, I am still stuck at work," Viktor explained. "A serious operation is in progress, very serious. I don't know when I will be able to stop by. Can I talk to Leonid?"

"Let me check if he is awake." Viktor heard the mouthpiece hit a hard surface and his mother's fading steps. A few minutes later, she was back. "Here he is."

"Hi Cousin, I guess we have to postpone our brotherly talk until later." Obviously, Leonid was disappointed. "Perhaps, around the New Year holidays, I'll be able to swing by."

"It would be great, brother." Viktor felt sad. "It would be even better if you could stay a day or two longer. They are not going to stop building BAM without you, are they?"

"I don't know. I have to get back to work." Leonid sounded hesitant. "I'll sleep on it."

Viktor kept pushing. "Please stay. Then we will be able to catch up, we know so little about each other and our families."

"Oh, by the way, I had a lovely time with your mom today." Leonid changed the subject. "I called my wife and told her everything about our reunion. She was so happy for us. Your mom talked with my older son. He was confused, though."

"I don't blame him. I would be too." Viktor laughed. "I wish my mom could see all of your family sometime soon. She is not young, you know."

"I hope she will—sooner than we think." There was a smile in Leonid's voice. "As the wise people say, 'Man may presuppose, but only God can dispose of.' "

"I really hope so. I must run." Viktor cut the conversation short when he heard a loud crackling and some distant voices coming from his portable radio. "Go back to sleep; we'll talk tomorrow."

He grabbed the microphone from its cradle of the portable radio and began calling, "Copy; can anybody copy?"

"Copy, Major Vitas." It was Oleinik on the other end, breathing heavily. "It's over, Major. Unfortunately, he got away. He vanished into thin air. No idea how, we had the entire perimeter airtight. But we got her. When we got inside, she was in bed alone. His side of the bed was still warm. The bastard gave us the slip at the last moment."

"Have you searched the entire flat? It was on the first floor, wasn't it? Start searching the immediate area at once." Viktor was trying to take command, but he was stunned. Were all these efforts for nothing? "Search the premises well, collect every piece of evidence, everything indicating his presence. Bring the woman and all evidence to me. Don't give up the manhunt until I give the order. He won't get far. Copy. "

"Copy that, Major. There's a lot of junk here—blood-soiled bandages, alcohol bottles, newspapers, theatrical announcements, all kinds of junk. You want everything?"

"Theatrical announcements? Yes, everything. Pack it all up. See you soon. Over."

"Over and out, Major."

Viktor felt his stomach in knots. He reached for the telephone again, this time dialing Lieutenant Toropko.

"Lieutenant, I need your help. Meet me here in an hour. I'll see you soon." Viktor hung up and leaned back in his chair, closing his eyes for a moment.

What a long day it was, and it wasn't over yet. He was sure Lieutenant Toropko would help to sort out all this junk, as Oleinik called it. *It may help determine Stepanov's physical condition and predict his next move after losing another partner. This son-of-a-bitch is becoming a real pain in a neck, isn't he? Not for long, though. He doesn't have the resources or the people to assist him anymore. This could make him even more desperate. And dangerous. We may need to ask Petukh for additional help. He will have no choice but to return to the other address, if he doesn't know we raided that place too. Unless he spots our men watching it—then what?*

Viktor knew he must stop agonizing over things he couldn't control. He had to. He pulled from the desk drawer the shoebox given by his mother with "Dad's stuff" written on it and began rummaging through the pictures and documents. Viktor had already viewed most of them, and he couldn't concentrate on anything but the thought of Stepanov, still at large with his stolen pistol.

Then, suddenly, some familiar pages grabbed his attention—the letter from his dad's old friend General Arutyunov, Viktor's mentor while he studied in Leningrad. He meant to read it several times before but didn't have a chance. Then he totally forgot about it.

Viktor read page after page, totally absorbed, and deeply fascinated by what the man had written—a man personally involved in implementing the policies of the country's most powerful security apparatus. After finishing the letter Viktor started shaking; it was familiar: he needed a drink. A shot of vodka would do, to subside the madness. But it was out of the question.   So, Viktor pulled the lighter from his pocket and dragged over the metal trash can, placing it between his legs. He rolled up the pages and lit them up; the thin paper caught flame quickly.

A phone call interrupted Viktor's feverish actions. He dropped the burning bundle into the bucket and grabbed the phone. Major Oleinik reported his arrival with the arrested woman and the bag of collected evidence. There was a hint of slight sarcasm when asked where Major Vitus wanted to place each of them. Viktor appreciated his colleague's humor especially after spending several hours in brutal cold. However, he wasn't in the mood for a laugh and gave specific directives: the woman was to remain in a temporary holding cell, and the evidence was to be sent immediately to the Forensic Lab.

Viktor didn't plan to talk to Stepanov's girlfriend before Lieutenant Toropko analyzed everything collected in her apartment. Hoping that Nina was already there, he hastily poured some water from a decanter over the fire and headed to the Lab.

Nina Toropko had just arrived. Her face was red, and her eyelashes and eyebrows were covered in frost. She glanced at Viktor and said, "Please turn on the electric heater, will you? I am freezing. What is the matter with you? You look terrible."

"I didn't have a chance to go home at all," Viktor explained. "The operation was a disaster. Stepanov escaped at the last moment. It's still unclear how. Perhaps it was my fault? I wasn't there, and made Oleinik wait too long for the go-ahead."

"Come on, Viktor. You know that outcome was possible. He is a slippery one." Nina tried to reason with him. "Field operations are always unpredictable. As I understand, we have the woman, don't we?"

"That is true—not a bad consolation prize." Viktor smiled for a moment. "I had to call you because the stuff in these bags must be analyzed before I can talk to her. So, let's not waste any time."

"Okay, Comrade Major. I am on it," Nina responded, as she quickly began opening up the evidence.

Soon, Lieutenant Toropko called Major Vitus back to the Lab and presented her findings. All pieces of evidence were laid out on the stainless-steel table, processed, and labeled.

"As you see, there aren't too many relevant items," Nina commented. "I sifted through everything very carefully. Most of the stuff is garbage. Believe me, Major."

"Of course, I believe you, Lieutenant," Viktor nodded and began inspecting one item on the table after another, asking for a more detailed description.

"This pile contains used bandages with bloodstains. I compared these samples with the samples I collected at the crime scene in Izmailovsky. The blood group is the same, and many other chemical elements match too. Everything points to Stepanov."

"So, there is no question it was him. He was at the apartment we raided," Viktor concluded and made some notes in his notebook. "Go on please."

"The next is a few local newspapers. Honestly, I didn't find any significance in any of them."

"Perhaps, they were looking for stories about their assault on the *apteka*?" Viktor speculated. "What else?"

"Here is a pile of oily rags." Nina pointed to it. "I tested them and determined Stepanov used these rags to clean the pistol. The rest of the stuff, as I mentioned before, wasn't interesting, except these theatrical programs. There were three of them. Each one features a different performance. Look at this one—The upcoming Shakespearean play at the Russian Drama Theater. Look at the woman on it."

"It's Katerina." Viktor almost whispered, bringing the program closer to the light. "That son of a bitch! Now I can talk to Stepanov's girlfriend. I am sure she will talk." Viktor was just about to leave.

"Wait, Major. There is one more piece of evidence that might have value. Look at this."

Nina handed Viktor a crumpled scrap of paper.

"Look what is sketched on it—a floor plan. It is quite amateurish, but nevertheless a crude layout." Viktor glanced it over and then placed it between the pages of his notebook as well.

"I'm taking this, Lieutenant. Please don't say anything."

* * *

Major Vitus stared across the interrogation room table at a woman wrapped in a green wool blanket over her long flowery nightshirt. Her dark, grey-streaked hair was a total mess. Her face had drab grayish skin, with a few deep wrinkles on her forehead, and narrow eyes with heavy eyelids that were rather unattractive.

"Please state your first and last name and your age," Viktor began, after looking at the first page of a passport the officers found while searching the woman's apartment.

"You have my passport, Comrade Major, don't you?" She smirked. "Why did your people raid my home and arrest me? I didn't do anything wrong."

"Relax! Let's do this one step at a time," Viktor interrupted her rudely. "First, answer my question, so I can be sure this is, in fact, your document. So, state your name and age. Then we'll talk about your arrest."

"All right, Comrade Major, I will do what you ask." The woman nodded agreeably. "My name is Glasha Kazakova. Actually, my given name is Glafira. I am 38. I reside at—"

"Is this your apartment, or does it belong to someone else?" Viktor interrupted again, just to keep her off balance.

"It belongs to my late husband Pavel Kazakov and me. We came here ten years ago from Stavropol, a city in the Kuban Region. He worked as a lathe machine operator for one of those secret factories until his last day."

"What happened to him?"

"Bad heart, the doctor said. He collapsed next to his lathe. That was almost four years ago." The woman paused, sighing. "The miserable drunk left me with nothing. I couldn't even go west, back to my family."

"So, how do you survive? What do you do for a living?" Viktor sounded sympathetic.

"One of my neighbors, Aunt Olga, got me involved in selling stuff at the flea market—you know, on the black market." Glasha started fidgeting in her chair. "Can you get me a cigarette, Comrade Major?"

"I don't smoke anymore. However, I'll send a guard to fetch a cigarette for you, but only after you answer all my questions. Agreed?"

She changed her tone. "Agreed, dear Nachalnik; you can ask me anything."

"And one more thing. If I catch you lying, you go right back to your cell without a smoke. Understood?" Viktor insisted.

"Yes. Don't worry, Nachalnik, I'll be telling only the truth. Cross my heart." She quickly made the Sign of the Cross over her chest and forehead.

"Who was with you before the Militia came in?" Viktor asked and looked at her fixedly.

"Nobody," she spat out, turning her head away.

"Hey, hey, look into my eyes!" Viktor expected such an answer but pretended he was angry. "You forgot so quickly your promise not to lie, haven't you?"

"Okay, okay, dear Nachalnik, there was someone with me—my boyfriend." Again, the woman was quick to answer. "All of sudden, the man got up from the bed, grabbed his clothes, and vanished. No goodbye, no nothing."

"Just like that? Okay, slow down and tell me more about your mysterious boyfriend. Describe him first." Viktor insisted again.

"He is a big strong man. Handsome too." She smiled, but only for a moment. "Bad temper, though. I am always afraid of him. He can snap your head off easily with his bare hands."

"Does he have a limp and a scar?"

"Yes, Nachalnik, yes. Ivan has a nasty scar on his face, and his left leg is a bit shorter than the other, so he walks a little funny. It looks like you know him, don't you?"

"How did you meet Ivan?" Viktor asked, ignoring her guess.

"We met at the flea market, where else? Come to think of it, I've met all my boyfriends there—since I became a widow, of course." Glasha sounded as if she was surprised.

"How many boyfriends have you had?" Viktor couldn't help but ask her but then lowered his eyes and added. "You don't need to answer that."

"I am not ashamed. Four or five, Nachalnik. It's tough for a single woman without a man, you know, especially one like Vanya," she sighed, smiling.

"So, his name is Ivan? And what about his last name?"

"He never told me his last name. I guess I never asked, either." Glasha paused before continuing. "Ivan picked me up, not the other way around as it usually happens. He told me he needed me to help him. I knew he meant business. So, I did what he told me to do and didn't ask him about nothing."

"What kind of help did he need?" Viktor felt he was getting closer to important information. "Be more specific."

"The moment I brought him home, I realized there was something wrong." Glasha got a worried look on her face. "As soon as his coat was off, I noticed a big wet bloodstain on his shirt and pants. He was bleeding. I insisted that he undress and lie down on the couch, and he didn't object. The poor guy was weak. His skin was losing color, becoming very pale. I recognized immediately there was a bullet wound in his right upper hip area and somewhere else."

"How did you determine there were bullet wounds? You are not a nurse, are you?" Viktor kept probing.

"I had some experience as a nurse. After school, I had extensive training and worked at the local hospital before getting married and moving here. I saw wounds like that." She sounded quite confident. "It wasn't a serious injury; luckily, the bullets went all the way through the flesh without damaging any organs or bones. However, the metal particles from the bullets were still there. The wound hadn't been properly dressed to begin with and had been totally neglected for some time. So, it had become infected. I suggested he needed medical attention, but he refused any doctor's involvement. Ivan expected I would take care of his wound."

"What gave him the idea you could?"

"I must've slipped a few words about my nursing abilities into our conversation during our initial interaction. I wanted to impress the man; you know." Glasha paused for a moment. "Come to think of it now, that is why this son-of-a-bitch picked me in a first-place!"

"So, you regret getting involved with Ivan, do you?"

"Not really, Nachalnik, I do not." It sounded more like a revelation to herself than to the interrogator. "Yes, he made me do things I shouldn't have done, like robbing the *apteka*. And he can be a violent man—often moody and unpredictable. A man with a dark past, I must admit. After all, he shot that poor innocent drugstore attendant. And yet there were moments when I could swear that deep inside, he had a gentle and extremely sensitive soul."

"Gentle and sensitive soul, you say?" Viktor interrupted, becoming angry. "I guess Ivan Stepanov—that is his last name, never told you how he viciously killed innocent people, in cold blood? Including his previous girlfriend and his elderly relative? He tried to kill me too."

"Oh my God!" Glasha exclaimed in desperation and covered her face with her hands. "I can't believe it's true, Nachalnik. I can't believe it."

"I shouldn't tell you that, but I am glad I did." Viktor paused to calm down. "Unfortunately, it is true. I am not playing games with you, Citizen Kazakova. And you know what is more unfortunate? He will kill again if we don't stop him!"

Glasha kept covering her face. Leaning forward, she put her head on the table and began crying hysterically. Viktor called the guard and asked him to bring a pack of cigarettes. When the door was closed, Viktor stretched his right hand and gently tapped the woman's shoulder, "Listen, I understand your frustration. However, you can make things right. Please, help us to catch this killer."

After a rather long pause, she raised her teary face and asked, "How do you think I can help? He is very clever, but reticent. He just used me. He didn't tell me much. Most of the day, he usually soaked in the bathtub, nursing his wounds. It didn't change much; the flesh around the wound was getting more and more infected. He constantly ran a high fever. I couldn't help him without antibiotics and dressing materials. After another sleepless night, Ivan ordered me to follow him to a nearby apteka. You know what happened there. That's all I can say."

"I need you to focus for moment. Try to remember any detail, even an insignificant one, which may give us a clue as to where he is now. Let's start with what places Ivan might know about, beside the two we raided yesterday." Viktor let her calm down and concentrate for a moment. "Where else could he have gone to hide?"

"I don't know, Nachalnik, I swear to God." Glasha was still visibly agitated. "He knew only two addresses, mine and my sister-in-law's place. She trusted me with a key to her apartment while spending the winter at her mom's place in Stavropol. We never stayed anywhere else. Although a few times Ivan would muster up the strength to go somewhere for a couple of hours. Sometimes in the day, sometimes in the evening. I noticed each time he would dress differently. He never shared where he was going."

"Did he ever tell you about his plans, what he would do next after getting healthier?" Viktor decided to approach the subject from a different angle but stopped when he heard a knock on the door. "Please come in, Sergeant."

The guard entered the room with a pack of "Pamir" filter less cigarettes and some matches. Viktor thanked him and waved him to leave.

"You see, Citizen Kazakova, I kept my promise." He pulled one cigarette from the pack and lit it with the match. Then he handed it to Glasha. "You can smoke. It may help you to calm your nerves and concentrate on what I am asking you."

"Thank you, Nachalnik, thank you. It will definitely help." She smiled before inhaling the first deep drag and closed her eyes in a rather exaggerated look of pleasure.

After Glasha exhaled a long plume of smoke, she opened her eyes and unexpectedly declared, "Now I know for sure he will kill again."

"Can you be more specific? Do you know who his next victim will be?" Viktor asked anxiously. Suddenly, he felt like he couldn't catch a breath.

"This I am not sure, Nachalnik. Except, most likely, it will be a woman—a rather young woman." Glasha looked at Major Vitus victoriously and forcefully exhaled another puff of smoke.

"Explain." Before saying it, Viktor tried to take hold of his anxiety. "How do you know this?"

"After one of his evening excursions, Ivan returned with these theater programs." She began carefully choosing words as if she were afraid to say something wrong. "He sat at the table and started drawing something with a pencil on a page he ripped from my old notebook. Apparently, he didn't like how it turned out, so he crumpled it and threw it on the floor. Then he picked up one of the programs and stared at it for a rather long time. I tried to find out what it was all about, but he angrily protested, chasing me away from the table. However, I heard what he whispered: 'I'll kill you, bitch!'"

"Was it this young woman he promised to kill?" Viktor pulled the program he kept between the pages of his notebook and laid it in front of Glasha. "Take a good look."

She nervously extinguished her cigarette butt on the table surface and glanced at the booklet.

"Yes, Nachalnik. It's her. Only, I don't know who she is, swear to God." Glasha crossed herself over not once, but twice.

"I believe you. Relax now. You've helped us a lot." Viktor was convinced he had extracted from this woman everything she knew about Stepanov. "Nevertheless, you still will be charged as a participant in the crimes of armed robbery and attempted murder. I hope you understand."

"I didn't mean to commit this crime, Nachalnik, I was forced. Didn't I tell you already?" She began sobbing again.

"Yes, you did, and this might be a mitigating circumstance, which will be taken into consideration by the prosecutor," Viktor informed her calmly. "I'll talk to him, though, I promise. Now you will be returned to your detention cell. You can keep the cigarettes."

Chapter 21

The Major ran upstairs to his office. His heart pumped blood to his brain so hard that his head felt as if it was about to explode. A feeling of impending disaster threatened to overwhelm him. He realized now it was up to him and only him to figure out how to protect Katerina and eventually catch this vengeful monster. However, to do that, he needed to take hold of his fear, to put aside his personal emotions and think rationally. There was enough useful information at his disposal. He must connect the dots.

As soon as he got behind his desk, Viktor put all his notes from the interrogation and the other relevant pieces of evidence on the table in front of him and closed his eyes, leaning all the way back in his chair. He put himself in Stepanov's shoes, asking what had changed since yesterday. And Stepanov would answer: *I have no more warm shelter, no partner in crime, no woman nurturing my injured body or catering to my needs. I am a wounded lone wolf in the wilderness, hunted again by the law. I am a killer with the blood of several people on my hands, people who threatened to reveal my identity. I am a desperate man with nothing to live for, driven only by vengeance toward the person who, in my mind, stole everything I held dear to my heart all these years. It doesn't matter that this person is my half-sister.*

Yes, she is his sister. Although some pieces of the puzzle were still missing, Viktor had finally concluded that Ivan Stepanov was Ivan Rogozhin, the son of Fyodor Rogozhin and half-brother of Katerina Rogozhina. It was Ivan Rogozhin who, in a rage, viciously murdered his own father because he had failed to save him from prison. And then his father again refused to accept him, to help him cover up his crime. And if that wasn't enough, the stubborn old man rubbed his nose in the existence of his other child, a daughter from another woman, whom he raised alone, whom he loved and cherished - a daughter to help him forget his evil firstborn, a daughter of whom he was proud.

Viktor's theory was no longer just the fruit of his imagination. He hadn't told anyone about his discovery yet, waiting for the last piece of information he expected to receive from the village where Ivan Stepanov had been born. But Viktor was sure all additional details would confirm it. Why was it so important? Because he knew that no one could solve a murder or convict a murderer without presenting a motive. Of course, the physical evidence was equally important, but the proven motive was the foundation of the whole case. He learned this from his teachers, the best jurists in the country at Leningrad University, and from his own father. Every homicide investigation starts and ends by determining the possible motive, period.

Still, the perpetrator of a crime must be in your custody. Isn't that so, Comrade Major Vitus? Viktor continued the conversation in his head. To catch him, I need to anticipate his next move. But how? What would be my move in his place? Okay, I know what is left for me to do: hurt, even kill Katerina. The question remains—how? I tried to get into her apartment. I even sketched a floor plan, but my first attempt failed because the security in her building was too tight.

Suddenly, it dawned on Viktor, — I assumed this sketch was about Katya's apartment. What if it was meant to depict some other place, where it would be easier to mount an assault? How stupid of me not to consider such an option! But where?

Viktor opened his eyes and reached for the wrinkled piece of paper with pencil scribbles on it. He flipped the sketch every which way, yet, for the life of him, he could not guess what place it might represent. Desperation was beginning to settle in when he heard the steps of someone approaching his desk. It was Lieutenant Nina Toropko, standing behind him and looking over his shoulder.

"Oh, I was thinking about this sketch too. I couldn't get it out of my mind. On my way home, I finally remembered where I had seen a similar layout. So, I returned to tell you that, Comrade Major."

"Where?" Viktor asked, moving his eyes away from the tatter toward Nina.

"The backstage of the Drama Theater," she said slowly. "Remember when I told you about my visit to Katerina the other day? While I waited by the dressing room to see her, I noticed on the corridor wall a framed fire escape plan, like you find in any public building. So, I guess I stared at this drawing for a few minutes."

"And you memorized it?" Viktor couldn't hide his skepticism.

"Yes, Comrade Major." It was hard to determine whether Lieutenant Toropko replied casually.

"Remarkable! Is that what they call a 'photographic memory', Lieutenant?"

"I am not sure if I would call it that, Comrade Major. But my visual memory was always very good."

"Very good is an understatement! If you are correct, your memory is quite extraordinary!"

"I appreciated your praise, Comrade Major. To answer your question: yes, both images have stuck in my mind, but only in the last thirty minutes did I realize how close they are," Nina explained.

"So, this means that Ivan Rogozhin plans to attack Katerina where her security protection is the most vulnerable… in the Theater."

"Wait. You meant Stepanov, didn't you?"

"His real name is Ivan Rogozhin. Stepanov is a name he took from a dead soldier." Viktor paused for a moment. "I'll tell you about that later. Now we have to make sure his plan will fail."

"If Stepanov is Rogozhin, he is Katya's half-brother, isn't he?" The discovery stunned Nina.

"Then why does he want to attack her? He still thinks she has the stolen gold, doesn't he?"

"He might think that, but this is not what drives him," Viktor replied. "He is obsessed with revenge, and Katerina is the only target left. I became quite positive about his state of mind after talking to the woman who spent the last week or so with him."

"What is your plan, Comrade Major?" The Lieutenant sounded extremely concerned. "We might be pressed for time."

"I am afraid we are, especially after we flushed out this wounded animal into the cold," Viktor agreed, then continued to analyze the developing situation out loud. "The fact that he drew the floor plan of the theater's backstage area tells us he was there in person at least once. This means he can easily find his way in there again."

He paused and slapped his forehead with his hand, exclaiming: "He is in the Theater already! It was his overnight hideout. We must warn Captain Mukhin immediately. Katerina must stay home until Rogozhin is apprehended!" Viktor glanced at his wristwatch, feverishly grabbed the telephone, and began dialing. After six or seven rings on the other end of the line, Viktor realized nobody would answer his call. He slammed down the mouthpiece angrily.

"They already left. I can't believe it. I must run to the Theater! Lieutenant, call Colonel Guzyev and alert him of the situation. Find Captain Golovin so he can provide backup over there with Captain Oleinik's field personnel. Do it quickly, Lieutenant!"

He grabbed his coat, hat, and weapons, and then ran downstairs, where he hoped Sergeant Uvalov would be waiting with his *kozyol* warmed up and ready to go. His heart raced, and his head pounded like a war drum. The thought that he might be too late terrified him; he could lose this battle.

Viktor found his car at the entrance door, already running and enveloped in a steamy cloud coming from the exhaust pipe. He jumped in the front seat: "To the Theater! Hurry up, Petya!"

On the way, Viktor dumped his heavy winter coat on the back seat. Next, he checked his pistol and his revolver for ammunition and slid the Nagant into the holster hanging under his uniform jacket at his left shoulder. The backup Makarov went back into the holster hidden inside his right high boot.

"Where is your weapon, Sergeant?" he asked his driver. "You will need to back me up until reinforcements arrive, understand? Park the car at the back door in the alley and leave it running. And be careful inside."

"Yes, Comrade Major, I am ready."

When the *kozyol* pulled up at the back door of the Drama Theater, they noticed a man in the alley holding a shovel. He looked like a *dvornik*, a maintenance worker. He seemed stunned by the sudden arrival of the car, but seeing the Militiamen jump from the car, he came out of his stupor and pointed to the door.

"Someone inside is shooting a gun."

"Step aside, papasha, and be on the lookout. When you see more Militia, show them where we are," Viktor instructed calmly.

The back door was wedged open with a broken-off wooden plank. Viktor slowly pulled the doorknob and let the Sergeant in through the open crack. Then he followed him into the darkness of the backstage corridor. Why wasn't it lit up? Perhaps it was too early in the morning, and the building manager hadn't switched all the lights on yet. Or perhaps someone deliberately kept this area dark. They'll find out soon enough. For now, they crept forward carefully, keeping as close as possible to the opposite walls. Soon, the corridor made a ninety-degree turn. Vitus halted and peered around the corner, his revolver in hand. Pyotr stopped across the path a bit behind him with his own Nagant at the ready and cocked.

The silence seemed so fragile and frightening. Viktor and Pyotr both took a deep breath and then moved to a new position around the corner. They found themselves in a wider hall with several doors facing each other. Dim light from a corridor further down took away their cover of darkness. Near one of the doors across the hall, they saw a man lying on the floor, face down in a puddle of blood. While Pyotr covered him, Viktor knelt and checked the man's pulse. There was none—the man was dead but still warm; he had been shot very recently. Viktor lifted his head and immediately recognized him as Alexandre Garanin, the Drama Theater's artistic director. The bullet that killed him had entered his left eye and gone through his brain; a stream of blood trickled from a jagged hole in the back of his skull. The man they were after was a crack shot!

As soon as the Major straightened up his body, Pyotr pointed to a trail of blood leading into the next corridor. Viktor noticed bloody footprints, small and pointy, most likely belonging to a woman.

They could be Katya's, Viktor thought, as his heart dropped to the pit of his stomach. She may be wounded. But where is Mukhin, or some other officer guarding her? Perhaps it was he who had been wounded and yet shielded Katya from the assailant's fire? He prayed it was true, wondering where they could be now.

Reaching the next corridor, they realized it led out onto the stage. They would be totally exposed there, sitting ducks for anyone who knew even a little about shooting a gun. On Viktor's signal, they quickly dashed across the darkest part of the corridor, hugging the wall until they reached the entrance to the stage. Viktor saw the entire area in front of the backdrop, the whole stage, the narrow orchestra pit, and the front seats of the house. But he still saw no sign of the survivors from the shootout.

Then, as his eyes adjusted to the brighter light, he noticed the heavy curtain across the stage swaying slightly. Someone was behind it. Viktor signaled to Uvalov to watch that area closely. Then, out of the corners of his eye, he saw moving shadows near the stage steps just to their side.

Moving instinctively, Vitus jumped the distance from the corner of the stage. In midair, he heard the loud pop and felt a sting in his right hip as he crashed into the front of the orchestra pit, rolling onto his back. For a moment the sharp pain paralyzed him. Viktor struggled to stay conscious as he spotted one of the shadows moving toward him. His hand struggled to find his revolver, but the pain made it hard to focus. Things were going black, as he cursed his own weakness. When he was finally able to wield himself to full consciousness, Vitus saw Katya hovering over him, trying to stop the bleeding from his wound. Viktor touched her arm, indicating that he wanted her to help him to sit up. Without a word, she propped him against the outer wall of the orchestra pit and turned her attention back to the wound.

"Are you okay, Katya?" Viktor whispered. "You need to leave here immediately. Do you hear me?"

"I am fine," she replied in a very low but strangely calm voice... "Mukhin is badly hurt. He tried to get me away, but…. I am not sure he'll make it."

"We saw Garanin in the corridor," Viktor continued in a whisper. "He is dead. What happened?"

"We arrived as always. Garanin met us at the door of my dressing room." Katya spoke erratically.

"A very large man came out of nowhere and began shooting. Alexandre stepped in front of me. He saved my life. Mukhin shot this man twice but was wounded, too. The big man retreated and hid behind the curtain, while we found cover behind the stairs. Mukhin couldn't go any further."

"Can you tell me how many times this man fired his gun?" Viktor closed his eyes, trying to gather his strength.

Katya paused to think for a moment. "Five, I guess. Yes, the last shot was at your driver. So yes, five shots. I'm not sure! Oh, my God, I can't stop your bleeding!"

"I'll be fine." Viktor tried to sound reassuring. "Katya, dear, listen to me carefully. You must get out of here. Pyotr and I will apprehend him. Use the main door. Call for help. Wait for my signal, and then run. Run!"

"I am afraid Pyotr is down too," Katya informed him. "Is this man the one who killed my father?"

"Yes, he is." Viktor sounded confident. "It doesn't change anything—you must get out of here. Do you hear me? Please prop me up a little higher so I can see the stage. Then wait for my signal. My pistol. Where is my fucking pistol?"

Looking around, Katya picked up the Nagant that lay a meter away and put it in Viktor's hand. Then she grabbed a folding chair and pushed it against the inner wall of the orchestra pit. Using the back of the chair, Viktor pulled his body up with both hands and put his left knee onto the seat. From this position, Viktor could see over the edge of the stage while presenting a minimal target.

Now he began calculating how many bullets were left in the clip of the gun Ivan Rogozhin was using. *Let's see: two shots in the pharmacy and five shots here, according to Katya. So, there was one more bullet left at his disposal—unless he got hold of additional ammunition, which was very doubtful. Yes, it must be his last bullet!*

He peered over the edge, quickly scanning the entire stage. Momentarily, he heard a loud pop and saw a flash from the gun muzzle. The bullet zinged by his right ear, less than an inch away. He smelled the hot gunpowder. Viktor wrenched his head down, thanking God that Rogozhin had missed. He signaled to Katya to run, then pulled the trigger of his weapon again and again, sending a hail of bullets in the direction of the flash. Katya scurried up the aisle, disappearing behind the heavy auditorium door. Viktor stopped shooting and exhaled with relief. *Now Katya is safe.*

Viktor peered again over the edge of the stage and froze. Rogozhin, covered in blood, his gun in hand was crawling quickly towards him, his bearded face twisted into a murderous scowl. With no time to think, Viktor pushed himself off the wall just as Rogozhin lunged for his throat. He tumbled from the chair backwards to the floor, landing painfully on his back, pulling the trigger.

The bullet struck Rogozhin's shoulder, near the neck. He shrieked like a wounded beast. Then, the momentum still pushing him forward, he slid off the edge of the stage, hitting the floor hard with his large, heavy body. The two bleeding men lay no more than a meter apart, their guns leveled at one another. They pulled their triggers almost simultaneously.

Both guns clicked impotently. *Dammit,* Vitas swore at his own incompetence. *Why didn't I count my own rounds?!* Rogozhin smiled and let his empty gun drop to the floor. With a low roar, the big man began crawling toward Viktor, clutching at his legs and reaching for something in his own belt.

A knife! I'm a dead man. Viktor's mind raced. His shattered right hip had left his leg in an awkwardly twisted position, and he suddenly remembered the spare Makarov in his right boot. He grabbed at the pistol, thanking God - again - that he'd made sure to chamber and leave the safety off. But it was too late as Rogozhin was upon him, clutching at his throat and raising his blade high over his head for the killing stroke. *Crack! Crack!* The Makarov barked twice, and the bullets ripped through Ivan's torso just as his huge hand brought the blade down on Viktor's chest. He stumbled backwards. Then, both men collapsed…

Viktor regained consciousness first. He had no idea how much time had passed since he fainted. Propping himself up on his elbows, he dragged his body back to the stage wall and leaned against it. He inspected himself, finding the knife wound in his upper chest, bleeding. But it was the wound in his hip that was the real issue. He was losing a lot of blood.

He unbuttoned his jacket, ripped a long strip from his white linen undershirt, crumpled it into a tight ball, and pressed it against the hole in his hip. With effort he repeated the action and applied the second strip to the knife wound. How long could he last? Five minutes, if he was lucky.

Viktor cursed quietly and looked around. Ivan Rogozhin was a motionless hulk about two meters away. A thick gray lock of his long hair covered his mouth, moving up and down. For some inexplicable reason, Viktor felt relief as he realized the man was still alive, even with the blood stained knife still in his hand.

Viktor picked up his Makarov, knowing that he had plenty of ammo left to finish his opponent, who was bleeding from at least four wounds that he could see. Three of them, from his guns, Viktor thought with a tinge of pride. Then, he began considering whether help would arrive before they both bled out.

Just then, Rogozhin stirred. He opened his eyes and looked at Vitus, who was now propped against the stage wall, gun in hand, pointing unsteadily in his direction. Ivan tossed his knife aside with a whispered profanity. Then he rolled over and crawled to the stage wall, propping his back up against it, mirroring Viktor. They sat like this for some time, with only the toppled chair between them, until Rogozhin spoke in a calm baritone voice: "You got me, Nachalnik. You really did. You can celebrate if you survive. Good work, Nachalnik."

Viktor leveled his Makarov and replied: "Tell me, Rogozhin, why did you kill your father?"

"I didn't mean to. I guess I was drunk," Rogozhin answered after a pause. "He betrayed me twice, though. I hated his righteousness. He was always a two-faced Godly man. Why am I telling you all this? You wouldn't understand it anyhow."

"Try me, Ivan. I know something about difficult fathers. And I know a lot about your father," Viktor said calmly.

"Then you should know that my father treated my gravely ill mother like dirt. He chose his God over my mother; he chose his God over me too. We didn't rape that poor girl. I told him! My cousin Dima told him, but he refused to believe us; his own kin!" Ivan almost choked. "He threw us to the wolves. Our lives were fucked ever since."

"Did you know that he spent almost seven years behind a barbed wire fence not far from here?" Viktor countered.

"What for?"

"For nothing. For being a godly man, as you put it." Viktor wanted to see his reaction. "It was there, by the way, that he met the woman who later became the mother of his daughter."

"Hmm—interesting story, Major. It doesn't change my feelings about him or my half-sister."

Viktor took a moment to digest this admission in silence, and then asked, "Did you kill Stepanov to get his identity?"

"He was already dead. We were hit by our own artillery shelling. What do they call it—friendly fire?" Rogozhin paused again, perhaps gathering his strength. He sounded weak. "Hey, Nachalnik, if I was feeling better, I would tell you more about that terrible war—you only know what is written in your schoolbooks."

"So, tell me, Ivan. Nothing else for us to do." Viktor suggested.

Rogozhin went silent. With effort, Viktor raised his left hand and looked at his wristwatch. It was only a quarter after eight. The entire incident had taken no more than ten minutes. Jesus! It had seemed like a lifetime.

Where was Katya now? he wondered. *Did her call for help get a response? Were the medics and reinforcements already on the way? They better be here sooner than later! The lives of several people depended on it. Petya! Petya's been shot! Is he alive?* He closed his eyes and took a deep breath, trying not to waste any strength. He needed to stay conscious as long as possible. Rogozhin's strangely calm voice brought Viktor back to the moment again.

"You have no idea what war is all about. My cousin and I volunteered to join the Red Army on the second day after the war broke out. They didn't trust us. They put us in the hands of the NKVD and placed us in its *Zagrad Otryad*, the so-called special defensive squad. The first few months of the war, when it was total chaos, we were ordered to shoot our own soldiers - imagine that - just because they dropped their rifles and ran when the Germans first attacked. It was awful; a lot of us lost our sanity right there and then." Rogozhin paused to gain strength. "Later, in the winter of '41 to '42, when the Red Army finally mounted the counterattack near Moscow and Stalingrad, they used our *shtrafbat* detachment as a smokescreen. It was mostly former convicts like us, pure cannon fodder. We lost 85% of our men. My cousin Dima was killed. So, when I saw a chance, I took it. You would have done the same if you were in my place."

Viktor couldn't find the words to respond. He had to admit: Ivan did get the short end of the stick.

"I was wounded there too; got this nasty limp and this ugly scar," Rogozhin continued. "But that turned out to be my ticket out of that hell, a way to start a new life."

"And what a life it has been!" Viktor said sarcastically; the old interrogation technique to provoke a reaction. "Theft, murder, God knows what else."

"You have no right to judge me, Major. It was my life on the line. I did what I had to do to survive." The scowling smile came back to his face. "I should've killed you too when I had a chance. It was my mistake."

"Perhaps it was," Viktor persisted, "Regardless, here we are now, bleeding to death side by side. Seems like a perfect time for the truth."

For the next minute, there was silence, Finally, Ivan coughed a few times, spit out a gob of bloody phlegm, and then asked, "What truth do you want, Major?"

"You know."

"That stinking rat inspector had some documents which could prove that I wasn't Stepanov." Rogozhin began his confession. "I had to make him disappear. Even Grishka didn't know about it. At least, I thought he didn't. Now, my girlfriend—who, as you put it, loved me—she was a real piece of work. She fooled me. This bitch somehow found out about our loot and got this crazy idea to poison us, so she and her father could take it. Thank God I figured out her plan first. We buried her alive in the *Taiga*."

"Why did you kill shift-master Mazur?" Viktor asked.

"I didn't kill him—Grishka did," Ivan replied. "He had a beef with Mazur regarding some woman. Grishka also suspected him of spying on us. At the end of the shift, he lured him into the woods away from the rest of the crew and hit him a few times on the head with a shovel. He didn't bother to hide Mazur's body because we decided to split that night anyway. This is the truth, Major Vitus."

Frankly, none of this proved very revealing to Viktor. It was just further proof of the viciousness and brutality of those criminals. *How easily they shift the blame to each other and, at the same time, how casually and proudly they brag about their evil doings. It is disgusting. It doesn't make any difference who killed whom, although Ivan's version of murdering shift-master Mazur is more plausible,* Viktor supposed; he was certain that his colleagues in Blagoveschensk had never considered this twist in the disappearance of Ivan's girlfriend.

However, none of that mattered to Viktor. He wanted to get one last honest answer from Rogozhin. He mustered all his strength to remain conscious just a little longer.

"Why did you decide to go after Katerina? Do you still think she has your stolen gold? Or that she ever had it?"

"Back at Izmailovsky, when we couldn't find our loot after that last confrontation with my father, I had this idea," Rogozhin explained with some hesitation. "It was logical that Fyodor would only pass on such valuable stuff to someone he really trusted. His daughter was the one. So, I told Grishka we had to go to Khabarovsk and look for her as quickly as we could. That's when your guys wounded me and grabbed my partner. That's how I ended up in Khabarovsk alone with no connections and no help."

"How did you track Katerina in Khabarovsk?" Viktor interrupted.

"I had her picture from the old man's house, and he bragged once that she was an actress. I noticed theatrical posters all over the city. I recognized her. Finding where she lived was simple. But when I saw that she was tightly guarded, I knew my loot was gone."

"And yet, you continued pursuing her. Why?"

"Because I hated her, and I couldn't let her live!" Ivan raised his voice for the first time.

"Why did you want to kill her, Ivan? Katya is your sister by your father; doesn't that mean anything to you?" Viktor's voice was fading fast.

"She is nothing to me! A welp from a woman who took my father away. She stole everything from me. She stole my whole life."

"Did you really want to murder an innocent person? A woman of your own blood?" Viktor was barely holding it together.

"Major, you wanted the truth? Here's the truth," Ivan paused and looked intensely into Viktor's eyes. "If I could do it all over again, I would kill that bitch and you along with her. And I swear to you right now that if God - or the Devil - should spare my life today, I will not rest until she is dead."

Ivan smiled again, leaned his head against the wall and closed his eyes.

The room began to spin and grow dark. Major Vitus took a deep breath before consciousness left him. Then he raised the Makarov and fired a single shot, point-blank, at Ivan Rogozhin's head...

Chapter 22

Viktor opened his eyes and immediately felt he had seen all this just a few days ago: the same off-white ceiling and square light green ceramic tiles for the walls, the same small windows. Only now, there was no daylight in those windows, and the two electric bulbs hanging in the middle of the room were dimmed. Viktor's upper body was elevated and propped up by several pillows. He tried to move, but heavy bandages across his neck and torso restricted him. His left arm was securely tightened to the bed rail. A needle stuck from it, connecting him by narrow plastic tube to several bottles hanging on hooks attached to metal poles standing next to the bed.

How long had he been in this room? He had no idea. He felt lightheaded and nauseous. In such murky surroundings, his eyes hurt. He closed them, and his head went into a spin, which made him even more nauseous. Viktor threw up some slimy, bloody fluid and began coughing. The nurse on duty heard his loud cough and rushed in.

"Relax, relax!" she said, helping Viktor to straighten his upper body. "Let me clean you up, dear boy. Now, drink this water slowly. Good boy. Everything will be fine, you'll see."

When his cough subsided, she lowered Viktor back on the pillow and gently tucked the blanket around him. She was an older woman, perhaps in her late fifties, with a round face, kind smile, and soft hands.

She introduced herself. "My name is Galina Pavlovna; I am your night shift nurse; you can call for me any time. And now, go back to sleep. You need a lot of rest, Sonny!"

"Wait, what day is it?" Viktor asked.

"Tuesday, November 29. Six o'clock in the morning," the nurse replied calmly and touched Viktor's forehead with her palm. "You are still running a slight fever, Sonny. I'll bring you a couple of aspirins."

"Thanks. But first, can you tell me what happened?"

"Doctor Bolshakov will tell you everything you want to know later in the morning, okay?" Galina Pavlovna informed him. "He and two other surgeons operated on you and on your fellow Militiamen all day Saturday and Sunday. I know only that you lost a lot of blood and were unconscious until now."

"You mentioned my fellows—how are they?" Viktor wouldn't let her leave.

"Not much different from you, Sonny, not much. The doctor hopes you all will survive, God willing." She crossed herself and hurriedly left the room to fetch the medicine Viktor needed.

She must be a very religious person, Viktor thought, closing his eyes again. This rather short conversation with the nurse left him tired. He tried to sort out the last events he remembered until Nurse returned with the pills and a cup of water. Then Viktor dozed off again.

* * *

Boris Andreyevich Bolshakov, the head surgeon of the city hospital, and two of his colleagues, Aleksandre Moiseyevich Gurevich and Yaroslav Dmitriyovich Zheleznyak, started their routine morning rounds in Viktor's room.

"Hello, Viktor Raymondovich. It doesn't happen very often that I operate on the same patient twice within a few days." Doctor Bolshakov greeted the Major with a smile. "Are you looking for trouble, or is trouble looking for you? Don't bother—I think I know the answer. How are you feeling?"

"A bit woozy. Otherwise, I am alive." Viktor assured him.
"You are not out of the woods yet after losing so much blood." Bolshakov carefully inspected Viktor's bandages. "I took two bullets out of you but stopping the bleeding from that new knife wound was actually the hardest part. We used a lot of blood transfusion. I guess in the next day or two, we should see how good my needlework was."
"Thank you, Doctor," Viktor replied with sincere gratitude. "I thought there was only one bullet wound, in my hip, but you said you had removed two bullets..."

"Something like this often happens in the heat of battle, so to speak, Comrade Major."

Bolshakov sounded a little puzzled too. "The second bullet was lodged in your left shoulder. It could've been a ricochet bullet. I am not a forensic expert. You will get them to keep as souvenirs. For now, all you have to do is rest. Understood?"

"Yes, Doctor. Can you tell me, though, how are Mukhin and Uvalov doing?"

"I'm sorry Major, but Comrade Mukhin did not survive his surgery; he had lost too much blood and there was massive internal damage. We did everything in our power…"

Viktor was not surprised. He recalled seeing Mukhin in the theater, and his motionless body seemed already dead. What surprised Viktor was how emotionless he felt at this moment. Then he remembered Freckle.

"How is Sergeant Uvalor?"

"With Sergeant Uvalov... There was only one wound. However, the bullet was lodged in his lower spine. If we try to extract it, it may result a complete paralysis. The next few days will tell. We are optimistic that we can save his life, but the likelihood of the Sergeant walking again is… low."

"And what happened to the fugitive?" Viktor asked casually. "Did you fix him?"

"The fugitive is quite dead, Major."

Bolshakov smiled and left the room, with Gurevich a step behind him.
Viktor fell back on his pillow and instantly descended into a dreamless unconsciousness.

* * *

The following three days were a blur of activity. With a constantly changing cadre of nurses, doctors, and visitors. Viktor's mother and sister appeared and disappeared at regular intervals bringing food, news and constant concern. The attention made Viktor uncomfortable; he hated his helplessness and the worry he brought to his family. Though his mind was often in a hazy, drug-induced semi-consciousness, he clearly remembered the excitement with which his sister presented the news of receiving a confirmation for an interview at OVIR — the Department of Registration and Visas.

Katya's presence was somehow both calming and exhilarating to him. Her melodic voice, the subtle smell of her perfume and her smile worked miracles for his general state of mind. But between the visits and the constant prodding of the nurses and doctors, Viktor drifted in and out of a deep narcotic sleep and the dream that had been haunting him.

* * *

He floated over the *Taiga*, but so low he could touch the tips of the pines and spruces. A patchy fog prevented him from seeing anything between the trees below him. Suddenly, the masses of white cotton broke up, revealing the glassy surface of the swampy permafrost. It was impossible to say whether this surface was ice or just water. Right beneath it, he could see hundreds of faces. He flew for some distance and couldn't recognize any of them, although their wide-open eyes seemed to ask the same question: *why?*

He tried to stop the dream, but it was no use. He kept floating in total silence, until an image of a handsome old man with a long, snow-white mane and beard appeared before him. His naked, muscular body, washed in white, extended from the trunk of a strong pine. It was Fyodor Rogozhin. An ax was lodged in the back of his head, but he was alive. He glanced up at Viktor with a sad smile. He turned his head in the direction of another nearby tree. The pale, naked form of his father, Raymond Vitus, extended from its trunk. Despite a bullet hole in his temple, he was also alive, smiling sadly. He pointed to the next living statue, in which Viktor recognized General Arutyunov.

What does all this mean? Viktor kept thinking. *Do they want to tell me something?* There was nobody to explain it to him. Some of those poor people below him weren't completely swallowed by the swamp: their heads and torsos stuck out from the surface, their hands waving in a desperate call for help.

In horror, Viktor began to recognize the faces below. There was Melekhov and his wife, Alyona! Not far away, he noticed Nina Toropko, Captain Nesterenko and his wife Lyuba, his driver Pyotr, and many others—some he had known for a long time, some he had just met.

Why are they all here? He thought again. *What was the meaning of all this? What must I do?*

Viktor couldn't help them. He had no control of his weightless body; he had no voice, nor could he hear their voices.

He was suddenly closer to the surface of the permafrost—closer to the faces. Now he could better see their features, their moving lips. He could no longer see Rogozhin, Raymond Vitus, or Arutyunov; new personalities showed up as extensions of the pine's trunks. Some were familiar to him.

Viktor recognized his grandfather, Alfred Vitus, as he remembered him from the old photographs. Slowly passing through the patchy fog, he noticed the fading visions of Dzerzhinsky, Lenin, and Kirov. They all had that same sad smile. This time, the dream was somehow both more real and more mystical.

Then, he saw Yulia. He recognized her immediately. Her broken body was visible under the shimmering surface. Viktor could see a web of blood vessels through her skin. His first impulse was to dive down, grab her, and pull her out of this swamp. But just like before, he could do nothing.

*   *   *

His dream was interrupted by a touch on his arm. It was Nurse Nadya, who whispered in his ear, "I am really sorry, but you have a visitor."

"Visitor? Who?" Viktor reluctantly opened his eyes. "You said no visitors after ten, didn't you?"

"Yes, I did. It is the rule, but this is not a regular visitor." She waved her head in the direction of the door and helped Viktor move his upper body so he could see too.

Melekhov stood still at the entrance to the room, dressed in his full General's uniform.
"My apologies, Comrade Vitus, for such a late visit. I realize you should've been resting by now."

Nurse Nadya jumped in before Viktor could even react. "It's all right, Comrade General. Patient Vitus needs to take his medicine and have some cleaning up before going to sleep."

"I see. Shall I wait?"

"No, no. You can remove your coat and sit here, Comrade General." She pulled the chair closer to the bed. "What I have to do isn't going to take long."

By now, Viktor was totally awake. There was a smile on his face, as if in apology for the bossy woman. The General smiled back, letting him know he understood his intention. Melekhov sat down and leaned back in his chair. The nurse left the room in haste.

The two men looked at one another in silence for... to Viktor, at least, it felt like an eternity.

"Here it goes…" he thought to himself and broke the impasse.

"Comrade General," he began formally, "I, of course, knew this conversation was inevitable after what had transpired. First, I want to say that I deeply appreciate your patronage and protection over the past few years. It was more than I deserved." Melekhov's face remained neutral. He nodded but remained silent. Viktor nodded back, took a deep drink of water from his glass, and continued:

"My actions in the theater along with the actions that led up to what happened in the theater were inexcusable. I disobeyed direct orders, I endangered my colleagues, and - to my eternal shame - committed what amounts to… murder, Comrade General. I am fully prepared to face the consequences, whatever they may be."

Melekhov's reaction was surprising to Viktor. He held up his hand to stop his monologue and furrowed his brow, more in annoyance than anger:

"Comrade Major, I'm severely confused by what you are saying; perhaps the heavy dose of medication you are on is distorting your perception of reality…"

"General, please allow me to finish…"

"There is nothing to finish, Major!" The general raised his voice slightly, but remained poised, "Your actions in the theater were nothing short of heroic. You not only saved the lives of your fellow officers - along with the lives of involved civilians, you - with minimal regard for your own safety, I may add, also neutralized a dangerous multiple murderer who was on a crime spree that would have claimed many more lives…"

"I shot an unarmed, wounded man, Uncle Misha! In cold blood."

"You did no such thing, Major!" The General's voice was harder now, more forceful. No warmth or personal feelings shone through his words. "You acted appropriately and - indeed - heroically. I am personally recommending you for a commendation. You will be promoted and decorated for your bravery under fire. I will also predict that the events of the previous day and your selfless actions will be taught to young Militia officers for decades to come. You are a hero, Viktor.

Before Viktor could muster a reply, Melekhov stood up, draped his heavy overcoat over his left arm and stepped briskly toward the door. Then he half-turned toward the speechless Viktor and said with quiet authority: "Rest, Viktor. Stop blaming yourself, and don't ever bring up this idiocy again. This conversation… and this case is over. By the way, I've just met Citizen Rogozhina in the waiting room," he said casually. "She is quite stunning, I must admit. She seemed very concerned about your speedy recovery."

The door closed behind him decisively, leaving Viktor confused and exhausted. He needed to shut himself off from the turmoil and let his mind idle for a while. He closed his eyes, hoping to descend gradually into a long, sound sleep that would heal his body and soul. But it wasn't meant to be. The *taiga* brought his mind back to where it wanted him.

When he woke up in swat, his thoughts reverted to his family. He didn't pay enough attention to mom and Raisa. They might leave the country very soon. This bothered him a lot. Yesterday, he practically ignored Leonid. Did he go back to New Urgal or decide to stay here one more day? All these questions—Viktor wished he had definite answers for each of them, but he did not.

He desperately tried to put these thoughts from his mind, replacing them with images of Katerina or his mother. But other images kept coming back every time Viktor closed his eyes. And with them, the dreadful, bone-chilling dream returned as well.

This time he flew lower, much closer to surface of the permafrost—closer to the faces. Now he could better see their features, their moving lips. He could no longer see Rogozhin, Raymond Vitus, or Arutyunov; new personalities showed up as extensions of the pine's trunks. Not all of them, though, were familiar to him. This dream wasn't the same as his previous one. It was more like a movie sequel, set on the same mystical stage.

However, the people beneath the transparent surface looked real. Their eyes were either closed or open but lifeless. Most of those people seemed as if they had been killed violently, just like his Yulia. But just like before, he had no control over himself; he couldn't even feel his limbs.

Will I also see Katerina here? The terrifying thought popped into his mind. At that moment, he saw Garanin. His head was cracked open; there was a black hole in place of one of his eyes. Katya knelt next to him, her head covered by a black veil. Viktor couldn't see her face, but he knew she was crying.

This frightened him so much that he screamed, making a desperate effort to slip out of the nightmare. He felt someone watching over him.

Chapter 23

Morning. Viktor opened his eyes, but it took a while to bring them into focus. A man stood next to his bed with a look of concern on his face. He was nicely dressed and well-groomed, holding a box of chocolates. It took Viktor a few moments to recognize him.

"Denis, is it you?" Viktor spoke faintly, still groggy from his drug-induced sleep.

Denis replied with a big, charming smile. "I am sorry for the early visit, Nachalnik. Did I wake you up? You were moaning. Bad dreams?"

"Very bad. How did you know that I was here? And how did they let you in?"

"Chocolates are a very effective method of entering any facility guarded by women, Nachalnik." Denis said with a wink, "Where do you want these, by the way?"

Viktor pointed at the table in the corner of the room, knowing he wouldn't touch a single candy. What he really craved was a cigarette, but he didn't want to ask for one. Denis put the box down and continued.

"The entire city is talking about what happened in that theater. It's big news! I got worried, Nachalnik. Nikolai too."

"Nikolai?"

"My nephew, my sister's kid. He told me about your talk with him," Denis explained.

"Oh yes, I remember." Viktor confirmed. "He is a good kid. I hope he stays out of trouble."

"Thank you for straightening him out. And also, for helping him get out of that jam." Denis tried to grab Viktor's hand to express his gratitude, but stopped in midair, realizing he might accidentally hurt him.

"That boy didn't belong in jail," Viktor replied and pointed to the box of candy. "You shouldn't have brought that."

"Just a token of my appreciation. Not everyone in your position would agree to help someone like me," Denis said.

"If you really want to show your appreciation, Denis, you'd give me a cigarette" Viktor said, instantly feeling guilty at his own weakness.

Denis quickly pulled an old-style *papirosa* out of his inside pocket. Viktor accepted it with a smile, squashed its hollow end with his fingers, and put it in his lips. His unexpected visitor lit it for him. The sensation of smoke entering his lungs was heavenly, and Viktor let a few long moments pass by before speaking again.

"I think you are a decent man, Denis. And decent men don't survive the life you've chosen for very long," he finally said.

Denis smiled again but didn't respond. They stayed in silence for another long moment as Viktor smoked. Finally, he said, "I hope your sister gets better soon," and Denis understood that the visit was over.

"I'll be seeing you, Major! Thank you again for everything. And I'm glad that mad dog Rogozhin is dead."

"Yes. Me too."

Without any additional ceremony, Denis walked out of Viktor's room with another friendly wink.

A nurse rushed in almost immediately, nonchalantly taking the burning cigarette out of Viktor's hand and stubbing it out in an empty glass by the bedside. Viktor didn't protest. The nurse went on to fix his bed, pulling out and replacing the sweat-drenched cover sheet and pillowcases. Then she checked Viktor's bandages and IV.

"What's your name, nurse?"

"Melanie, Comrade Major," the woman responded flatly.

"Please call me Viktor. Tell me, how is my young friend Pyotr Uvalov?"

Melanie hesitated. "I cannot say precisely, Comrade Viktor. It's almost eight now. The neurosurgeon is expected at nine. Perhaps he can answer your questions." She was careful in choosing her words.

"In an hour or so, I shall come back with your breakfast, Comrade Viktor. You should take a nap in the meantime."

To fall asleep and see that horrible dream again? No thanks! Viktor thought as Melenie closed the door behind her. *And what exactly was the situation with Freckles? Why is she so cagey?*

Viktor forced himself to think of something more pleasant: the kid, Nikolai. Frankly, he wasn't sure that his relatively short conversation with the young man and brief inquiry into the case would convince the prosecutor to drop the charges. Nevertheless, Viktor was glad about the outcome and was touched by Denis' gratitude. Hopefully, his visit to the hospital would not raise any suspicion from Petukh. *Denis is too smart to jeopardize his life by being caught as my informant*, Viktor concluded.

All of a sudden, he was reminded of Arutyunov's letter. By now, he remembered it almost by heart and that memory was the only evidence left of its existence.

My Dear Friend,

I hope my letter finds you in good health and good spirits. How is your lovely, devoted wife Leya? How does she tolerate you around the house all day since you retired? How are your children and grandchildren? Especially Viktor: I have been worried about him.

You must be wondering why I decided to write this letter and deliver it in such a peculiar way. Before, we always communicated by phone, it was just fine. The thing is, I don't trust telephones anymore—too many ears listening. This letter must be for your eyes only.

Most likely, when you read it, I will be gone already. "Gone," meaning I will not be alive. You may ask, How do I know that? I know because ending my life will be in my own hands. Until recently, I thought my life was worth living. But lately, I realized, my family, my country, and my career—everything I held so dearly in my heart—failed me miserably. With help from a traitor, my father was executed by his enemies. My mother, whose last breath was given to the Revolution, disappeared one day behind the walls of the Lubianka. My only son, Frunzik, never returned from that terrible war, which was led by a cowardly leader and fought by his uneducated commanders because all the real military minds were deliberately destroyed for political reasons beforehand.

My wife Dora, the apple of my eye, being so young and so beautiful, didn't survive cancer because I was forbidden from taking her to Stockholm for a promising treatment. And now, it is my turn: I have been diagnosed with cancer—lung cancer. It is inoperable, the doctors say. My fate is a slow, painful death within the next few months.

I hear you saying that this is nobody's fault but yours, perhaps resulting from many years of heavy smoking. I agree. Believe me, I don't mean to blame anyone. I just want to explain why all this gave me pause and made me reevaluate my entire life. I wanted to share it with you not only because you are my closest friend, my only friend, as I finally discovered, but because you were always the most brutally honest man I ever came across, the man who would judge our lives and the history of our beloved country fairly and with an open mind.

So, let me start with the personal secret I never told you. Arutyunov is the last name of my stepfather, who my mother married soon after fleeing to Moscow from the city of Baku in 1918. I was only six years old then and learned about my real father nine or ten years later. His life story was directly connected to the fate of 26 Baku Bolshevik Commissars murdered by the counter-revolutionary White Guard soldiers.

My mother's first husband, my biological father, was among those twenty-six, and her version of those tragic events differed from the official Party version. Since my teenage years, I tended to believe my mom, who was there at the time, more than official Soviet historians. It was our family secret, which she and my stepfather took to their graves.

According to mom's version, it happened during the evacuation of Baku with the advancing Ottoman forces. The deputy from the Bolshevik faction Anastas Mikoyan, using threats and false pretenses, requested the release of the Baku Commune members for conducting investigations as part of the upcoming court trials. After release, they secretly boarded the ship to Astrakhan (held by the Reds). On the way there, the captain of the steamboat changed course to the city of Petrovsk (Makhachkala) that was held by the White forces. On arrival at Petrovsk, during the personal check, Mikoyan was caught with unlawful possession of a weapon and placed in a cell for questioning. While interrogating him, Major General Martynov, the chief of the counter-espionage team, offered Anastas Mikoyan a deal: his life for assistance in identifying all the Bolshevik Commissars among the 600 refugees. Mikoyan took this deal. All 26 Commissars, his comrades, were detained and brought to the Military court. As a result of a speedy trial, all Bolsheviks were sentenced to death by firing squad. Only Mikoyan was released unharmed under the condition that he would not engage in revolutionary activities anymore.

Ever since I could remember, my mom hated this man, and in conversations with my stepfather, whispered Mikoyan's name, always being afraid that one day he would, with the help of GPU or later NKVD, figure out who she really was. That day came in 1929. She was arrested and never returned home. My stepfather immediately took me to Petrograd (the city was already renamed as Leningrad). He left me with his sister-in-law, his late brother's wife, Maria Fyodorovna Arutyunov-Pankratova, a remarkable woman in her own right. An Old Bolshevik herself had been in the circle of friends with Nadezhda Krupskaya and knew Vladimir Lenin personally several years before the October Revolution. Pankratova, after the premature death of her husband, lived a lonely, although comfortable, life. Like Vladimir Lenin himself, she was never a fan of Josef Stalin and his supporters, or of Anastas Mikoyan in particular, knowing very well their methods of "treating" their political adversaries.

Maria Fyodorovna accepted me with open arms and full-heartedly as her orphan nephew. It wasn't easy, considering that I was quite a difficult teenager and not her true blood relation. Soon, she became my surrogate parent, my protector, my good friend, and confidant. Her love and wisdom helped me grow up and guided me for the rest of my life.

Regardless of my relatively happy and secure adolescent years, I never changed my feelings toward that man, Anastas Mikoyan, of whom I was afraid. Maria Fyodorovna shared my feelings too and had her own concerns. Perhaps therefore she supported my naïve notion that if I joined the Soviet State security "machine" and became one of them, it would spare me from the fate of my mother. Yes, I did believe it was my life's calling when

I joined the NKVD Academy at eighteen. I just didn't know yet how monstrous that machine was.

* * *

At that moment, a strange thought interrupted Viktor's recollection of the letter: Anastas Mikoyan had the longest political life. He was the only one who survived from *Ilyich Lenin to Ilyich Brezhnev,* as a popular anecdote described it. In the thirties, during his tenure as the Minister of Foreign Trade, Mikoyan implemented several useful technologies from the United States for the mass production of ice cream, hot dogs, and traditional American hamburgers. In the early forties, Mikoyan initiated and personally sponsored the very popular publication *The Book of Tasty and Healthy Eating*, a book found in almost every Soviet home despite the notoriously limited quantity and quality of food in the country.

In 1956, Mikoyan, joining his lifelong friend Nikita Khrushchev in a crusade against the personality cult of Josef Stalin, shed his loyalty to the "Father of the Nation." He also blamed Stalin for all the atrocities committed during the purges of 1934-40 and the "Enemies of the State" campaigns of 1946-52.

General Arutyunov had a different opinion about all this. That is why Viktor burned the letter, to keep it from the eyes of anyone else. And yet, the letter so thoroughly compelled Viktor's attention that he retained it in his memory even now. It kept coming back:

The years at the Academy were fun. There, I met you, Raymond. Despite my natural suspicious nature, I felt safe with you. I felt I could trust you. And you became my friend. I am sorry that I couldn't be totally open with you in the early years. I didn't want to put you in a compromising, even dangerous, position. Besides, you had your own family issues you had to deal with. Remember? First, your mother died in 1925 under strange circumstances, presumably from tuberculosis that was never diagnosed, staying at that time alone in Riga. And then it was your father, one of the original members of the Revolutionary Latvian Riflemen formation—the precursor to the Soviet Secret Service. I knew that he, one of the personal guards of Vladimir Lenin, was your role model, your hero. And while growing up, you never complained about not seeing him often enough, even after Lenin's death. I knew it was a blow when one day in 1930, he didn't come back home at all. You were told your father gave his life to the Proletarian Cause while on a special assignment. You believed this story because you wanted to and because there were no other options.

Now, with my sincere apology to you, I can confess that years later, I incidentally came across the file in the NKVD Archives with Alfred Vitus' name on it. From that file, I learned the real truth: "Executed as an Enemy of the People." This short verdict was signed by the Deputy Chairman of the GPU State Political Directorate Genrikh Yagoda.

* * *

Viktor imagined how his father, Raymond Vitus, would have reacted to this devastating revelation. *Should I tell Mom about it?* He thought. *It might give her a sense of closure, or it might not.* His mother was a very complex, sophisticated, and emotionally strong woman. Viktor had always suspected she possessed these qualities, and learning her life story left him with no doubts. His gut feeling was that she must've read this letter before handing it to him and was waiting for him to talk first.

At that moment, Nurse Melanie rushed into the room, holding a tray with a breakfast plate and a cup of tea.

"Sorry to break up your nap, Comrade, but you have another early visitor." She came right to the point: "It is almost nine. My shift is over, and yet I didn't finish everything I had to do."

"Everything's fine. Do what you need to do," he replied. Frankly, Viktor was happy to get away from this disturbing letter. "Who is here to see me?"

"I think it's your Mama. She brought a lot of homemade food for you, so you don't need to eat this hospital food."

"Then let her in quickly."

Leya Solomonovna didn't look good. She put two large sacks with an aluminum pot and a ceramic bowl, still steaming, on the table next to the hospital tray and literally sank into the chair closest to the bed.

"Have you slept, Mom?" Viktor asked with real concern.

"Not much, Viten'ka. I couldn't, so I decided to cook a little."

"I see. You call this a little?" Viktor asked, smiling. "Why couldn't you sleep? You left me yesterday in good spirits. Today, I feel even better. So, what is the worry, Mom?"

"Honestly, Son, I haven't slept well since your father's death," Leya Solomonovna replied after a long pause. "The last few nights, I couldn't close my eyes at all. I am worried about everything: your health, our departure, leaving you here."

"I beg you, stop worrying and concentrate on the task at hand." That sounded too cold to Viktor, so he added, "Sorry, Mom. I meant that you have to start packing. I'll be fine here."

"You look tired… and irritated too. Why? Is the pain bothering you?" Leya Solomonovna asked. "Or is it something else?"

"Have you read the letter, Mom?" Viktor blurted it out without giving it a thought. "Have you?"

"What letter, Son?" She was caught off guard.

"Arutyunov's letter to Father, have you read it? Tell me the truth, please," Viktor insisted.

"Why is it so important to you, Viten'ka?" Leya Solomonovna was buying time.

"Because, if you have, you will know what's bothering me—what gives me nightmares, the same damn dream." Viktor looked straight into his mother's eyes, whispering slowly, emphasizing every word.

"I found it in that box and read it. I was scared and I wanted to destroy it. The letter was discovered right after your father's suicide," Leya Solomonovna answered in a whisper. "I didn't know when exactly he received this letter. However, I noticed profound changes in his behavior about a week before the tragedy. He became overwhelmed with anxiety attacks, which were followed by periods of deep depression. He wouldn't discuss his feelings with me, but I noticed his anguish and fear. Do you think I still don't feel guilty for missing those signs?"

The day shift nurse, a woman in her mid-thirties with a pretty, round face and almond-shaped eyes, quietly entered the room. Mother and son immediately went silent. The nurse, realizing she had caused an uncomfortable situation, tried to defuse it.

"I'll be quick. I just need to check your temperature and pulse. By the way, my name is Masha."

"Good morning, Masha." Viktor replied politely.

The young woman nodded gratefully and shook the thermometer before sliding it under Viktor's armpit. Then, glancing at her watch, she gently grabbed his wrist and put her thumb over the artery. After pulling the thermometer out, she turned it to the light and wrote some numbers into his medical chart.

"Your temperature is normal. However, your heart is racing a little," Masha said with seriousness in her voice. "You must calm down. You didn't eat yet. The doctor will start his rounds in ten minutes."

As soon as the nurse left the room, Leya Solomonovna began fussing with the chicken soup in the pot she had brought.

"She is right—you must eat before the doctor sees you. We can continue our conversation later. And if you are wondering where Katya is, she called me at seven to tell me she would be here after twelve." Leya Solomonovna said all this as quickly as she could. "She's a lovely girl, I think."

Viktor couldn't respond because his mother had just pushed a spoonful of warm, thick chicken broth into his mouth. Nevertheless, he was happy.

During Dr. Bolshakov's visit, Leya Solomonovna made every effort to keep him at Viktor's bedside for as long as possible. She asked question after question about her son's injuries and the prospects for his recovery. While they were legitimate questions, Viktor understood perfectly well that his mother simply didn't want to resume their earlier conversation and couldn't find a better way to avoid it. Viktor played along, but it couldn't go on forever. Eventually, Leya Solomonovna ran out of questions.

Dr. Bolshakov made some notes in his medical chart, and Viktor asked him, "What was the result of the neurosurgeon's consultation for Pyotr Uvalov?"

"He approved the surgery to remove the bullet; I'll do it tomorrow," Bolshakov replied without hesitation and moved on to see the next patient. Nurse Masha followed the doctor out. The son and his mother were alone again in silence.

Leya Solomonovna began slowly. "Speaking of your father, he had similar episodes of deep depression at least twice in the past. The first time was in 1938, right after he returned from that meeting with NKVD boss Yezhov. I think Arutyunov reminded him about it in the letter. At that time, its consequences weren't severe. Perhaps he was young and very determined to hide it. After all, he survived—he even got a promotion. And, because he was more preoccupied with my pregnancy troubles."

"What about the second time?" Viktor asked.

"The second time, it was much worse. It happened after Yulia's accident." Leya Solomonovna again lowered her voice almost to a whisper. "He was in a panic, ready to fly to Leningrad. Arutyunov convinced him not to. Then he fell into such a deep depression that I had to take him to see Doctor Bolshakov. "

"And?"

"He put him in the hospital for observation," she responded. "Three days later, your father was back home with the diagnosis of stress-related cardiomyopathy and strong advice to get serious rest. I suspected that he had a minor heart attack just before you returned from Leningrad but recovered from it rather quickly."

"I had no idea," Viktor admitted regretfully.

"You were in a terrible state yourself, Son."

"Why didn't you tell me when the same symptoms became obvious the last time? I was here, wasn't I?" Viktor asked pointedly.

"I have no excuse. As I said before, I missed the signs." His mother paused for a moment before she exclaimed, "I hope you don't think that I gave you the letter to persuade you in your decision to emigrate!"

Leya Solomonovna was interrupted by her daughter. Raisa rushed into the room and kissed her brother. Nurse Masha ran in behind her, lamenting, "Citizen, Citizen! You cannot be here in your winter coat. You should've left it downstairs in the cloakroom. If our head nurse sees you, I'll be reprimanded."

"I am only here for a moment to pick up my mother," Raisa tried to explain. "We have a very important appointment in an hour. So let me help her gather her things and we will leave."

"Raya, dear, what's the rush? You'll get this lovely girl, who is looking after your brother, in trouble." Leya Solomonovna got up and started fussing with the pot again. "Say goodbye to your brother and wait for me in the hall."

"Okay, Mom, but please hurry up. They changed the time. You know how strict they are in OVIR with appointments." Raisa bent over Viktor and kissed him on the cheek again. "Sorry, Dear, we'll see you later… Hopefully with good news."

When Raisa left the room, Leya Solomonovna moved close to Viktor and said, "If you still love me, Son, listen to me. Forget this letter; don't go back to it looking for clues. This letter is a poison pill, although I am not questioning its veracity." She paused for a moment. "You've made the decision not to join us. It's unfortunate. I understand and respect it, but consider this: you have to live in this country, don't you?"

"Mom, I love you so much and value your wisdom so much." Viktor's eyes suddenly filled with tears. His voice cracked. "I burned the letter, and I wish I could forget about it. I can't. It has such a grip on me. I keep coming back to it whether I want to or not."

"Son, you are much stronger than you think. You can fight it off." Leya Solomonovna sounded gentle yet confident. "Do not end up like your father. Get back on your feet, create your own family with someone you love and be happy. No matter what life may throw at you. And believe me: one day we will reunite again. Let's hope it will happen sooner than not."

"Mom, you are not leaving yet. You are just going to OVIR." Viktor tried to lighten the mood. "We will reunite in a few hours." He wiped his eyes and smiled.

Nurse Masha came back into the room as soon as Leya Solomonovna left. She checked the IV solutions bottles, straightened Viktor's bed sheets and fluffed his pillow.

"I am sorry to chase your sister out of the room, but it is the rule," Masha apologized.

"Rules are rules. You don't have to apologize," Viktor said politely. "Better tell me, how is my comrade doing?"

She was glad Viktor had changed the subject, and her reply was more animated. "Sergeant Uvalov's condition is more complicated. He is fully conscious and can speak. By the way, he is asking about you all the time. Doctor Bolshakov is with him now."

"Please let me know when the surgery happens and what his prognosis is. Promise?"

"Of course, Comrade Major," Nurse Masha responded, and then left.

Viktor was alone again. The conversation with his mother had revealed something extremely important about his late father, something he had suspected but never fully understood. He did remember those mood swings, those long silent spells after his retirement. Viktor attributed the behavior to him missing his work. Now, however, there was no doubt that his father had been afflicted by a mental illness, which was never diagnosed or treated. The letter from his disillusioned friend was the trigger that set the tragic events into motion.

By now, he felt exhausted. If this was finally the answer to all his questions, why did he feel no relief? Why wouldn't this familiar pain go away? Perhaps now this pain was just the natural reaction to a tremendous loss, and it would dissipate with time. Perhaps. It seemed his mom and sister had learned how to live with this loss long before him. So, he must, too.

Both his injured body and tormented mind needed serious rest. He had to get some sound sleep. Viktor didn't want Katya to see him like this when she came. Unfortunately, every time he closed his eyes, that nightmare with its terrifying images and inexplicable symbolism returned. Asking for sleeping pills now would be useless; they would not allow such medications before nighttime. So, Viktor returned to Arutyunov's letter.

* * *

One of the significant reforms by Khrushchev in March 1954 was the transformation of the Ministry of State Security (MGB) into the Ministry of Internal Affairs (MVD) and the creation of a new, separate agency—the Committee of State Security (KGB).

Under the leadership of Ivan Serov, a close associate of Khrushchev, the KGB quickly grew into one of the largest and most powerful state security organizations in the world. It was created with only one purpose—to support and promote the Soviet leader's ambitions of world domination. The KGB became a very sophisticated, multi-pronged tool of internal security, protecting the Soviet elite and performing important counter-espionage activities.

The same tool was widely used in foreign affairs and external intelligence. Together, KGB Chief Ivan Serov and Marshal Zhukov crushed the anti-Soviet Hungarian Uprising of October and November 1956. Close to two thousand Hungarians were killed in only a few days of the bloody operation. Soviet losses: 72 killed, 1540 wounded, and more than 50 missing in action—not exactly a brilliant victory. However, both Zhukov and Serov were awarded the title of Soviet Union Hero and the Gold Star that comes with it. For Zhukov, it was his fourth Gold Star.

By the middle of 1957, Nikita Khrushchev ordered 18,000 field agents and operatives of the Soviet security forces to be purged from the service as a part of his consolidation of power. These people weren't just fired or sent into retirement. Some of them were executed, and many of them ended up in the GULAG. I was lucky again to survive these tumultuous times; I even landed a cushy position in the "Big House" of the KGB Leningrad headquarters.

I am sure you understand what I went through because you remember your own ordeal that took place in January 1938, when we didn't know if you would come out of Nikolai Yezhov's office alive. Thank God you survived. What you may not know was that on that day, your fate hung in the balance. As I found out later, what tipped the scales in your favor was a positive report on you, delivered three hours before your audience with Yezhov, from his protégé, the Chief of the Far East NKVD, Gennadi Lyushkov. Yes, the same Gennadi Lyushkov who, five months later, defected to Japan. You must remember him. In my humble opinion, it was that event that caused Yezhov's downfall. Just like in the case of Yagoda before him, Josef Stalin decided that his usefulness for the great purge had been exhausted. At the same time, the concentration of power in his hands and his possession of information on the subjects reached a critical mass. You know the history, but let's talk about more recent events that are also related to you and your family.

During the late 60s, especially after the victorious Six Day War, the distraction of Israel remained the cornerstone of Soviet geopolitical doctrine in the Middle East. Under the chairmanship of Yuri Andropov, the KGB continued its crusade against Israel. It supported Arab countries in the region, and especially the PLO, created in a training camp near Odessa, for their aggressive policies and terrorist activities against the Jewish State. It didn't go as well as expected after several failed attempts to push the Israelis into the sea, which caused a lot of grief for my new boss. But this was nothing in comparison with the headache our agency was experiencing at home.

In August 1967, activists from all over the country gathered in Moscow to create a National Committee to coordinate the work of the separate groups in collecting facts about human rights violations—first, against Soviet Jews who wanted to emigrate, and then other ethnic groups. In response, the KGB Head Yury Andropov decided to create a special Section 5 to neutralize the threat of Zionist ideas and squash general dissent. The order was passed down to the local OVIRs to reject as many applications for exit Visas as possible. This created a new class of Soviet people, "Refuseniks," with a peculiar situation in Soviet society. As a result, hundreds and hundreds of families were ostracized as traitors by their neighbors, usually losing any source of income and any prospect to regain meaningful employment. So, it came as no surprise when many of those Refuseniks joined local Zionist support groups to have a voice.

Eduard Kuznetsov and his group of Refuseniks fell under KGB scrutiny back in 1968, when some of their proclamations and manifestos were intercepted. The group was dubbed as the Leningrad Group and assigned to the Section 5 Leningrad office, although only one member, Mark Dymshets, was a resident of Leningrad. The rest of the participants and their families were from Moscow, Kyiv, and Riga. I read the reports.

One day, I learned of a young woman they had attempted to recruit from inside the close circle of Mark Dymshets. Naturally, I couldn't know who she was, only her code name. In some reports that crossed my desk, I sensed her handler's frustration; this recruit had tried to fool them by pretending she had real intelligence for more than three months. The situation required action, and Section 5 was getting ready to act. More details began trickling in about this woman, who happened to be a distant relative of Dymshets.

Finally, I figured out who she was. I literally went into shock when it became clear to me that the recruit was Yulia. I had known her well since she was a little girl; she was the daughter of my colleague, one of the best professors of Jurisprudence at Leningrad University. Yulia was an excellent student and the fiancé of my best friend's son. I couldn't think straight. My first reaction was to run and warn her. But I didn't. I couldn't help her anyway without jeopardizing Viktor and myself. And I could not warn you directly for the same reasons. I tried to pass the information to you through your deputy, Melekhov, who I knew had your fullest confidence. (By the way he was transferred from Leningrad to become your deputy. Wasn't he?). It was too late. Forty-eight hours later I heard about the hit and run accident on Gogol Prospect. The victim was a woman in her twenties. I knew it was Yulia. The fact that I could not prevent her death is one of my most shameful regrets, in a life full of them.

Now, you know what really happened in Leningrad. I called you after, but you were in the hospital, so I couldn't tell you the real story. I couldn't share the truth with Viktor either. He was devastated, suspicious, and obsessed with his own investigation. I had to protect him from danger, get him out of equation before the KGB began to focus their attention on him. I had asked for help from Melekhov again, and he came through very fast convincing Viktor to leave Lenindrad immediately!

* * *

When Viktor first read the letter, he stopped after this passage in shock and anger. He knew Arutyunov well enough not to doubt him. He finally knew the truth about Yulia's death, but not the whole truth. Now, as he dissected the letter in his mind, there was no blind rage anymore and no sense of helplessness that came from absence of really truthful information. He reflected on that horrible moment in his otherwise happy and trouble-free life in Leningrad. He remembered Yulia's smile, her green eyes, and the way she wore her hair. All those years ago, Viktor was angry and confused by the senselessness of her untimely death. Now, he understood that Yulia's death was far from senseless; it was a planned and premeditated assassination. But by whom? The KGB? Why would they kill their own recruit, even if the recruit was not fully cooperating yet? Was it the Refuseniks themselves, trying to silence a potential leak? An unlikely risk for them to take, that would endanger the entire movement. No. There had to be another reason. There had to be something else!

His mind drifted back to the letter's final paragraphe:

Later, I realized with sadness that Yulia had lost her life in vain. Eventually, the Section 5 agents spying on the Leningrad group intercepted a plan to fly to Sweden on a hijacked airplane. They could've arrested every one of them right away, quickly, and quietly, but the head of Section 5, Fyodor Bobkov, the first deputy of Yuri Andropov, ordered them to do this in another way. The decision was made to continue surveillance and make arrests when the group implemented the plan. They meant to catch all of them red-handed in the process of committing a terrorist act and then publicize the incident widely in order to have the activists condemned in the court of public opinion. It was Bobkov's plan to gain the people's support, to justify more severe security measures and mass arrests.

The day after the operation at Smolny Airfield, which Bobkov supervised himself, a series of arrests began in Riga, Kishinev, and Kyiv. More than 45 activists not even connected with the Leningrad case were detained, quickly pulled through the court system, and convicted. The goal was clear: to drive a dagger through the heart of the Zionist movement in the USSR — to crush it in a single blow. Such far-reaching implications explained the severity of the received sentences, including capital punishment, which is extremely rare in Soviet legal practice.

During the court proceedings in the Leningrad case, the most famous human rights activist Andrei Sakharov, the father of the Soviet hydrogen bomb, and his wife Yelena Bonner, never missed a single day of those proceedings. They were secretly passing detailed reports to Western journalists, telling the truth of what was going on inside the court.

The Soviet leaders didn't like this at all. It interfered with Brezhnev's grandiose plans for the future Moscow Olympic Games, enlarging his personal collection of foreign, primarily American, automobiles, his appetite for diplomatic soirées and international visits. To afford all that, the country needed stable Western currency, but without friendly trade with the West, there would be no dollars and no pound's sterling. Perhaps this was why Leonid Illyich Brezhnev listened very carefully and reacted appropriately when U.S. President Richard Nixon called him personally regarding the unfair legal treatment of the members of the Leningrad "Refuseniks" group and demanded a review of their sentences.

Dear Raymond, I apologize if my letter has made you upset. Believe me, this wasn't my intention. I have no one I can be open with, especially when it comes to our job and the nasty secrets that go along with it. You are my only friend, one who I always considered a brother, whom I can trust with my life. So, think of this letter as my last confession, my last and honest look at my life, our country, and myself.

The forty years of my career had its peaks and valleys. I am sure yours had them too, in the service of the Militia, which maintains law and order and represents integrity and transparency, even more so when it is far away from the politics of Moscow. Therefore, as I mentioned already, you were luckier than me in getting your job in Khabarovsk. No doubt you might disagree. I recall this case of the priest you told me about. I understood your disappointment when you couldn't save an innocent man. And yet, most of the time, you were taking on the hard criminals… murderers, rapists, armed robbers, and child abusers— the real bad guys.

It was not so clear-cut with the kind of people with whom my agency dealt: basically decent, unsuspecting citizens taken away from their families in the middle of the night. Many of them didn't even understand what they were guilty of! The kind of work that made me vomit for three straight days, and then eventually lose any shred of faith I ever had in the basic goodness of human nature. I don't know what kept me in this line of work. Although, throughout my entire career, my hands were clean — technically — I avoided having any connection with torturing or executing people. That's how I justified continuing my service in state security. But lately, my conscience does not allow me any sleep. Is it old age that makes us see everything, not for what we want it to be, but for what it really is? I think it is. Until recently, I thought I served the people of my beloved country. Now, I think all of us served the false gods we ourselves created; those mythical idols who controlled us—the leaders who never had any real interest in the people they led. The leaders who were drunk on power and used people as cannon fodder, whether during the construction of the Byelomor–Baltiyskiy Kanal or in the Great Patriotic War against Nazi Germany. They never cared how many Russians, Ukrainians, Byelorussians, Georgians, or Armenians perished. They never cared about any of us.

So, let me stop right here and say goodbye to you, my dear Raymond. I was always your loyal friend, as you were mine. Therefore, I ask for your forgiveness if I ever was selfish and not fully truthful with you. I am a weak man, and now, when I am this close to my death, I can admit it. What a liberating feeling, my friend!

Always your loyal Vartan A.

* * *

Viktor laid with his eyes closed, thinking. What did Uncle Vartan mean by calling himself a weak man? Was it because he "Spoke no evil, Saw no evil, and Heard no evil" while being in the middle of evil? But as Viktor remembered from his philosophy studies, there were many lessons to be taken from this ancient Japanese saying. One could view it as a way to turn the ears, eyes, and tongue away from anything judgmental and to never accuse anyone of anything which was morally wrong. While another interpretation may view it as "burying one's head in the sand" to protect their own existence; to deny the truth out of self-preservation. A far less kind perspective and one that was more likely in this case.

Viktor, while growing up well-shielded from everyday life, wasn't totally oblivious to the Soviet social realities. Therefore, in his thinking, he leaned toward the assumption that Arutyunov, in all his years of service, had been afraid to speak his mind and his conscience - of course, until he wrote this letter, his confession, as he put it, to a close friend. What a peculiar way of doing it, though. And what did he hope to accomplish? Maybe nothing except getting this heavy burden off his chest.

But Raymond Vitus must've known something much more revealing in the letter; something that Viktor had overlooked. Yes, But what? Viktor recalled that a few days following his father's funeral, there was also a phone call from one of Viktor's former fellow students, Misha Latynin, who, since his graduation, had resided in Leningrad and worked at the University Jurisprudence Department. Of course, being under emotional stress, Viktor took this call just like another traditional expression of condolences. He didn't pay much attention to the small talk, in which Misha had casually mentioned some old professor they both knew who had - like his father - recently committed suicide. He didn't name this professor, and that's why this news had escaped Viktor's memory. But now, it popped right back into his mind. Latynin was talking about Arutyunov! The old KGB General and guest-professor at Leningrad University had committed suicide soon after sending the letter to his closest friend, the retired MVD General Raymond Vitus. Most likely, Raymond had read the letter and called him right away, but it was too late. Or was it? Did his father speak to his old friend before Arutyunov killed himself? And what did they speak about? The letter was full of confessions, but knowing his father, Viktor realized that there was only one question - the only unanswered question that even Arutyunov didn't realize - that would draw the sharp investigative mind of Raymond Vitus: who murdered Yulia? Here it was, that missing link that could explain what triggered his father's suicide.

Suddenly, the blood rushed from Viktor's brain, leaving him dizzy and weak, drenched in a cold sweat. Even if his father never spoke to Arutuynov before he killed himself, the answer was right there in the letter. General Melekhov, Viktor's beloved godfather and protector, was responsible for the death of the woman he loved. It was the only answer! Arutyunov had tipped Melekhov off as to Yulia's role in the Section 5 investigation, and Melekhov had put it in motion… recruiting someone in Leningrad to stage a 'hit and run ' and remove the girl from the chessboard. When Raymond Vitus read the letter, he understood immediately what Malekhov had done. Father probably confronted his friend. "Why!? Why, Misha?"

"I did it for you, Raymond. For you and Viktor. I did it to protect you. Because once the girl's name became publicized in connection with the investigation, her fiancé, and his whole family - half of whom are Jews - would be implicated and destroyed. I did it for you, Raymond." This answer is what ultimately made my father, "the man of steel" take his own life.

In anguish, Viktor opened his eyes, desperately gasping for breath and looking for someone to help him. Everything was blurry and foggy. He wished his mom were here right this moment to save him. His dear mother, who had endured so much growing up, dedicated her entire adult life to her husband and children and continued to be the family's moral compass. Did she know?

Viktor's inflamed brain was on fire. His heart started pounding inside his chest, raising his anxiety. He had to make a noise, call a nurse to give him medicine to calm him down. If not, his heart would burst, and his head would explode. He could not die. He must see Katya, at least once more! "Nurse! Please help!" Viktor, sweeping with his left hand behind his pillow, finally felt the signal rope to call for help and yanked it with such force that it broke off from its socket on the wall. He thought he heard the voice of Doctor Bolshakov.

Then everything went black.

* * *

When he woke up, Viktor was alone. Rays of the low winter sun pounded through the blinds of the window. There were no nurses and no doctors near his bed. His head was still light but clear. He was breathing deeply and regularly. His heartbeat was steady. He felt alive. More alive than he had felt in years. And he knew exactly what he had to do. He had to leave this country. Perhaps that was the meaning of the dream. Yes! The faces in the permafrost, his own face and the faces of his family, the people he had loved, and the people whom he was yet to love. And they were screaming for him to act, to take back their lives, to be free. They were begging him to escape the system that kept them as helpless cogs in an indifferent machine that turned loyalty into betrayal and love into murder. They were begging him to release them from this dreadful permafrost…

Viktor's eyes opened wide, focusing on the door and a silhouette standing within its frame.

"Katya!" His lips moved soundlessly.

"Yes, my love. This is your Katya."

THE END

Made in the USA
Middletown, DE
13 November 2025